# Twain's
# THE ADVENTURES OF
# HUCKLEBERRY FINN

## THE MANGA EDITION

# Twain's
# THE ADVENTURES OF
# HUCKLEBERRY FINN

## THE MANGA EDITION

Adam Sexton • Hyeondo Park

**WILEY**

Wiley Publishing, Inc.

Published by Wiley Publishing, Inc., Hoboken, New Jersey



For general information on our other products and services or to obtain technical support please contact our Customer Care Department within the U.S. at (800) 762-2974, outside the U.S. at (317) 572-3993 or fax (317) 572-4002.

Wiley also publishes its books in a variety of electronic formats. Some content that appears in print may not be available in electronic books. For more information about Wiley products, please visit our web site at www.wiley.com.

***Library of Congress Control Number is available from the Publisher.***

ISBN: 978-0-470-15287-4

Printed in the United States of America

10 9 8 7 6 5 4 3 2 1

Book design by Elizabeth Brooks
Book production by Wiley Publishing, Inc. Composition Services

**Adam Sexton** is author of *Master Class in Fiction Writing* and editor of the anthologies *Love Stories*, *Rap on Rap*, and *Desperately Seeking Madonna*. He has written on art and entertainment for *The New York Times* and *The Village Voice*, and he teaches fiction writing and literature at New York University and critical reading and writing at Parsons School of Design. A graduate of Columbia University and the University of Pennsylvania, he lives in Brooklyn with his wife and son.

**Hyeondo Park,** at the age of 10, moved from Seoul, South Korea to Dallas, Texas with his mother and two brothers to reunite with his father. He had a special passion for comics growing up, and he sometimes waited until midnight at the local bookstore to get the latest issue. He loved the laughter, the excitement, the danger, and the suspense of comics, which he could read over and over again and could buy on his weekly allowance. It is one of many reasons why he attended and graduated from the School of Visual Arts in 2006 as a cartoonist. Now he hopes that his comics will provide the same excitement and entertainment value for others as they did for him when he was young. Visit Hyeondo's Web site at www.hanaroda.net.

# Huckleberry Finn and Manga

## by Adam Sexton

The great American novelist, journalist, and short-story writer Ernest Hemingway once wrote, "All modern American literature comes from one book by Mark Twain called *Huckleberry Finn*." Though Hemingway may overstate his case, it is true that *The Adventures of Huckleberry Finn*, published in 1884, has been enormously influential.

The book's author, Samuel Langhorne Clemens, was born in 1835 and grew up in Hannibal, Missouri, a town on the Mississippi River. At age twenty-two he became a riverboat pilot; later Clemens adopted the pseudonym Mark Twain, a term for water that is two fathoms deep. In 1869 his collection of often-humorous travel pieces, *Innocents Abroad*, became a bestseller and Twain became a celebrity. Novels including *The Prince and the Pauper* and a best-selling children's book, *The Adventures of Tom Sawyer*, followed.

Mark Twain's masterpiece, *The Adventures of Huckleberry Finn*, was published in 1885. Twain wrote *Huckleberry Finn* as a sequel to *The Adventures of Tom Sawyer*. The second book's language and its themes make it too difficult for children to comprehend, however. Twain intended it for adults.

A summary of the plot: In the small town of St. Petersburg, Missouri, in the mid-19th century, Huckleberry Finn has been adopted by the Widow Douglas and her sister, Miss Watson, who want to teach him religion and etiquette. Huck's brutal, drunken father shows up, though, and warns him to quit school. When Huck refuses, Pap kidnaps him and holds him captive in a cabin in the woods.

Huck fakes his own murder and escapes along the Mississippi River, discovering Miss Watson's slave Jim, who has run away for fear he will be sold. They find a raft and flee together down the river. Jim's plan is to reach Cairo, Illinois, where he will follow the Ohio River to the free states.

Huck fears he is behaving immorally by assisting a fugitive slave but sticks with Jim anyway. They encounter many characters: a band of robbers aboard a wrecked steamboat; two genteel Southern families involved in a bloody feud; and a pair of con men called the duke and the king. Eventually, Huck must rescue Jim, and he is assisted in the attempt by his pal Tom Sawyer.

At least three things make *The Adventures of Huckleberry Finn* especially suitable for adaptation as a *manga*, or Japanese-style graphic novel: First, the manga is an example of *popular culture* rather than *high culture*. Unlike a painting by Jackson Pollock or a poem by T.S. Elliot, most manga are intended to appeal to a mass audience. Similarly, *Huckleberry Finn* was one of the first novels to be written entirely in dialect—ordinary speech from a particular region, rather than self consciously "literary" language and syntax—and it is full of rollicking fun and lowbrow humor. Though some manga are beautiful and profound, they are not fundamentally *difficult* in the way that Modern-era paintings and poetry can be. They're easy both to begin and to finish, approachable—just as *Huckleberry Finn* is approachable. As devotees of the form well know, the best manga are more than mere comic books, and Mark Twain's novel transcends its humble origins as a sequel to a bestselling book for kids.

Secondly, many manga do not shy from depicting violence. (Quentin Tarantino's notoriously bloody film *Kill Bill*, starring Uma Thurman, was based on the title character of a Japanese manga called *Lady Snow Blood*.) And, although this is often played down in child-friendly adaptations for the screen,

*Huckleberry Finn's* world is a brutal one. From his own father's shack to the house of the apparently genteel Grangerfords to the Phelps farm where Jim is incarcerated and Tom is shot, Huck is immersed in deadly violence. Virtually the only place he finds tranquility is floating on the river with Jim. A manga is an ideal medium in which to depict Huck's rough, often life-threatening surroundings.

Finally, *The Adventures of Huckleberry Finn* is cinematic — though of course motion pictures had not been invented when Twain wrote the book. (They would be before he died in 1910.) Think of all the scenes in the novel that seem to have been written with the movies in mind, including the following:

* Huck's escape from Pap's house, especially the faking of his own death, played out in a series of images like those in a silent film.
* The episode on the steamboat that has run aground, in which Huck eavesdrops on plans for a murder — and quickly devises a plan of his own to prevent it.
* The long night in the fog on the river. In fact, all of the scenes on the Mississippi beg to be captured on celluloid.
* Huck's unsuccessful, and highly comical, masquerade as a girl.
* The spectacular destruction of the raft by the steamboat, at night.
* The bloody battle between the Grangerfords and the Shepherdsons.
* The slaying of Boggs by Colonel Sherburn, and Sherburn's contemptuous dismissal of the mob that gathers at his house seeking vengeance.
* The duke and the king presentation of the Royal Nonesuch.

Finally, Huck and Tom's attempted emancipation of Jim from the Phelps's farm is worthy of a Hollywood action movie.

As motion pictures and graphic novels resemble one another closely, it follows that *The Adventures of Huck Finn* and manga are something like a perfect fit.

A note on authenticity: In order to fit this adaptation into a book of less than 200 pages, the writers and editors of *The Manga Edition* have of course cut much from Twain's masterpiece. Virtually all of the dialogue that remains, however, comes directly from *The Adventures of Huckleberry Finn*. For ease of reading, the characters' words have been spelled conventionally rather than phonetically.

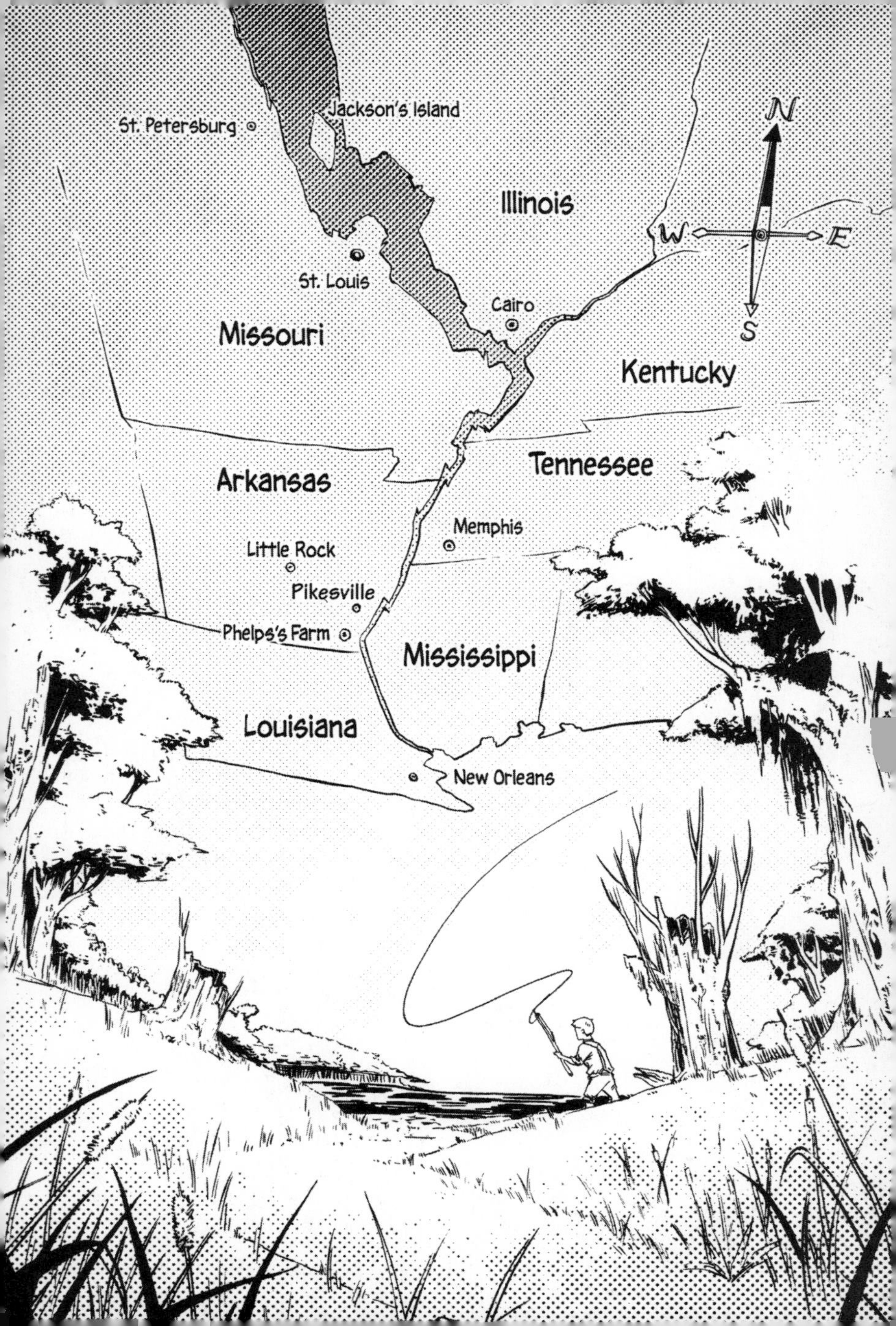
Jackson's Island
St. Petersburg
N
Illinois
W
E
St. Louis
Cairo
S
Missouri
Kentucky
Tennessee
Arkansas
Memphis
Little Rock
Pikesville
Phelps's Farm
Mississippi
Louisiana
New Orleans

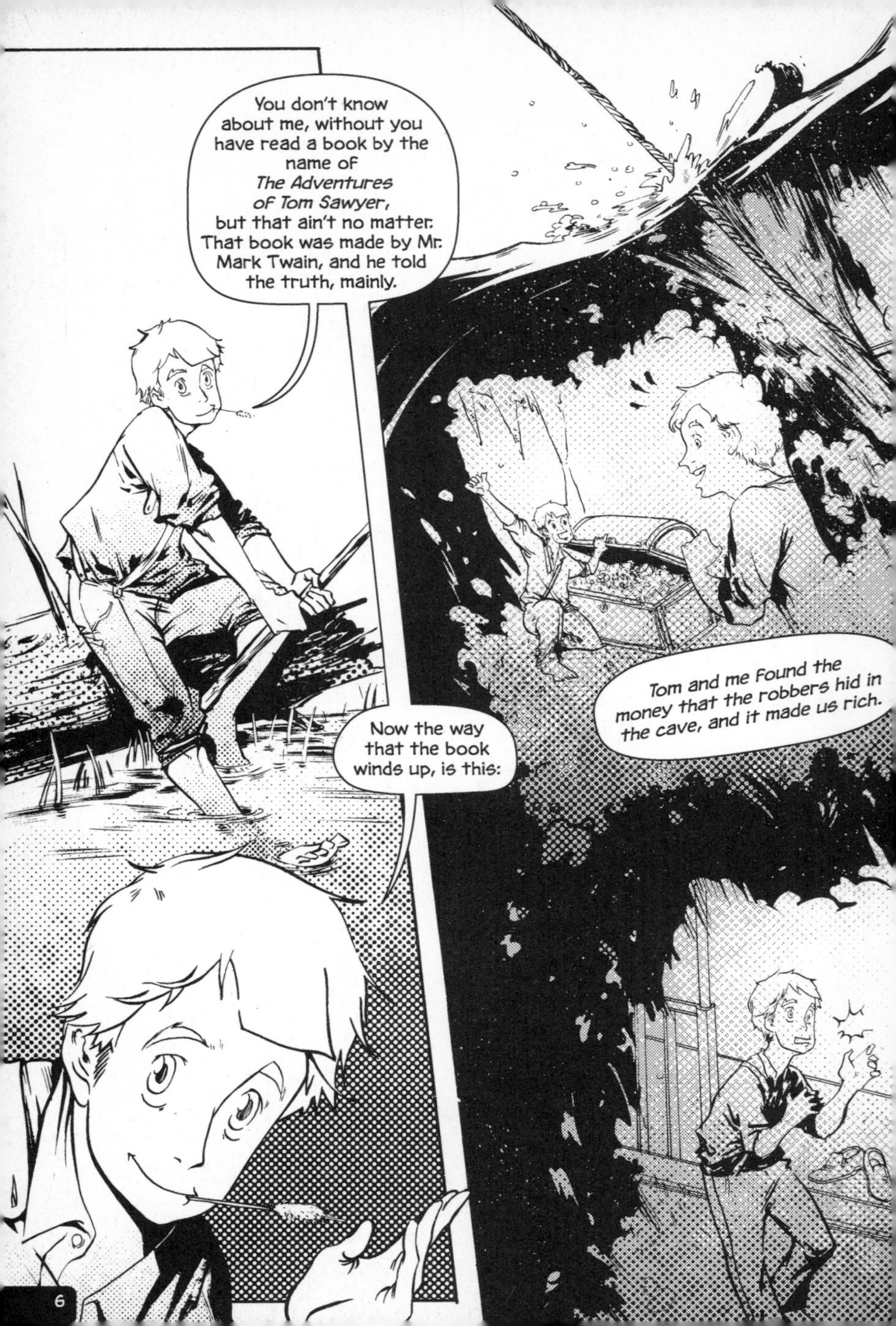
You don't know about me, without you have read a book by the name of *The Adventures of Tom Sawyer*, but that ain't no matter. That book was made by Mr. Mark Twain, and he told the truth, mainly.
Now the way that the book winds up, is this:
Tom and me found the money that the robbers hid in the cave, and it made us rich.

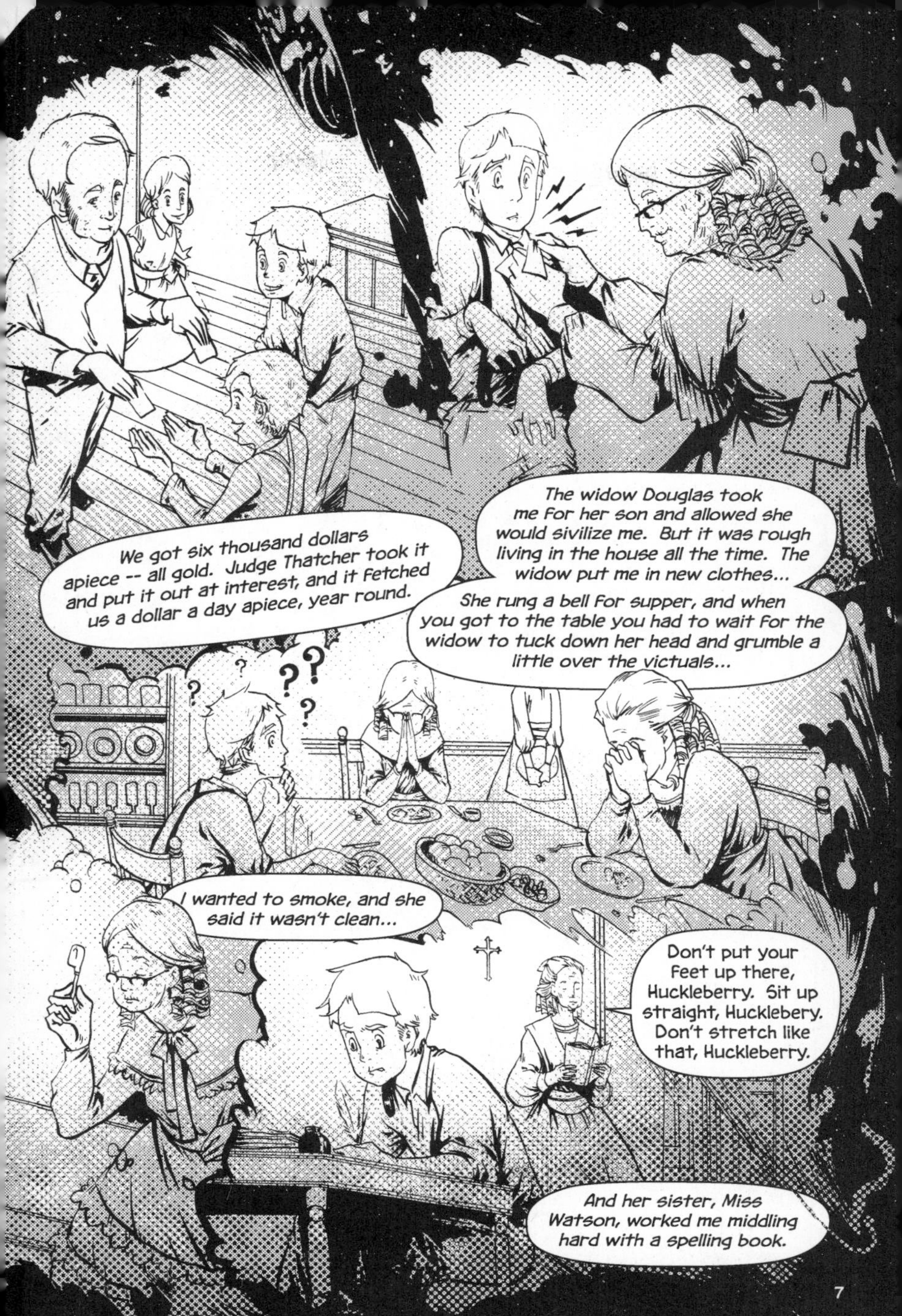
We got six thousand dollars apiece -- all gold. Judge Thatcher took it and put it out at interest, and it fetched us a dollar a day apiece, year round.
The widow Douglas took me for her son and allowed she would sivilize me. But it was rough living in the house all the time. The widow put me in new clothes...
She rung a bell for supper, and when you got to the table you had to wait for the widow to tuck down her head and grumble a little over the victuals...
I wanted to smoke, and she said it wasn't clean...
Don't put your feet up there, Huckleberry. Sit up straight, Huckleberry. Don't stretch like that, Huckleberry.
And her sister, Miss Watson, worked me middling hard with a spelling book.

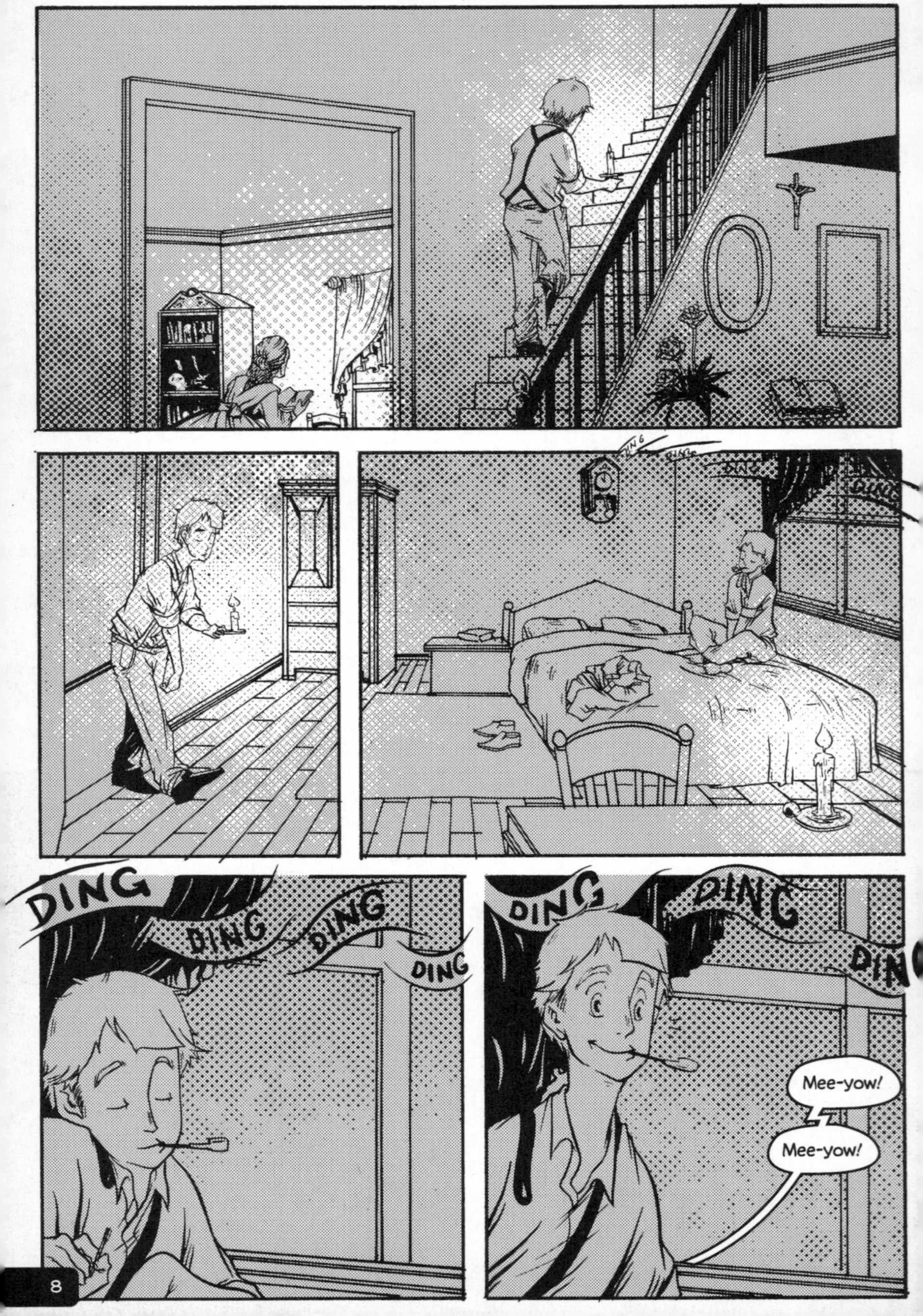
DING
DING
DING
DING
DING
DING
DING
DING
DING
DING
Mee-yow!
Mee-yow!

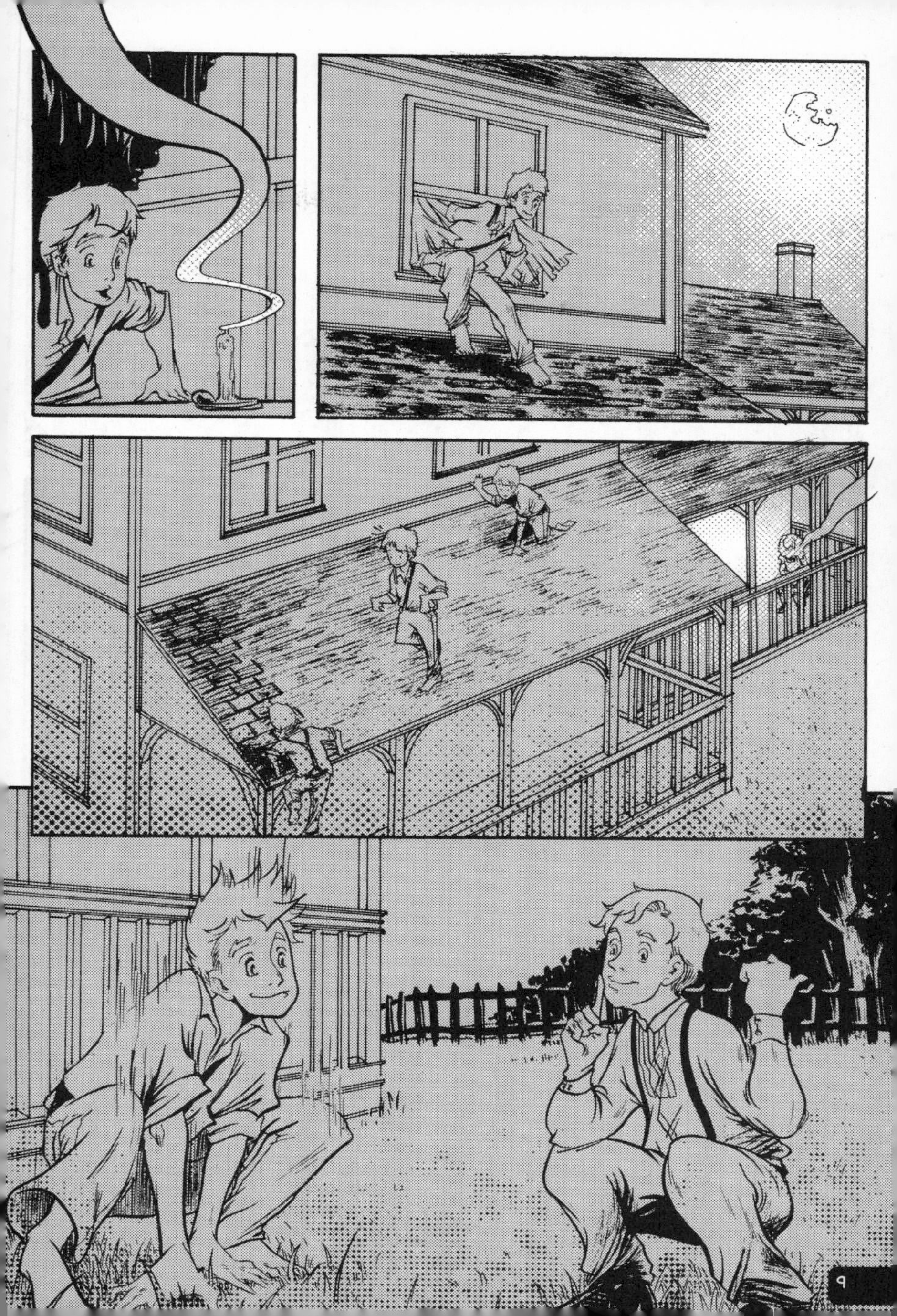

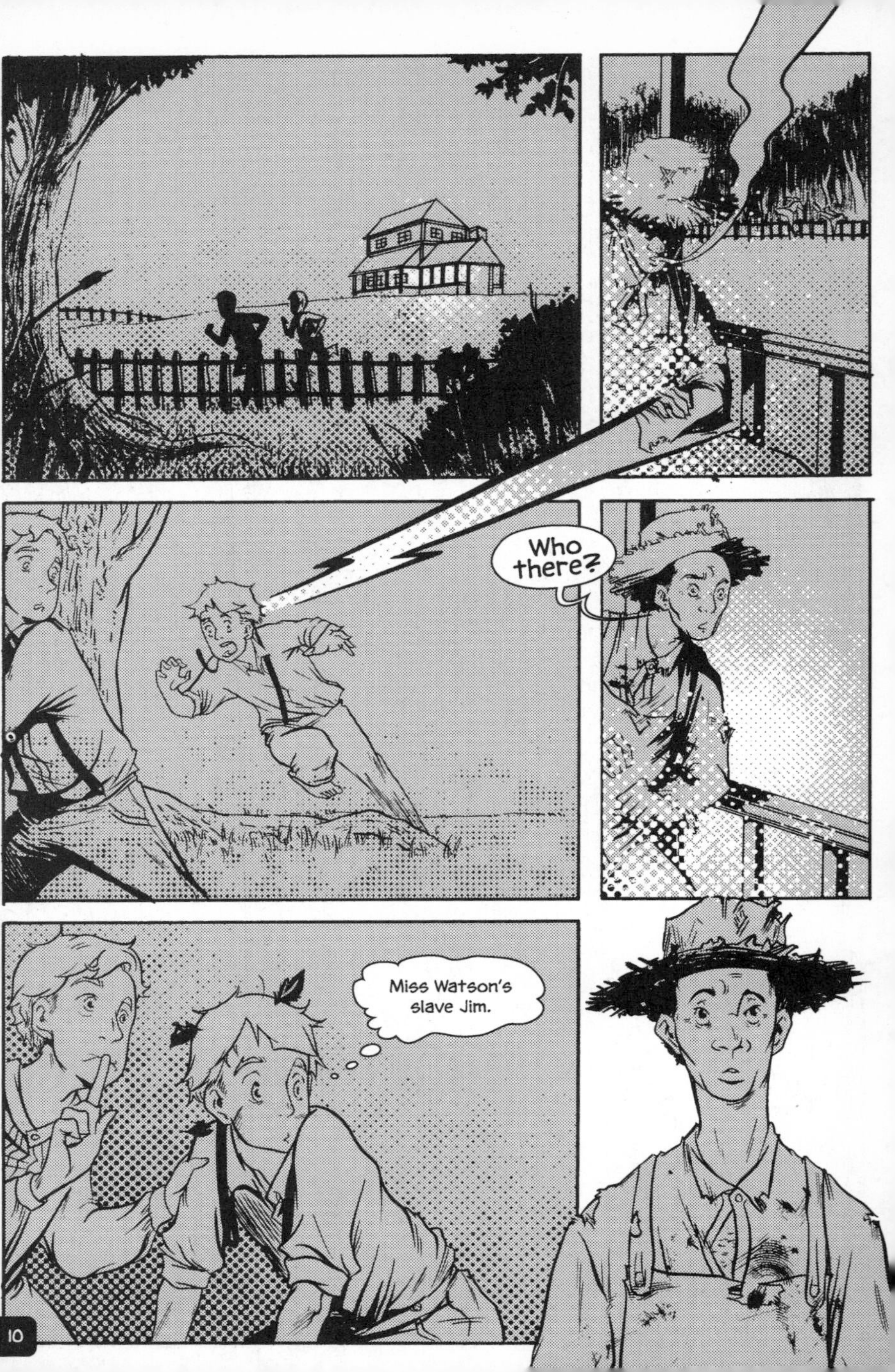
Who there?
Miss Watson's slave Jim.

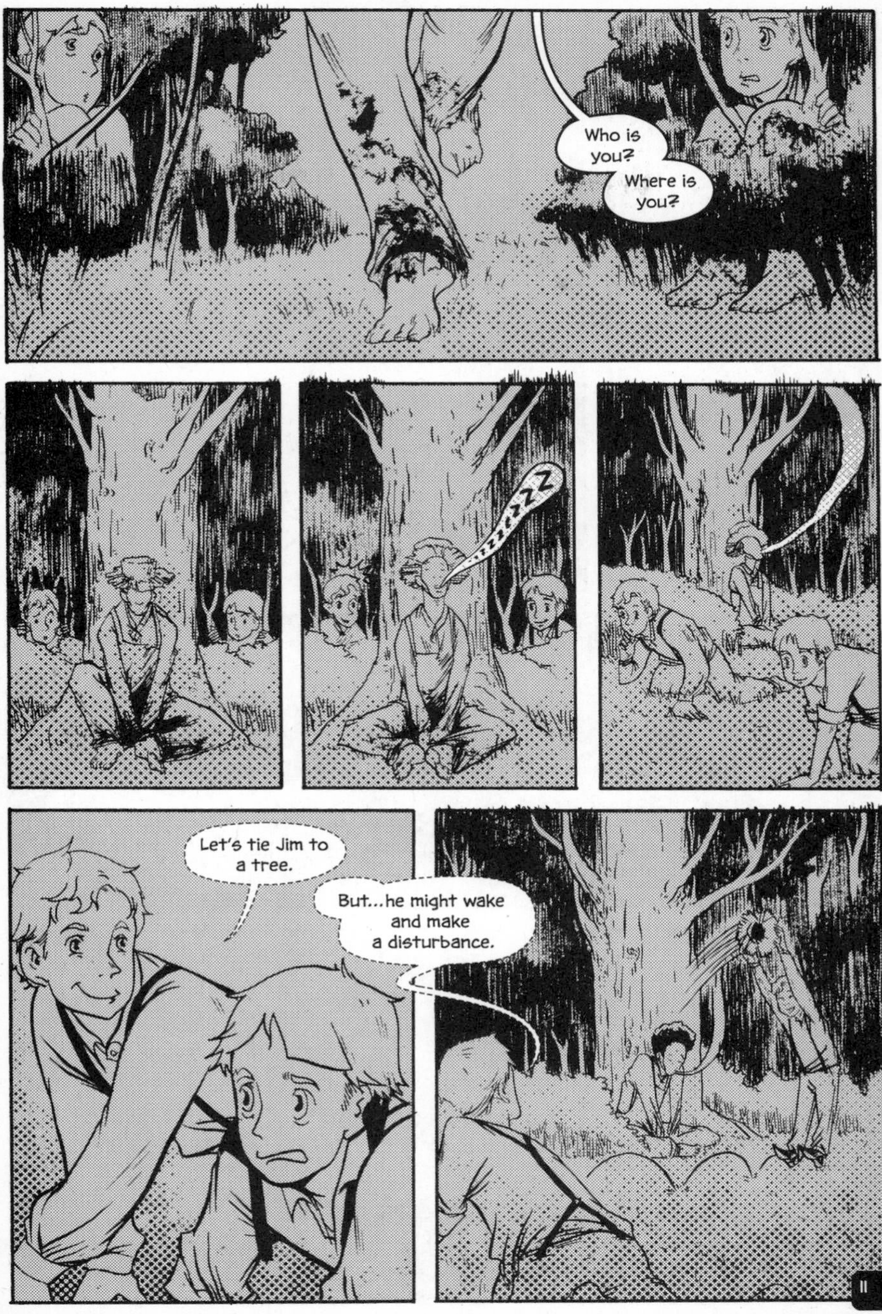
Who is you?
Where is you?
ZZZ
Let's tie Jim to a tree.
But...he might wake and make a disturbance.

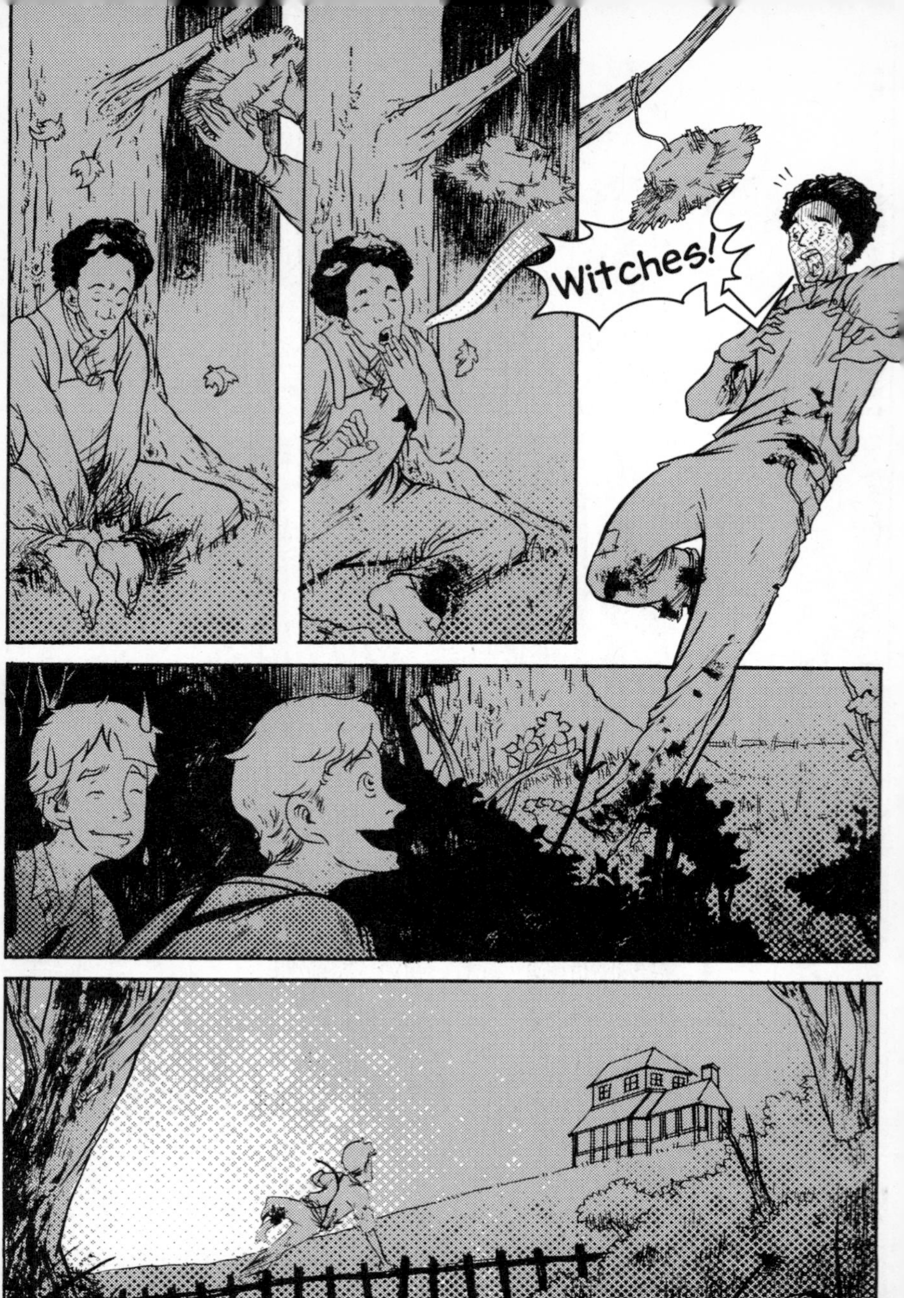
Witches!

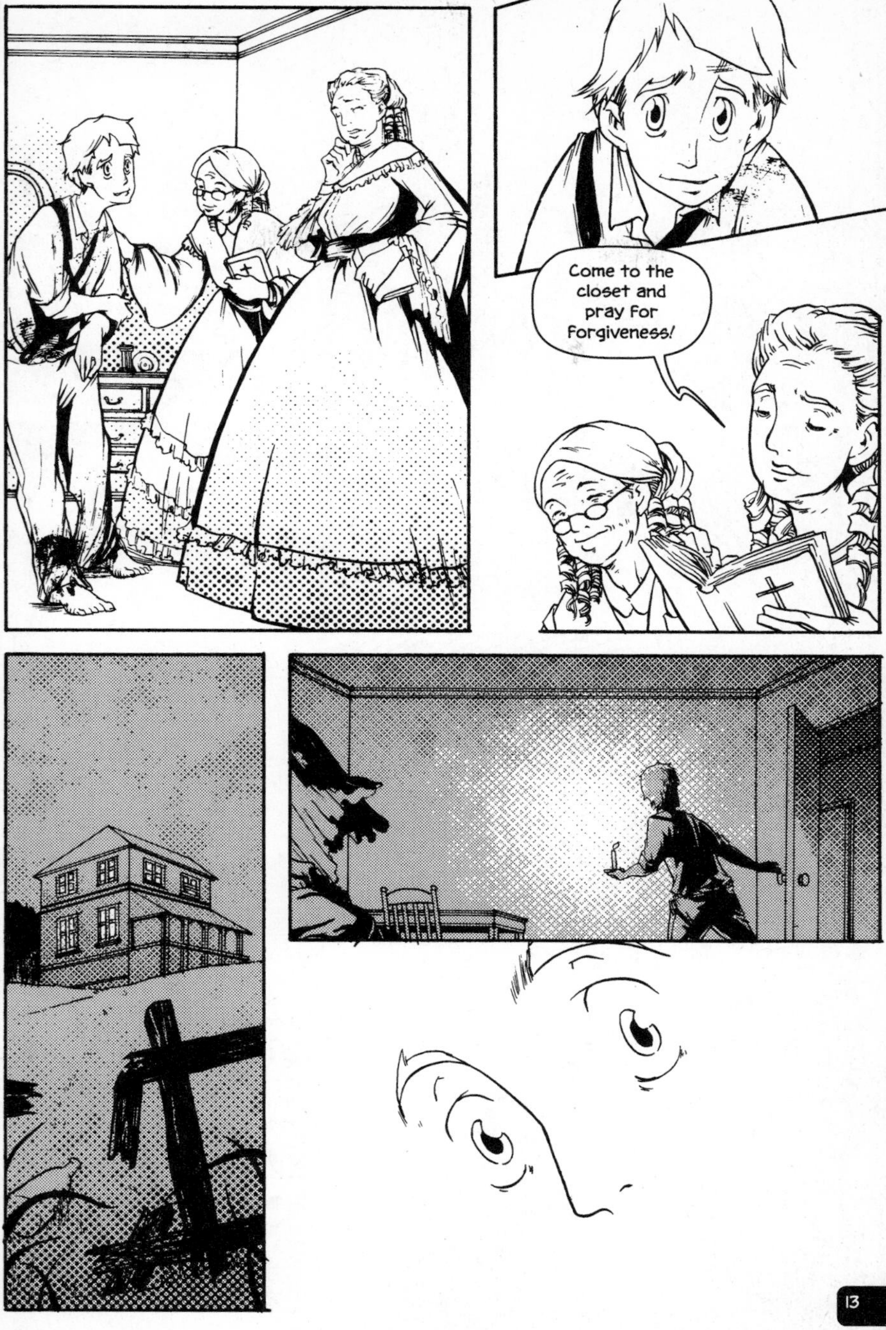
Come to the closet and pray for forgiveness!

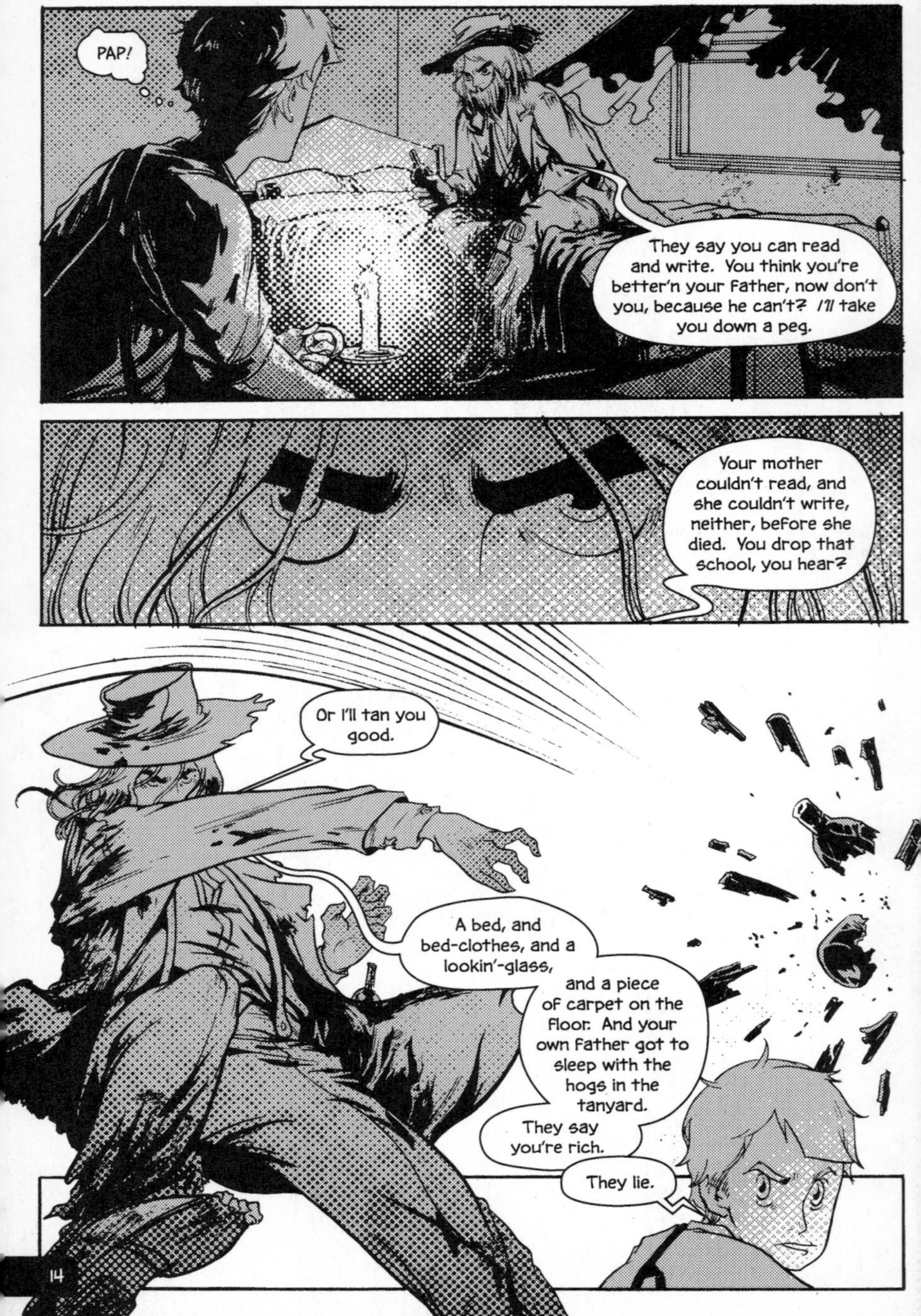
PAP!
They say you can read and write. You think you're better'n your father, now don't you, because he can't? I'll take you down a peg.
Your mother couldn't read, and she couldn't write, neither, before she died. You drop that school, you hear?
Or I'll tan you good.
A bed, and bed-clothes, and a lookin'-glass,
and a piece of carpet on the floor. And your own father got to sleep with the hogs in the tanyard.
They say you're rich.
They lie.

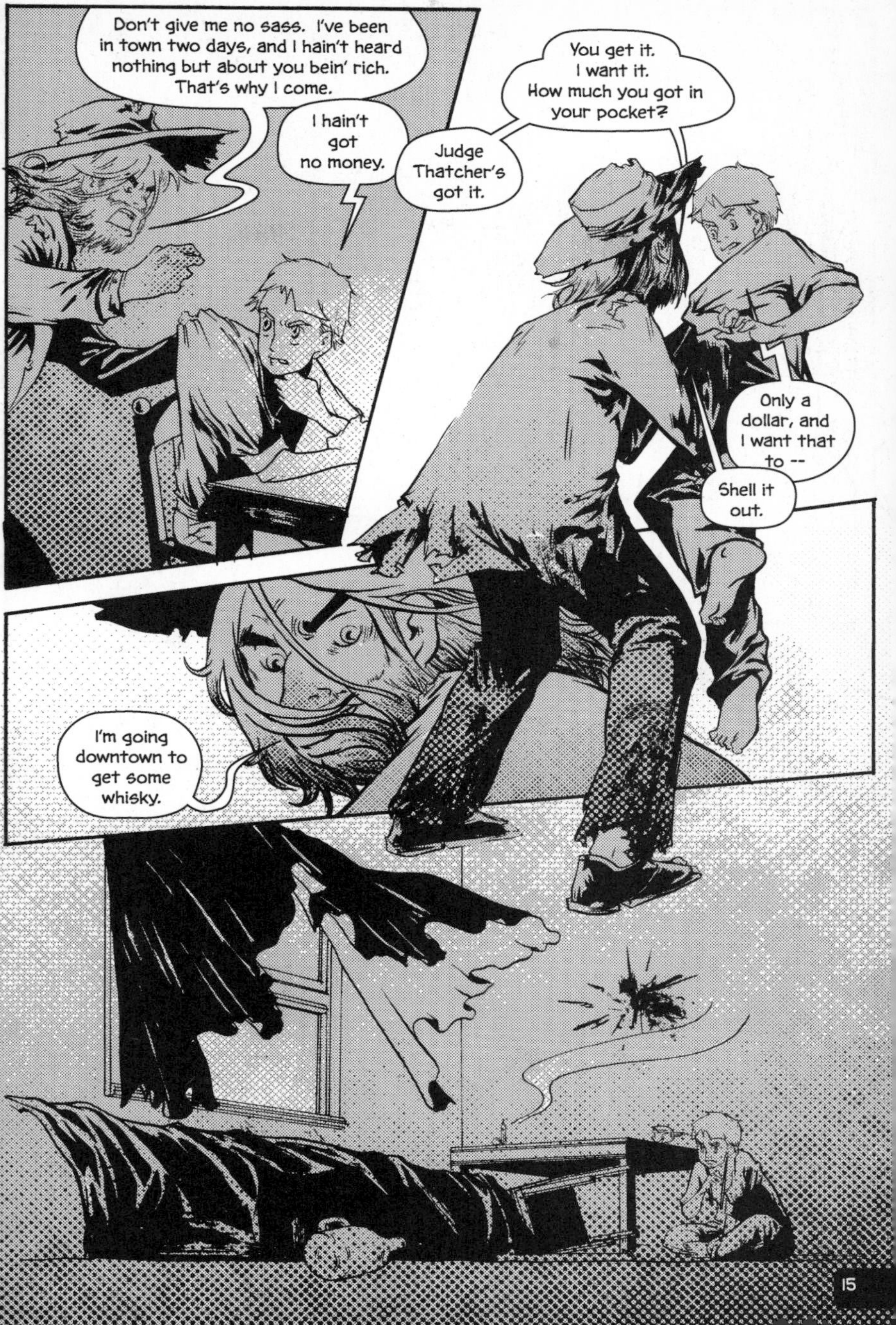
Don't give me no sass. I've been in town two days, and I hain't heard nothing but about you bein' rich. That's why I come.
I hain't got no money.
You get it. I want it. How much you got in your pocket?
Judge Thatcher's got it.
Only a dollar, and I want that to --
Shell it out.
I'm going downtown to get some whisky.

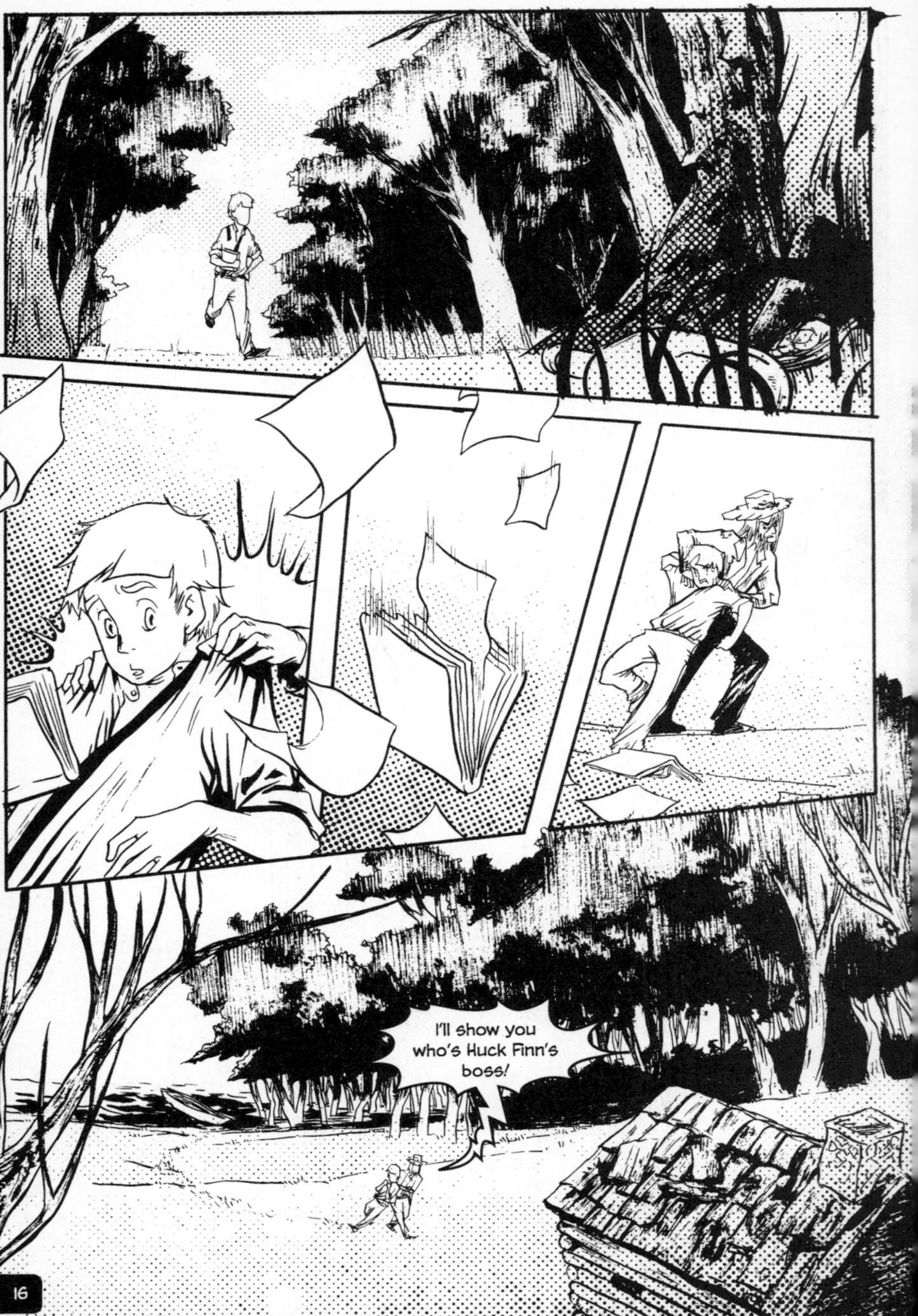
I'll show you who's Huck Finn's boss!

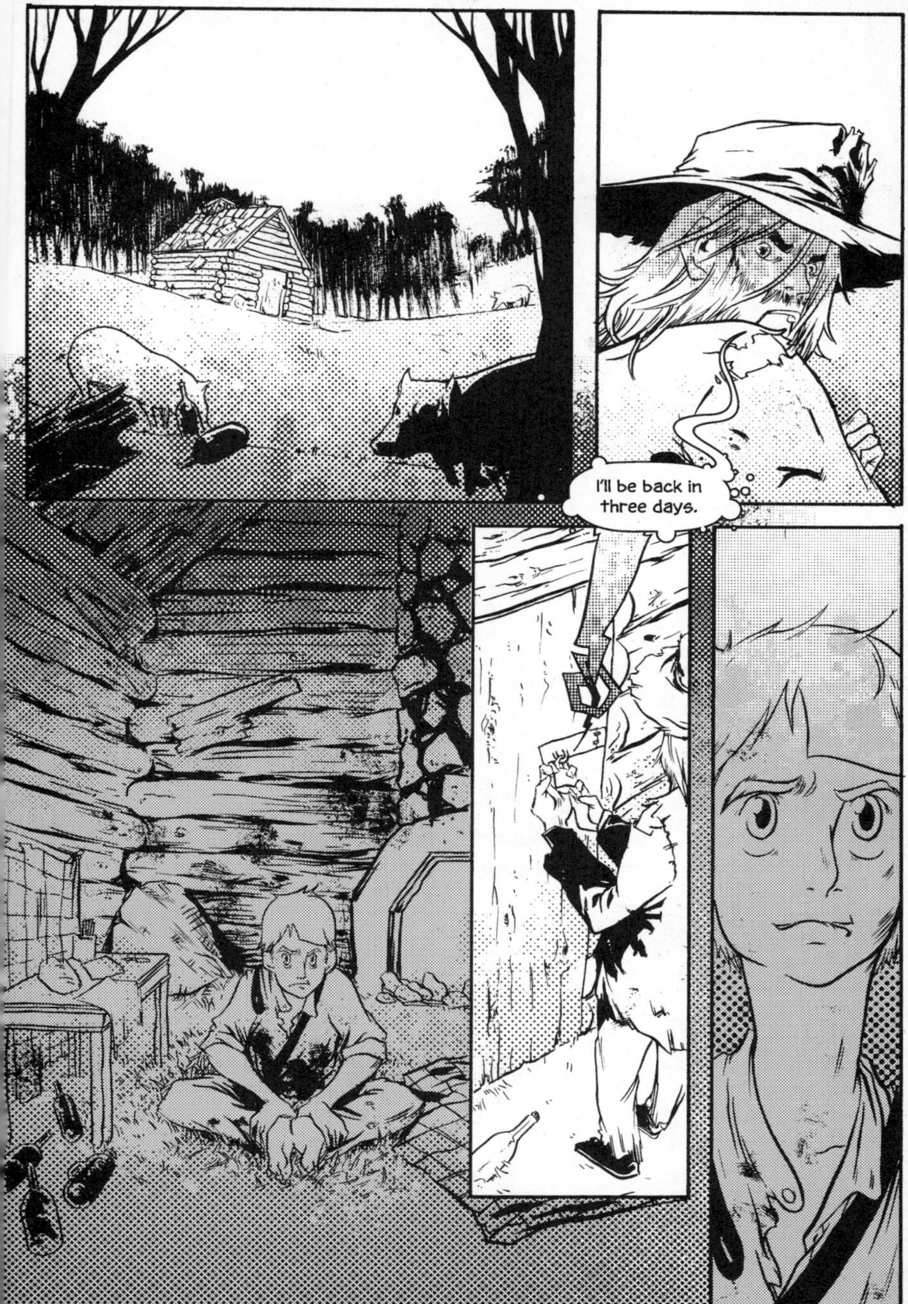
I'll be back in three days.

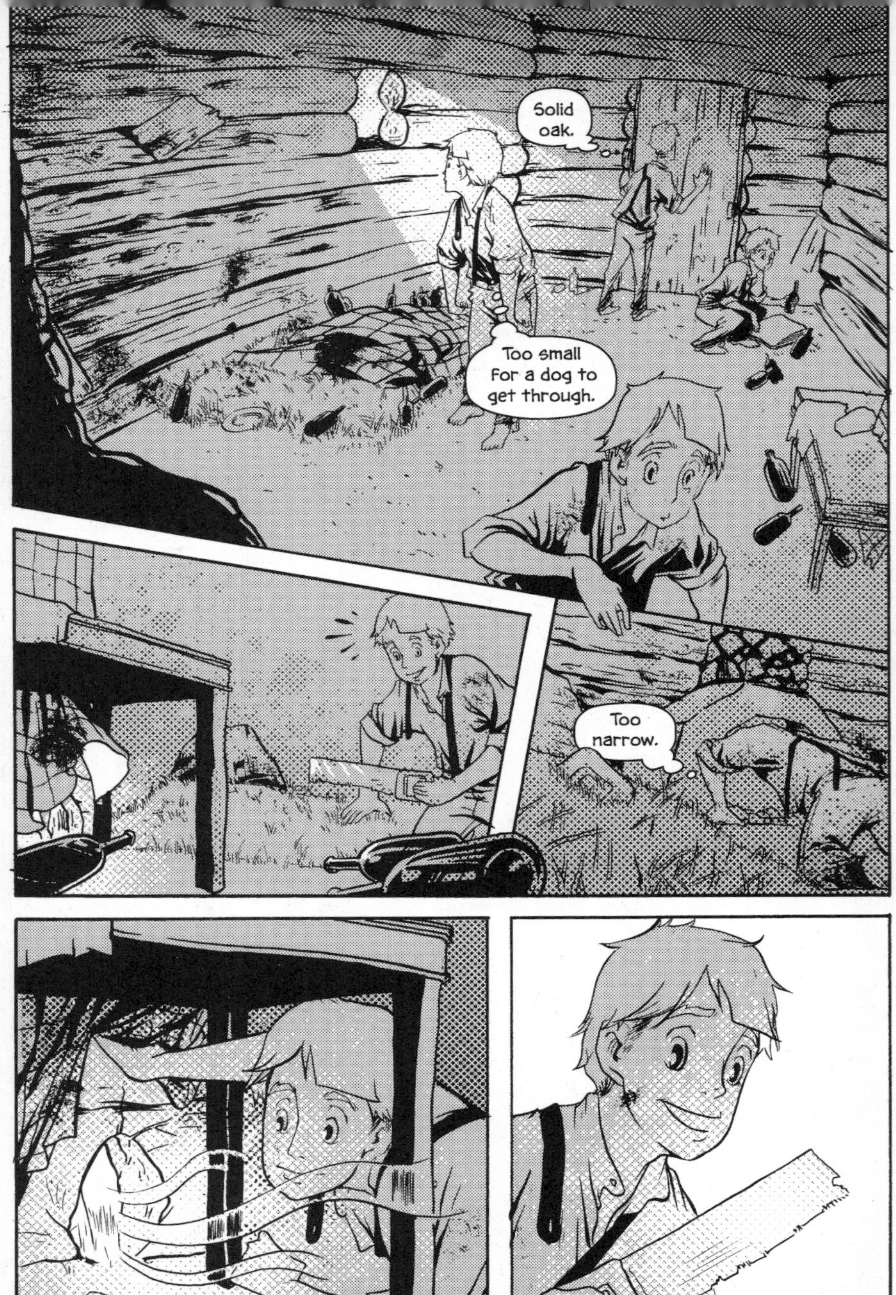
Solid oak.
Too small for a dog to get through.
Too narrow.

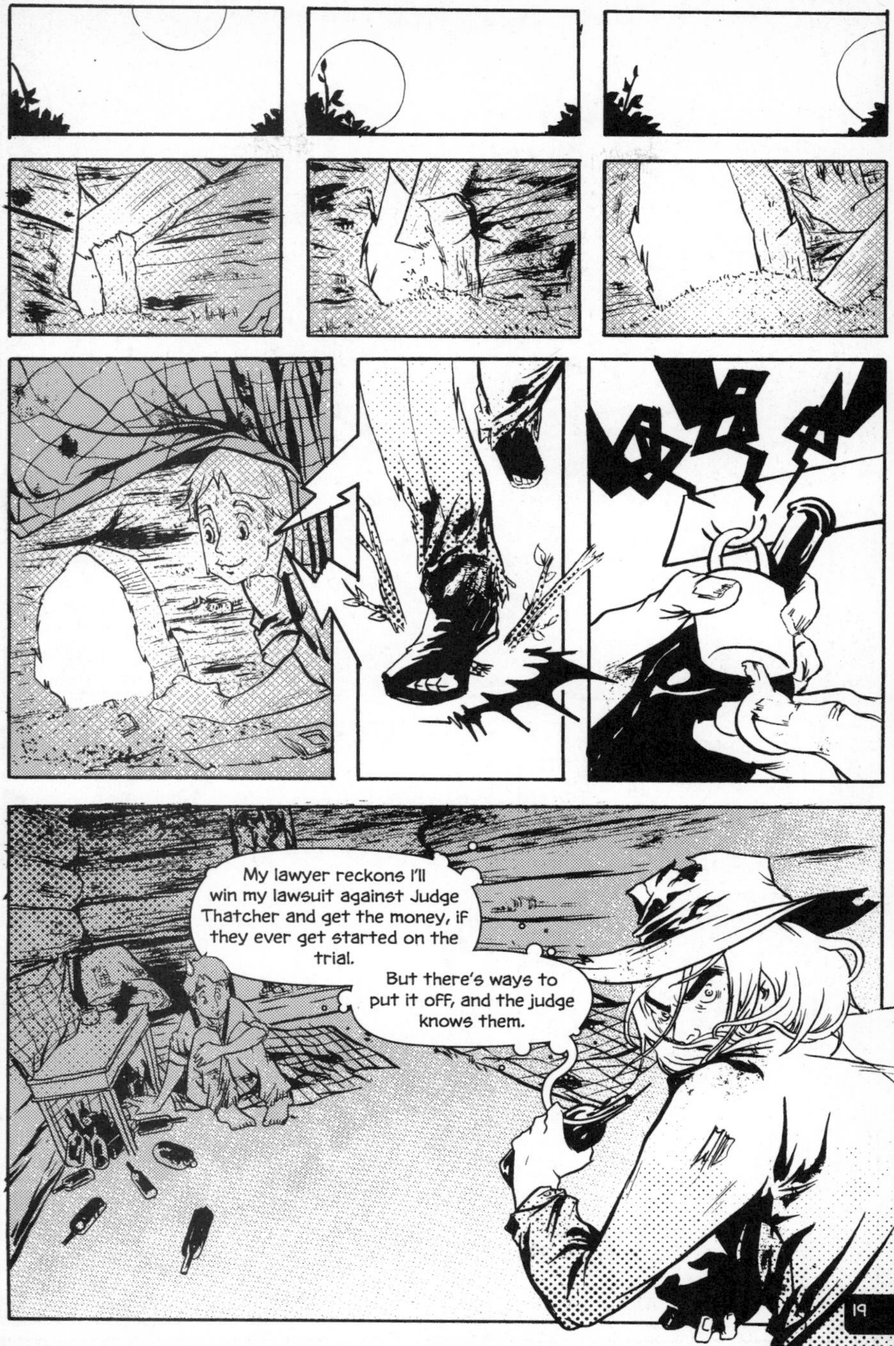

My lawyer reckons I'll win my lawsuit against Judge Thatcher and get the money, if they ever get started on the trial.
But there's ways to put it off, and the judge knows them.

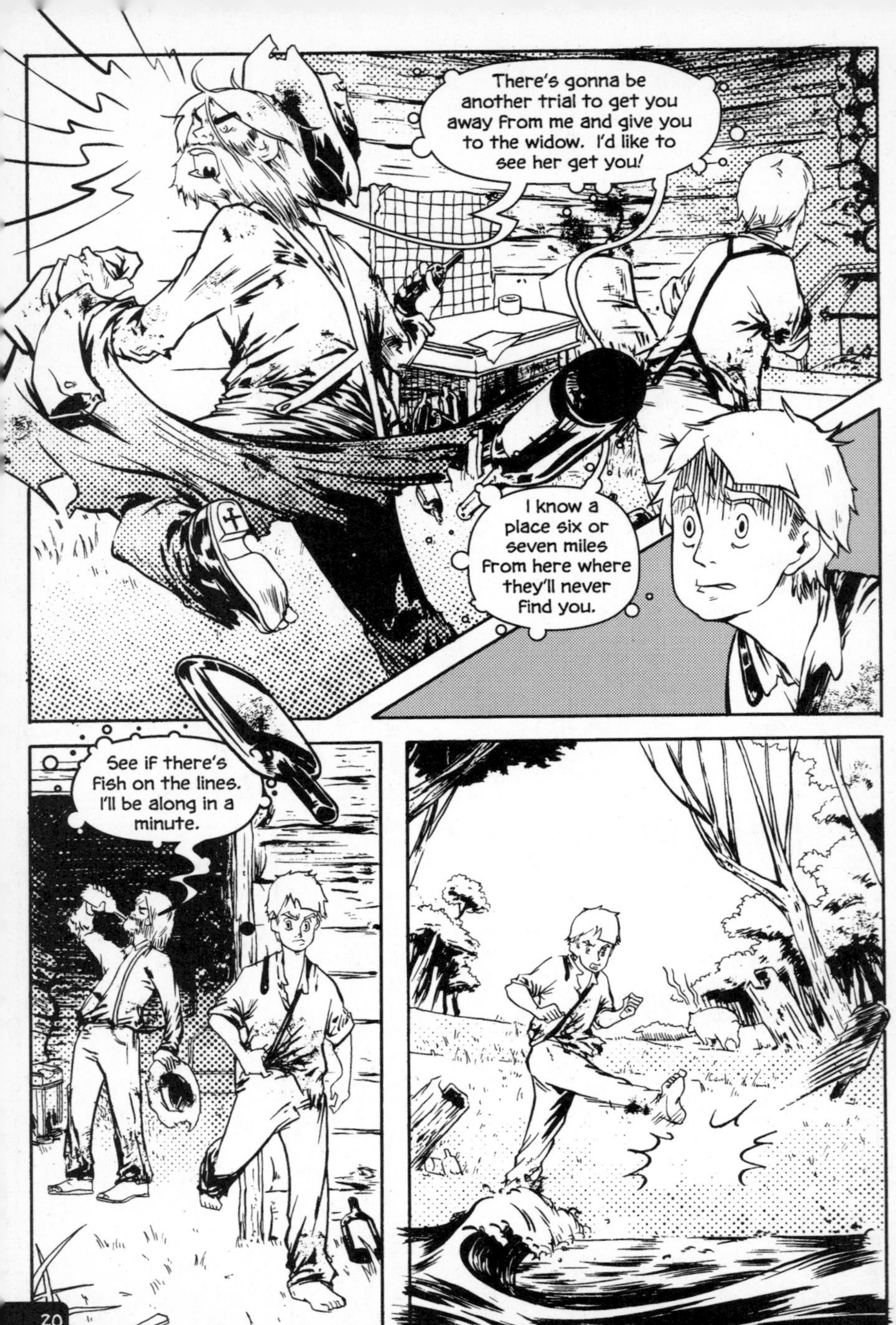
There's gonna be another trial to get you away from me and give you to the widow. I'd like to see her get you!
I know a place six or seven miles from here where they'll never find you.
See if there's fish on the lines. I'll be along in a minute.

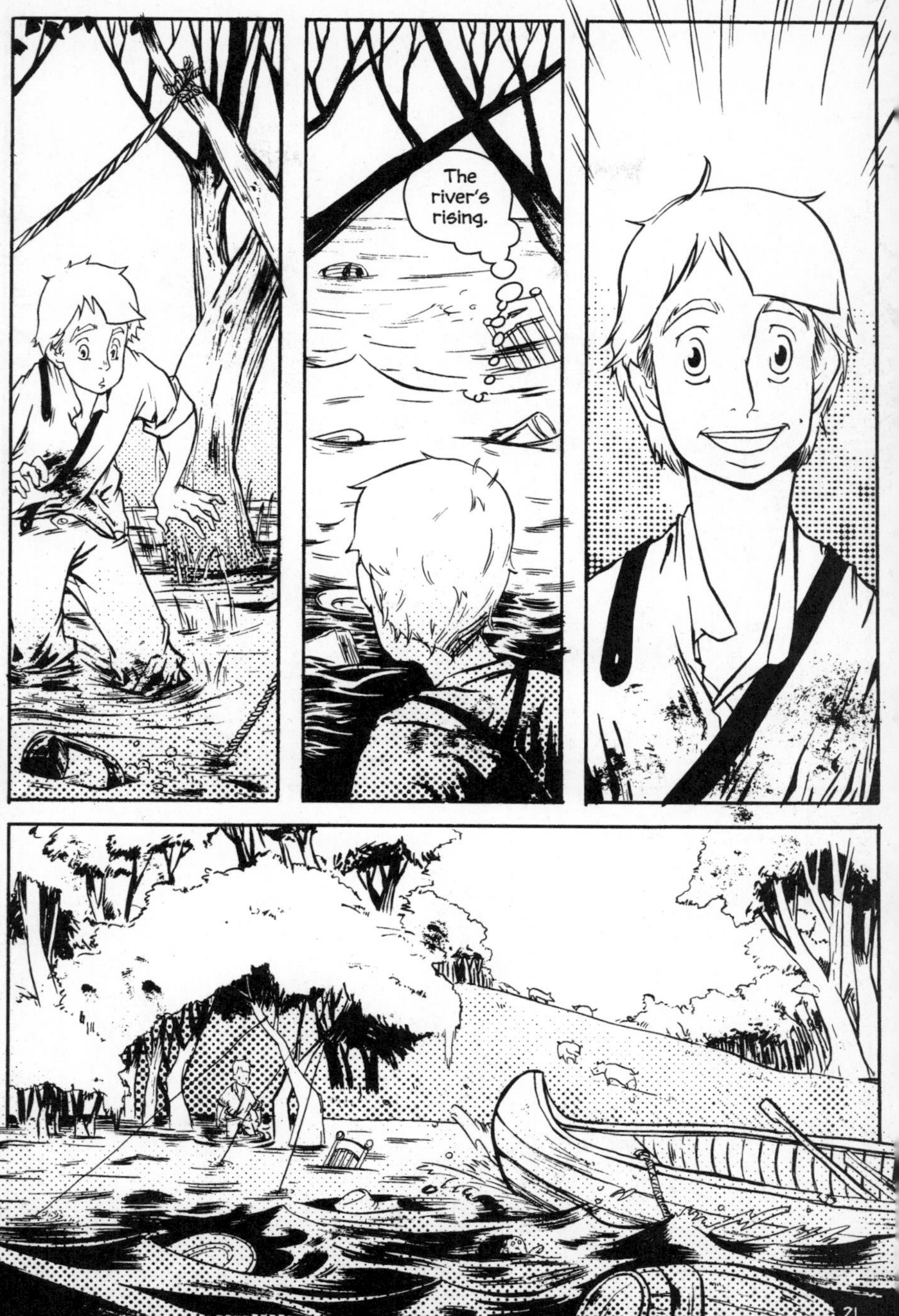
The river's rising.

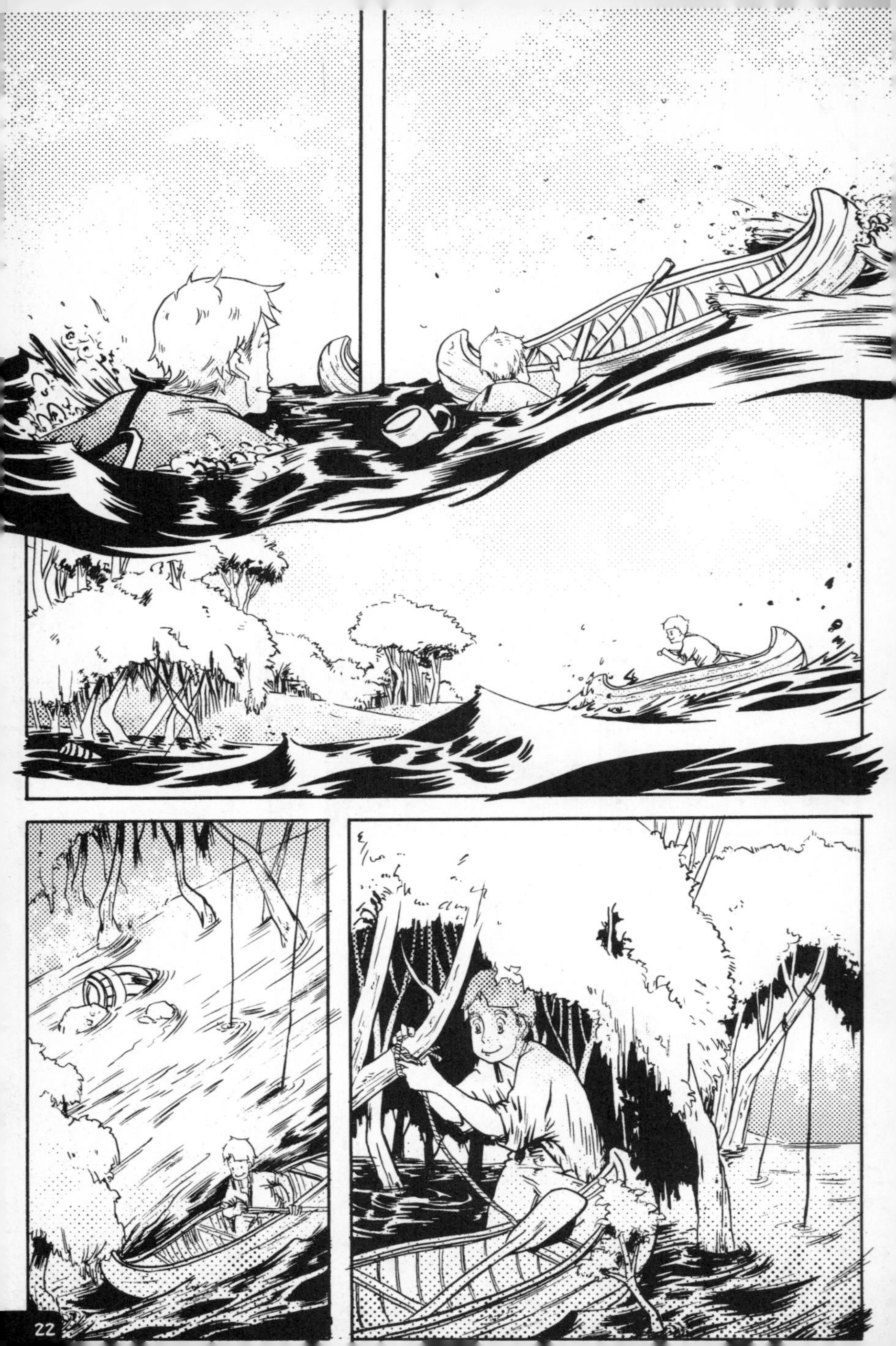

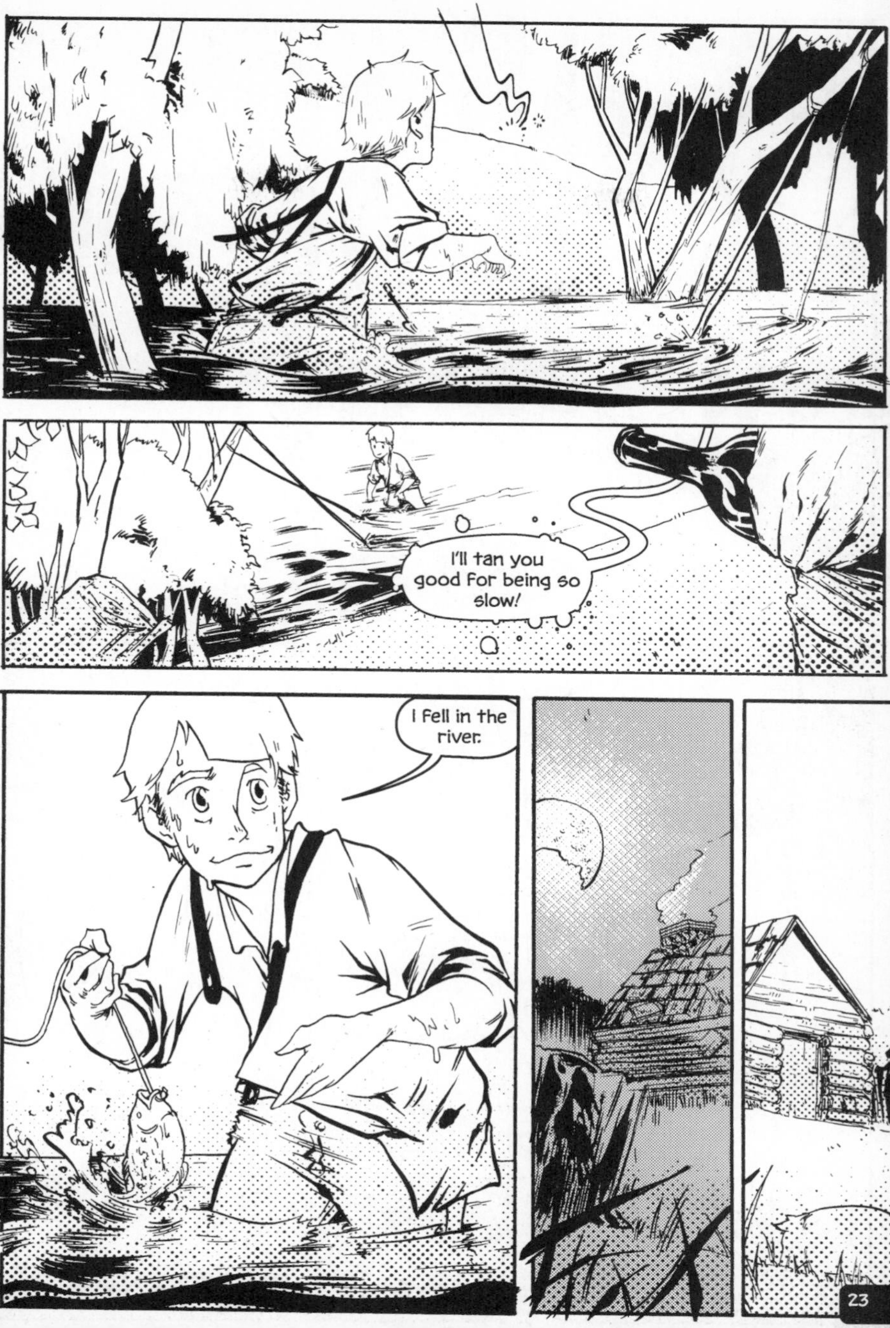
I'll tan you good for being so slow!
I fell in the river.

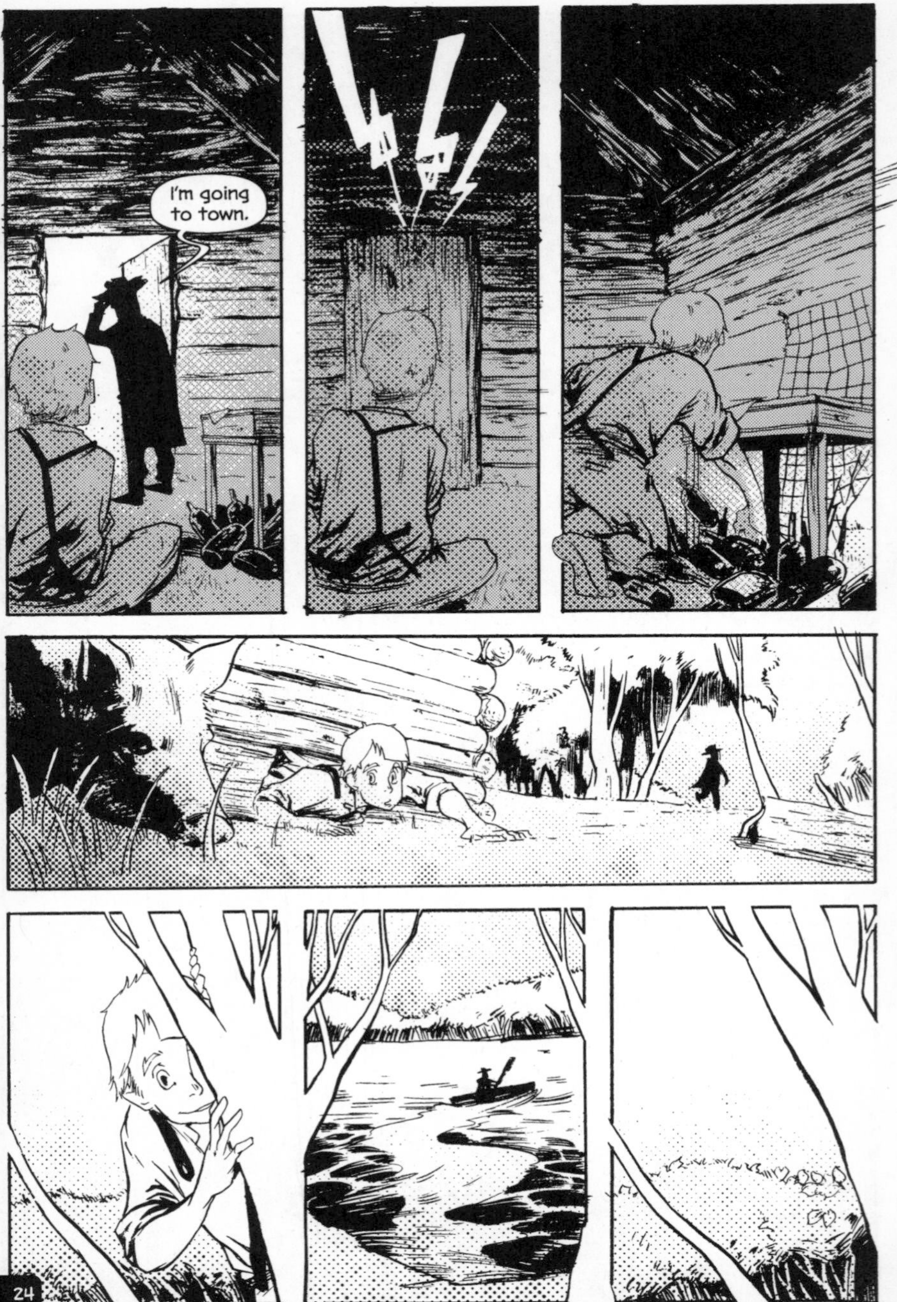
I'm going to town.

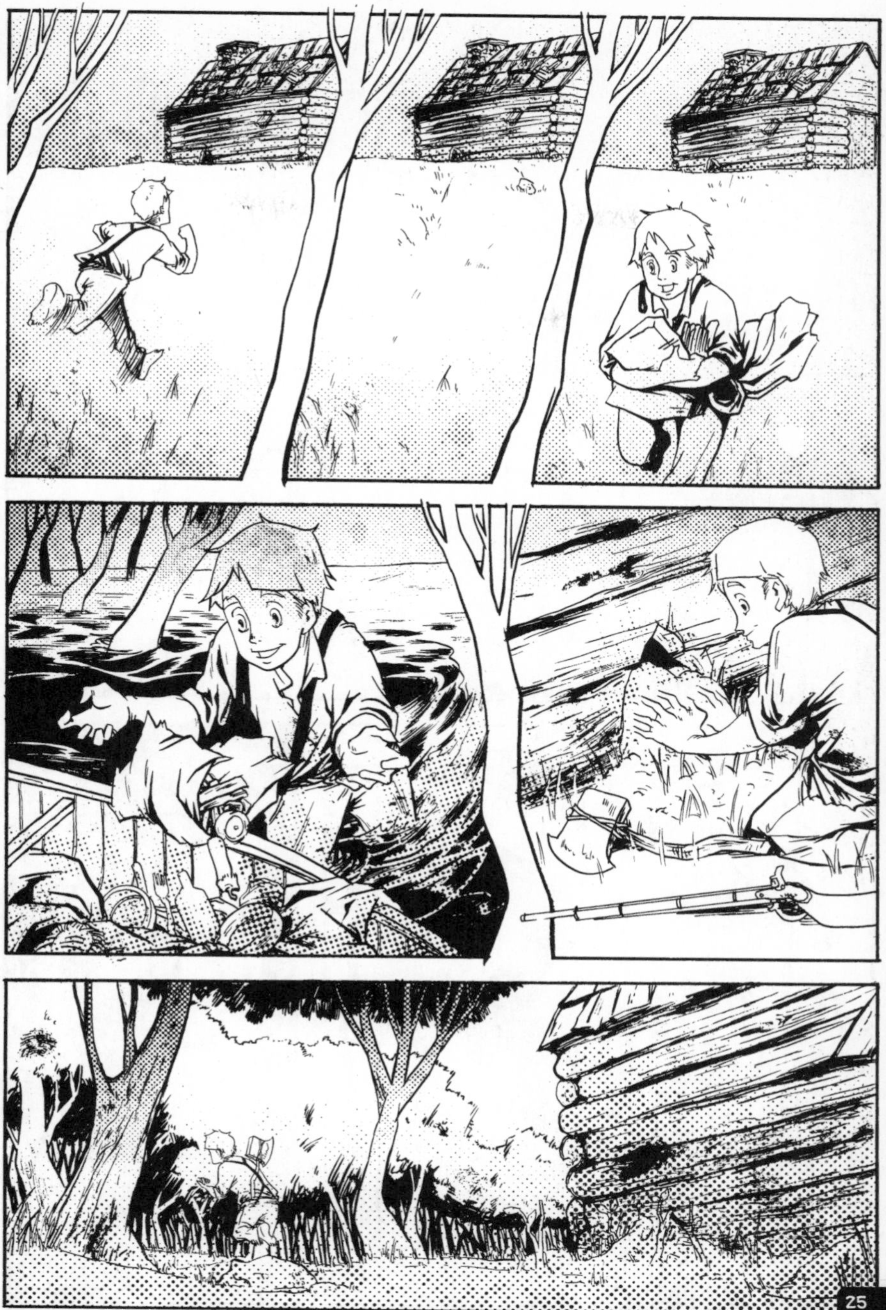

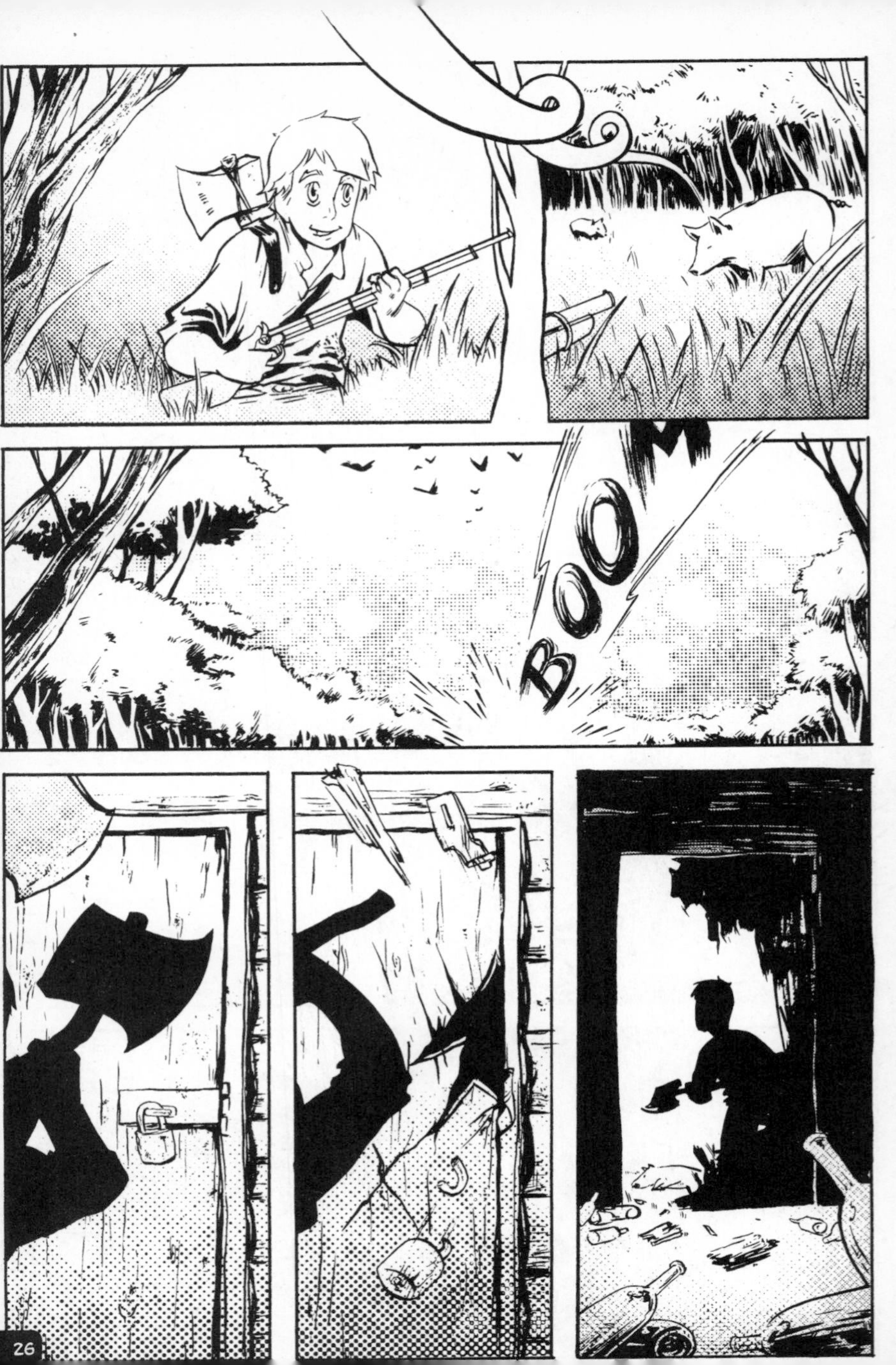
BOOOM

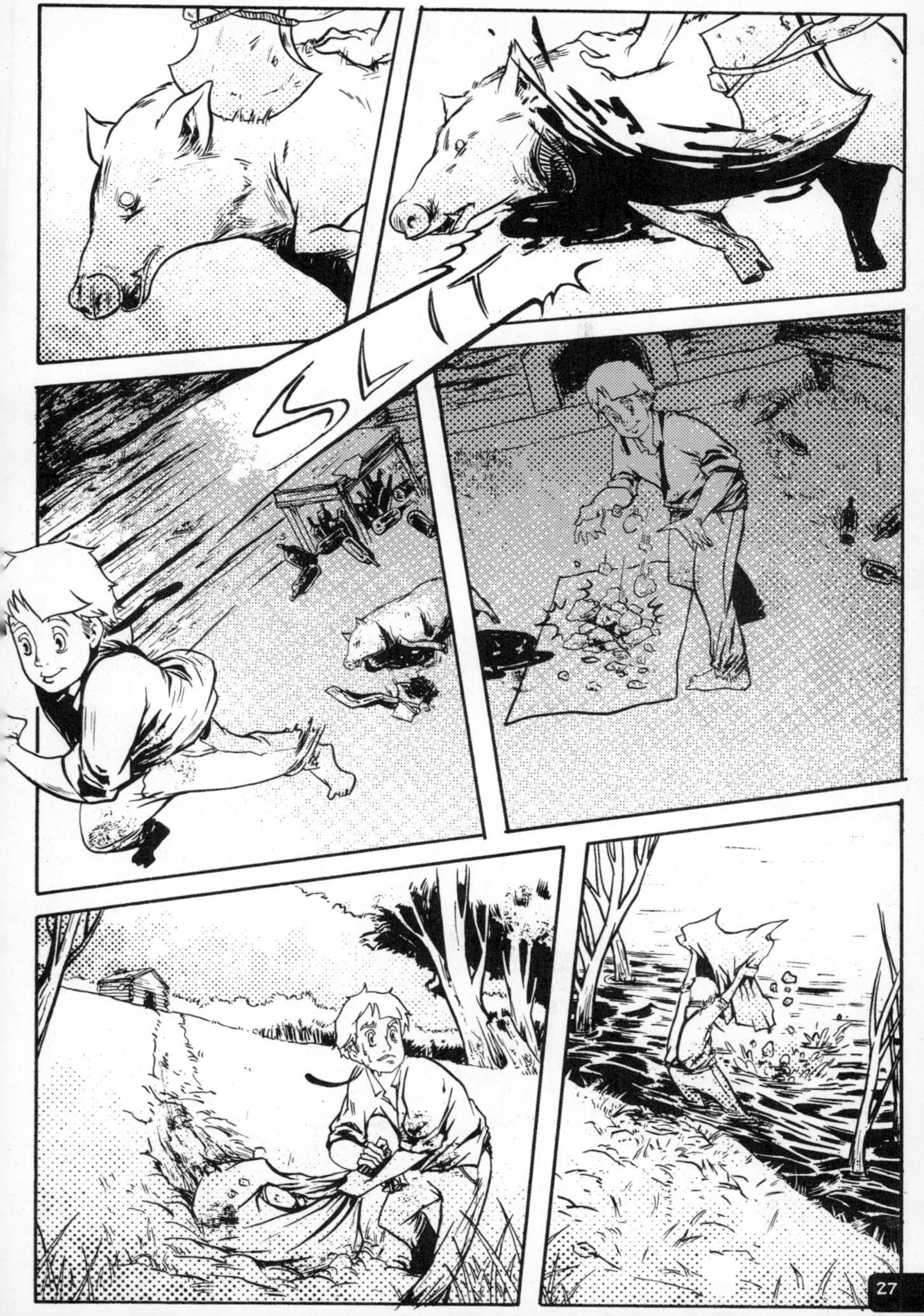
SLIT

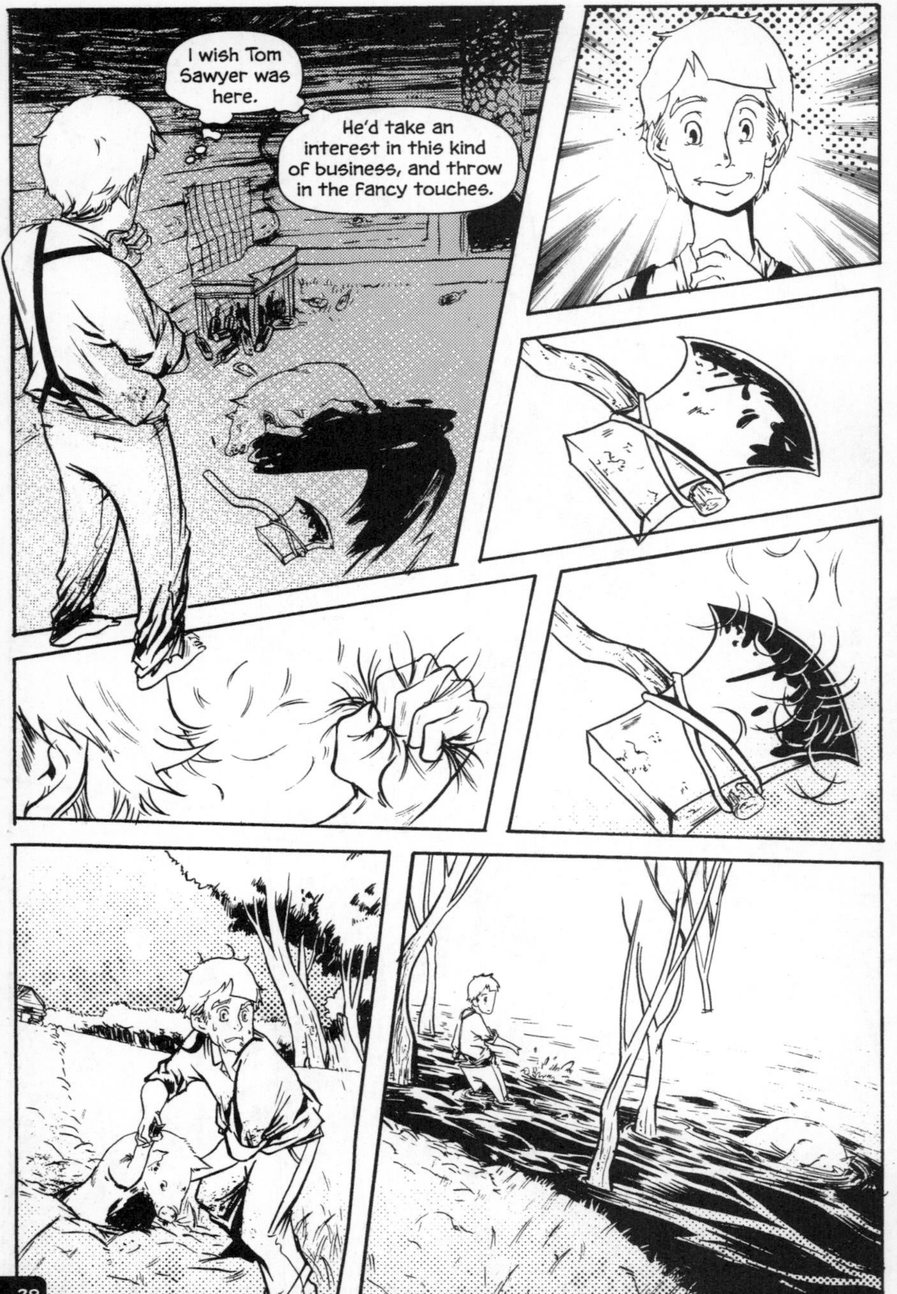

I wish Tom Sawyer was here.
He'd take an interest in this kind of business, and throw in the fancy touches.

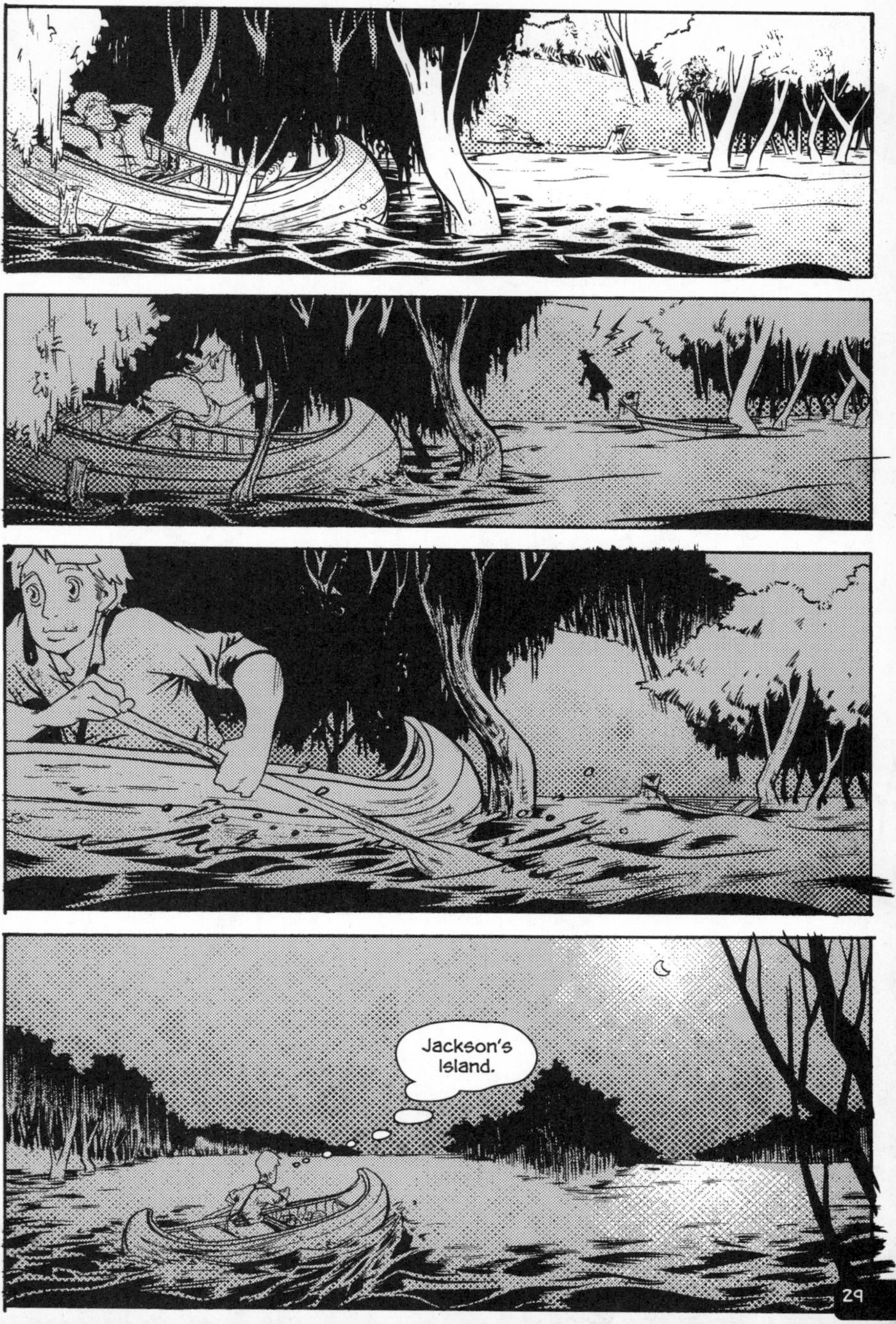
Jackson's Island.

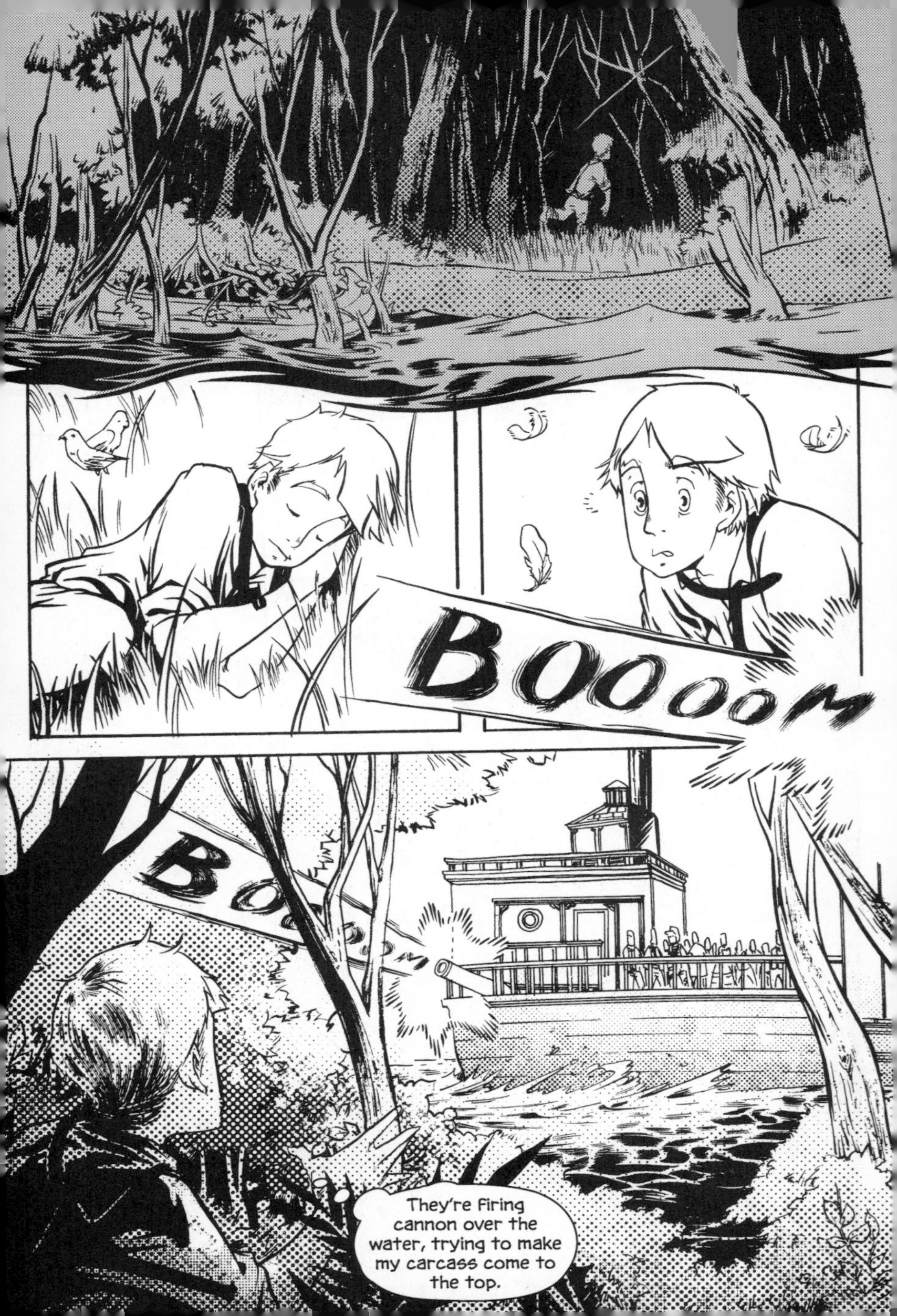
BOOOOOM
BOOOOOM
They're firing cannon over the water, trying to make my carcass come to the top.

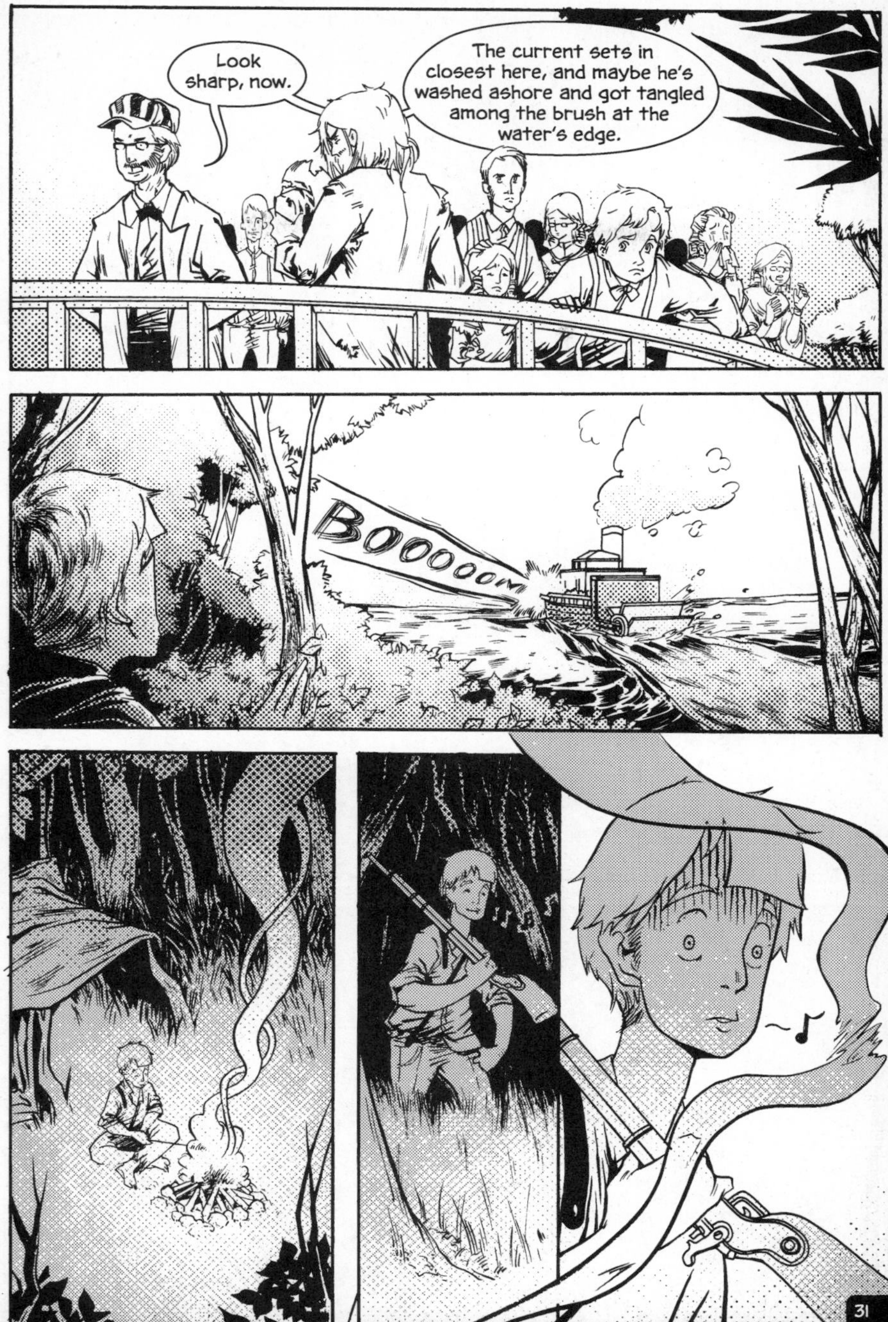
Look sharp, now.
The current sets in closest here, and maybe he's washed ashore and got tangled among the brush at the water's edge.
BOOOOOOM

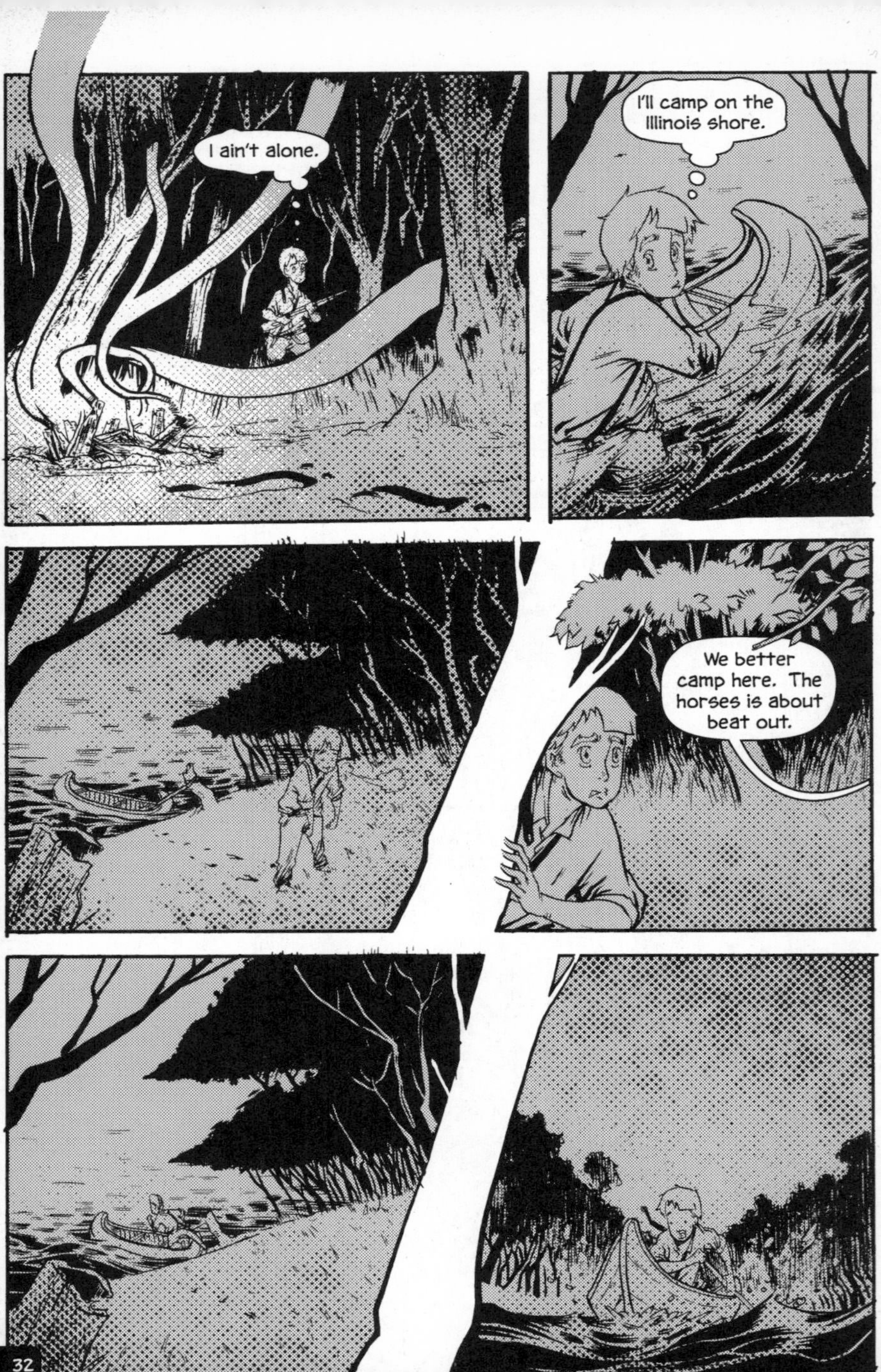
I ain't alone.
I'll camp on the Illinois shore.
We better camp here. The horses is about beat out.

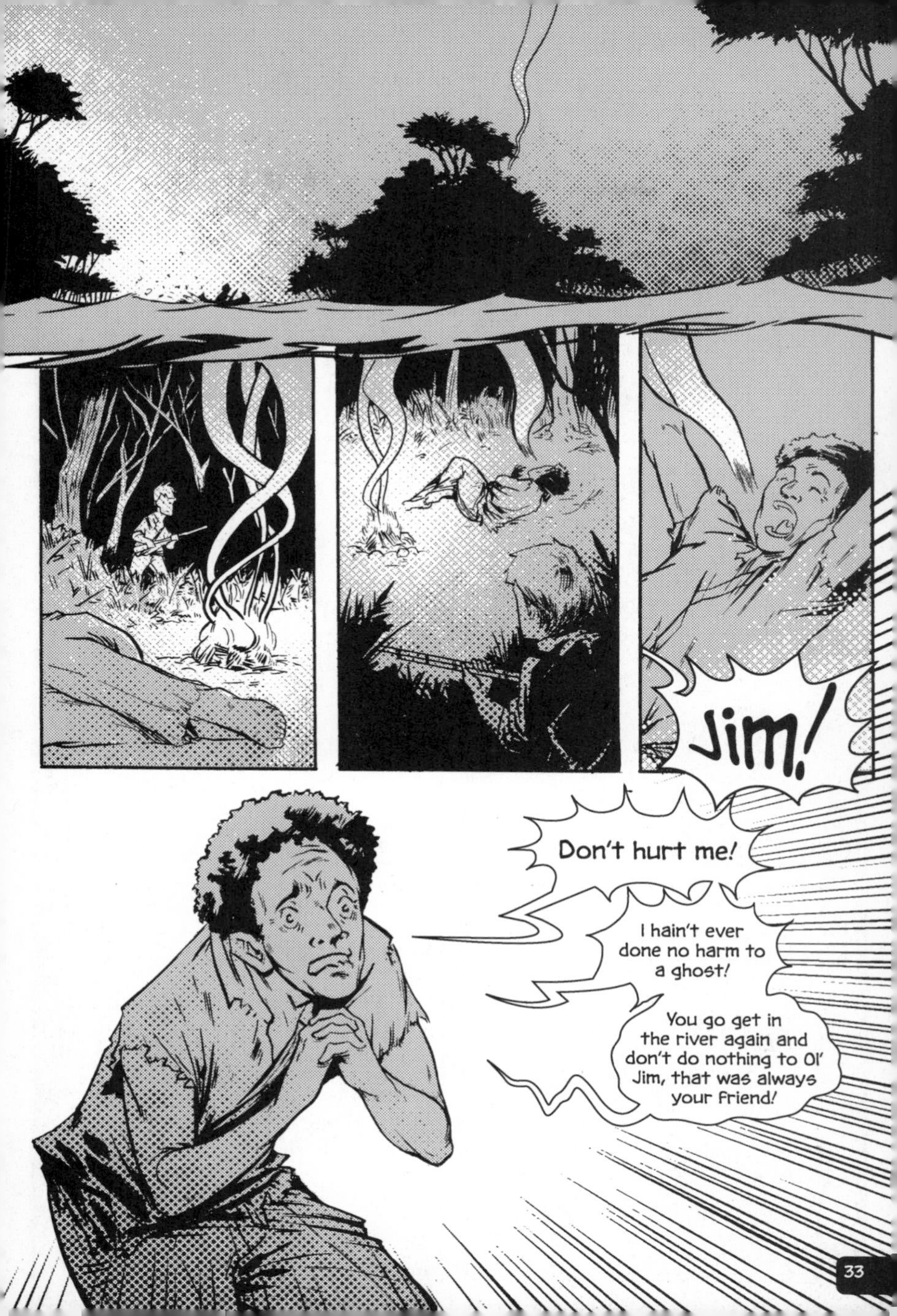

Jim!
Don't hurt me!
I hain't ever done no harm to a ghost!
You go get in the river again and don't do nothing to Ol' Jim, that was always your friend!

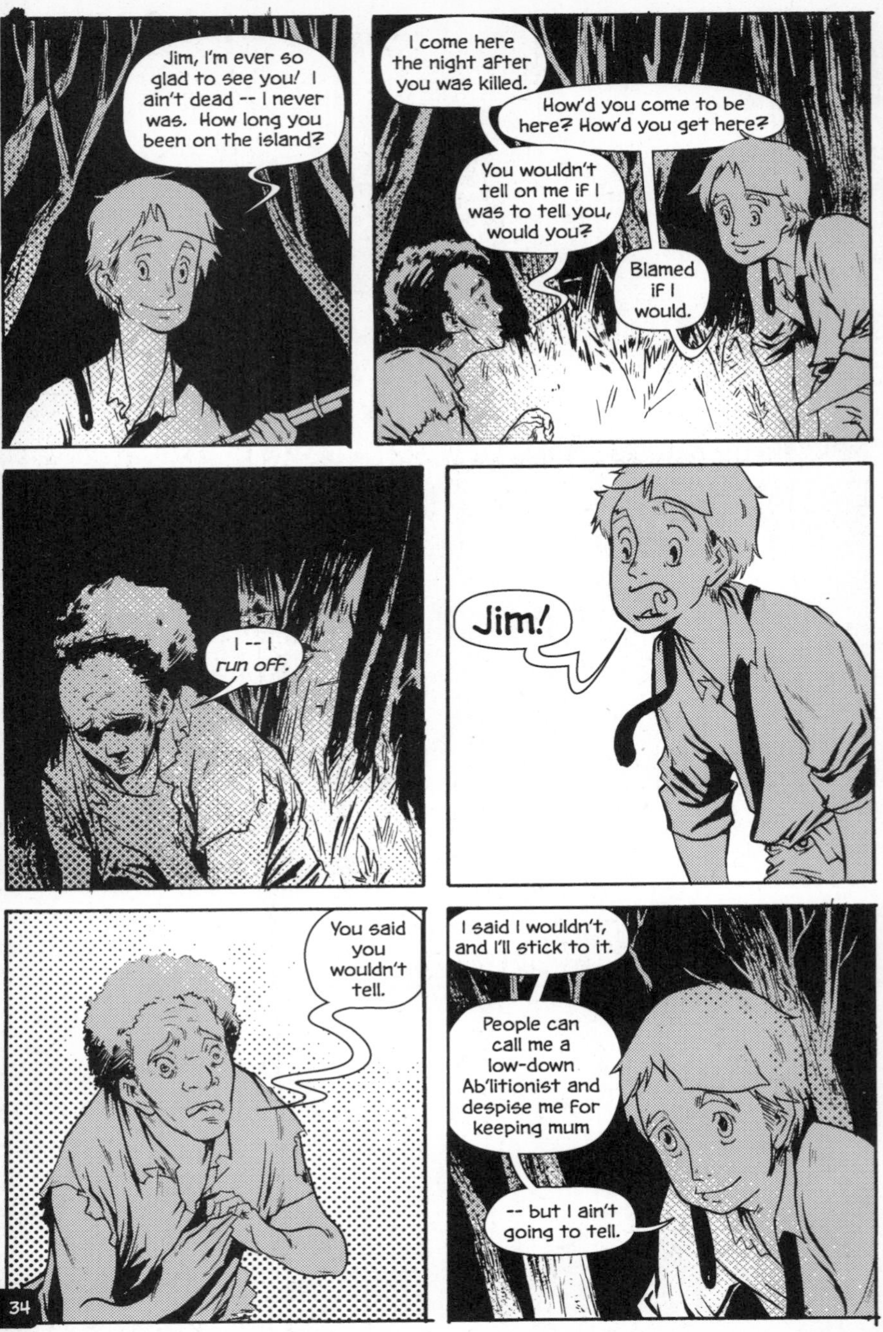
Jim, I'm ever so glad to see you! I ain't dead -- I never was. How long you been on the island?
I come here the night after you was killed.
How'd you come to be here? How'd you get here?
You wouldn't tell on me if I was to tell you, would you?
Blamed if I would.
I -- I run off.
Jim!
You said you wouldn't tell.
I said I wouldn't, and I'll stick to it.
People can call me a low-down Ab'litionist and despise me for keeping mum
-- but I ain't going to tell.

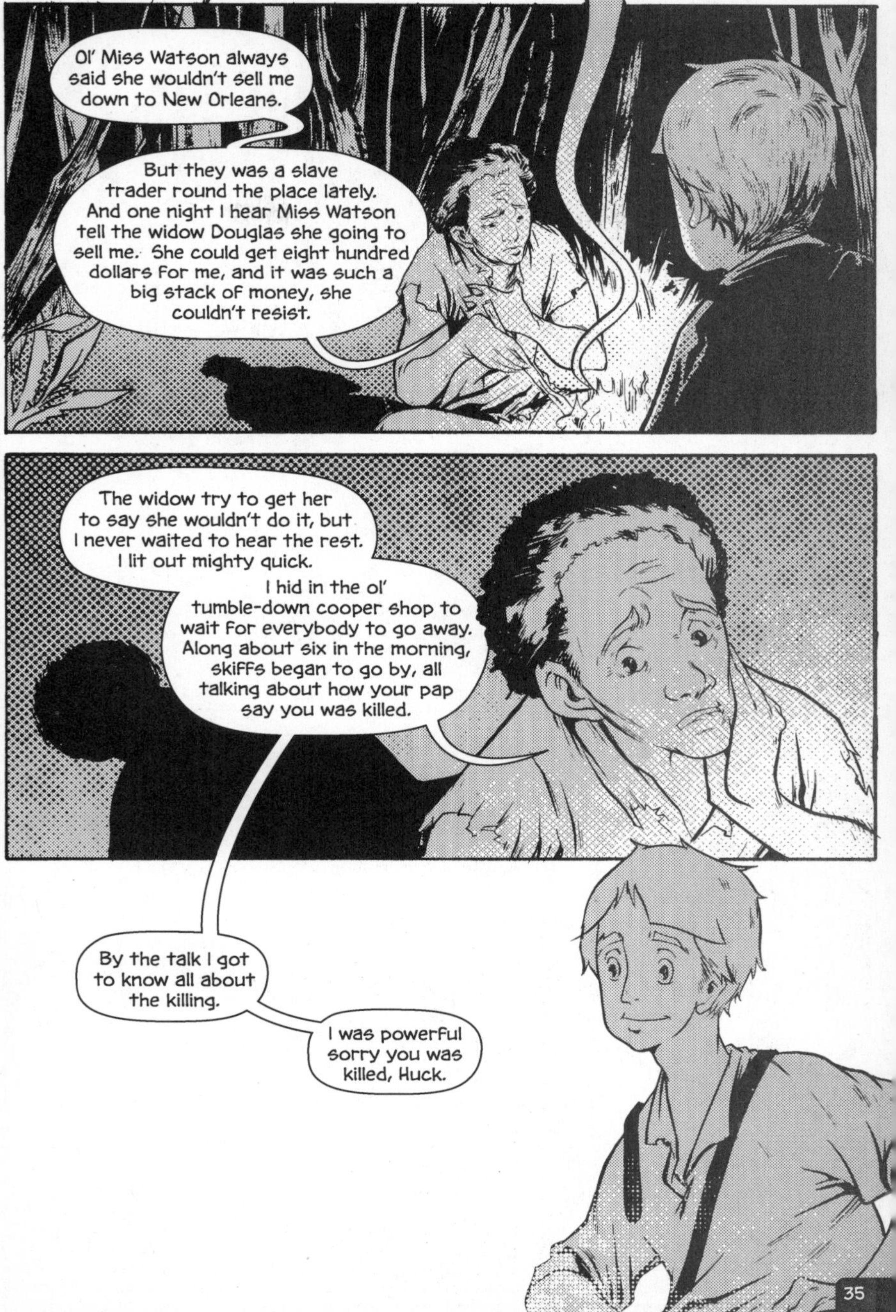
Ol' Miss Watson always said she wouldn't sell me down to New Orleans.
But they was a slave trader round the place lately. And one night I hear Miss Watson tell the widow Douglas she going to sell me. She could get eight hundred dollars for me, and it was such a big stack of money, she couldn't resist.
The widow try to get her to say she wouldn't do it, but I never waited to hear the rest. I lit out mighty quick.
I hid in the ol' tumble-down cooper shop to wait for everybody to go away. Along about six in the morning, skiffs began to go by, all talking about how your pap say you was killed.
By the talk I got to know all about the killing.
I was powerful sorry you was killed, Huck.

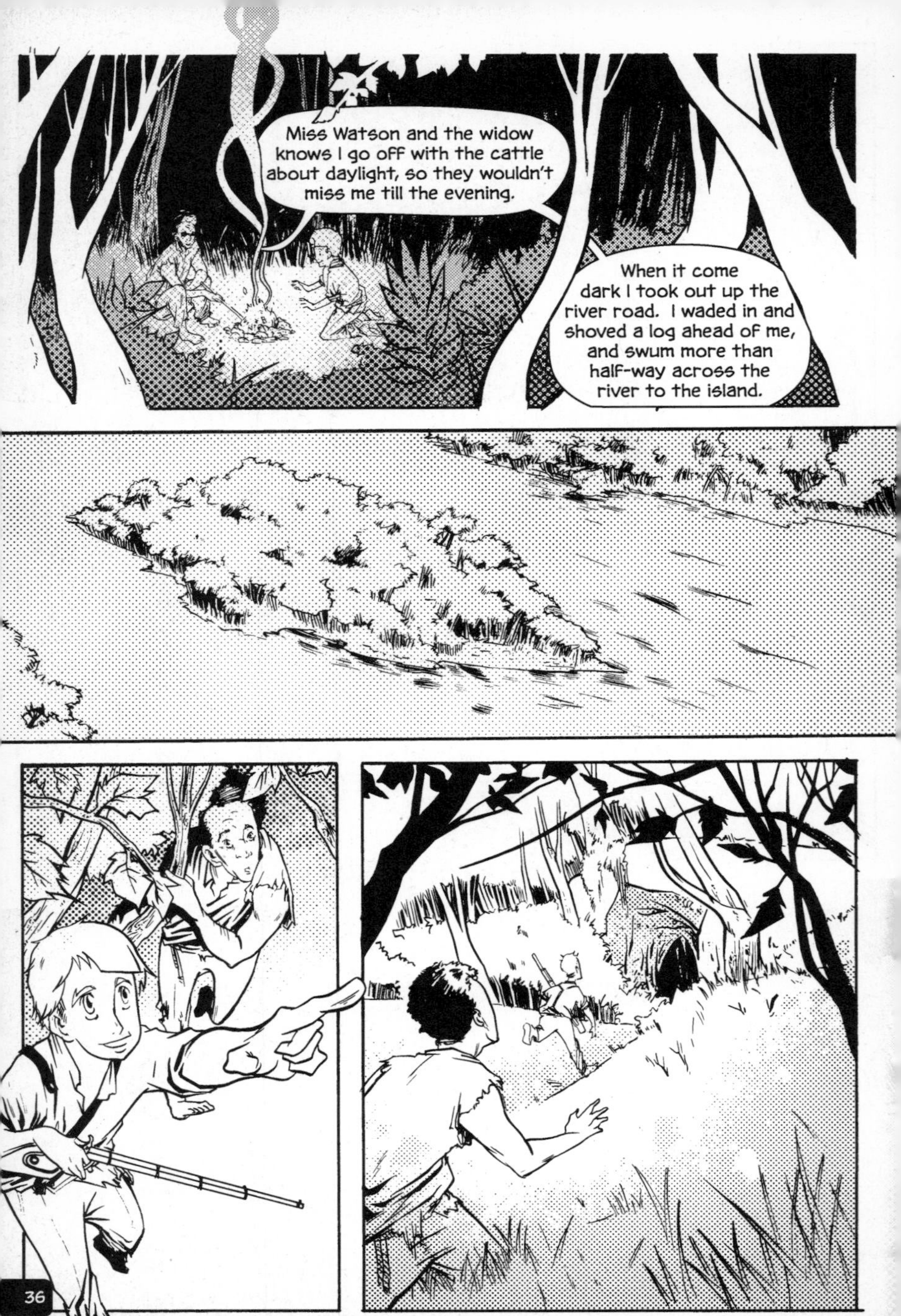
Miss Watson and the widow knows I go off with the cattle about daylight, so they wouldn't miss me till the evening.
When it come dark I took out up the river road. I waded in and shoved a log ahead of me, and swum more than half-way across the river to the island.

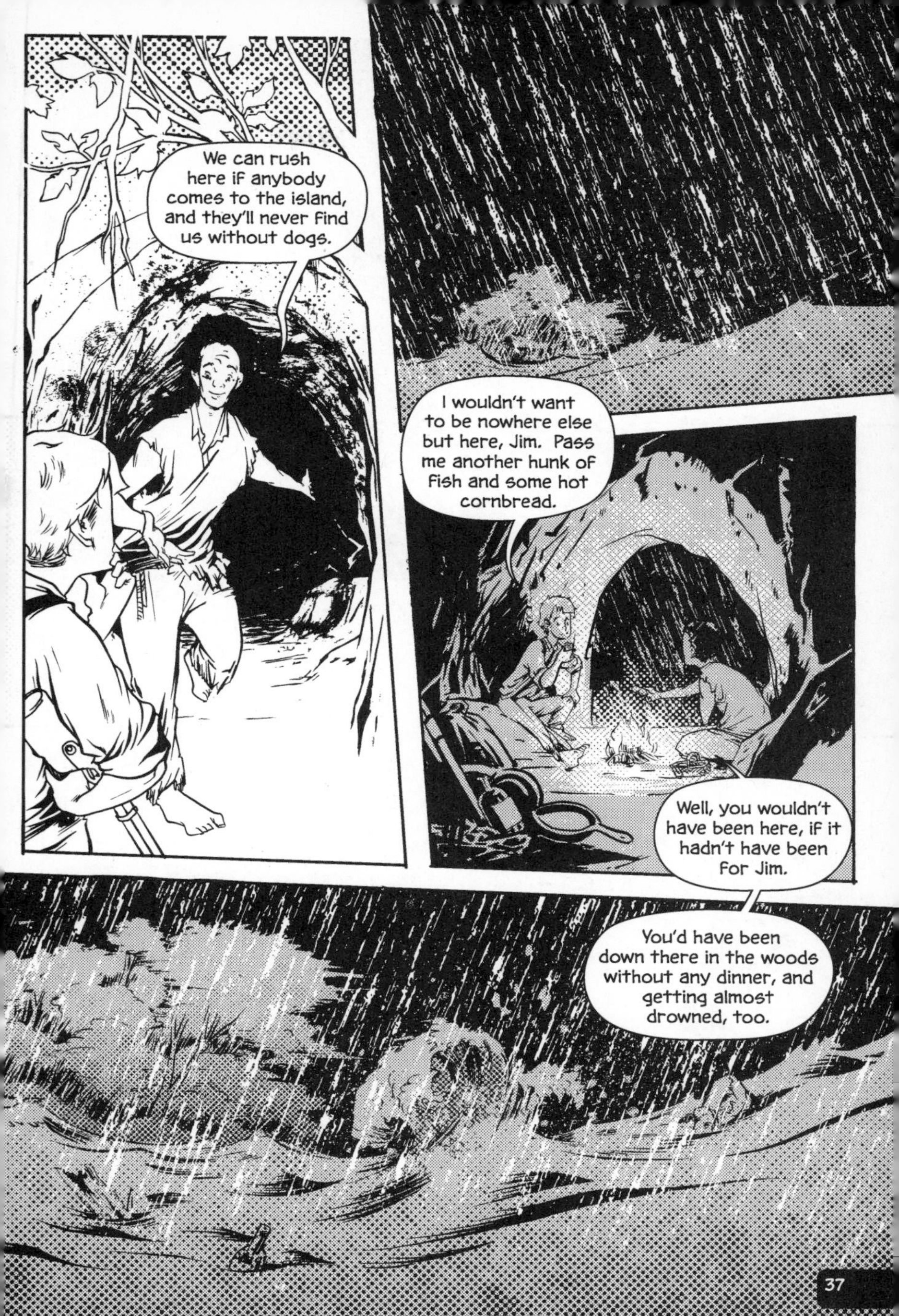
We can rush here if anybody comes to the island, and they'll never find us without dogs.
I wouldn't want to be nowhere else but here, Jim. Pass me another hunk of fish and some hot cornbread.
Well, you wouldn't have been here, if it hadn't have been for Jim.
You'd have been down there in the woods without any dinner, and getting almost drowned, too.

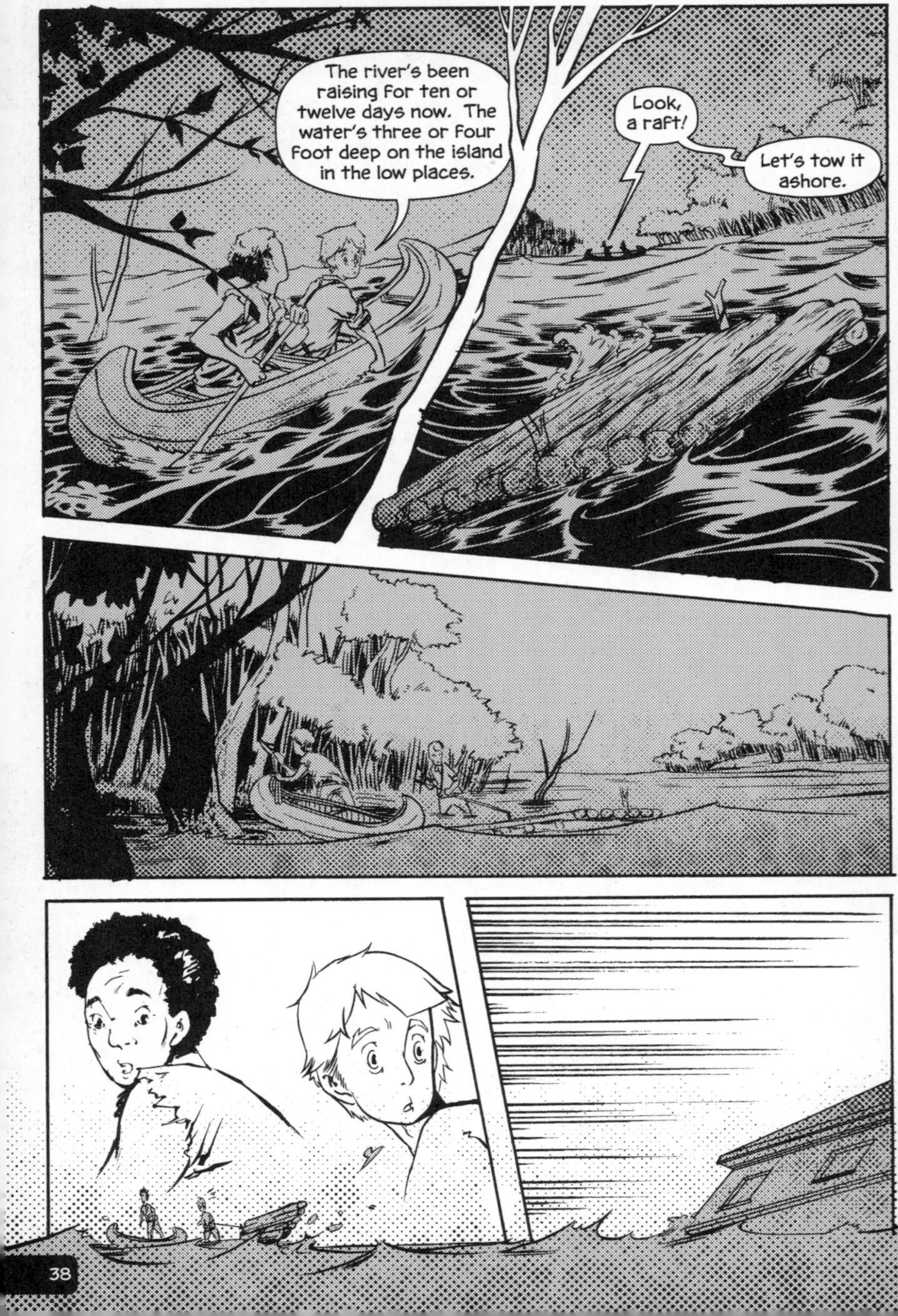
The river's been raising for ten or twelve days now. The water's three or four foot deep on the island in the low places.
Look, a raft!
Let's tow it ashore.

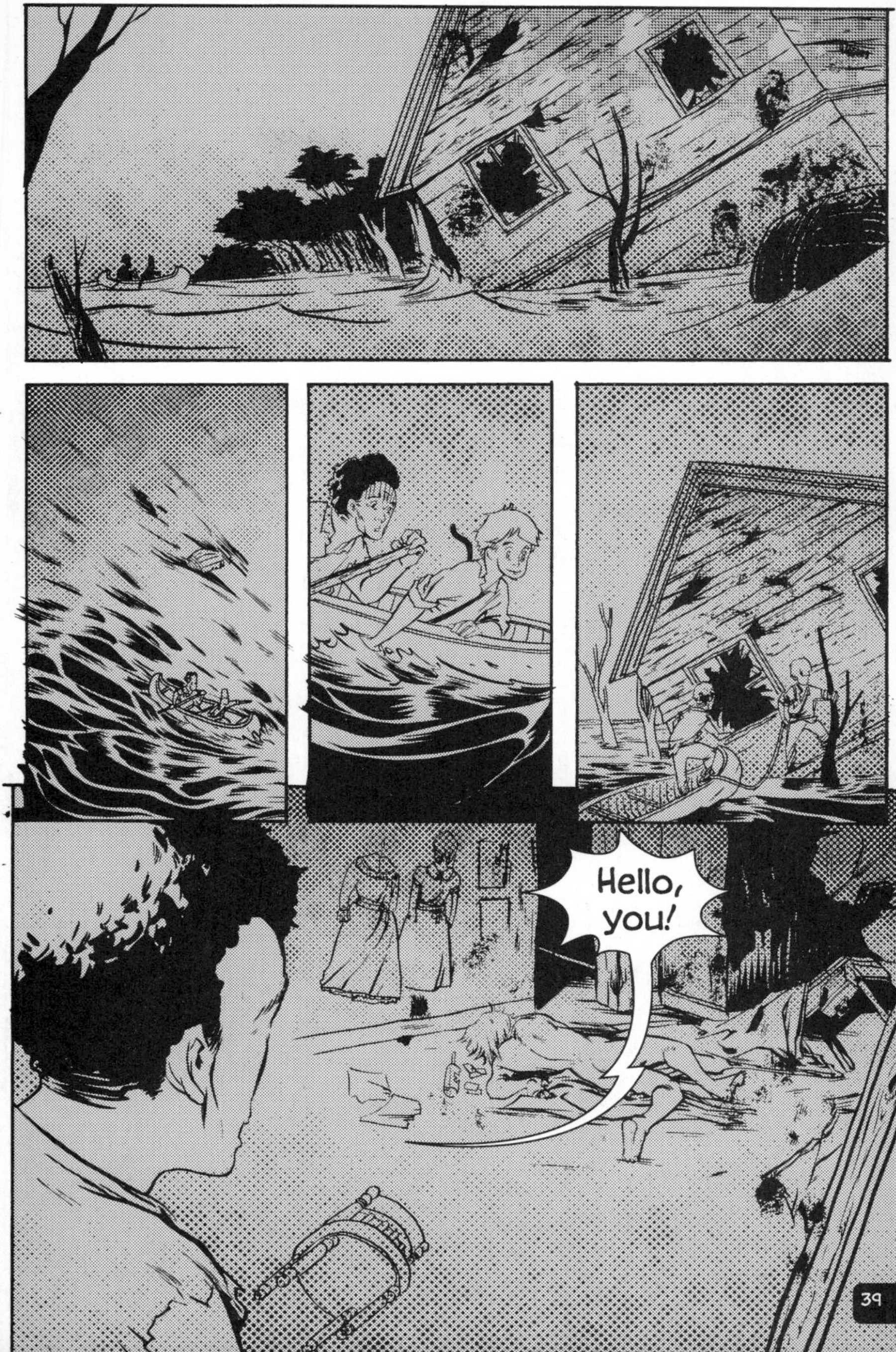
Hello, you!

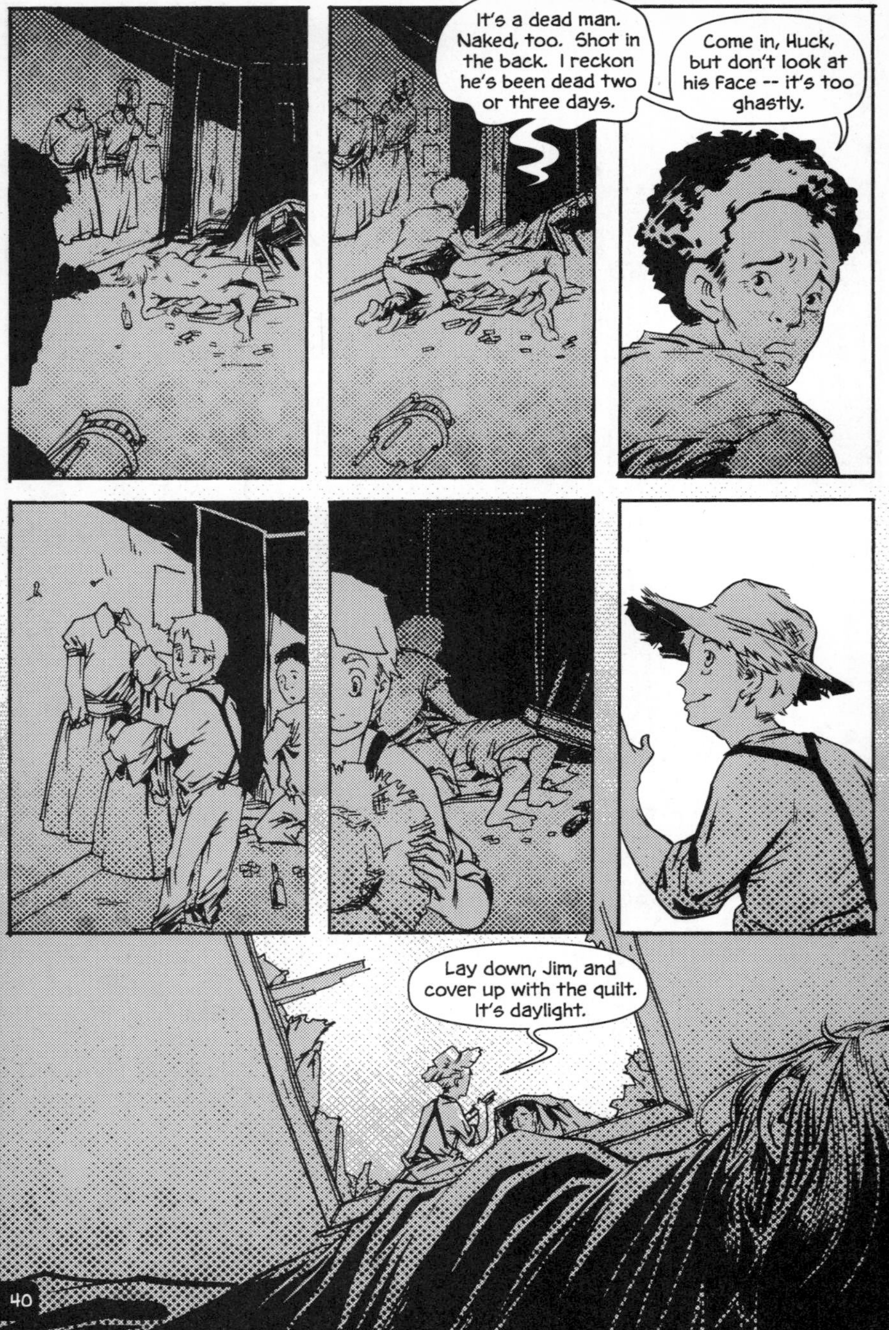
It's a dead man. Naked, too. Shot in the back. I reckon he's been dead two or three days.
Come in, Huck, but don't look at his face -- it's too ghastly.
Lay down, Jim, and cover up with the quilt. It's daylight.

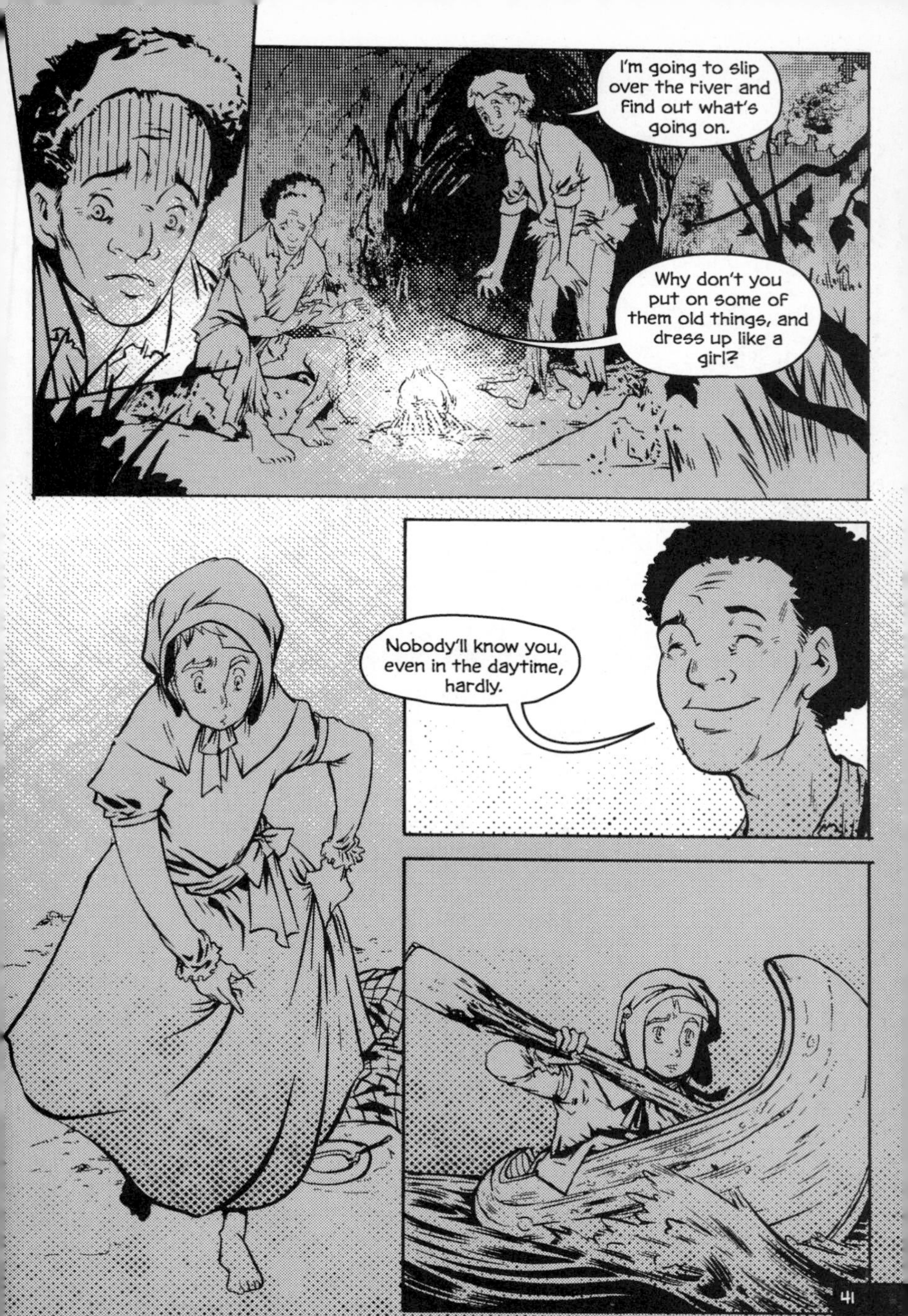
I'm going to slip over the river and find out what's going on.
Why don't you put on some of them old things, and dress up like a girl?
Nobody'll know you, even in the daytime, hardly.

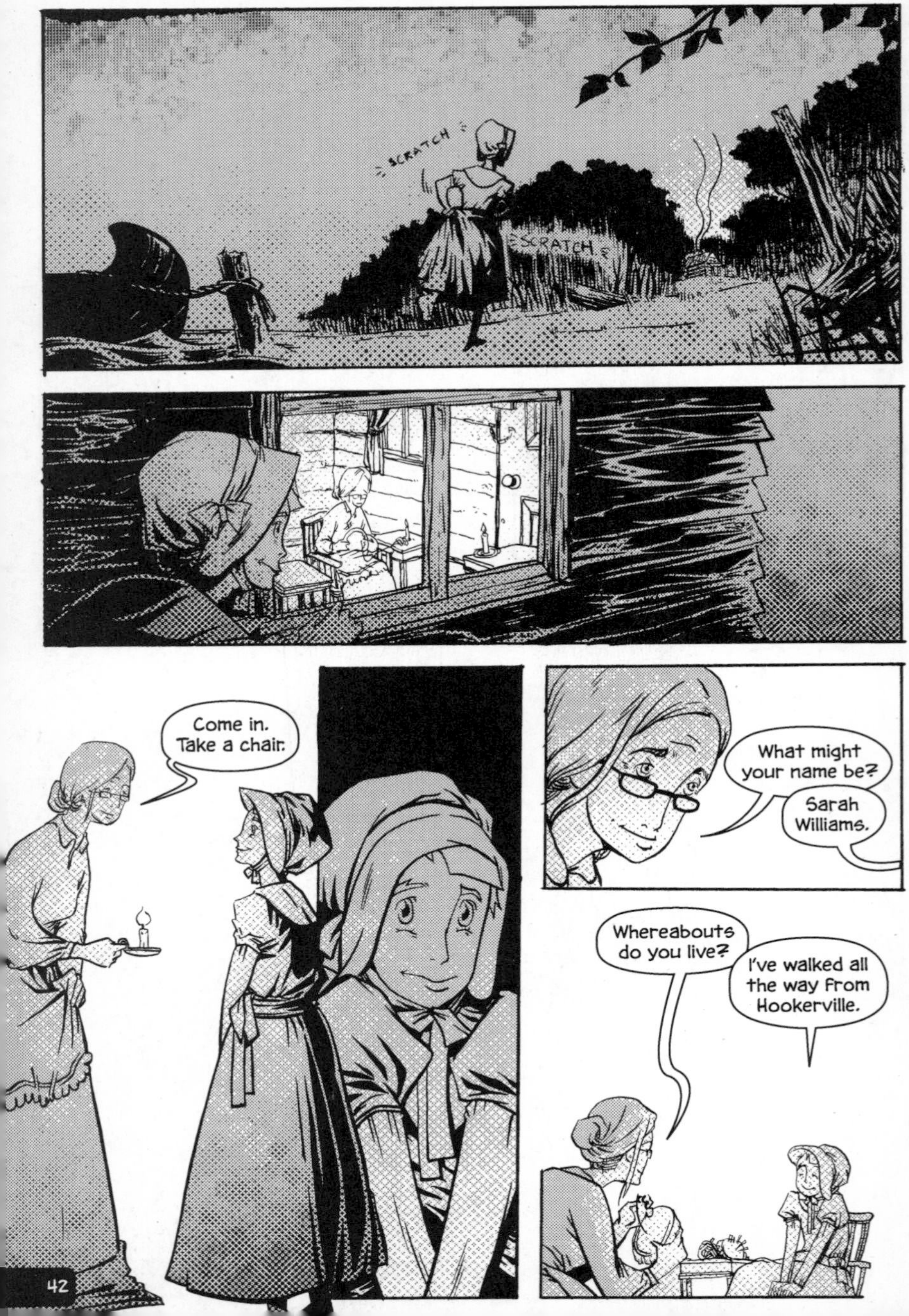
SCRATCH
SCRATCH
Come in. Take a chair.
What might your name be?
Sarah Williams.
Whereabouts do you live?
I've walked all the way from Hookerville.

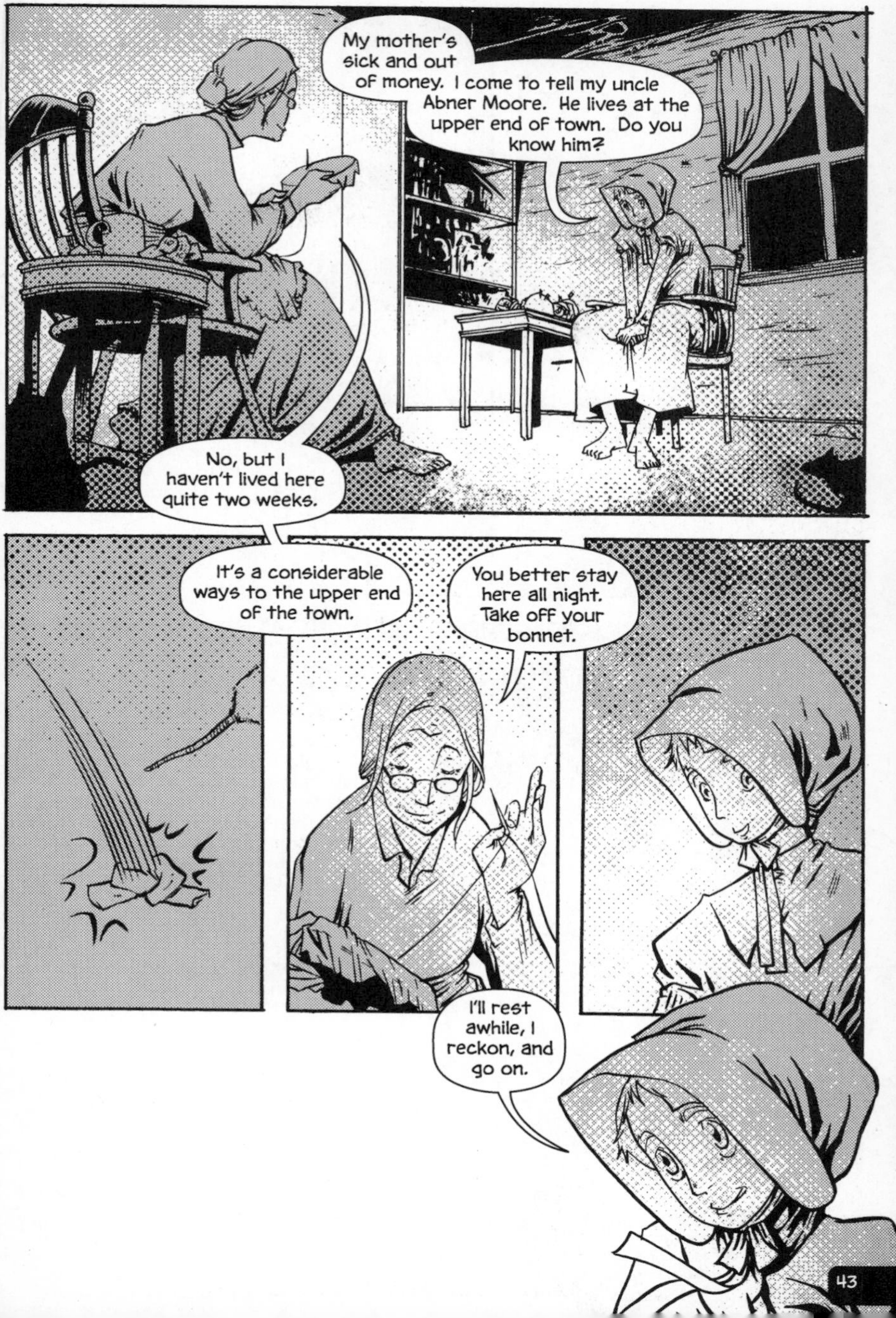
My mother's sick and out of money. I come to tell my uncle Abner Moore. He lives at the upper end of town. Do you know him?
No, but I haven't lived here quite two weeks.
It's a considerable ways to the upper end of the town.
You better stay here all night. Take off your bonnet.
I'll rest awhile, I reckon, and go on.

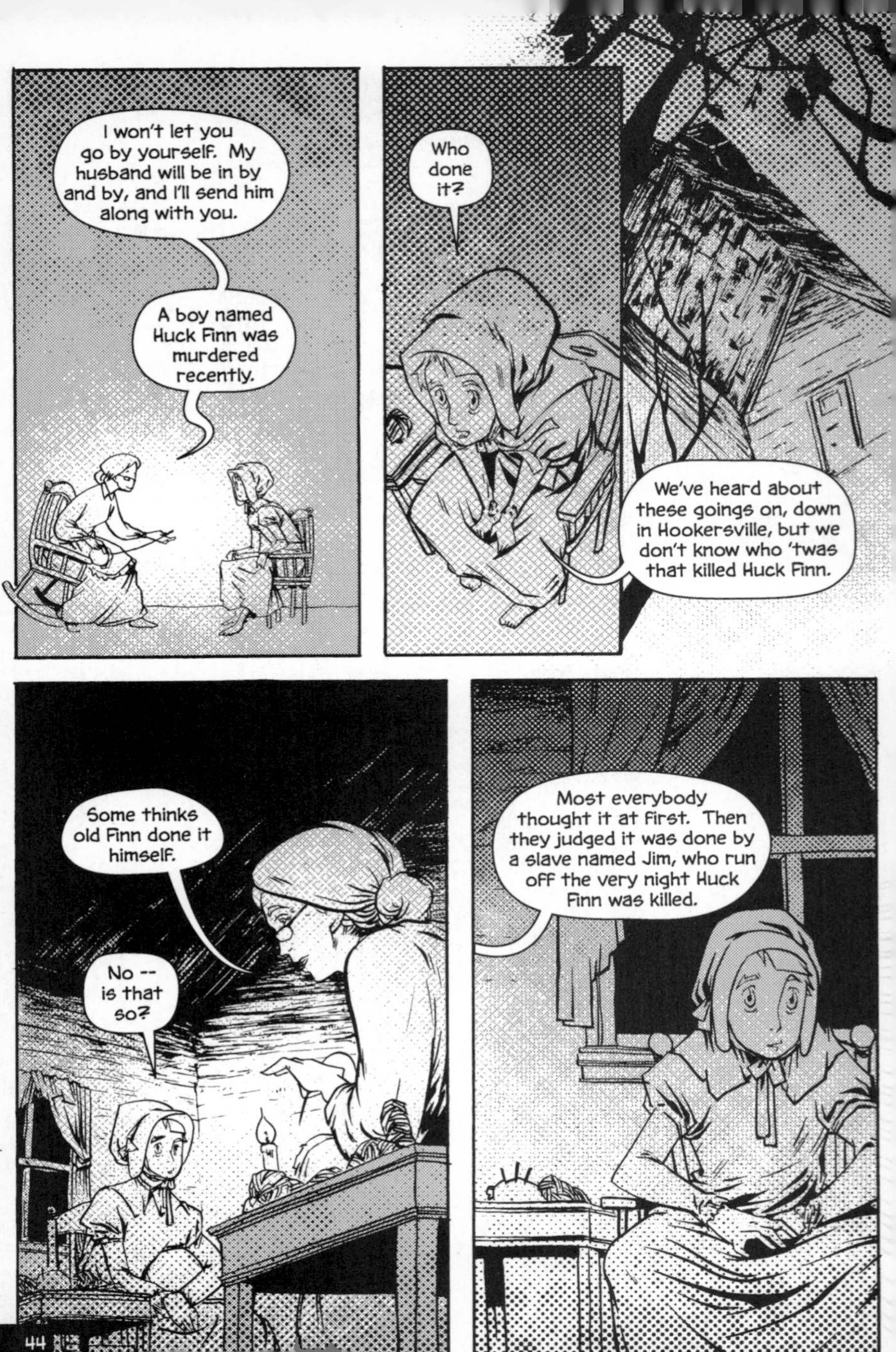
I won't let you go by yourself. My husband will be in by and by, and I'll send him along with you.
A boy named Huck Finn was murdered recently.
Who done it?
We've heard about these goings on, down in Hookersville, but we don't know who 'twas that killed Huck Finn.
Some thinks old Finn done it himself.
No -- is that so?
Most everybody thought it at first. Then they judged it was done by a slave named Jim, who run off the very night Huck Finn was killed.

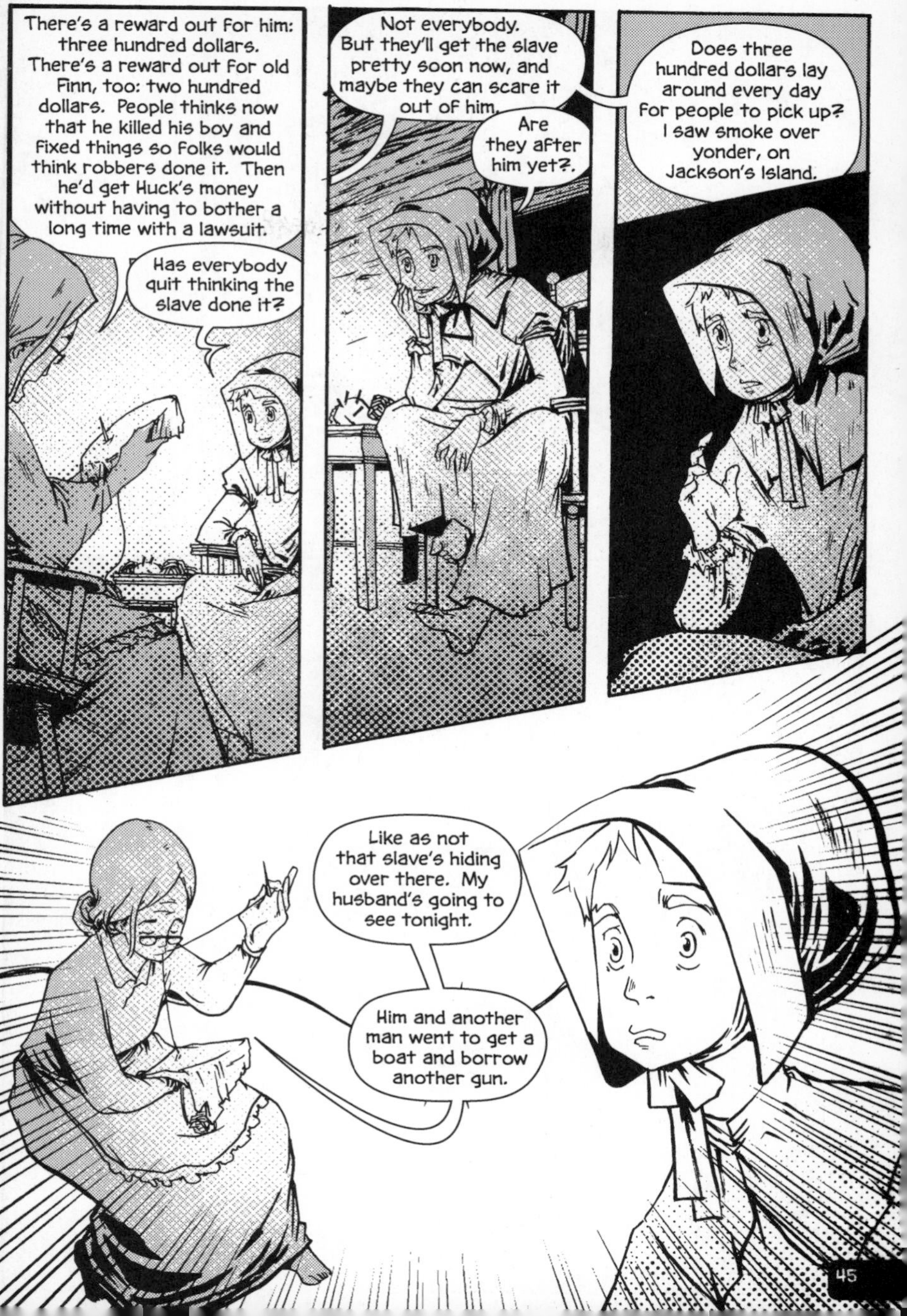
There's a reward out for him: three hundred dollars. There's a reward out for old Finn, too: two hundred dollars. People thinks now that he killed his boy and fixed things so folks would think robbers done it. Then he'd get Huck's money without having to bother a long time with a lawsuit.
Has everybody quit thinking the slave done it?
Not everybody. But they'll get the slave pretty soon now, and maybe they can scare it out of him.
Are they after him yet?
Does three hundred dollars lay around every day for people to pick up? I saw smoke over yonder, on Jackson's Island.
Like as not that slave's hiding over there. My husband's going to see tonight.
Him and another man went to get a boat and borrow another gun.

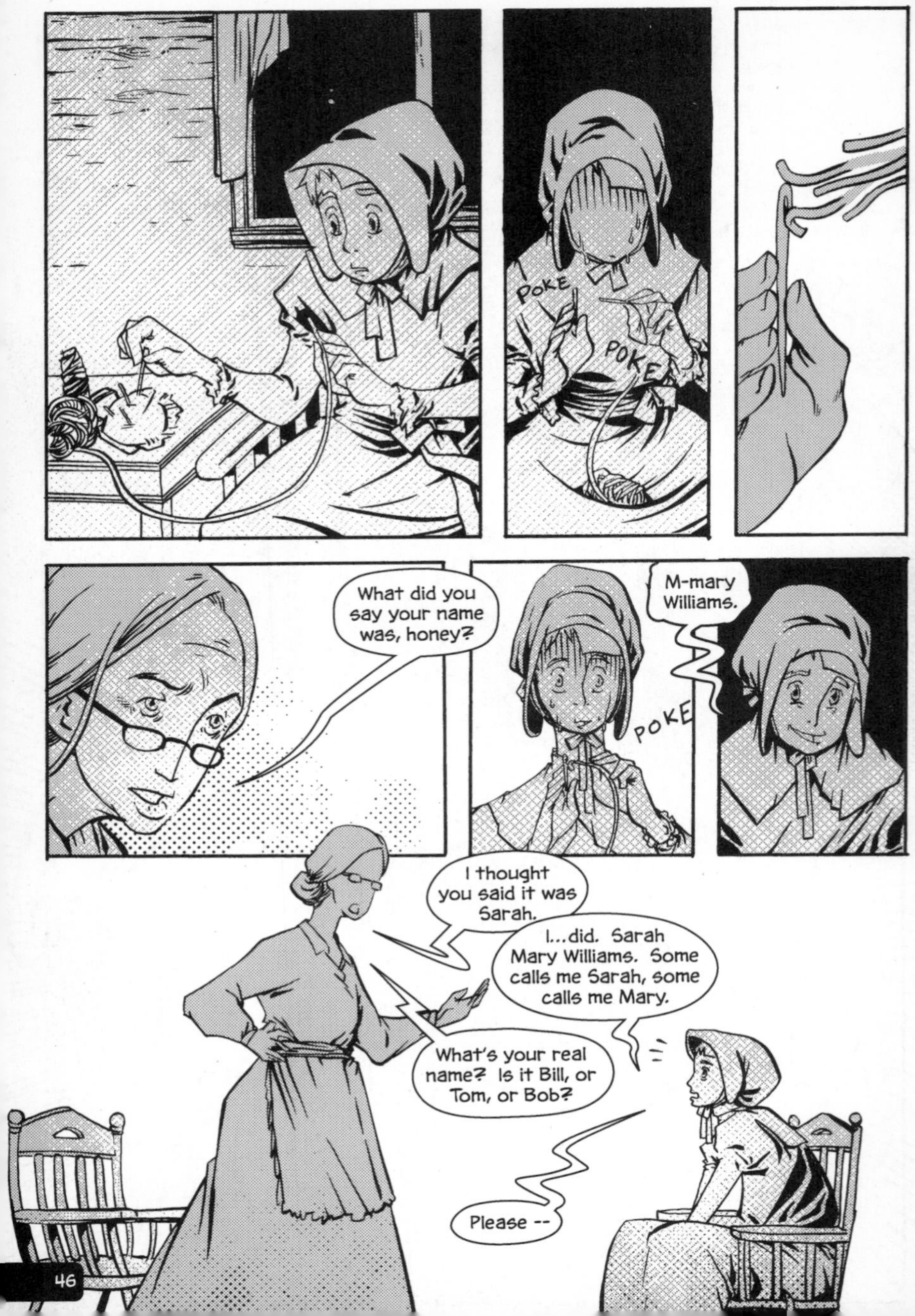

POKE
POKE
What did you say your name was, honey?
M-mary Williams.
POKE
I thought you said it was Sarah.
I...did. Sarah Mary Williams. Some calls me Sarah, some calls me Mary.
What's your real name? Is it Bill, or Tom, or Bob?
Please --

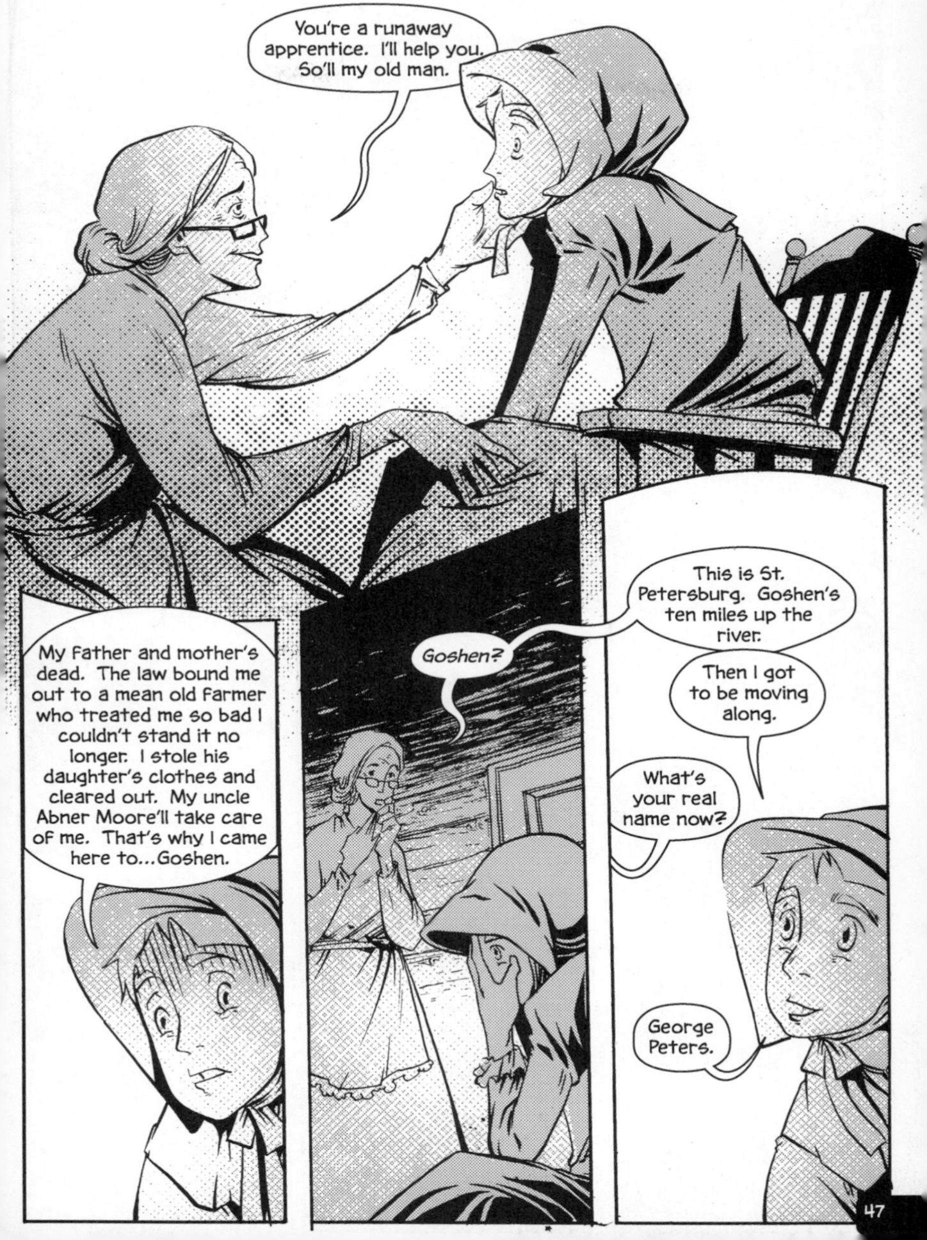
You're a runaway apprentice. I'll help you. So'll my old man.
My father and mother's dead. The law bound me out to a mean old farmer who treated me so bad I couldn't stand it no longer. I stole his daughter's clothes and cleared out. My uncle Abner Moore'll take care of me. That's why I came here to...Goshen.
Goshen?
This is St. Petersburg. Goshen's ten miles up the river.
Then I got to be moving along.
What's your real name now?
George Peters.

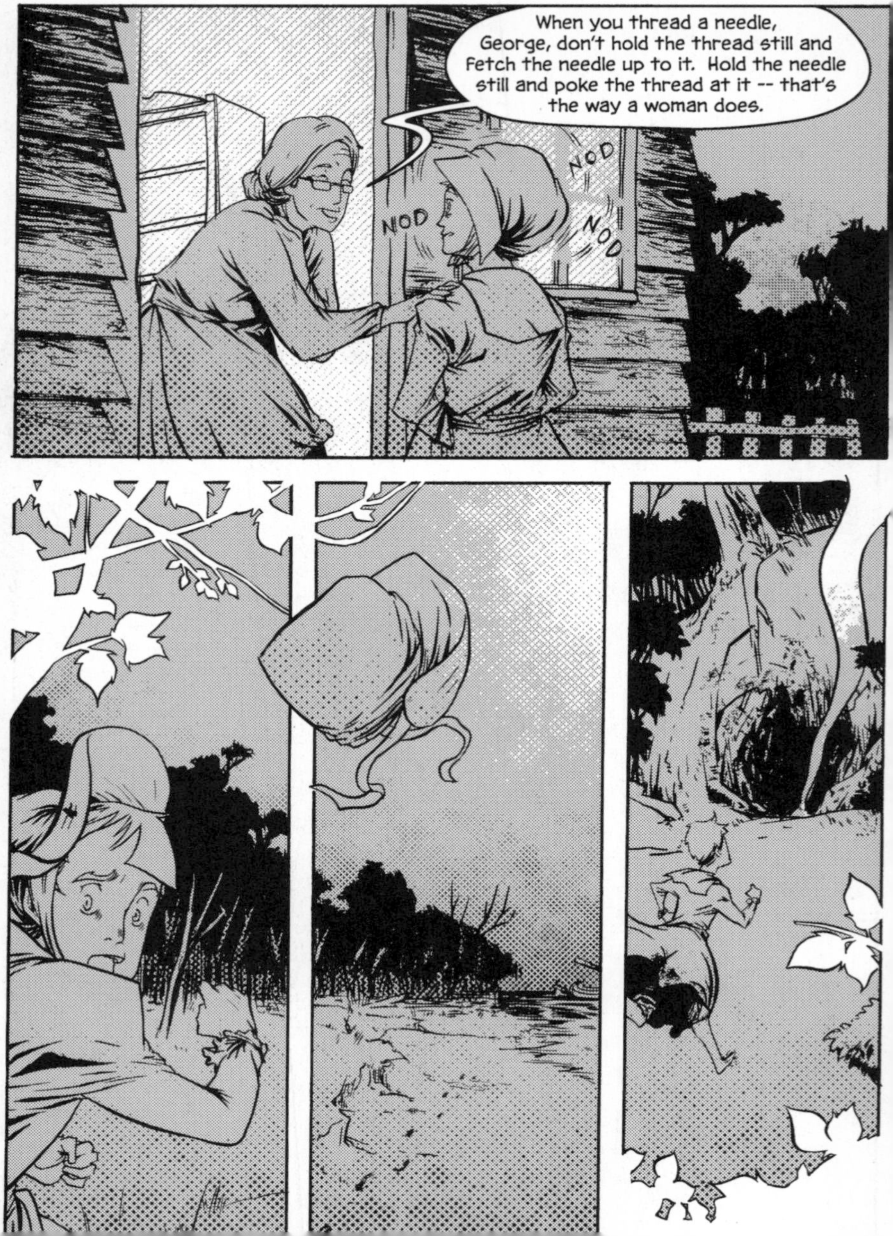
When you thread a needle, George, don't hold the thread still and fetch the needle up to it. Hold the needle still and poke the thread at it -- that's the way a woman does.
NOD
NOD
NOD

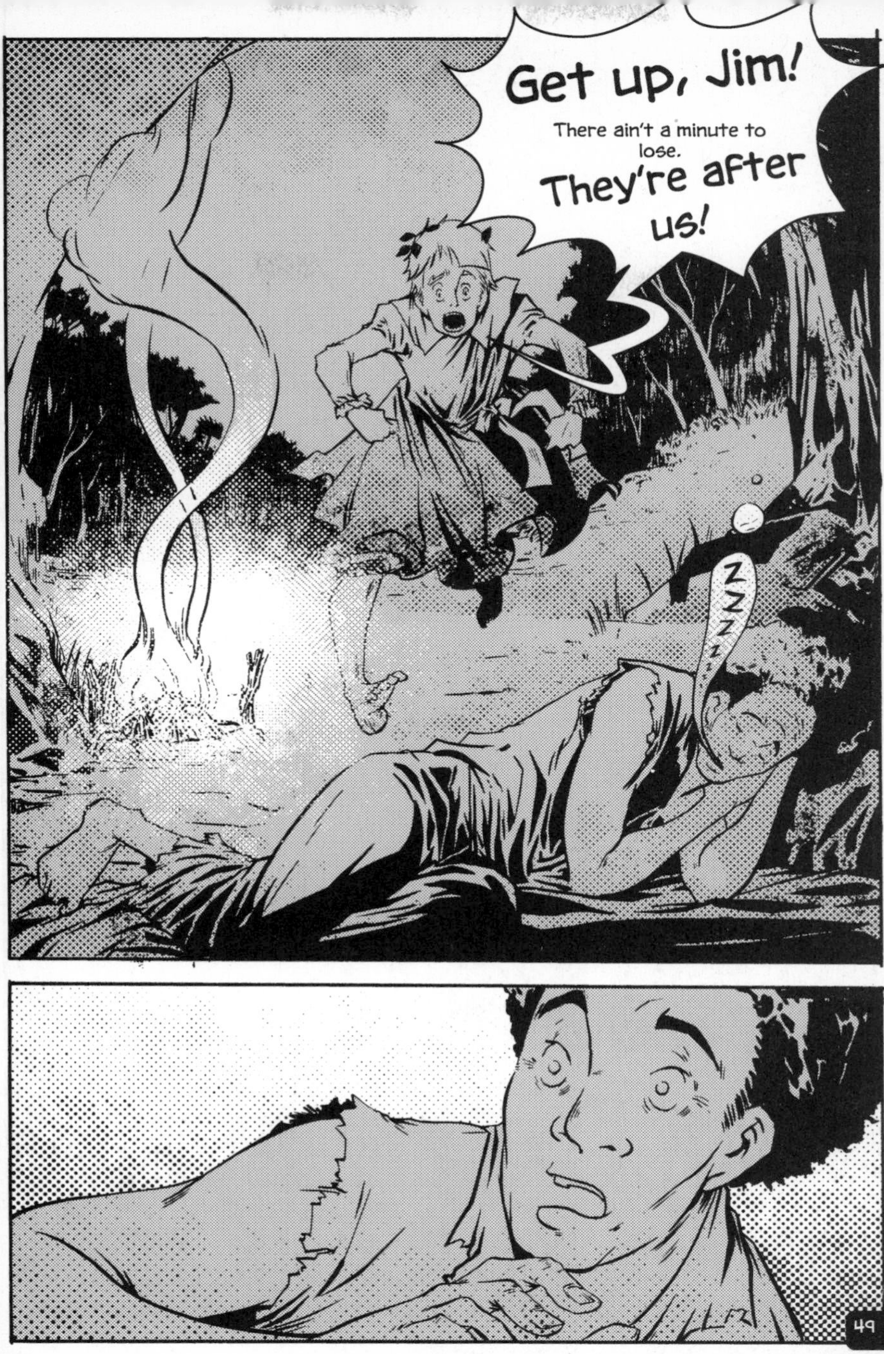
Get up, Jim!
There ain't a minute to lose.
They're after us!
ZZZz

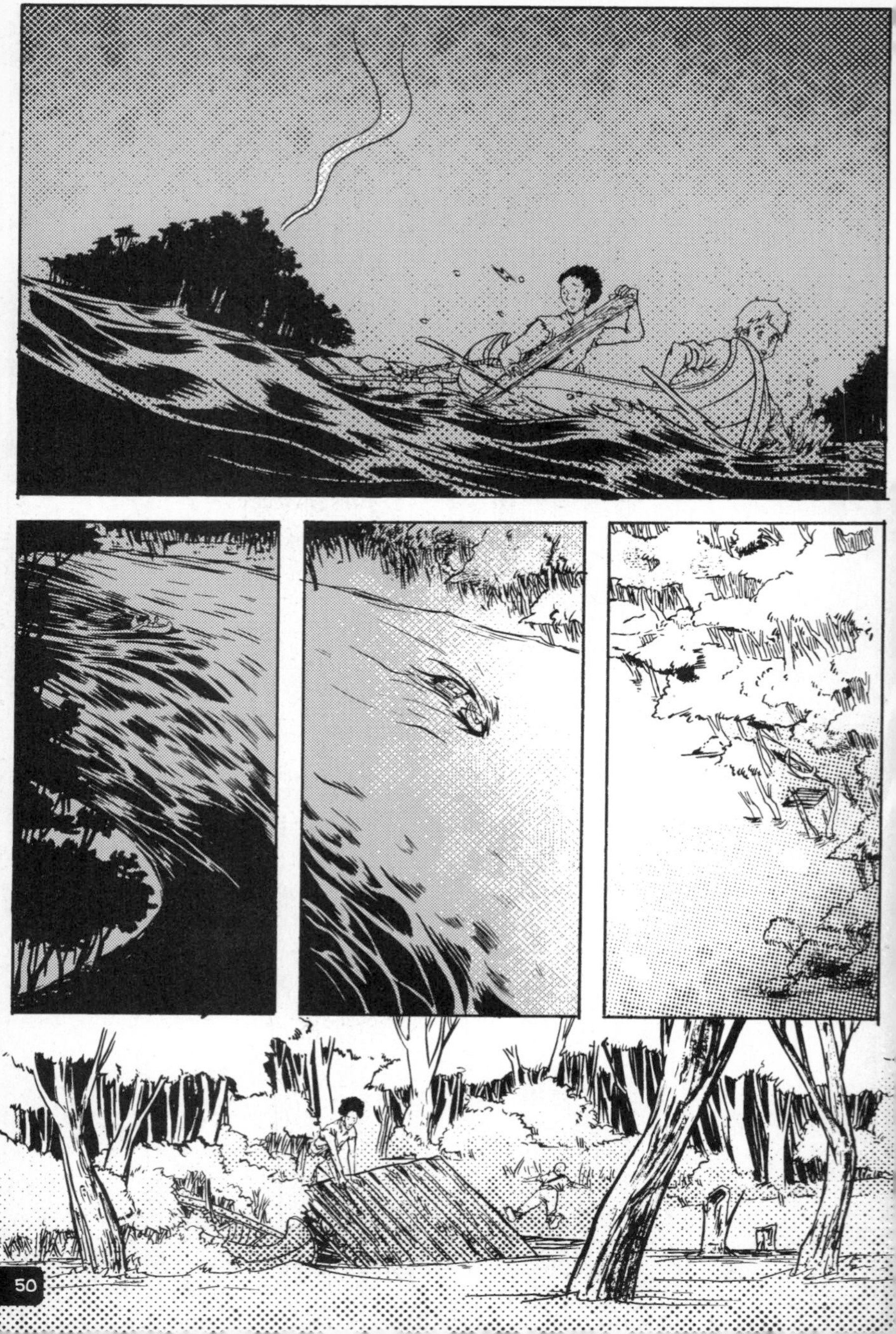

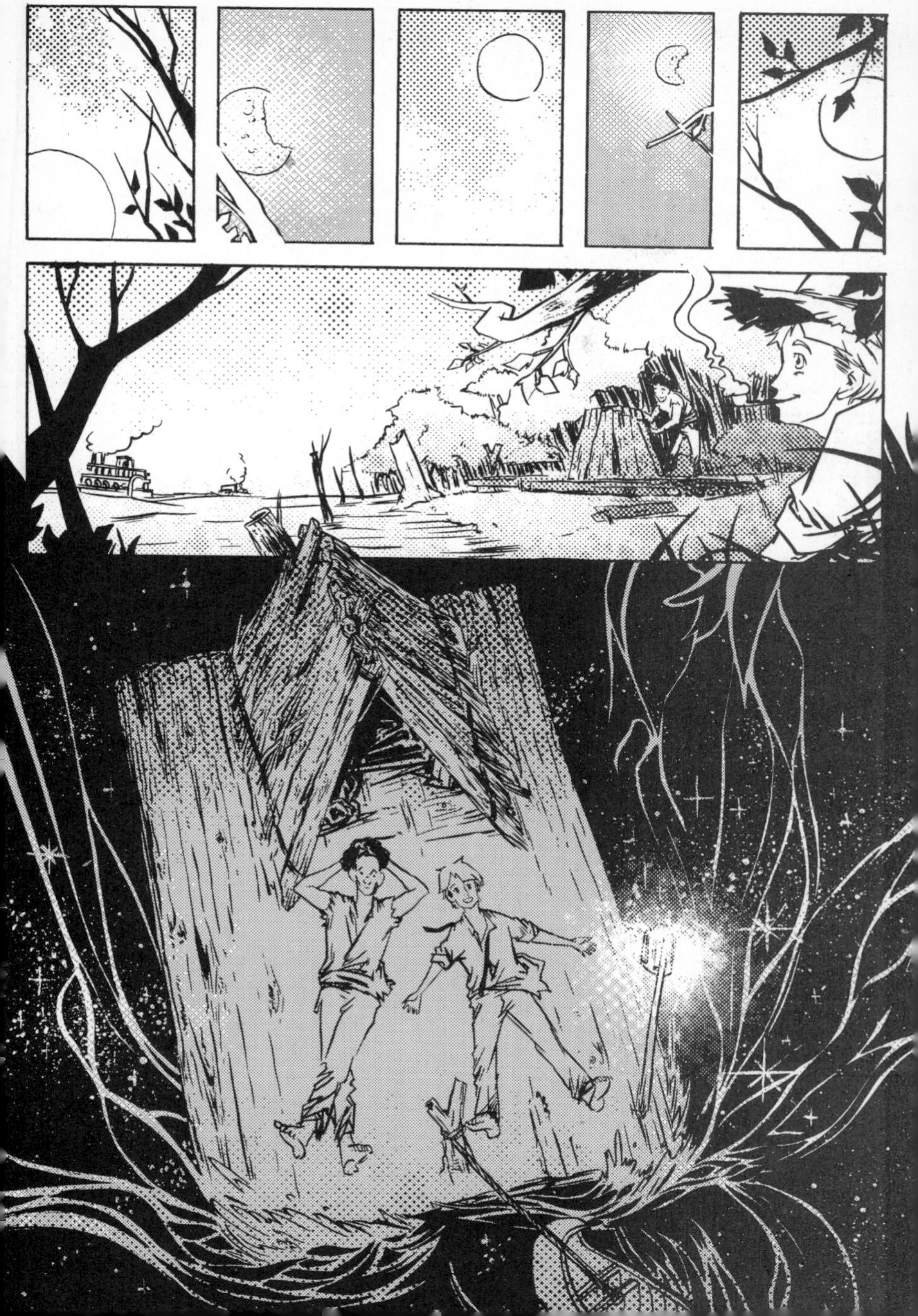

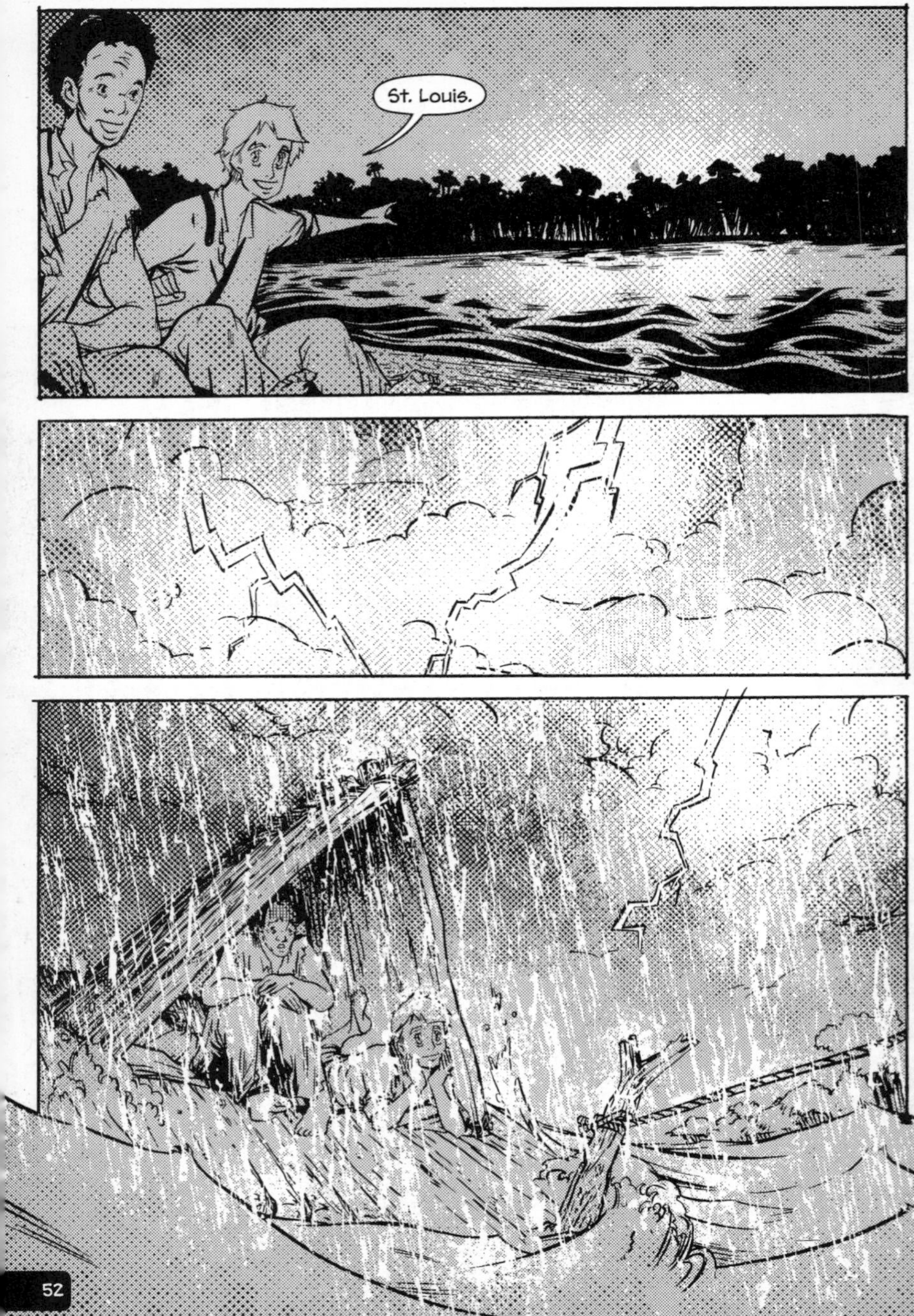
St. Louis.

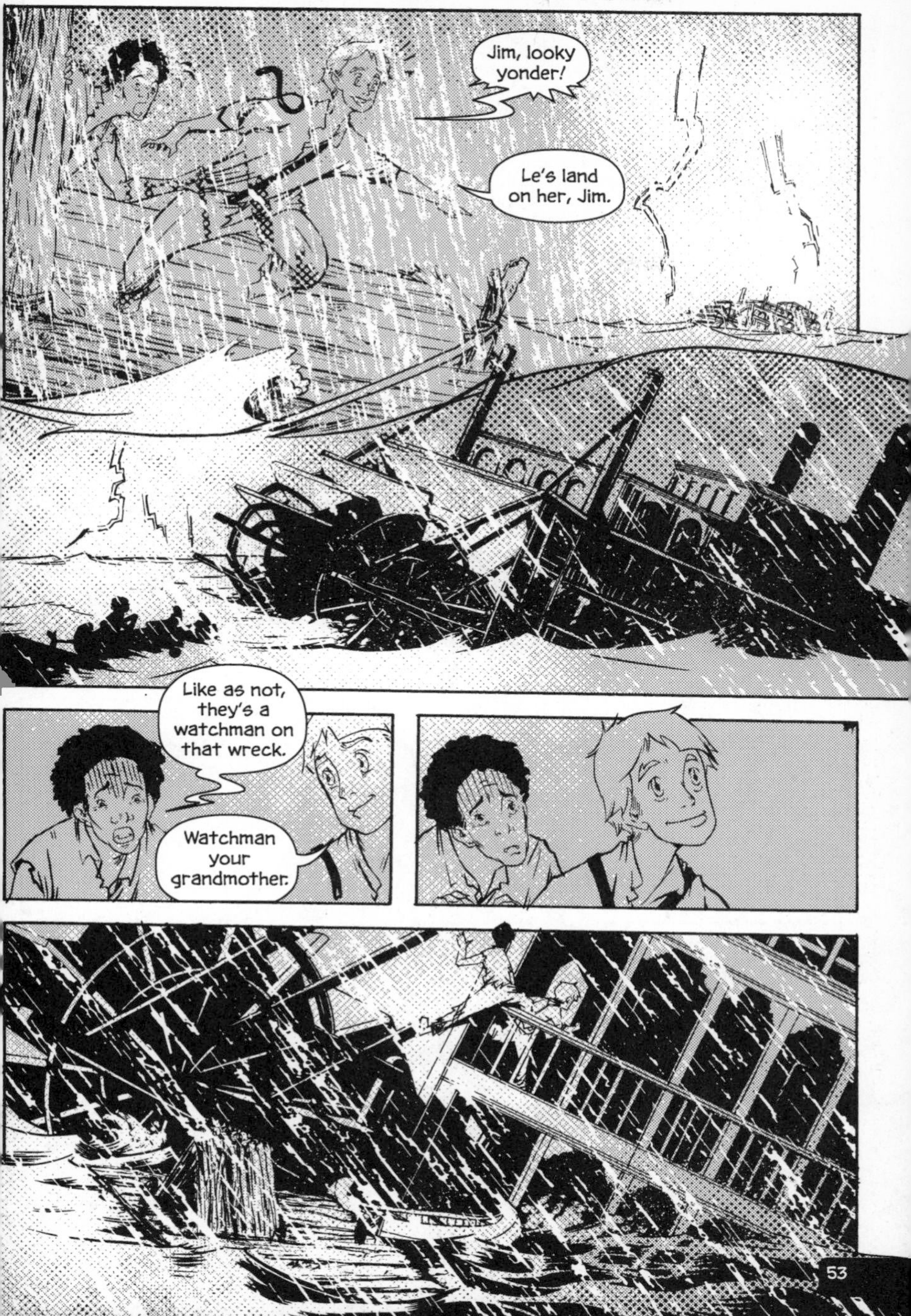
Jim, looky yonder!
Le's land on her, Jim.
Like as not, they's a watchman on that wreck.
Watchman your grandmother.

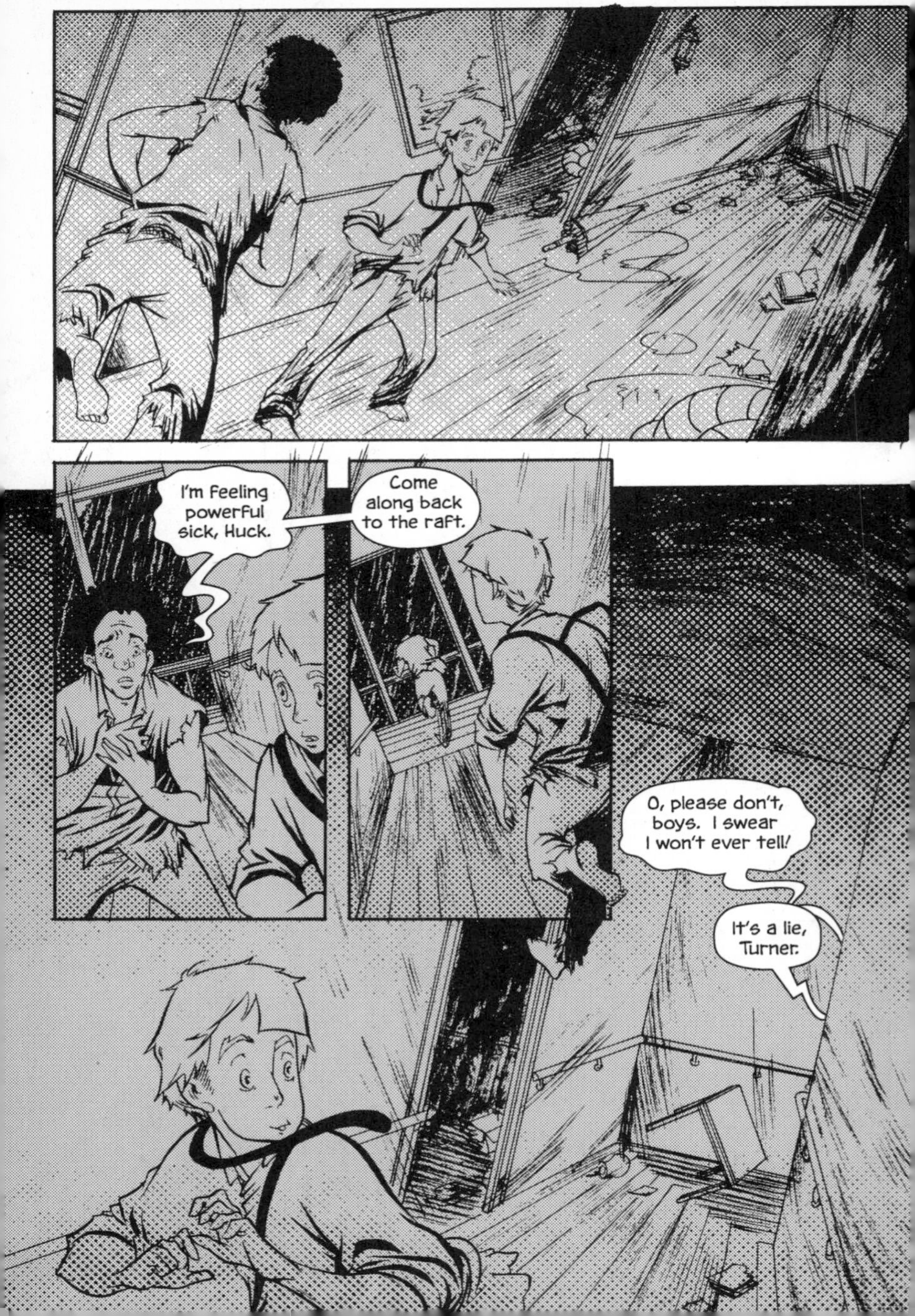
I'm feeling powerful sick, Huck.
Come along back to the raft.
O, please don't, boys. I swear I won't ever tell!
It's a lie, Turner.

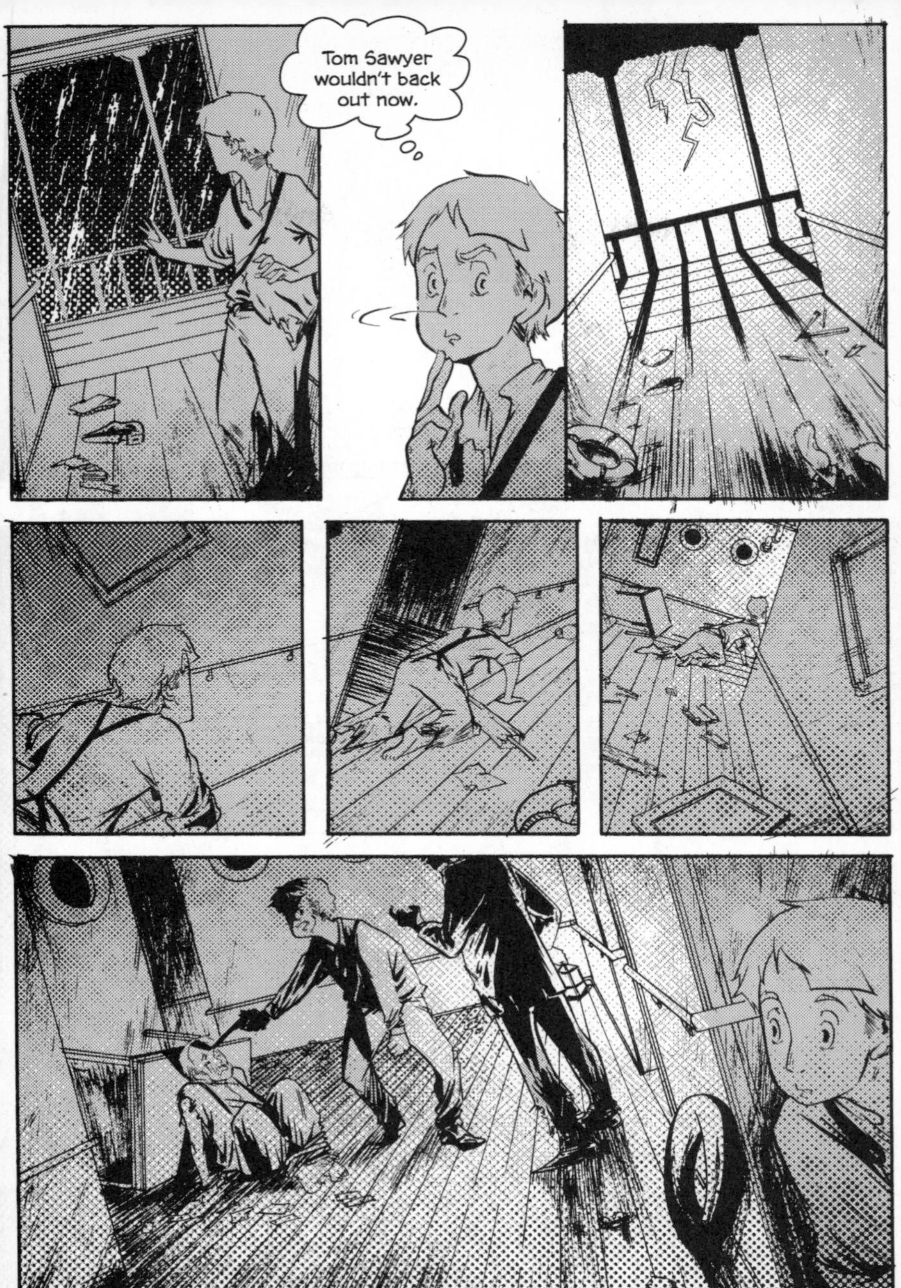
Tom Sawyer wouldn't back out now.

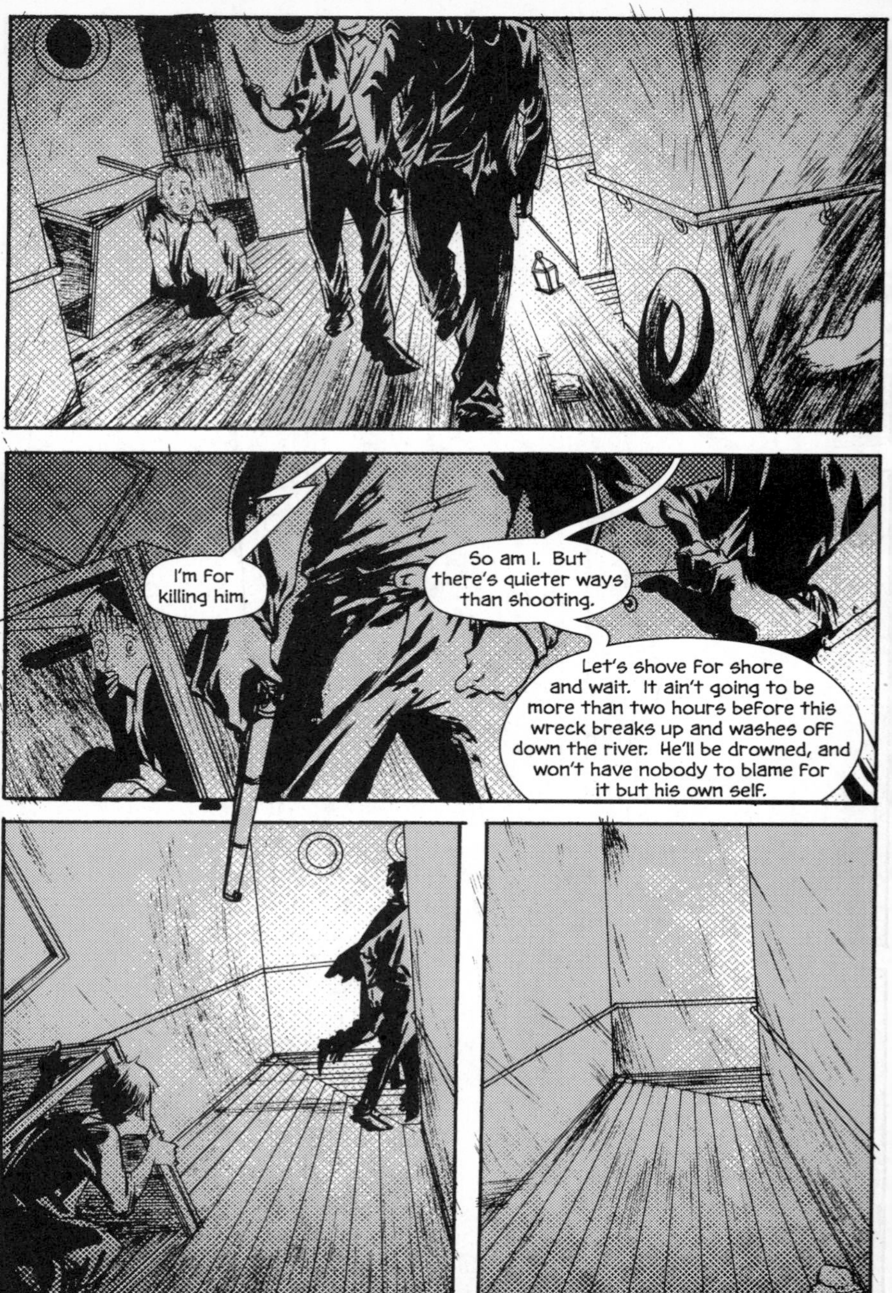
I'm for killing him.
So am I. But there's quieter ways than shooting.
Let's shove for shore and wait. It ain't going to be more than two hours before this wreck breaks up and washes off down the river. He'll be drowned, and won't have nobody to blame for it but his own self.

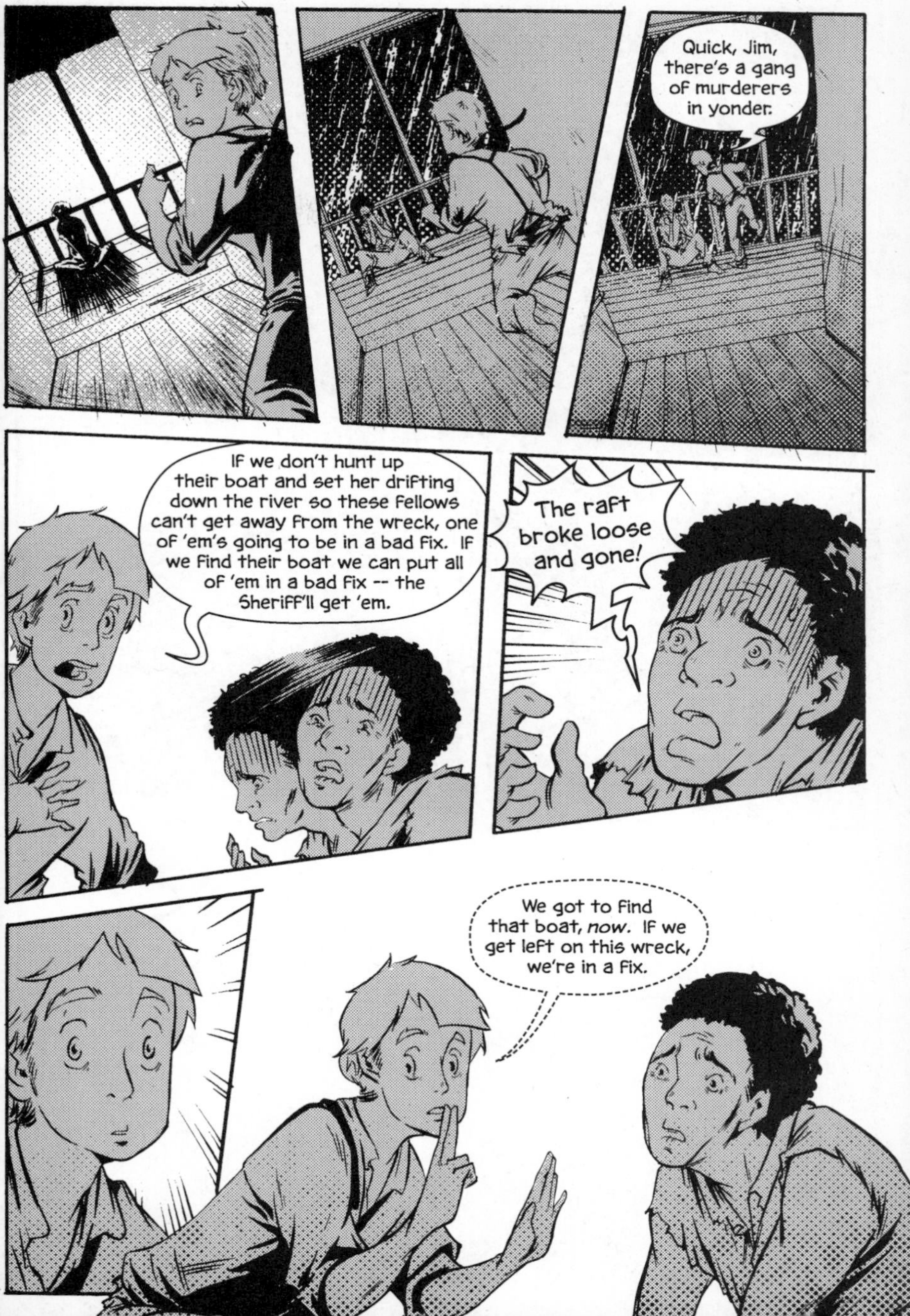
Quick, Jim, there's a gang of murderers in yonder.
If we don't hunt up their boat and set her drifting down the river so these fellows can't get away from the wreck, one of 'em's going to be in a bad fix. If we find their boat we can put all of 'em in a bad fix -- the Sheriff'll get 'em.
The raft broke loose and gone!
We got to find that boat, *now*. If we get left on this wreck, we're in a fix.

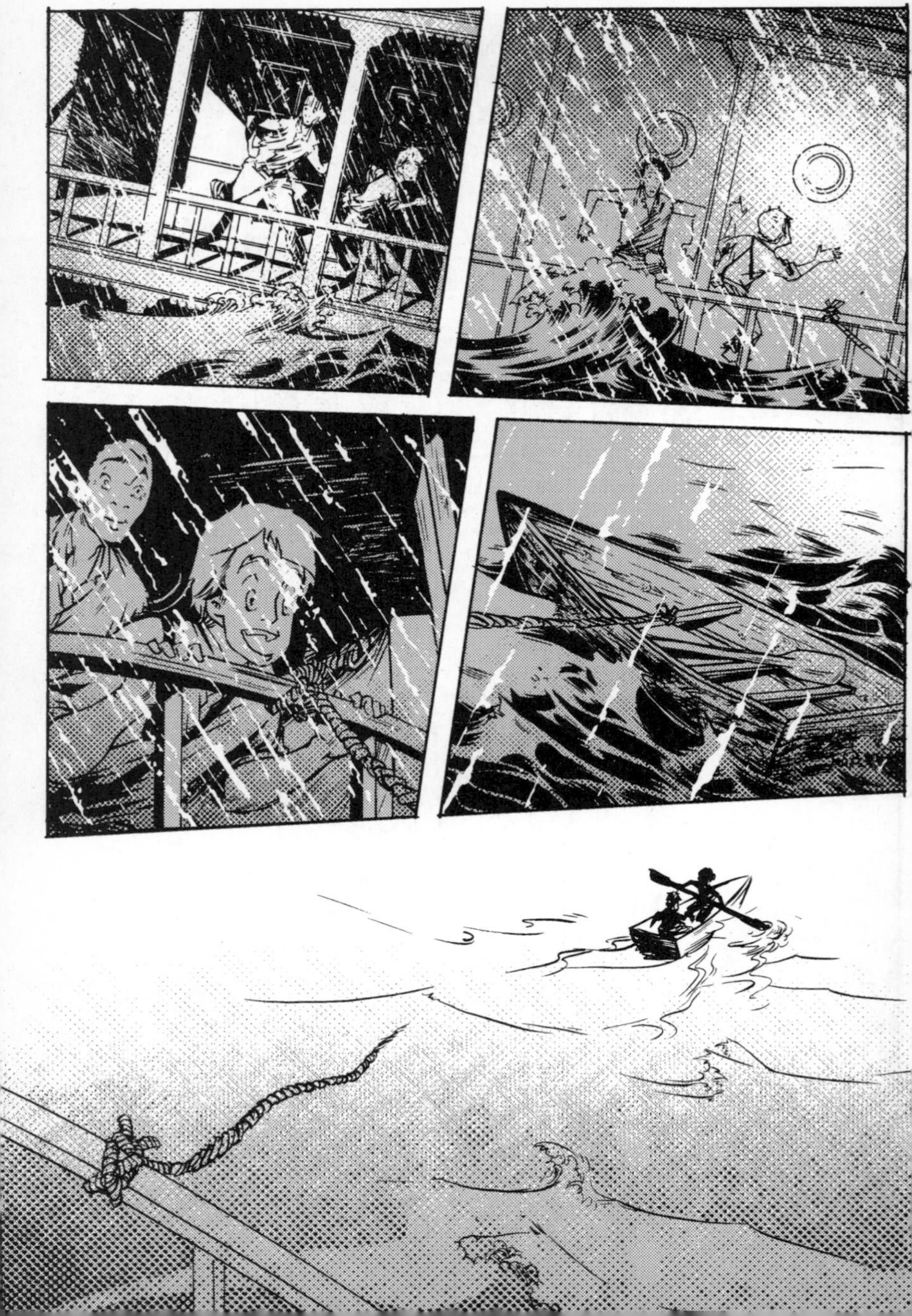

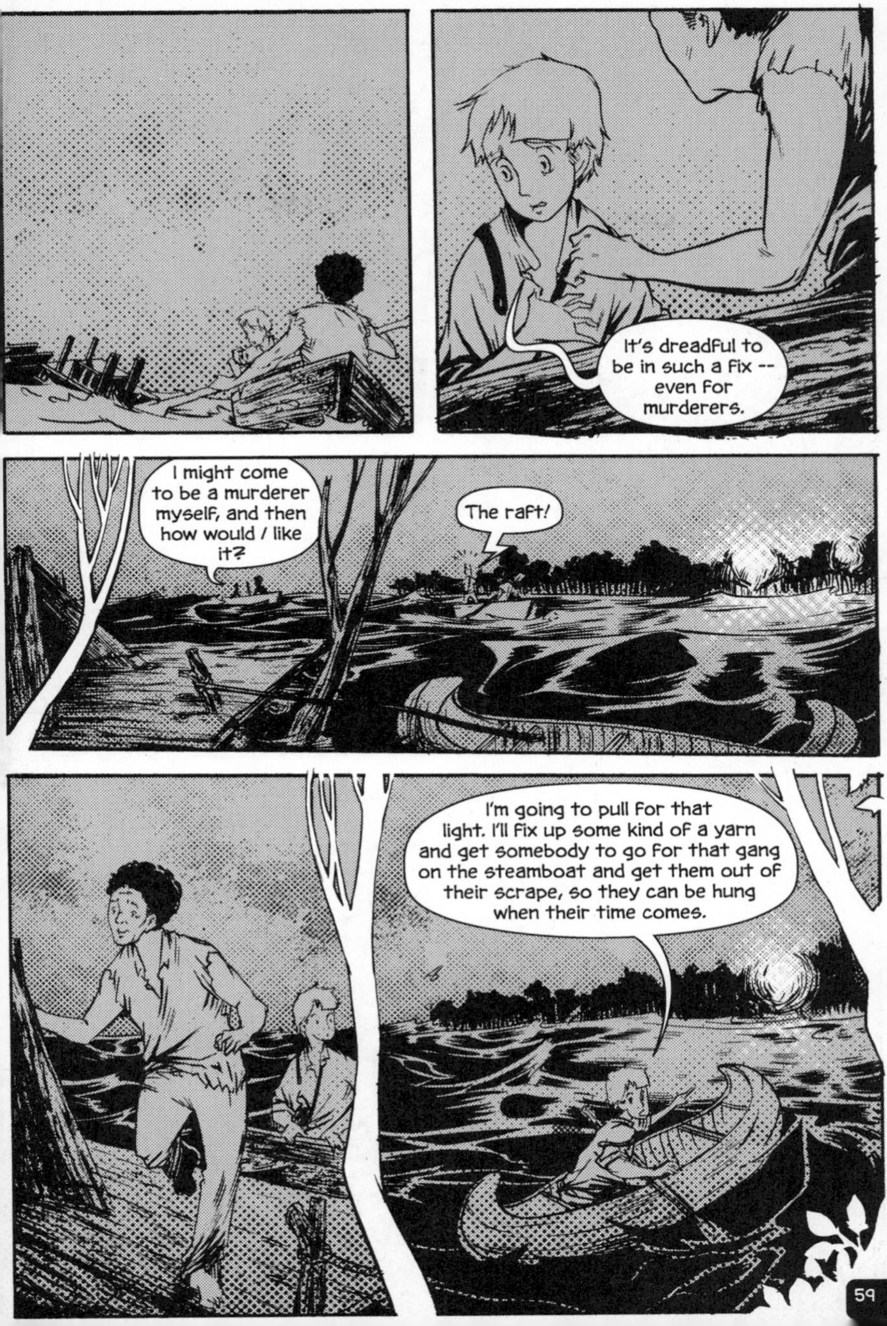
It's dreadful to be in such a fix -- even for murderers.
I might come to be a murderer myself, and then how would / like it?
The raft!
I'm going to pull for that light. I'll fix up some kind of a yarn and get somebody to go for that gang on the steamboat and get them out of their scrape, so they can be hung when their time comes.

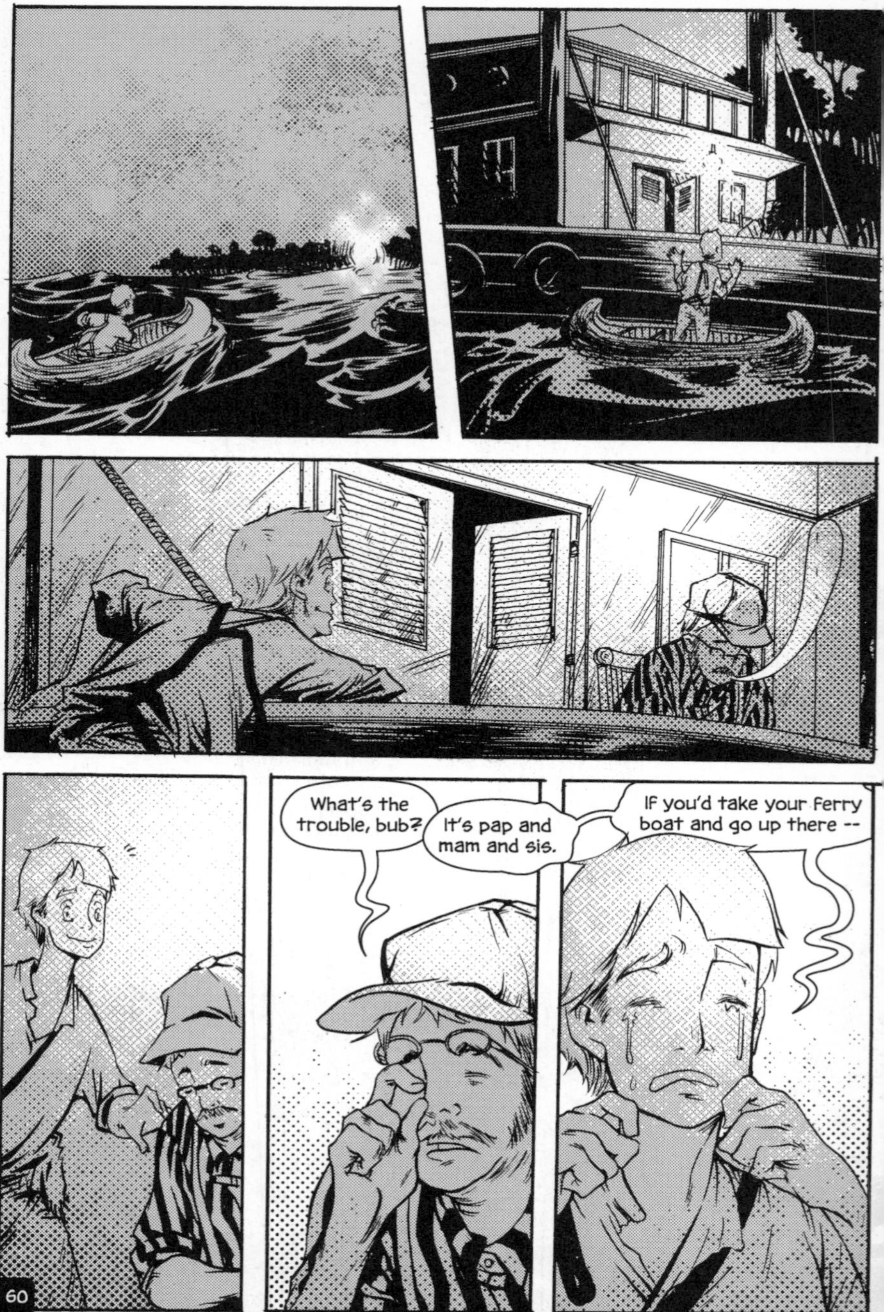
What's the trouble, bub?
It's pap and mam and sis.
If you'd take your ferry boat and go up there --

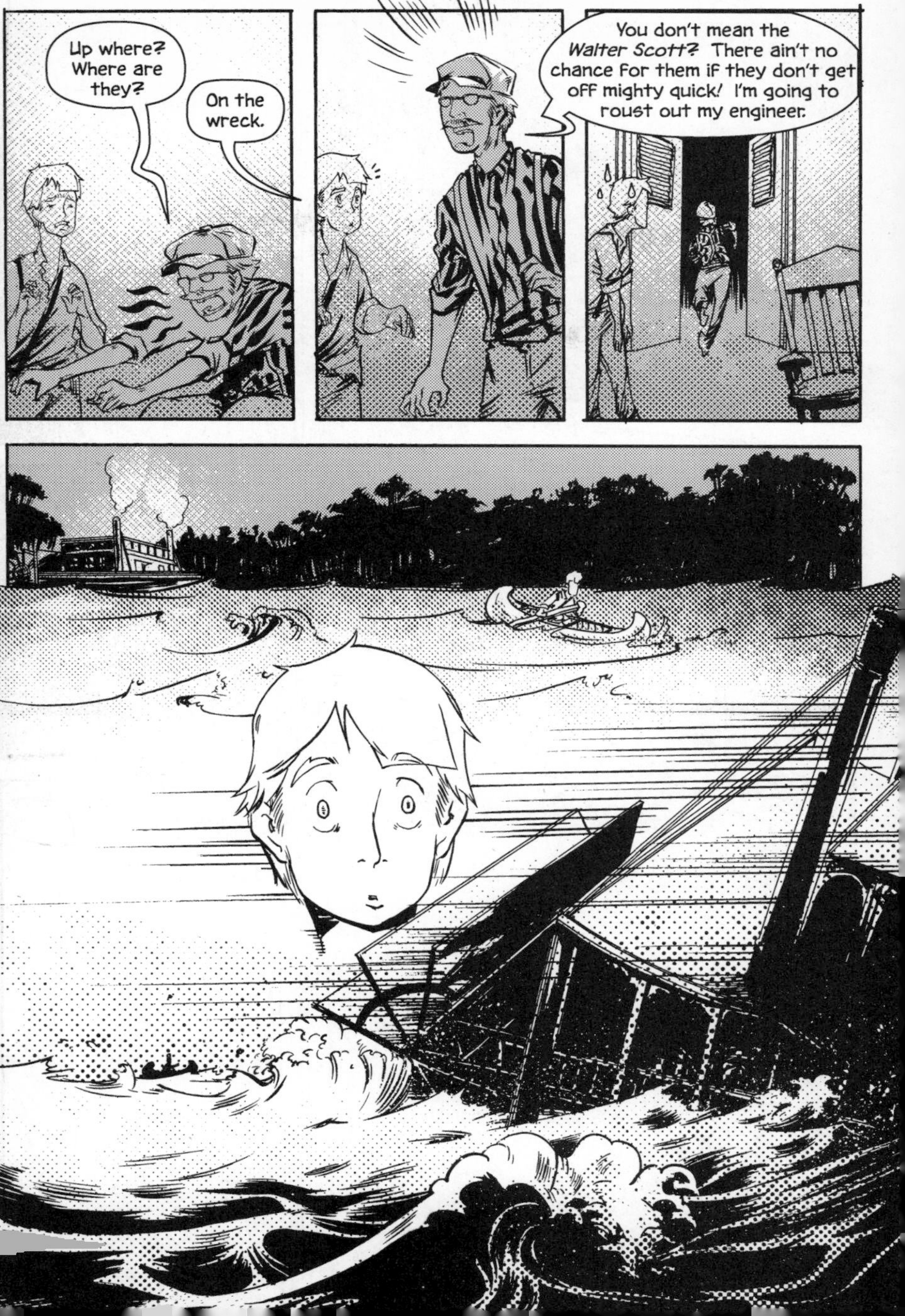
Up where? Where are they?
On the wreck.
You don't mean the *Walter Scott*? There ain't no chance for them if they don't get off mighty quick! I'm going to roust out my engineer.

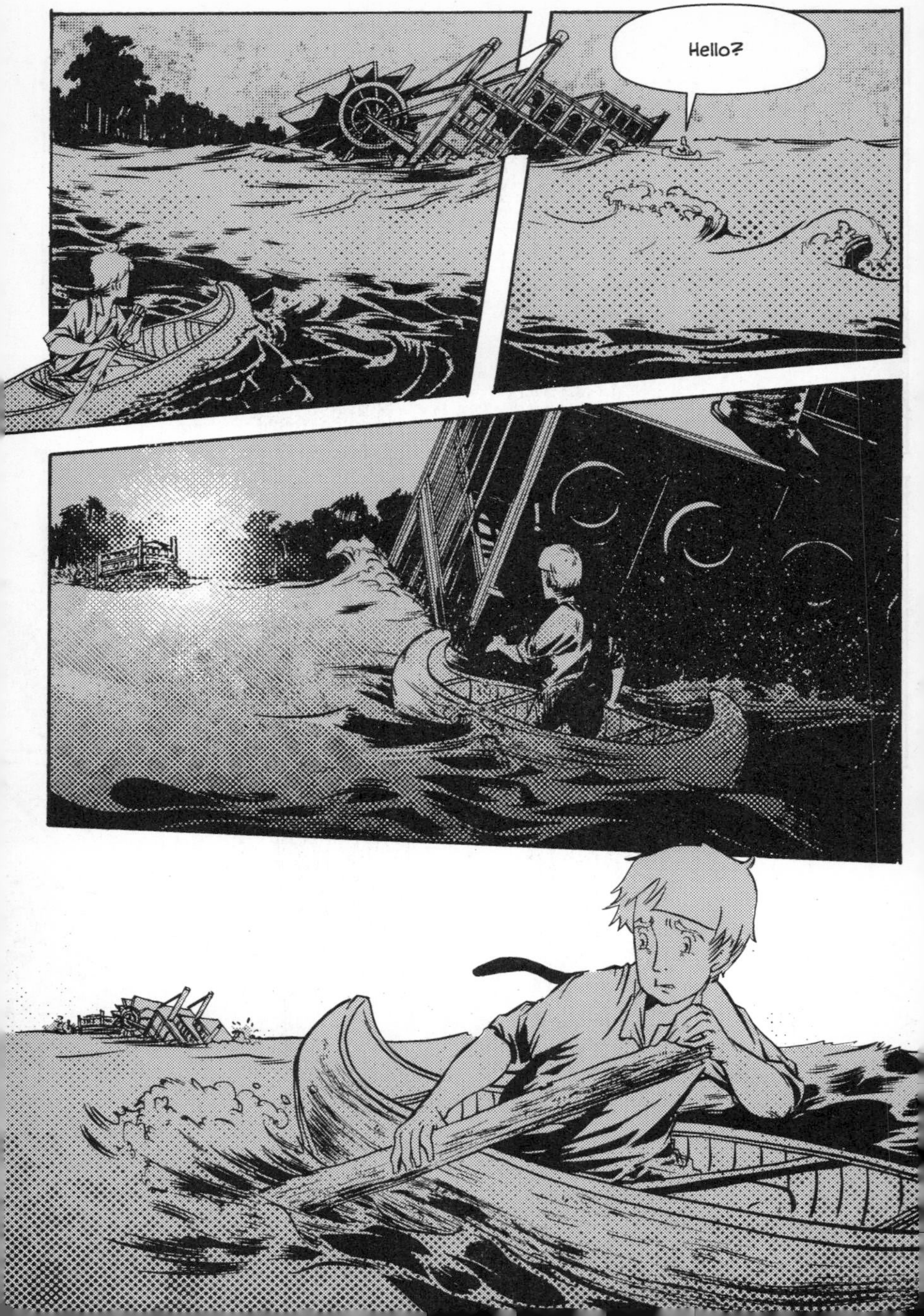
Hello?

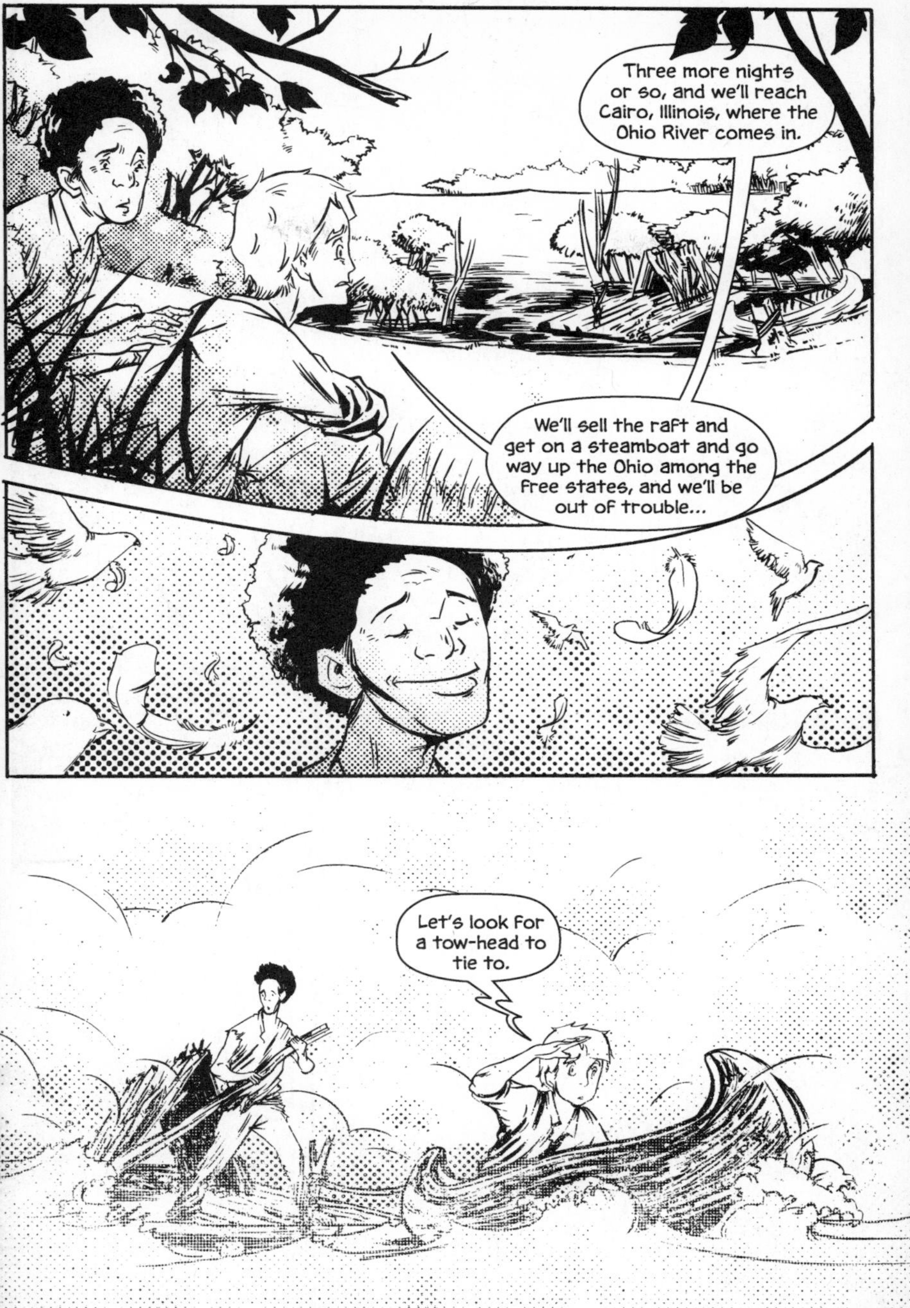
Three more nights or so, and we'll reach Cairo, Illinois, where the Ohio River comes in.
We'll sell the raft and get on a steamboat and go way up the Ohio among the free states, and we'll be out of trouble...
Let's look for a tow-head to tie to.

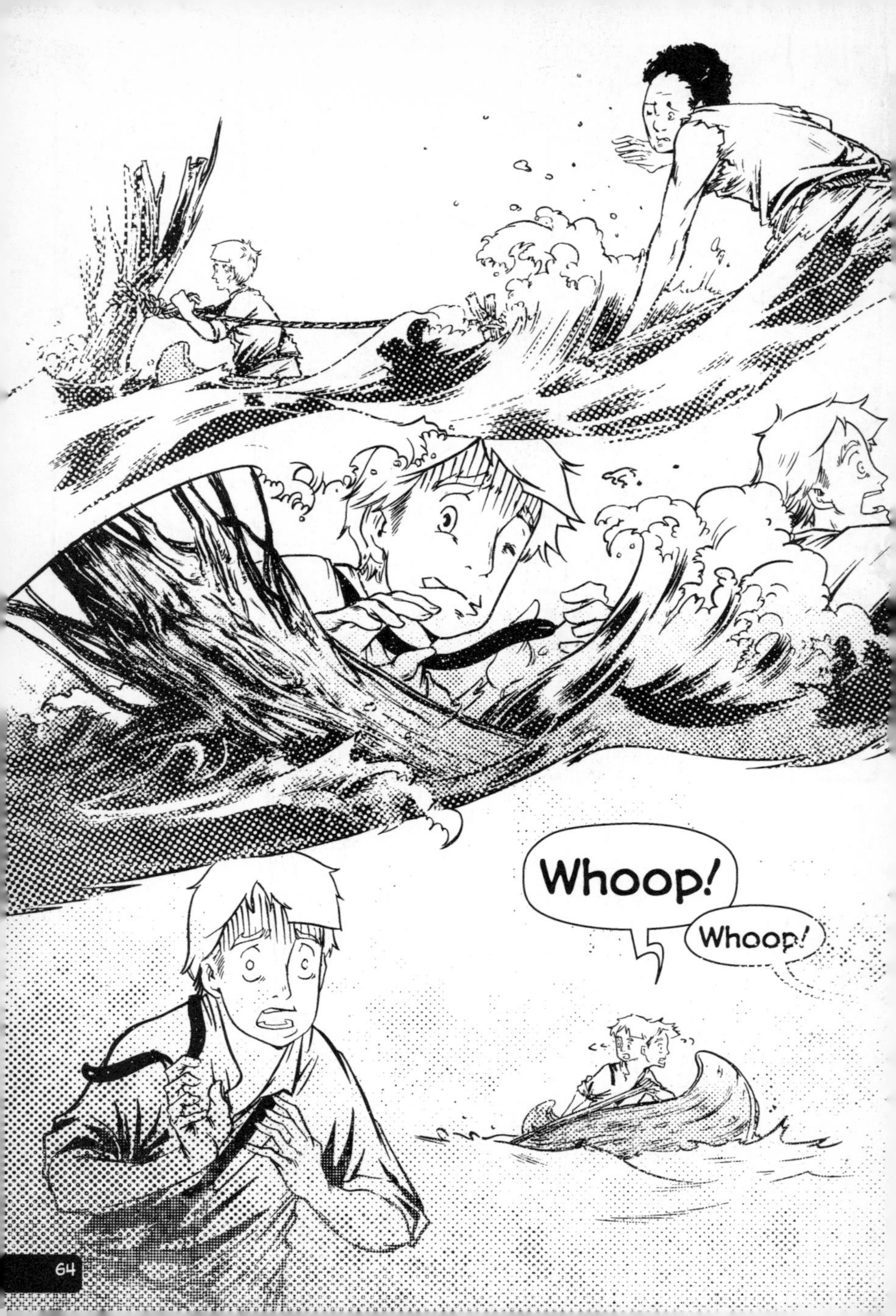
Whoop!
Whoop!

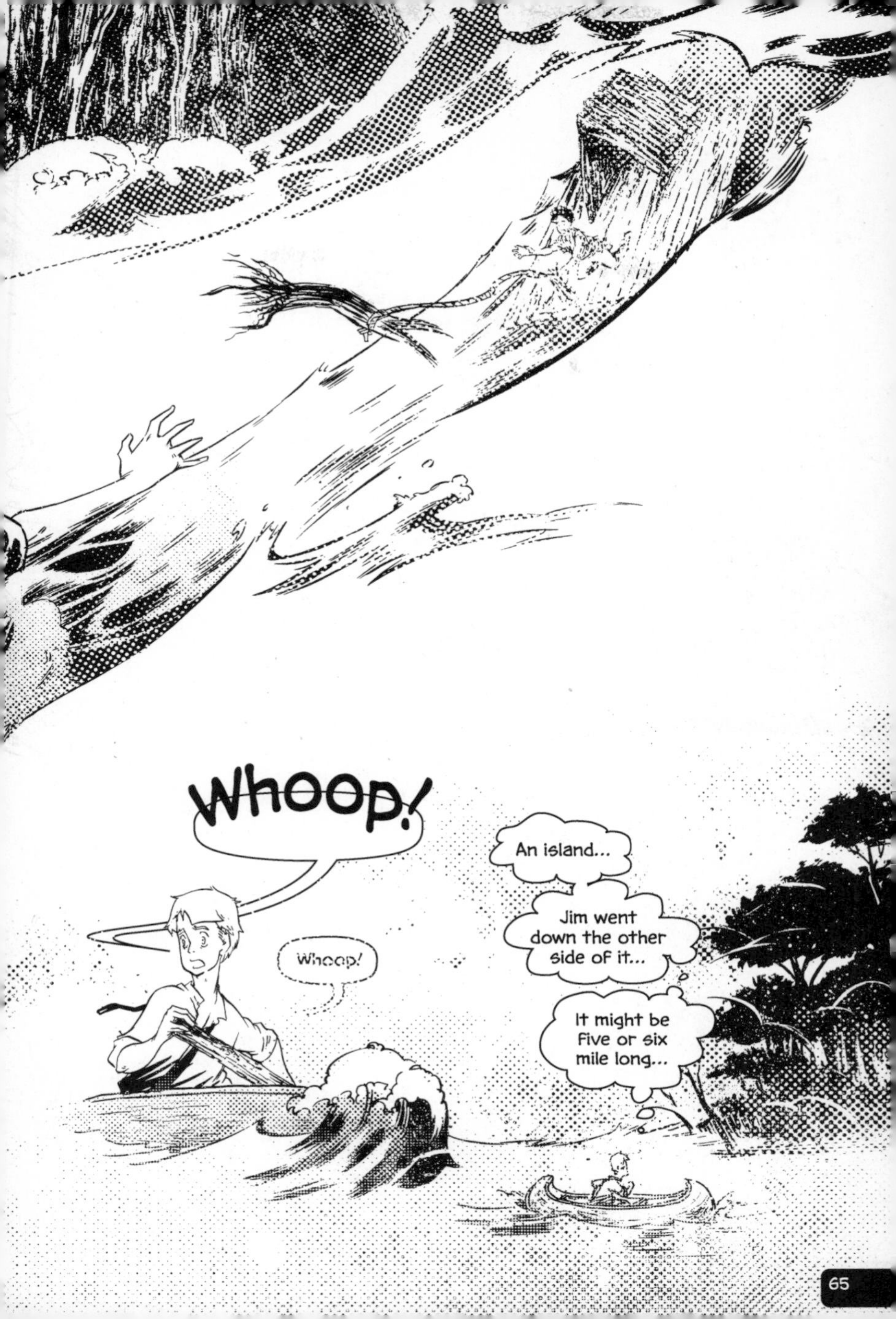
Whoop!
Whoop!
An island...
Jim went down the other side of it...
It might be five or six mile long...

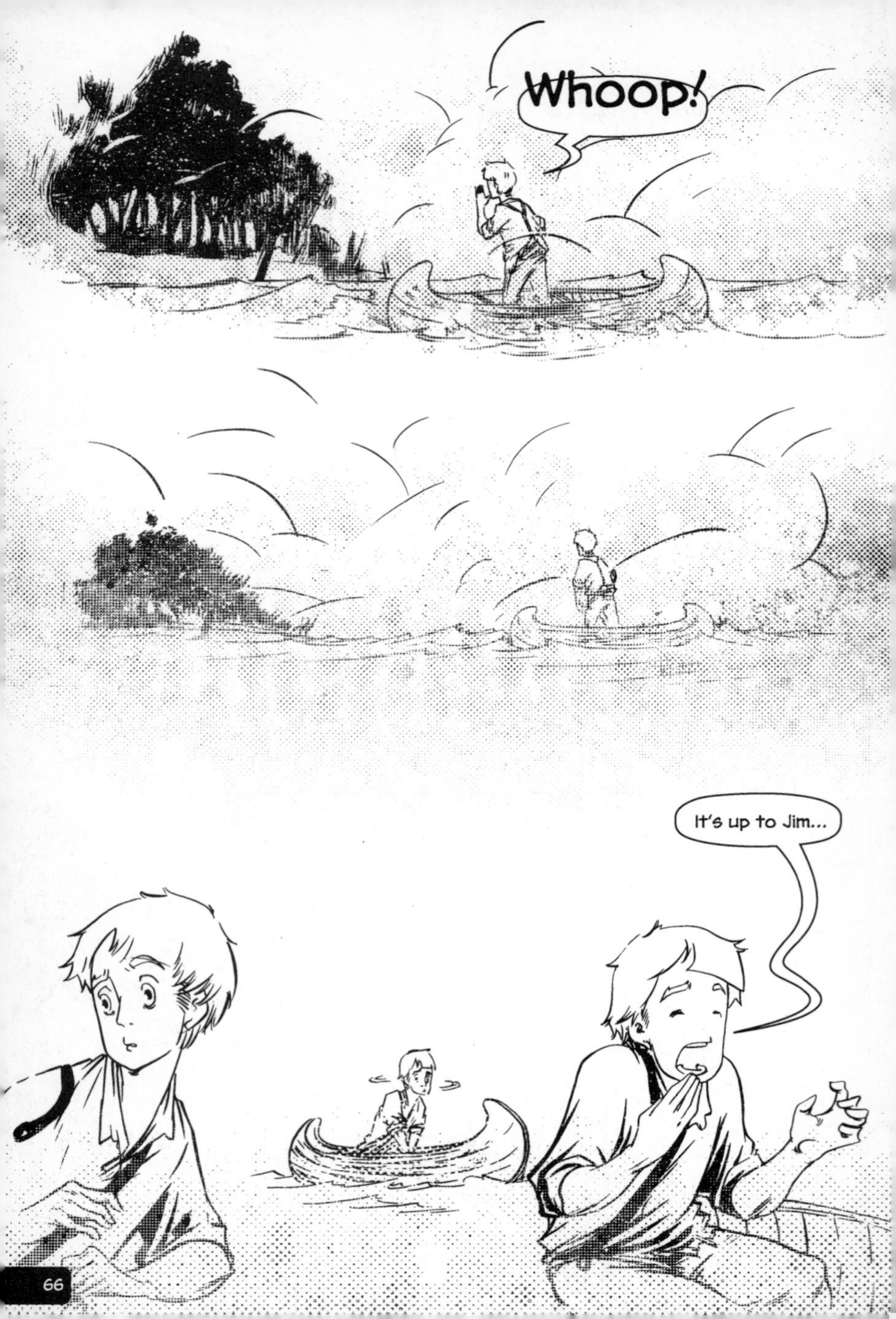
Whoop!
It's up to Jim...

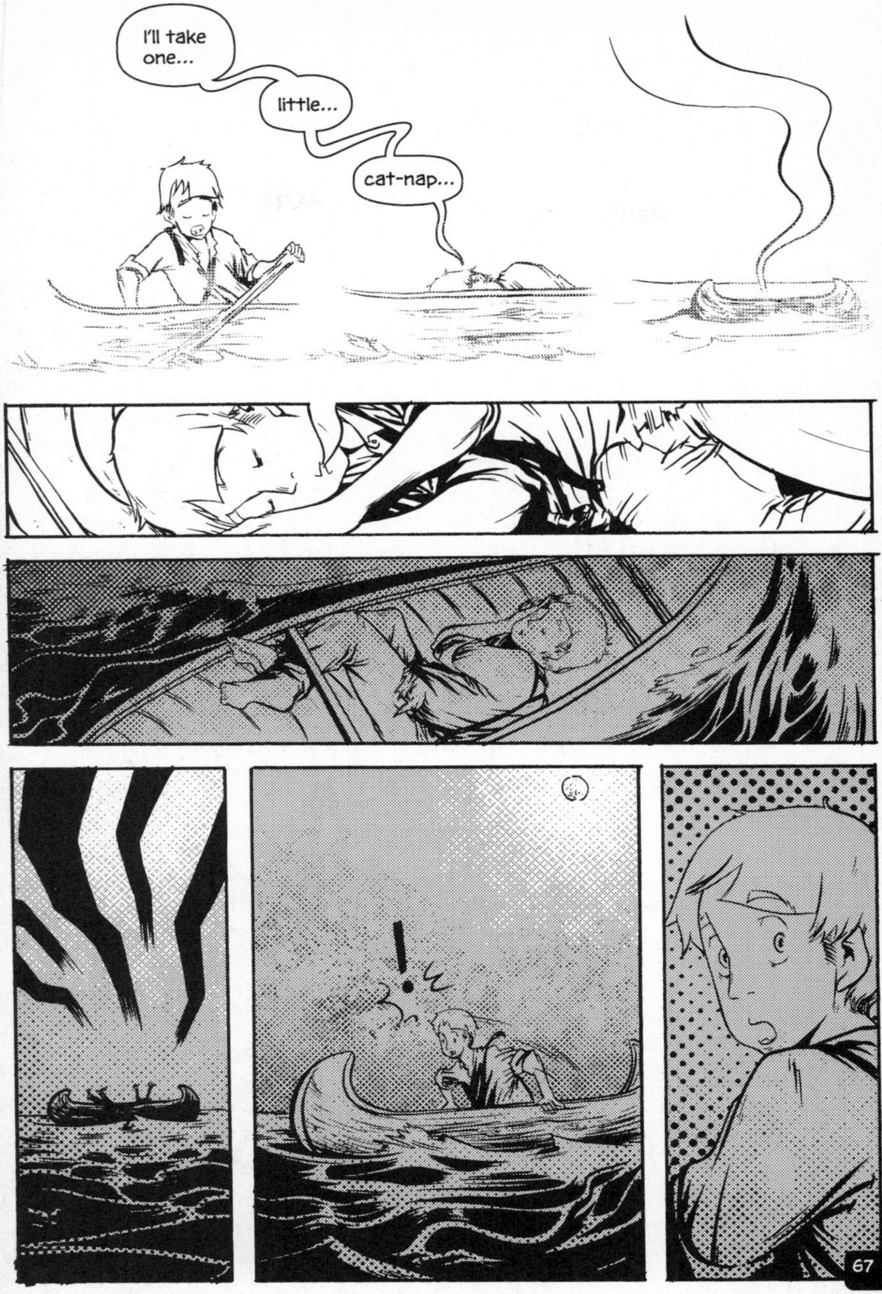
I'll take one...
little...
cat-nap...
!

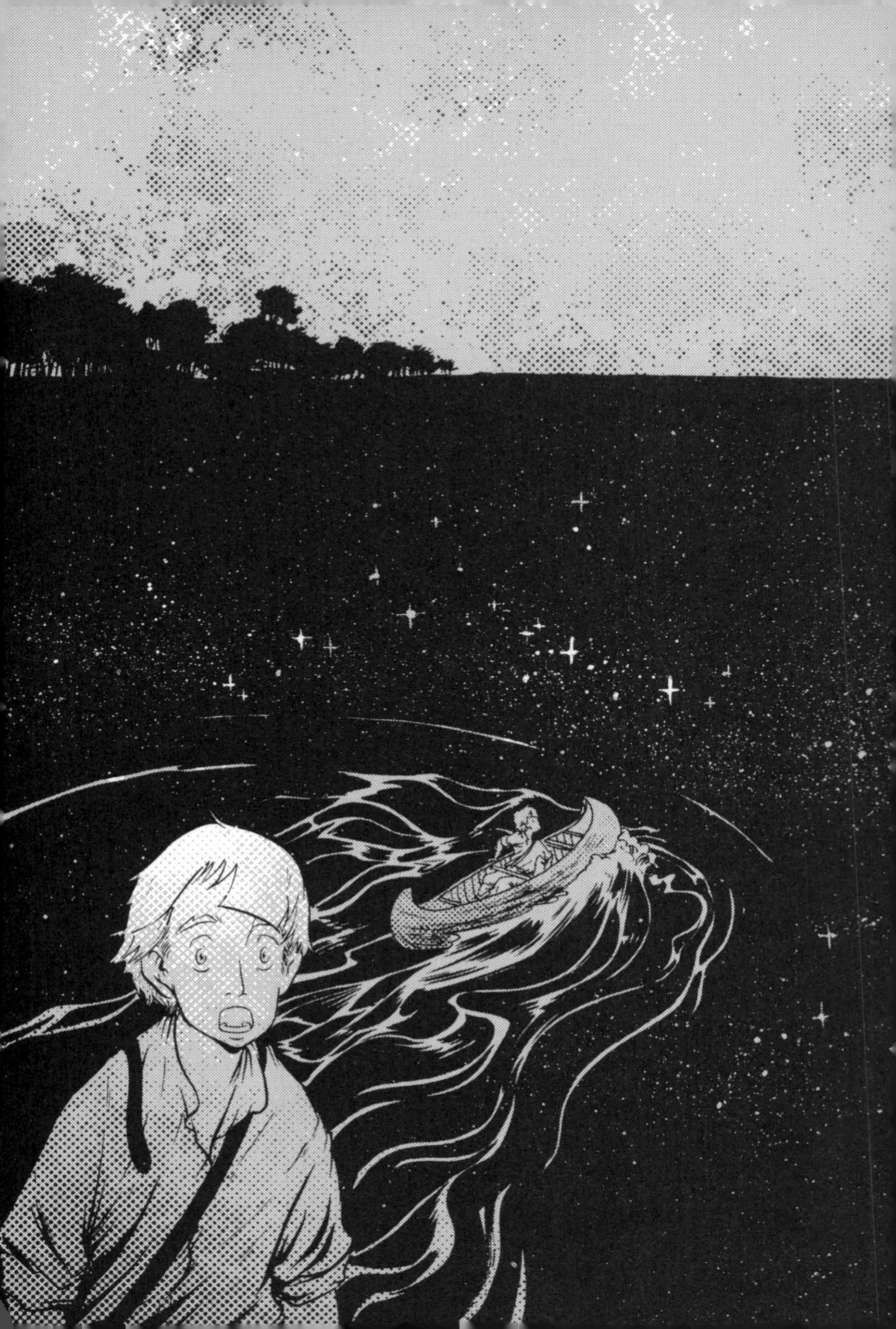

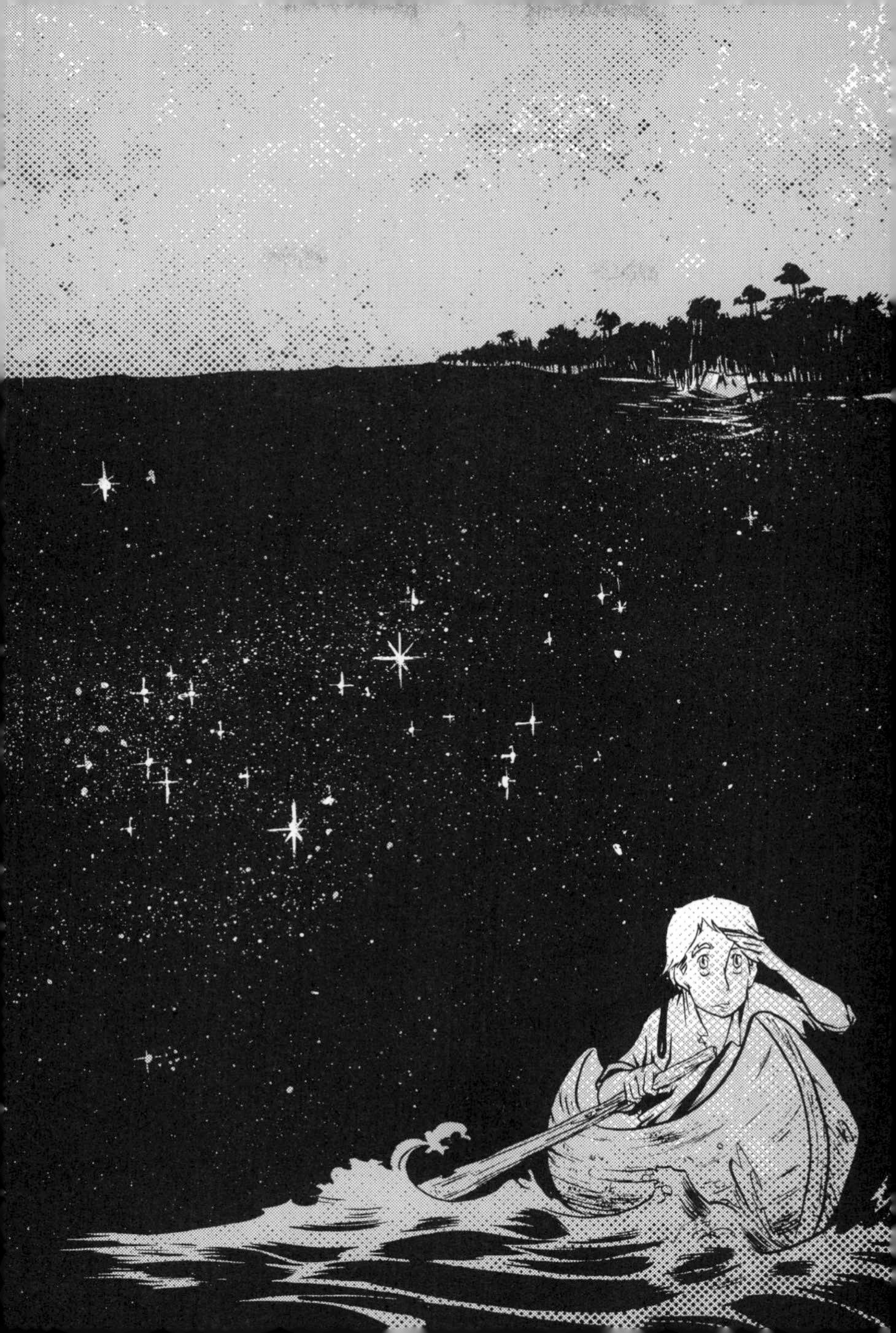

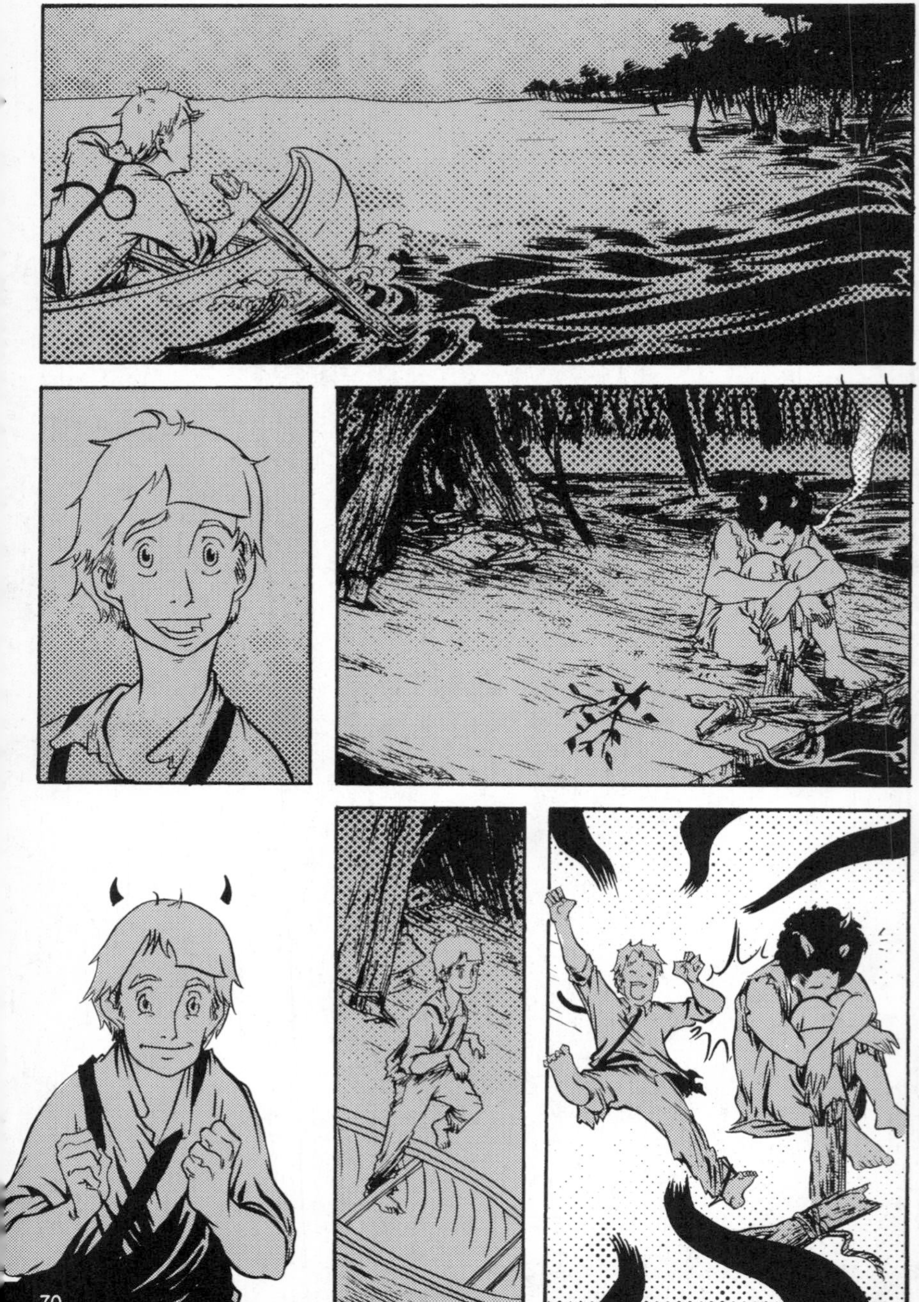

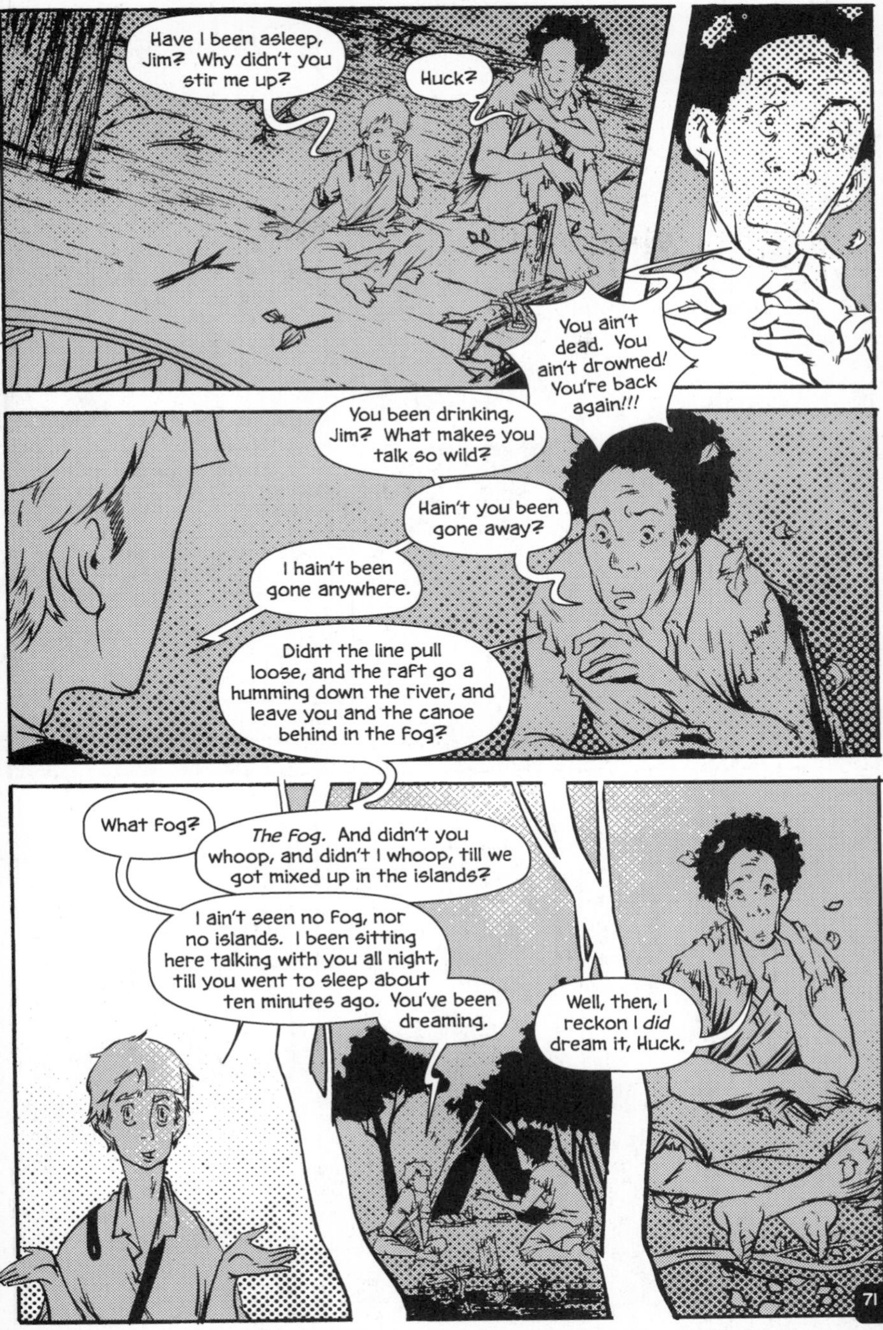
Have I been asleep, Jim? Why didn't you stir me up?
Huck?
You ain't dead. You ain't drowned! You're back again!!!
You been drinking, Jim? What makes you talk so wild?
Hain't you been gone away?
I hain't been gone anywhere.
Didnt the line pull loose, and the raft go a humming down the river, and leave you and the canoe behind in the Fog?
What Fog?
*The Fog.* And didn't you whoop, and didn't I whoop, till we got mixed up in the islands?
I ain't seen no Fog, nor no islands. I been sitting here talking with you all night, till you went to sleep about ten minutes ago. You've been dreaming.
Well, then, I reckon I *did* dream it, Huck.

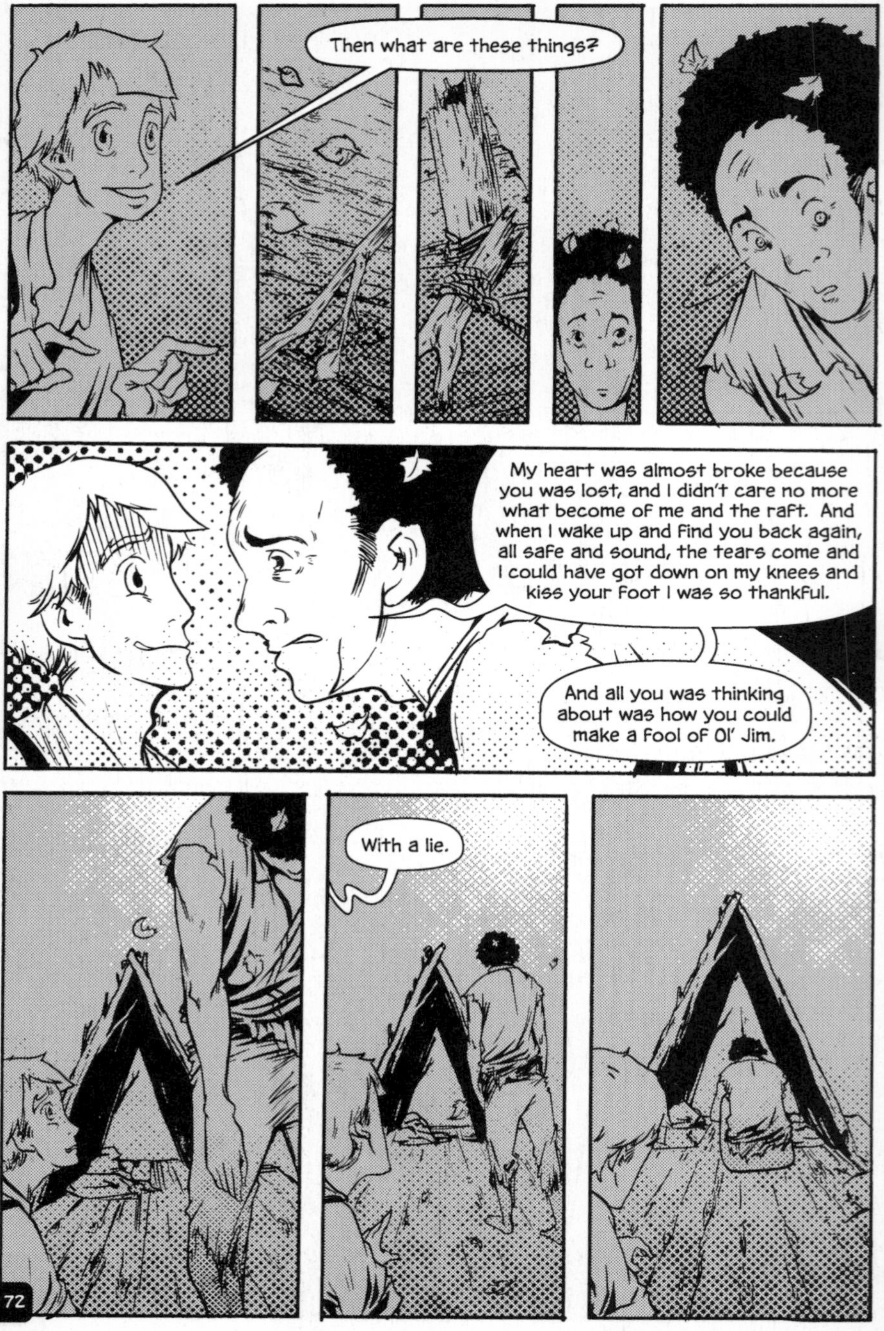
Then what are these things?
My heart was almost broke because you was lost, and I didn't care no more what become of me and the raft. And when I wake up and find you back again, all safe and sound, the tears come and I could have got down on my knees and kiss your foot I was so thankful.
And all you was thinking about was how you could make a fool of Ol' Jim.
With a lie.

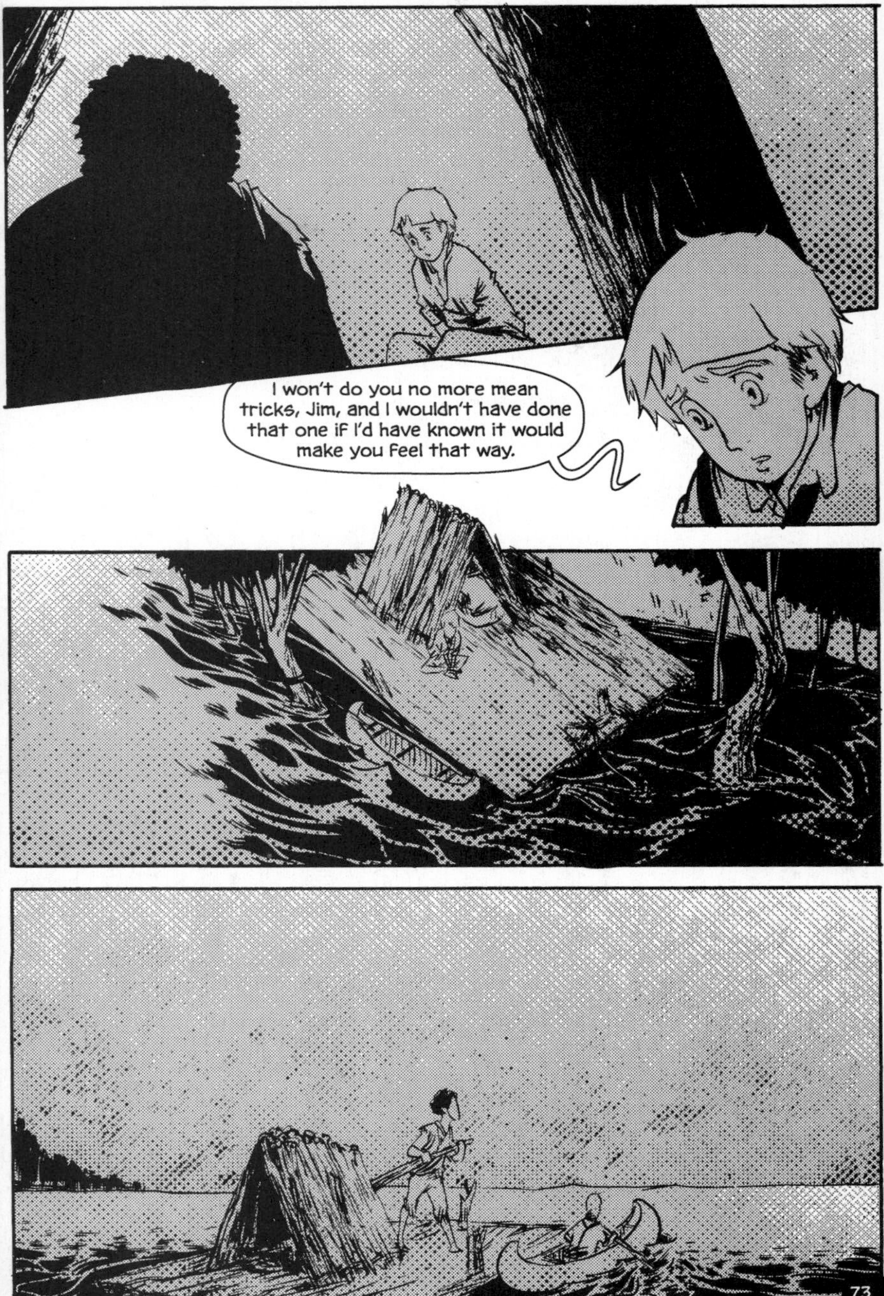
I won't do you no more mean tricks, Jim, and I wouldn't have done that one if I'd have known it would make you feel that way.

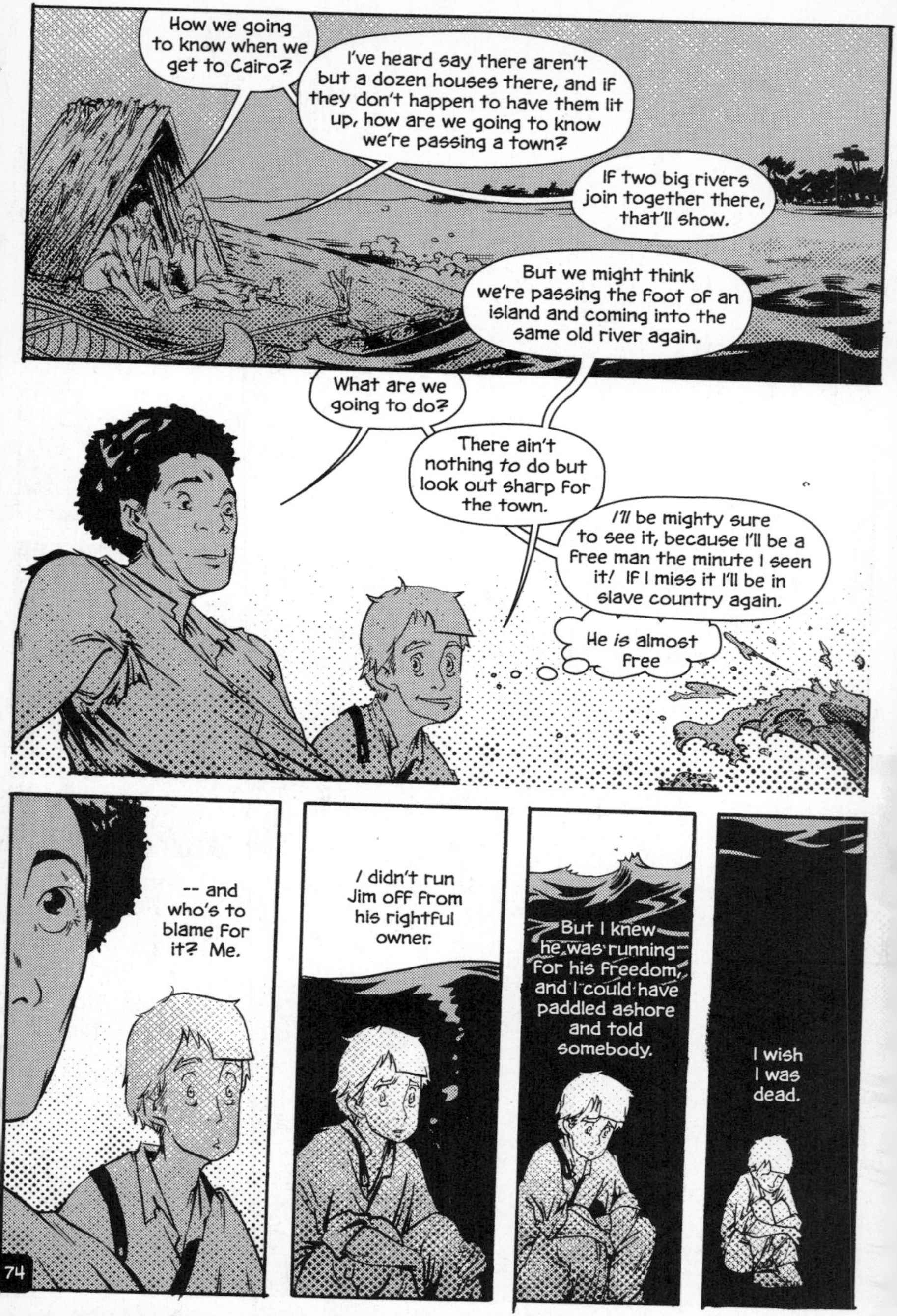
How we going to know when we get to Cairo?
I've heard say there aren't but a dozen houses there, and if they don't happen to have them lit up, how are we going to know we're passing a town?
If two big rivers join together there, that'll show.
But we might think we're passing the foot of an island and coming into the same old river again.
What are we going to do?
There ain't nothing *to* do but look out sharp for the town.
*I'll* be mighty sure to see it, because I'll be a free man the minute I seen it! If I miss it I'll be in slave country again.
He *is* almost free
-- and who's to blame for it? Me.
*I* didn't run Jim off from his rightful owner.
But I knew he was running for his freedom, and I could have paddled ashore and told somebody.
I wish I was dead.

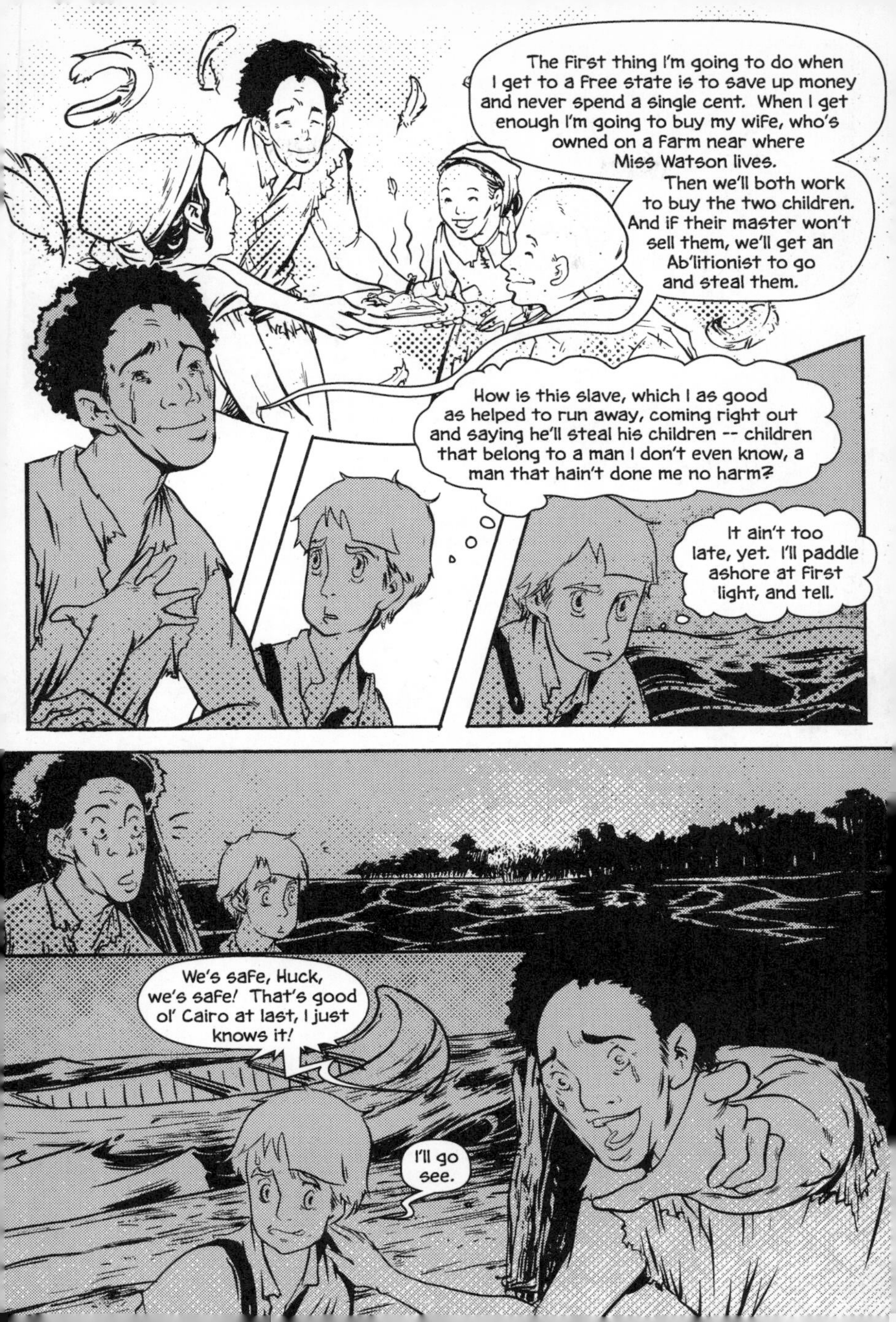
The first thing I'm going to do when I get to a free state is to save up money and never spend a single cent. When I get enough I'm going to buy my wife, who's owned on a farm near where Miss Watson lives.
Then we'll both work to buy the two children. And if their master won't sell them, we'll get an Ab'litionist to go and steal them.
How is this slave, which I as good as helped to run away, coming right out and saying he'll steal his children -- children that belong to a man I don't even know, a man that hain't done me no harm?
It ain't too late, yet. I'll paddle ashore at first light, and tell.
We's safe, Huck, we's safe! That's good ol' Cairo at last, I just knows it!
I'll go see.

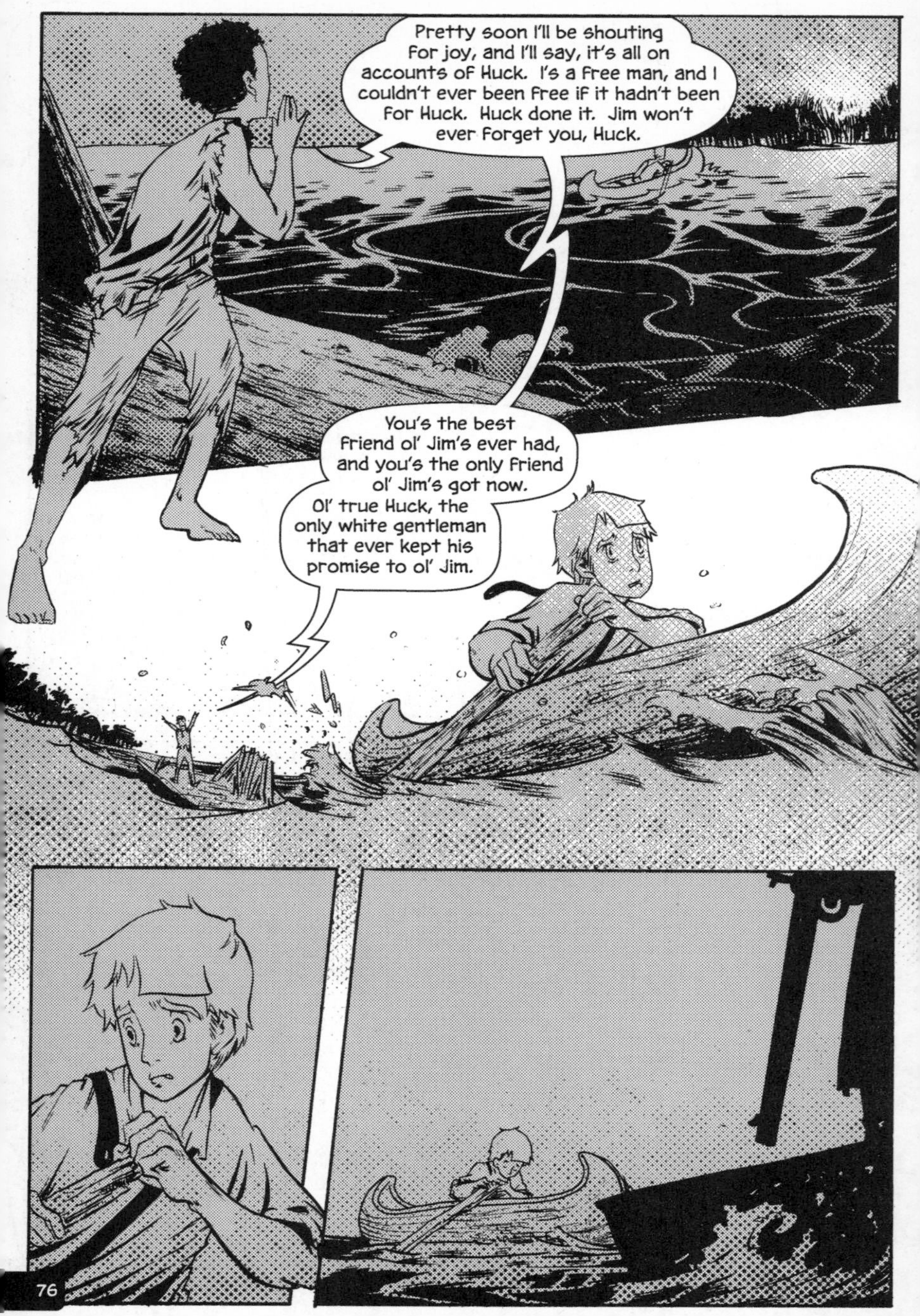
Pretty soon I'll be shouting for joy, and I'll say, it's all on accounts of Huck. I's a free man, and I couldn't ever been free if it hadn't been for Huck. Huck done it. Jim won't ever forget you, Huck.
You's the best friend ol' Jim's ever had, and you's the only friend ol' Jim's got now.
Ol' true Huck, the only white gentleman that ever kept his promise to ol' Jim.

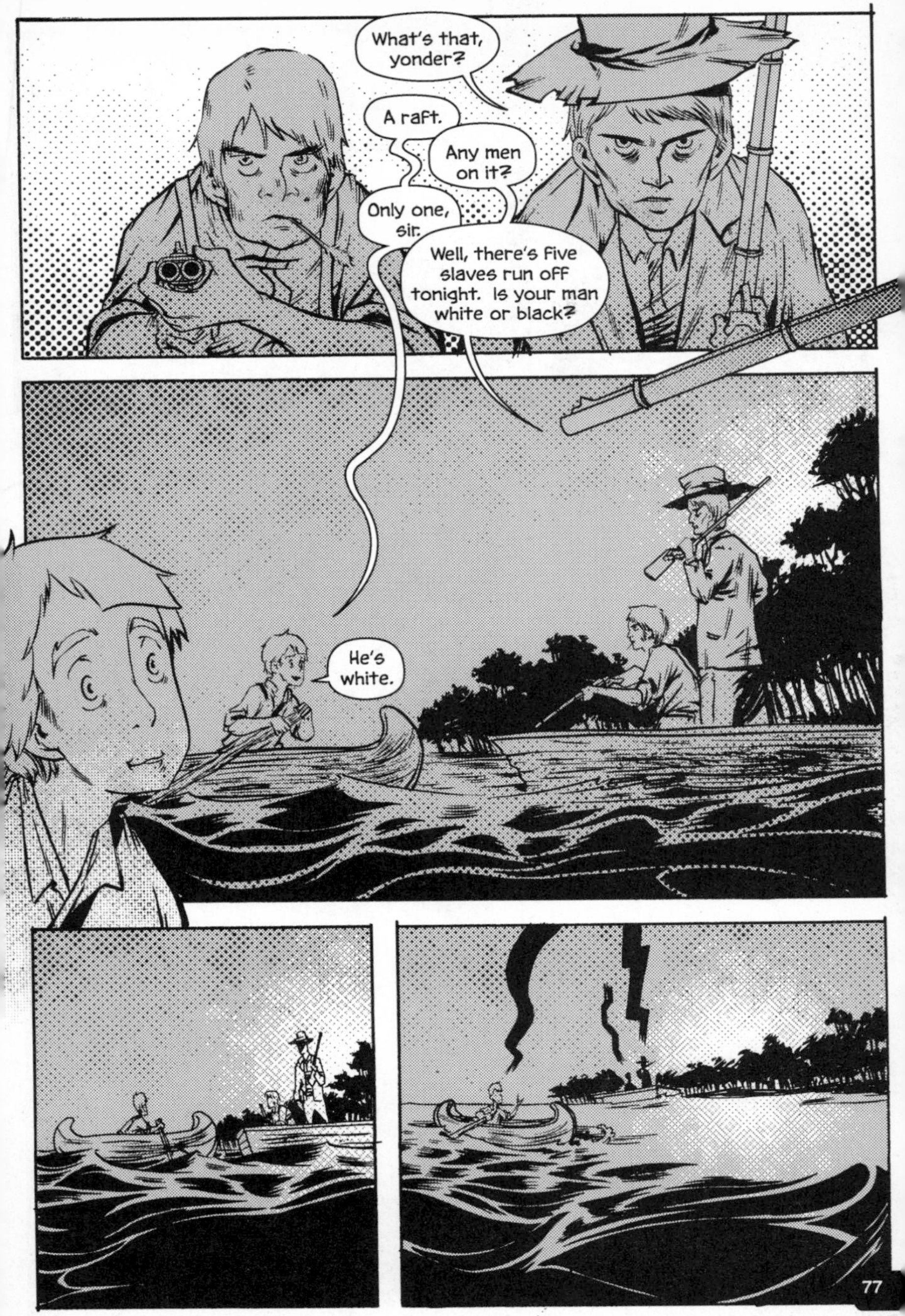
What's that, yonder?
A raft.
Any men on it?
Only one, sir.
Well, there's five slaves run off tonight. Is your man white or black?
He's white.

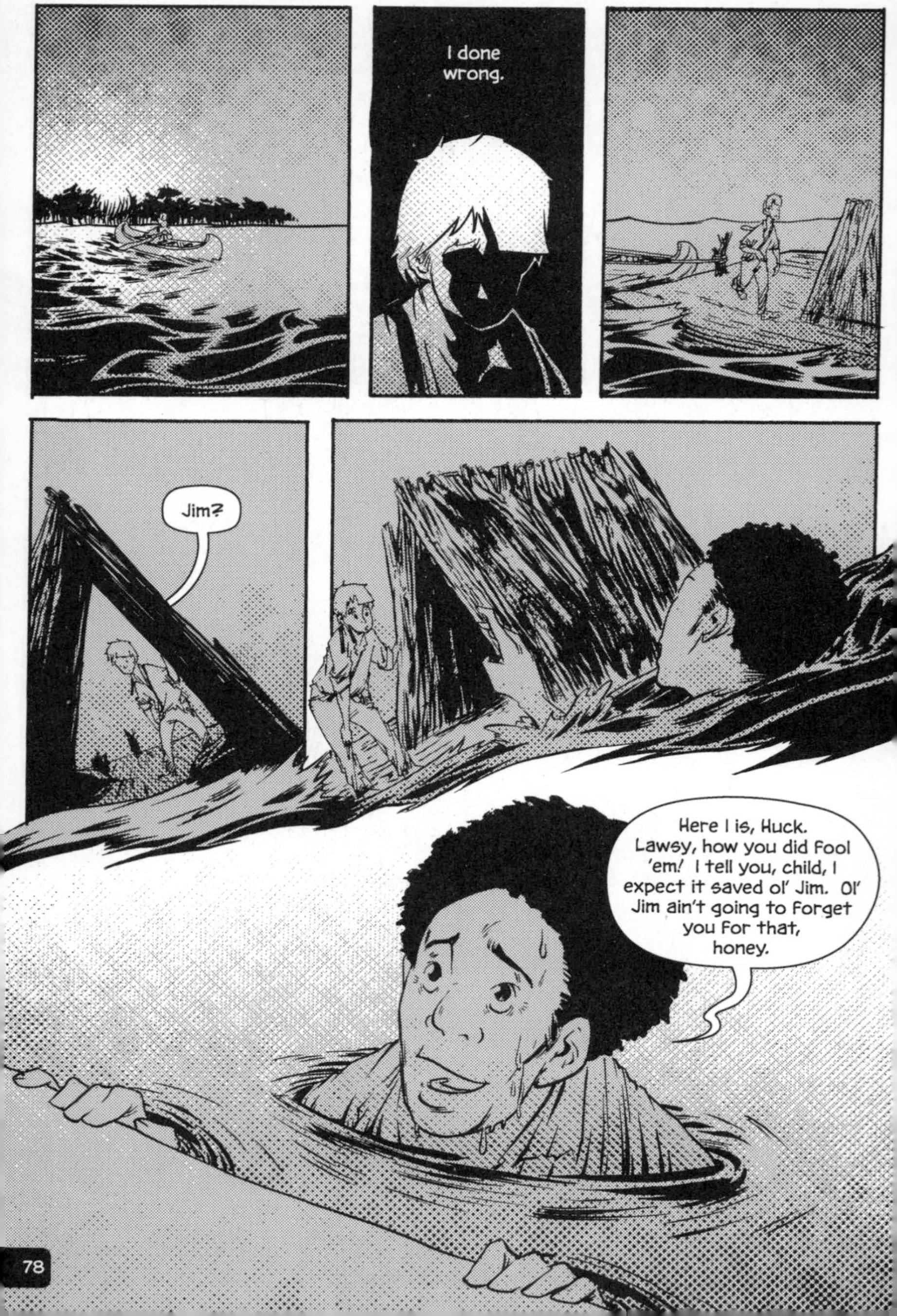
I done wrong.
Jim?
Here I is, Huck. Lawsy, how you did fool 'em! I tell you, child, I expect it saved ol' Jim. Ol' Jim ain't going to forget you for that, honey.

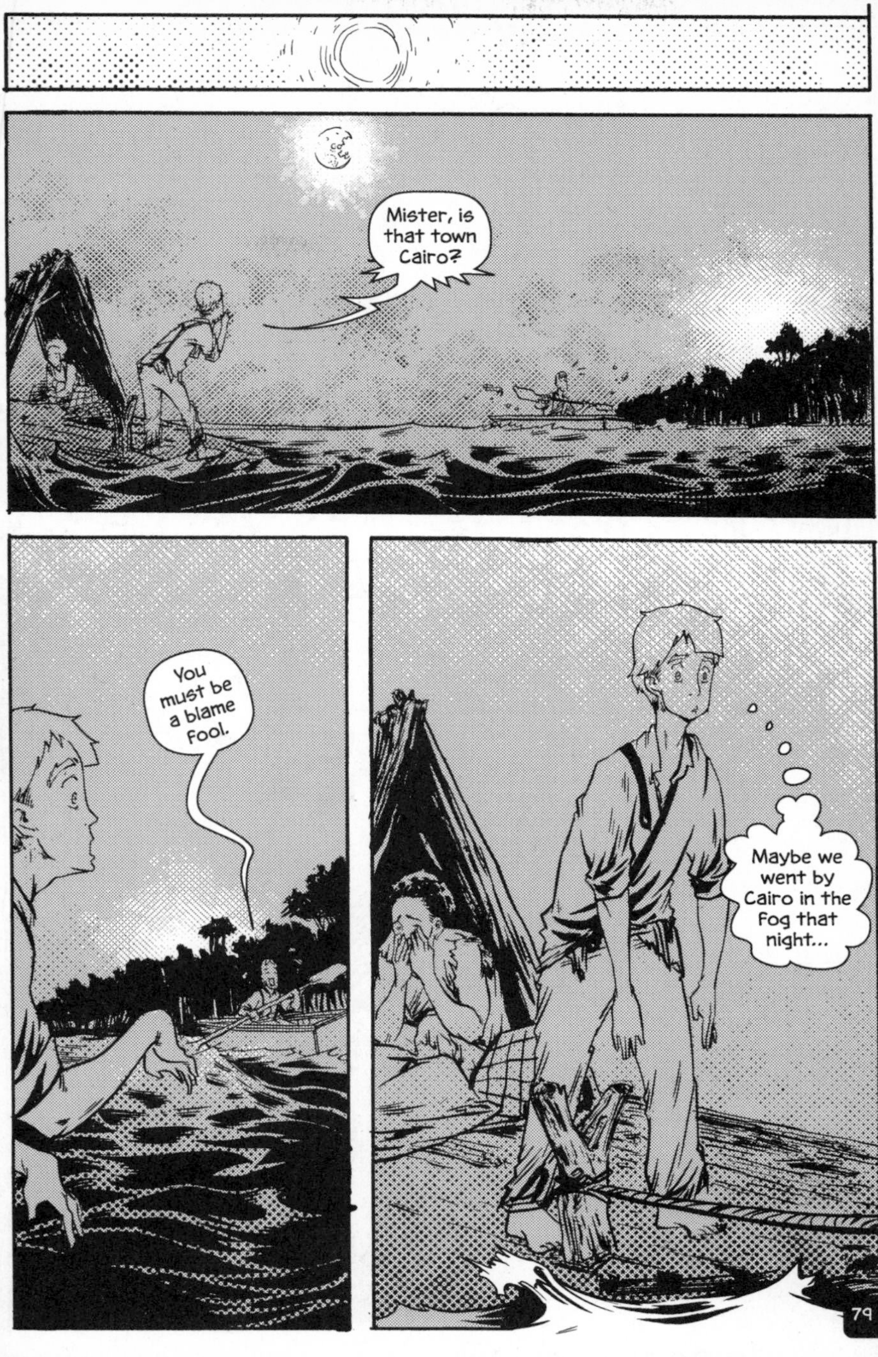
Mister, is that town Cairo?
You must be a blame fool.
Maybe we went by Cairo in the fog that night...

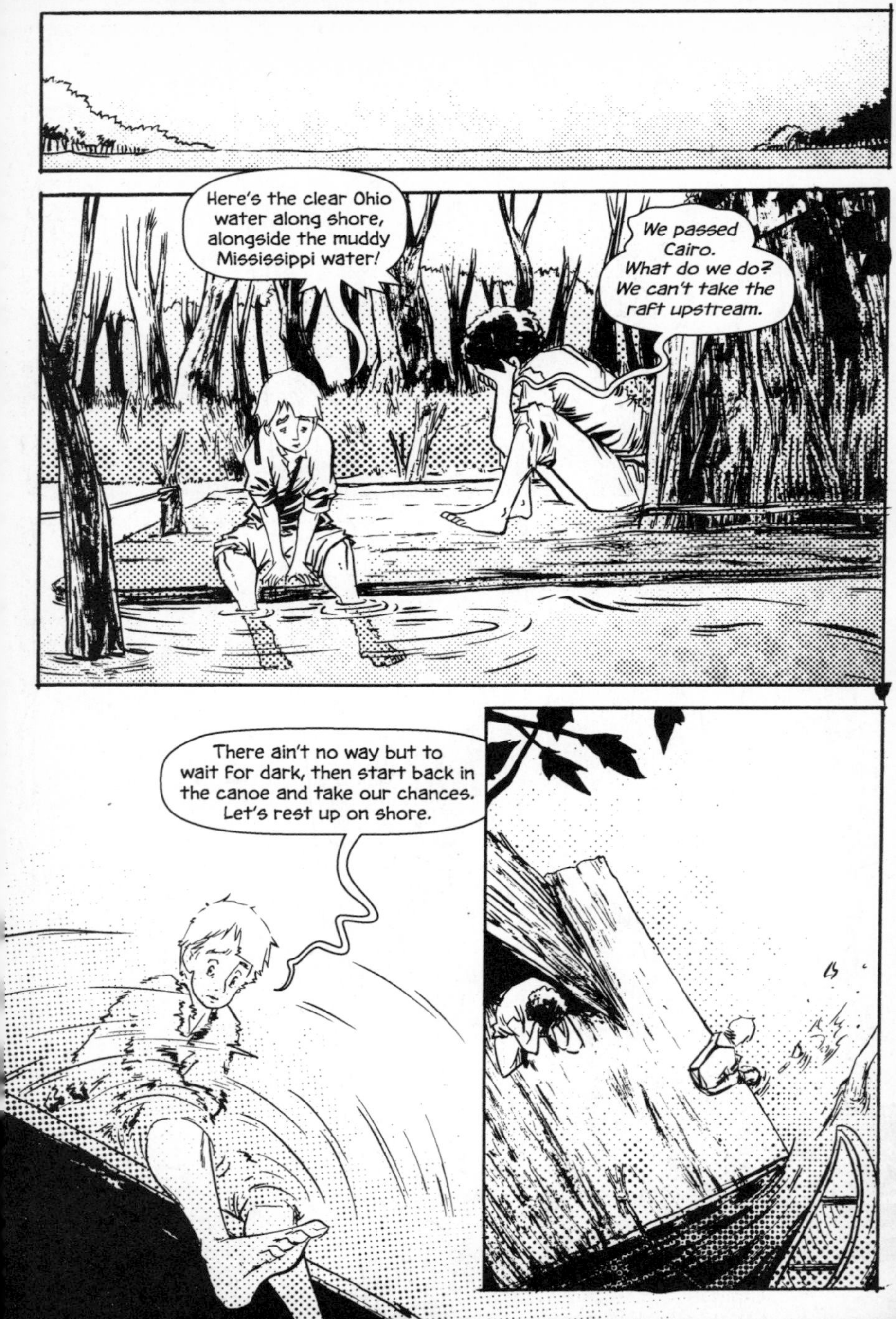
Here's the clear Ohio water along shore, alongside the muddy Mississippi water!
We passed Cairo. What do we do? We can't take the raft upstream.
There ain't no way but to wait for dark, then start back in the canoe and take our chances. Let's rest up on shore.

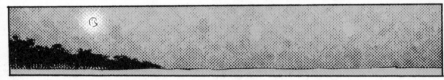

The canoe is gone!

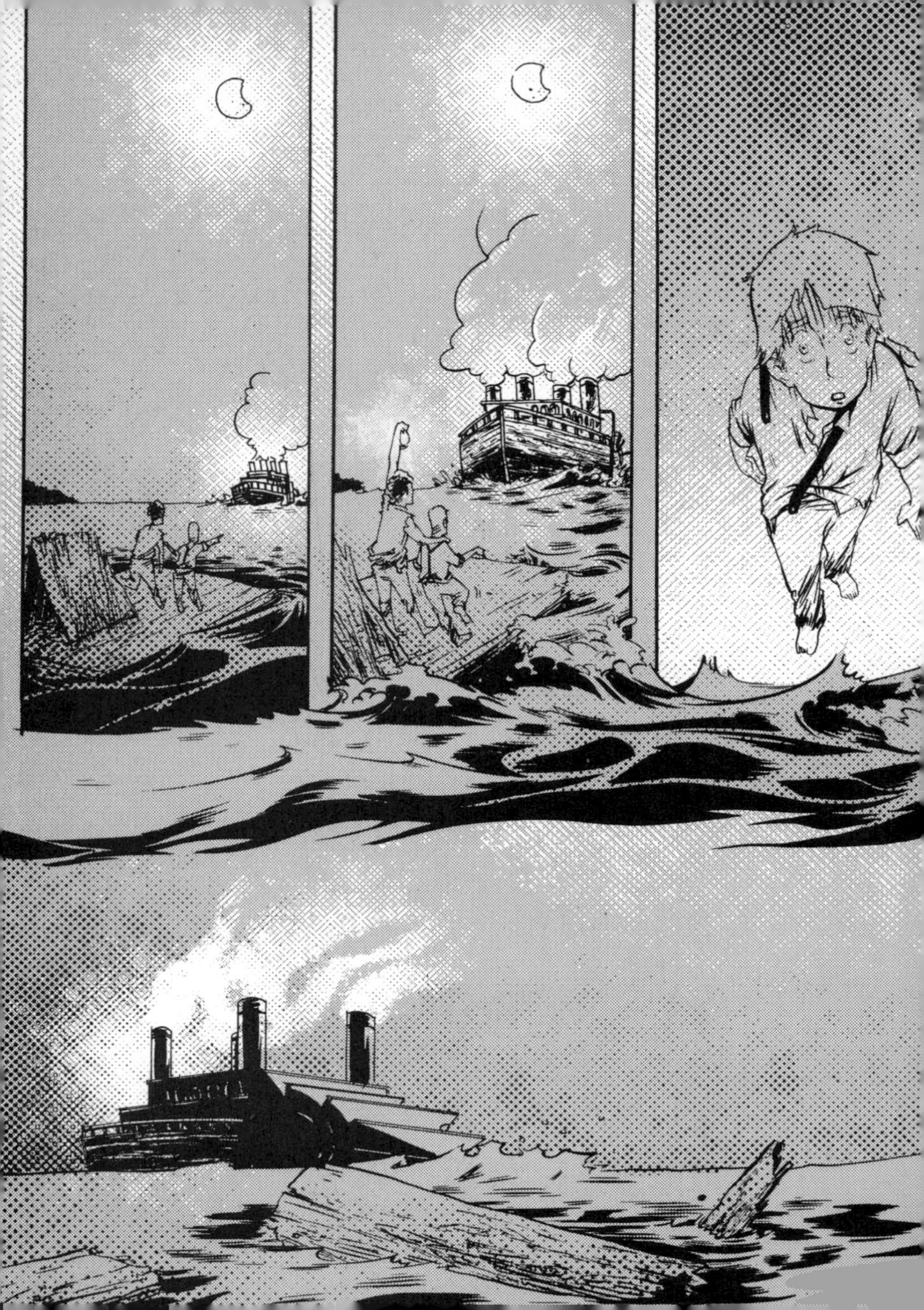

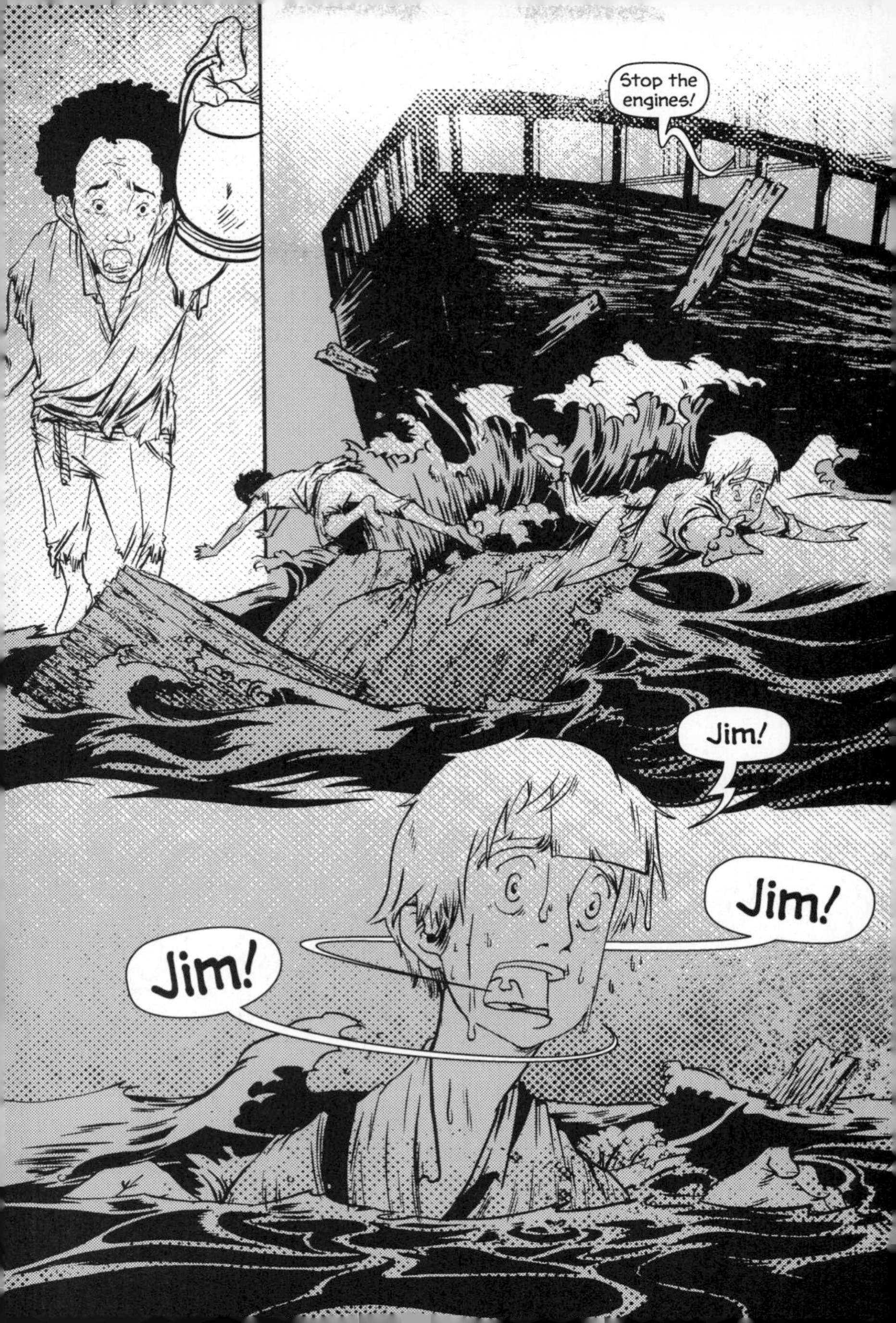

Stop the engines!
Jim!
Jim!
Jim!

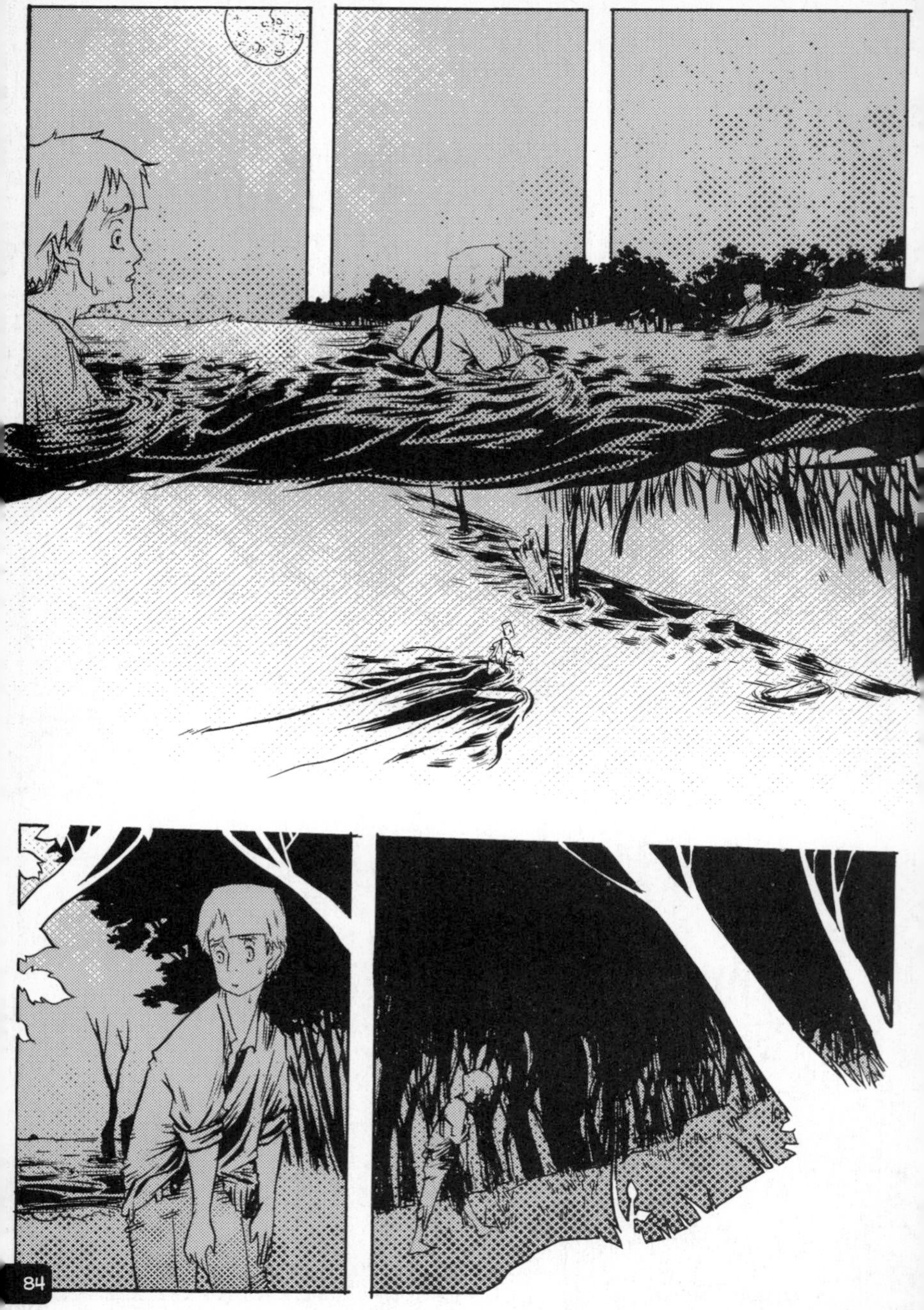

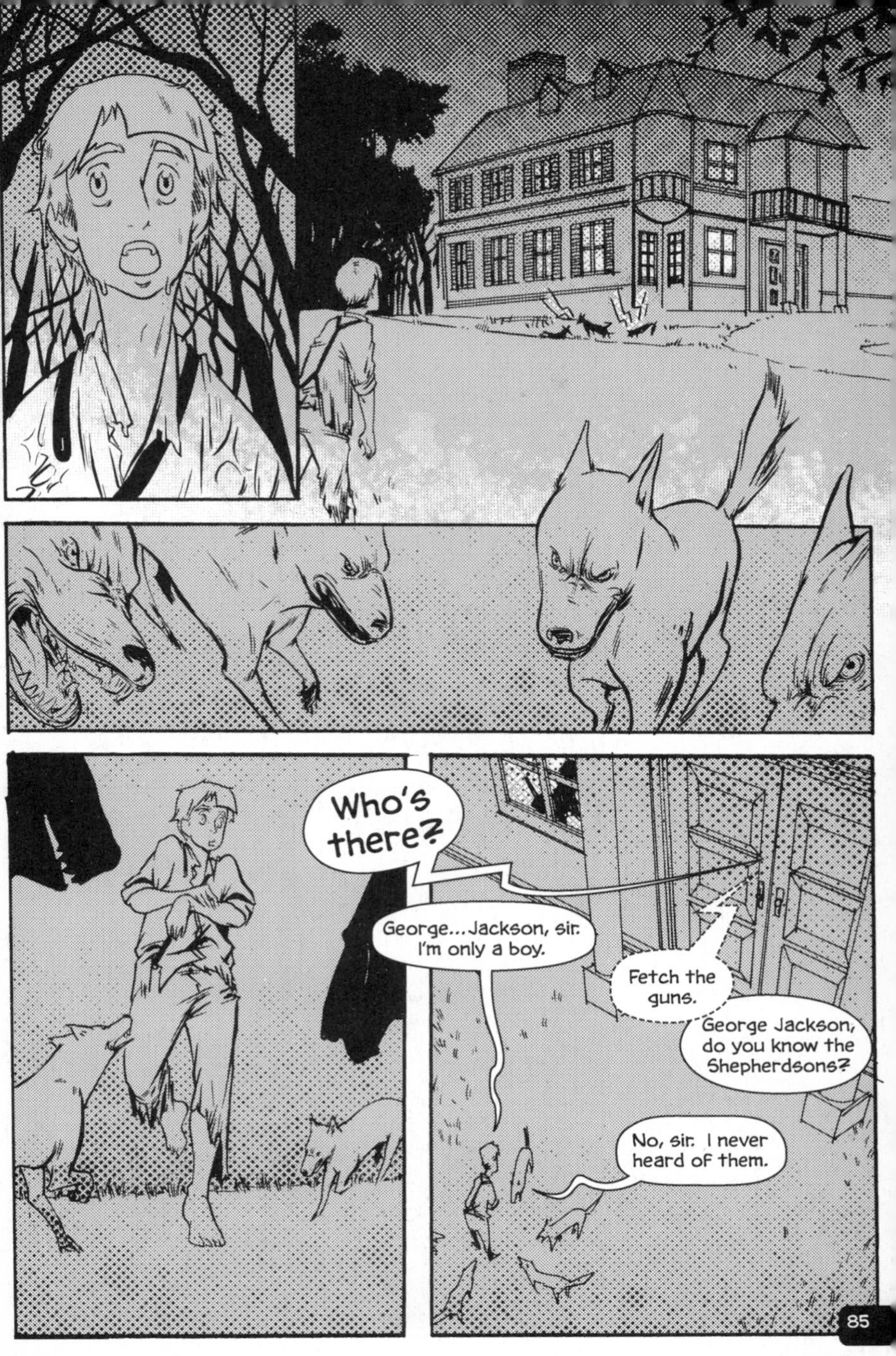

Who's there?
George... Jackson, sir. I'm only a boy.
Fetch the guns.
George Jackson, do you know the Shepherdsons?
No, sir. I never heard of them.

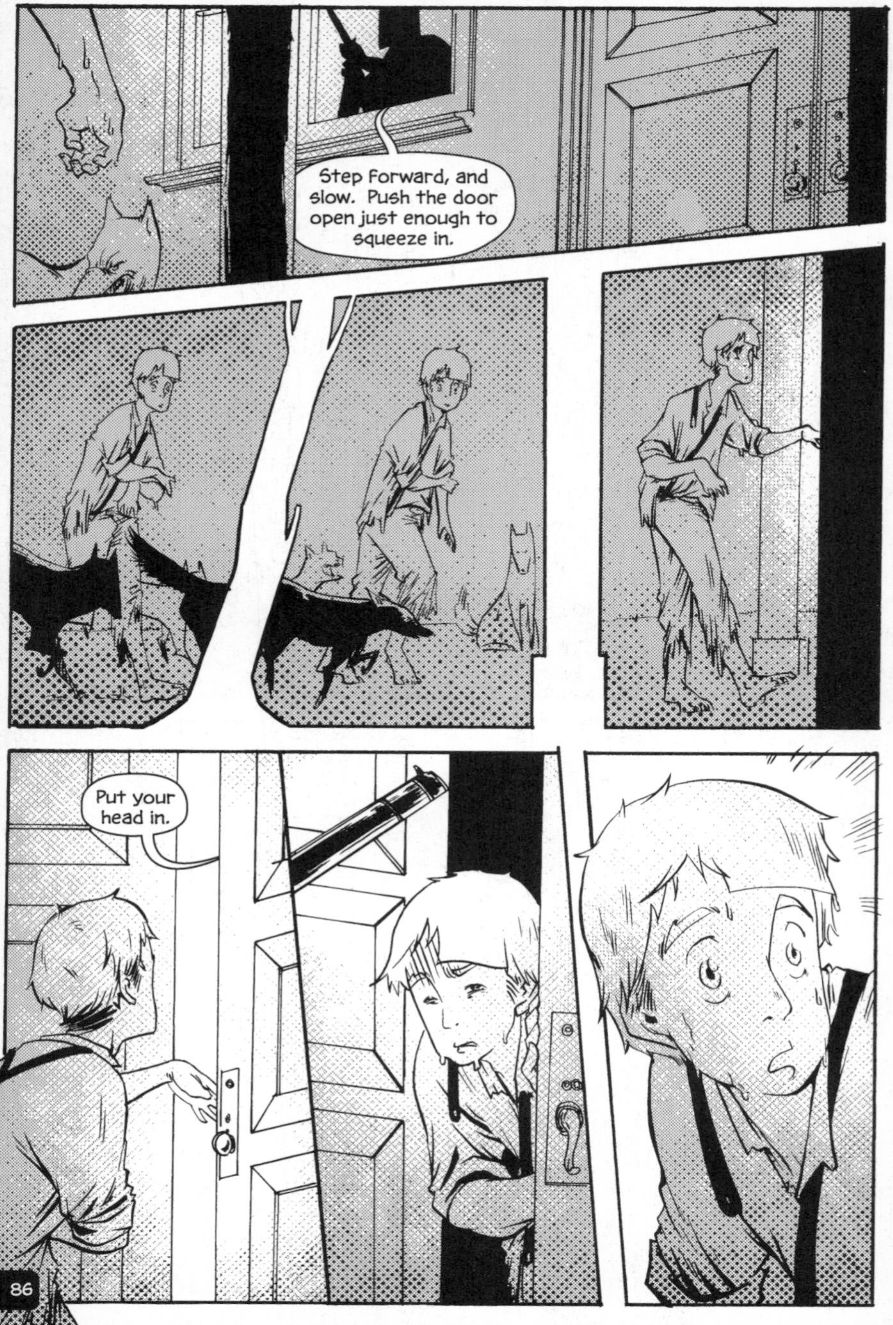
Step forward, and slow. Push the door open just enough to squeeze in.
Put your head in.

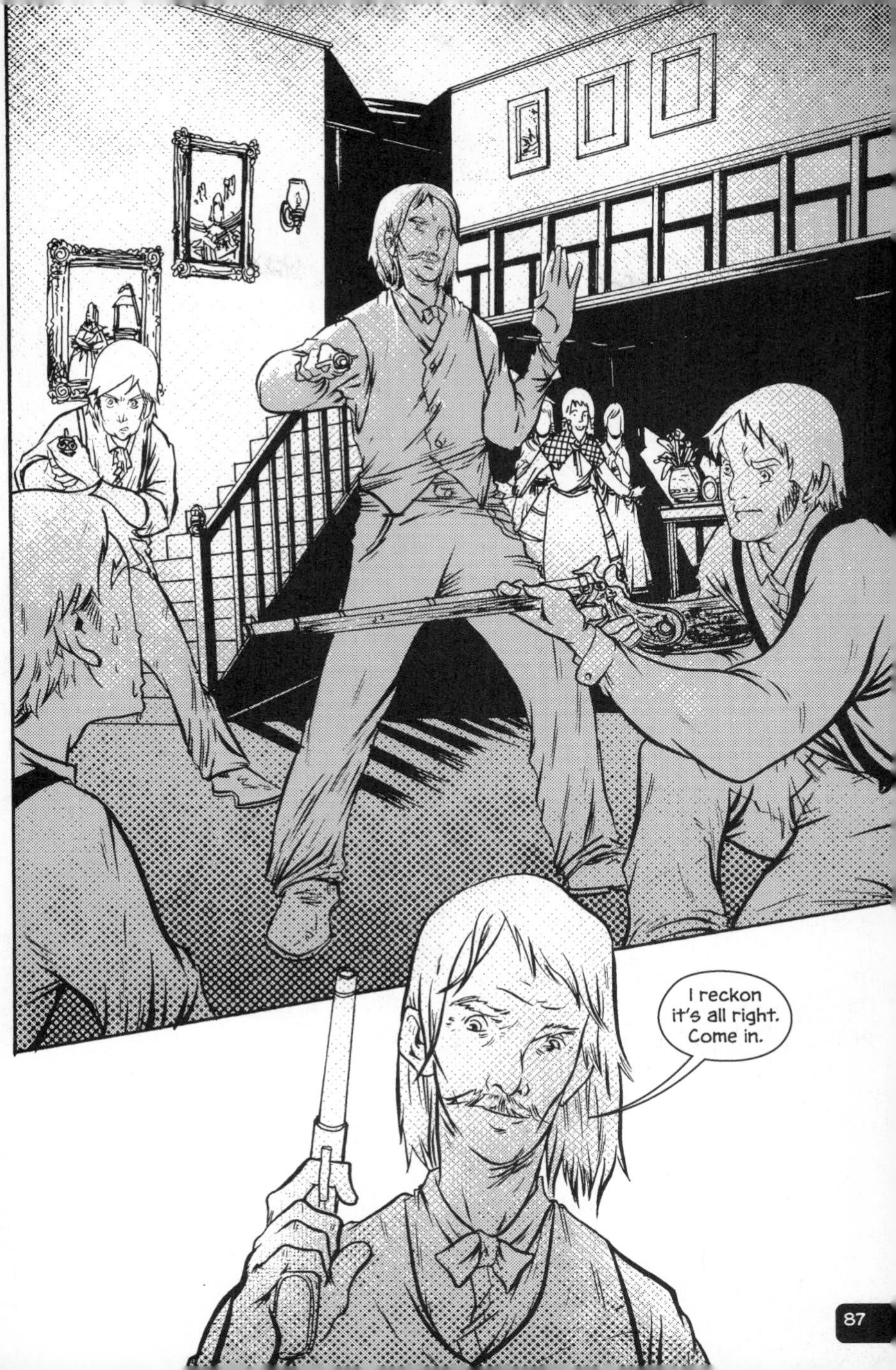
I reckon it's all right. Come in.

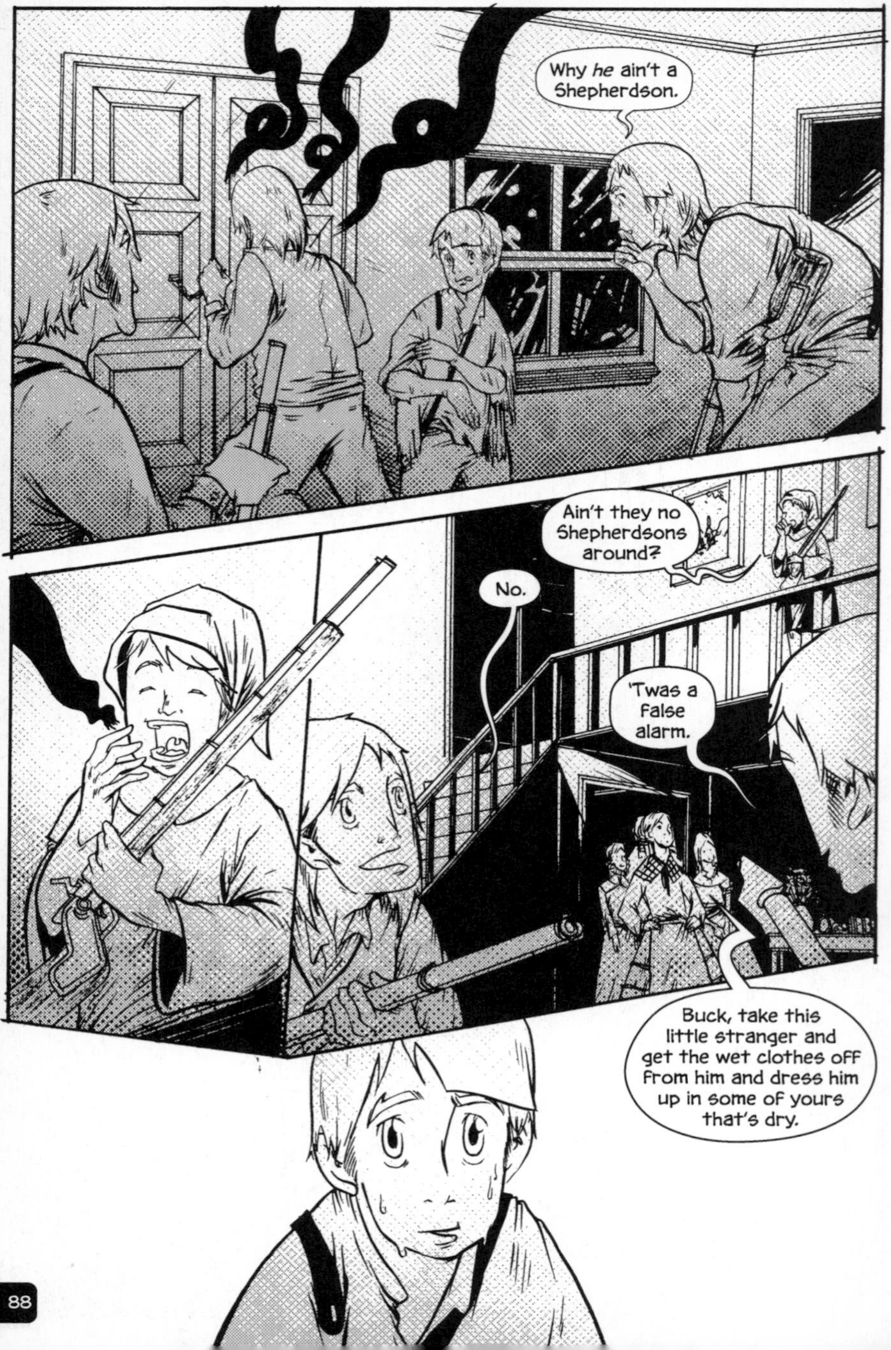

Why *he* ain't a Shepherdson.
Ain't they no Shepherdsons around?
No.
'Twas a false alarm.
Buck, take this little stranger and get the wet clothes off from him and dress him up in some of yours that's dry.

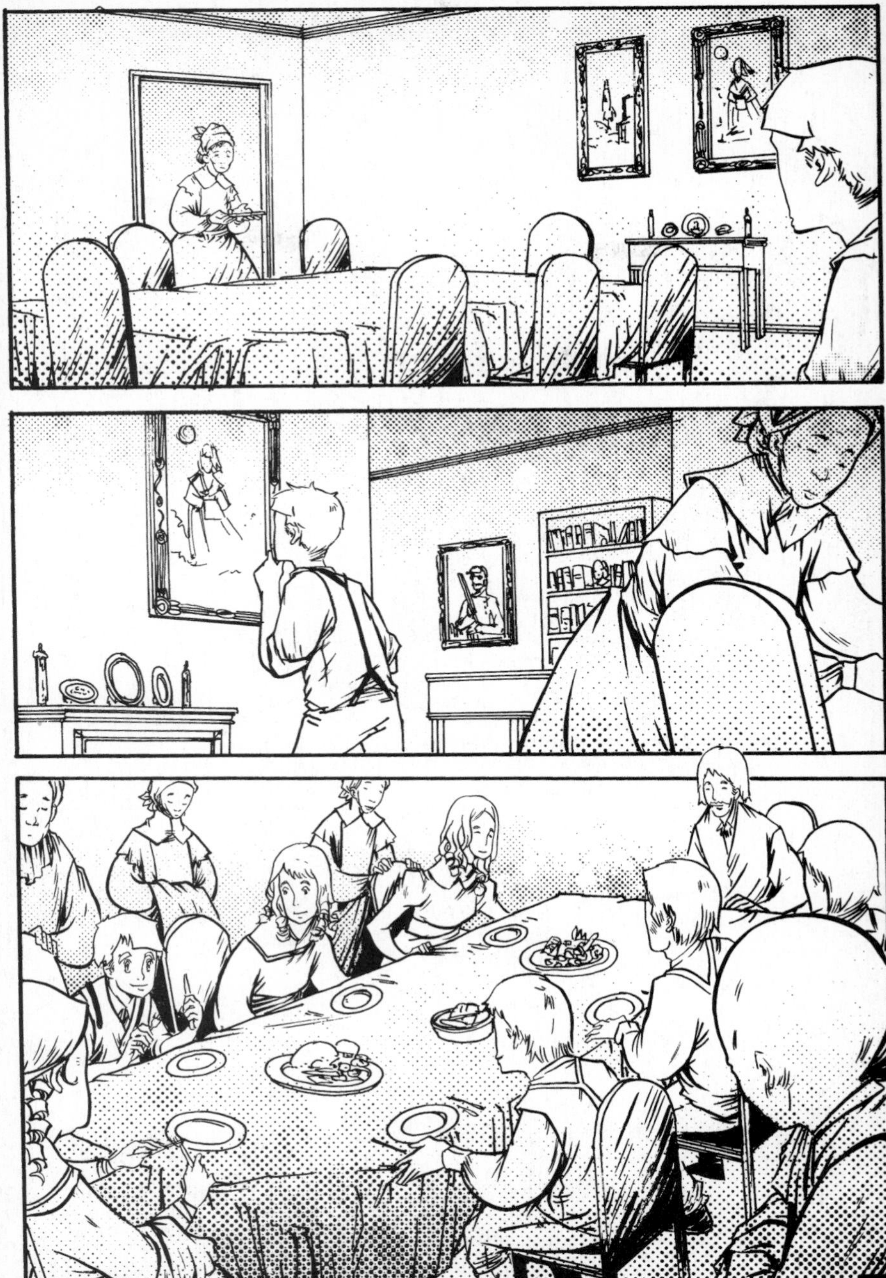

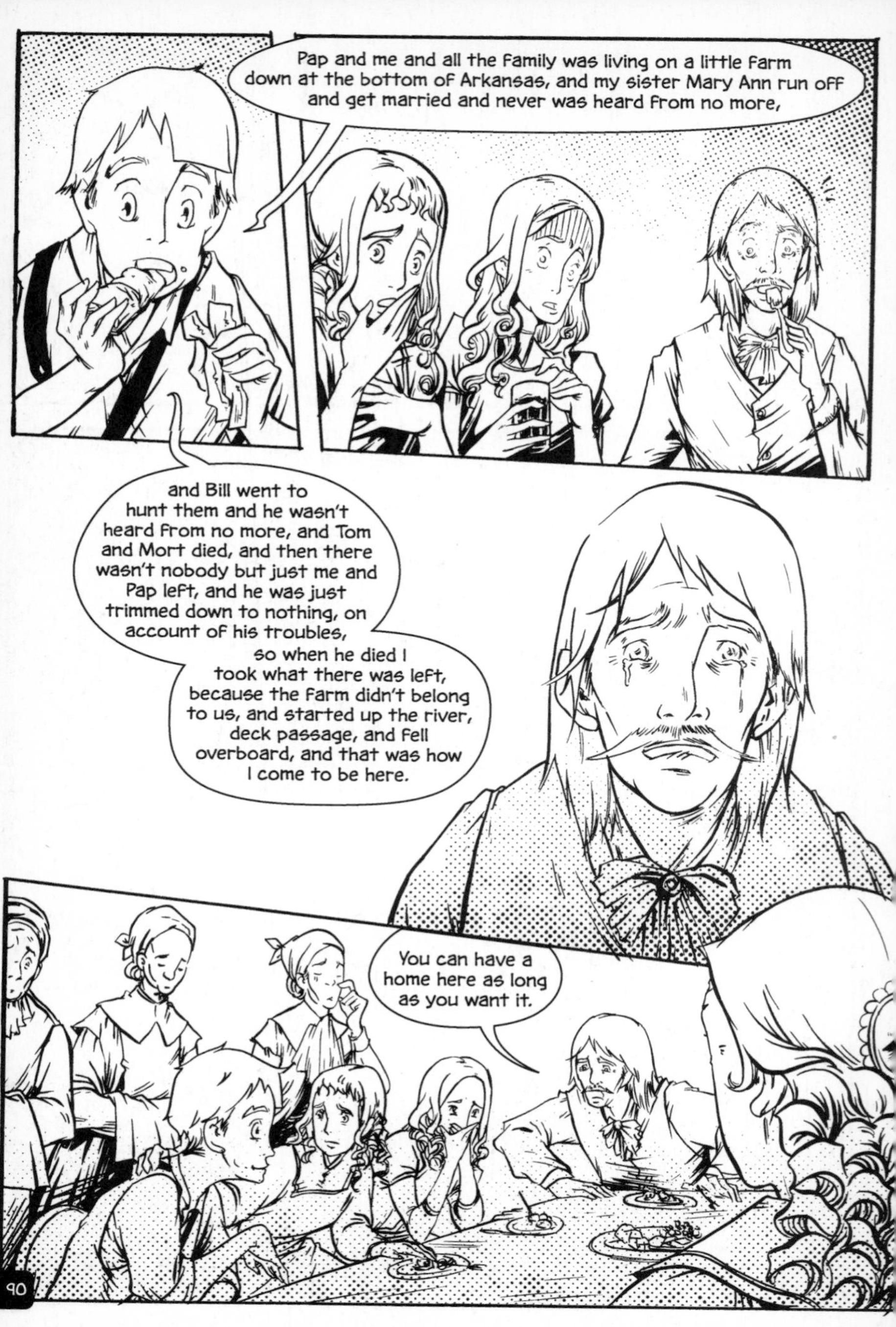
Pap and me and all the family was living on a little farm down at the bottom of Arkansas, and my sister Mary Ann run off and get married and never was heard from no more,
and Bill went to hunt them and he wasn't heard from no more, and Tom and Mort died, and then there wasn't nobody but just me and Pap left, and he was just trimmed down to nothing, on account of his troubles,
so when he died I took what there was left, because the farm didn't belong to us, and started up the river, deck passage, and fell overboard, and that was how I come to be here.
You can have a home here as long as you want it.

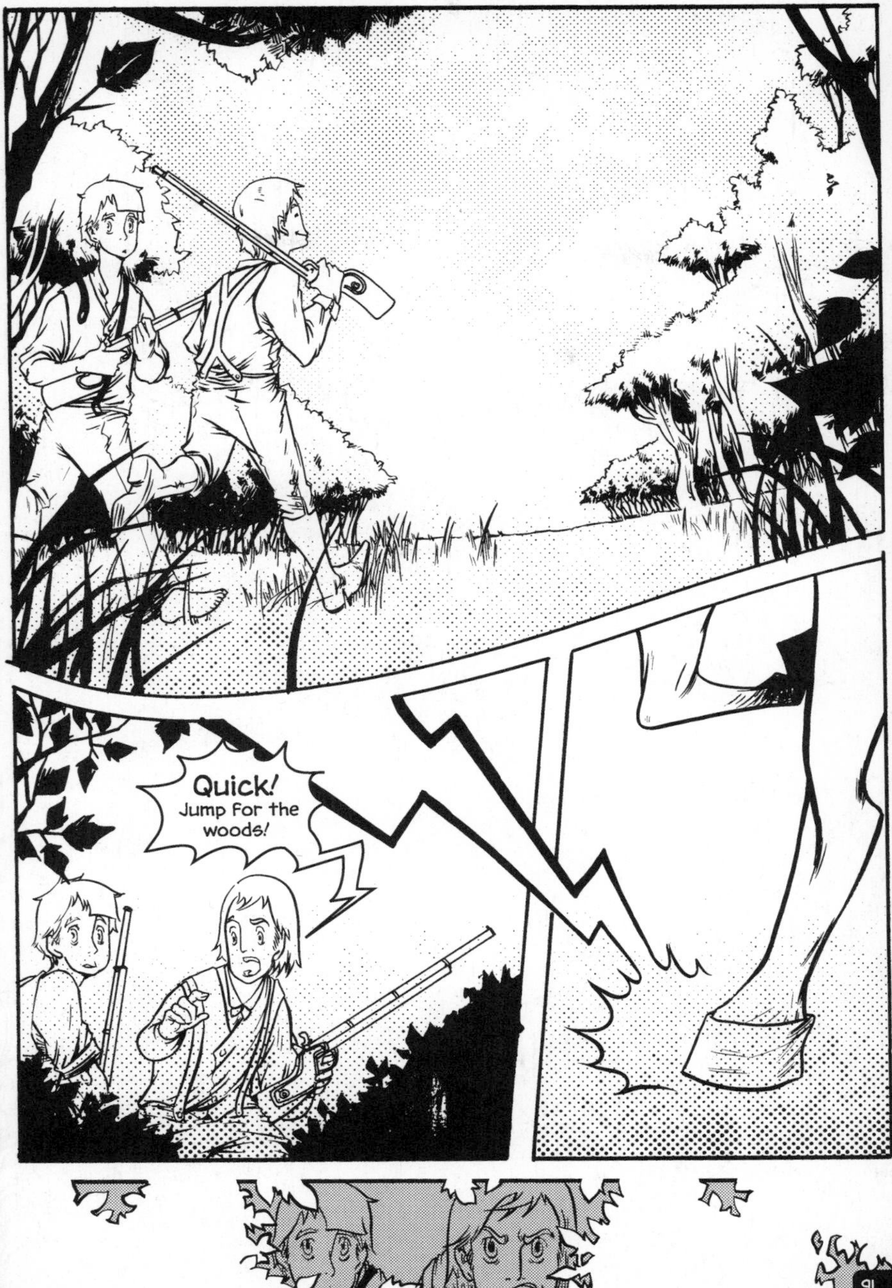
Quick!
Jump for the woods!

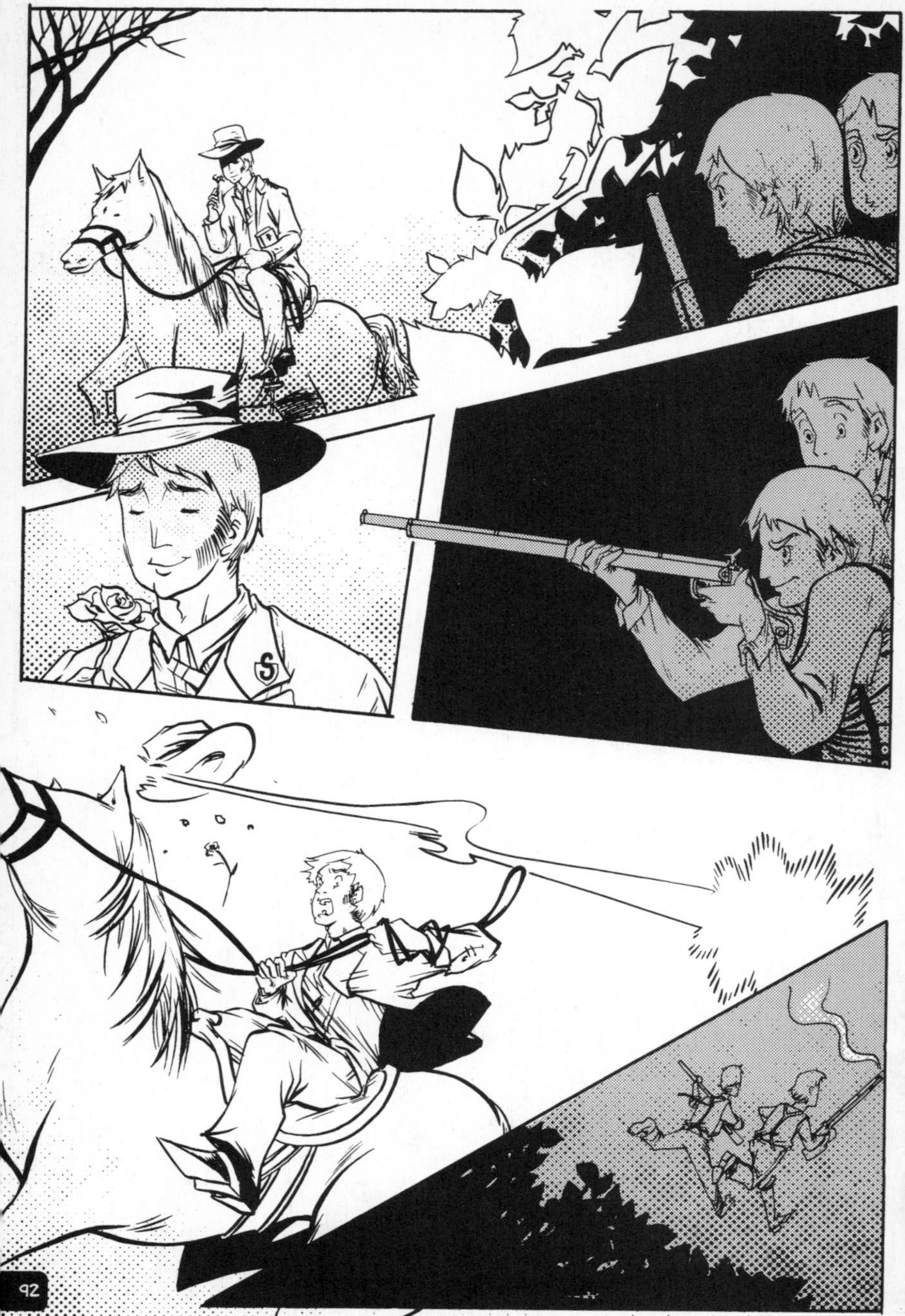

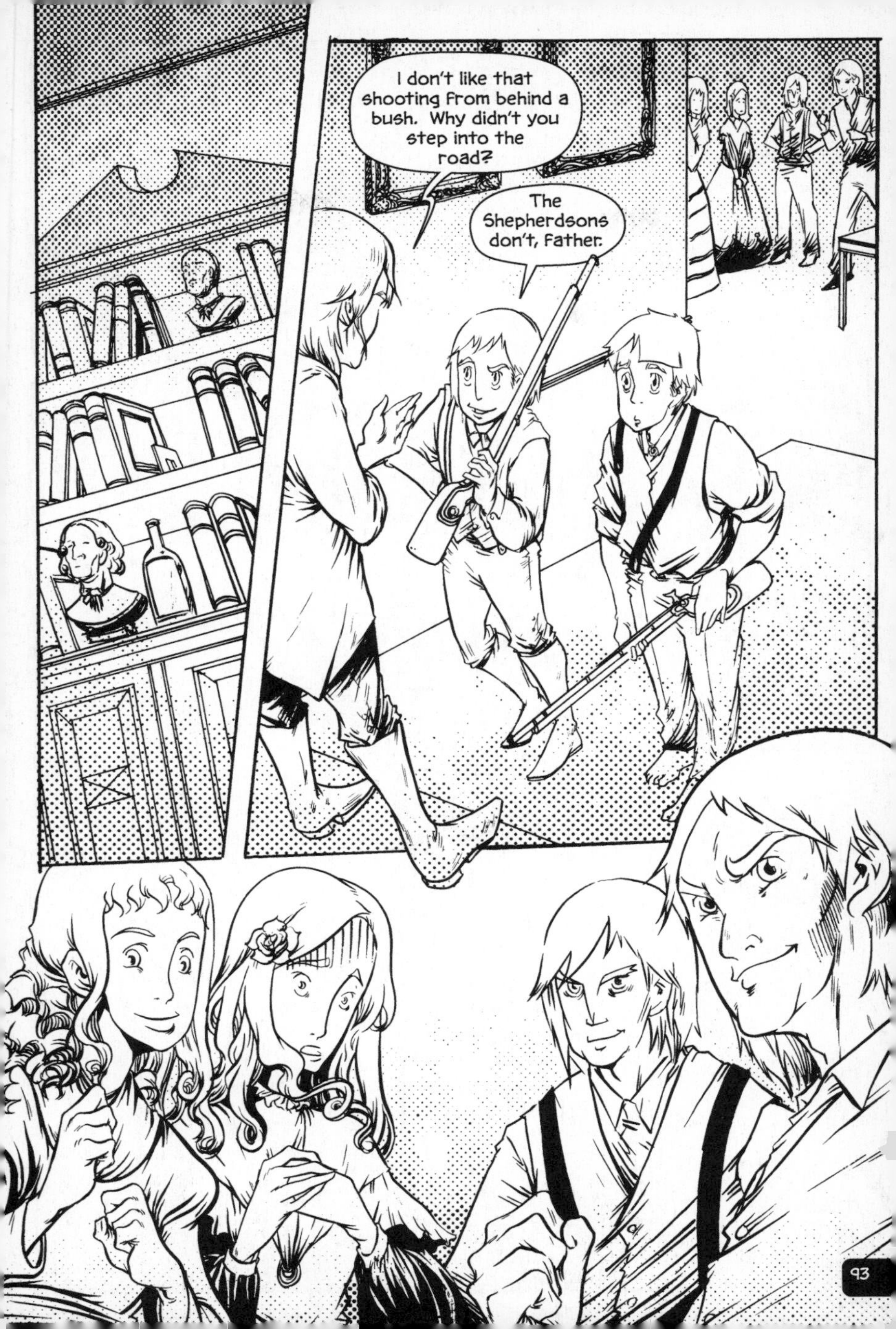
I don't like that shooting from behind a bush. Why didn't you step into the road?
The Shepherdsons don't, father.

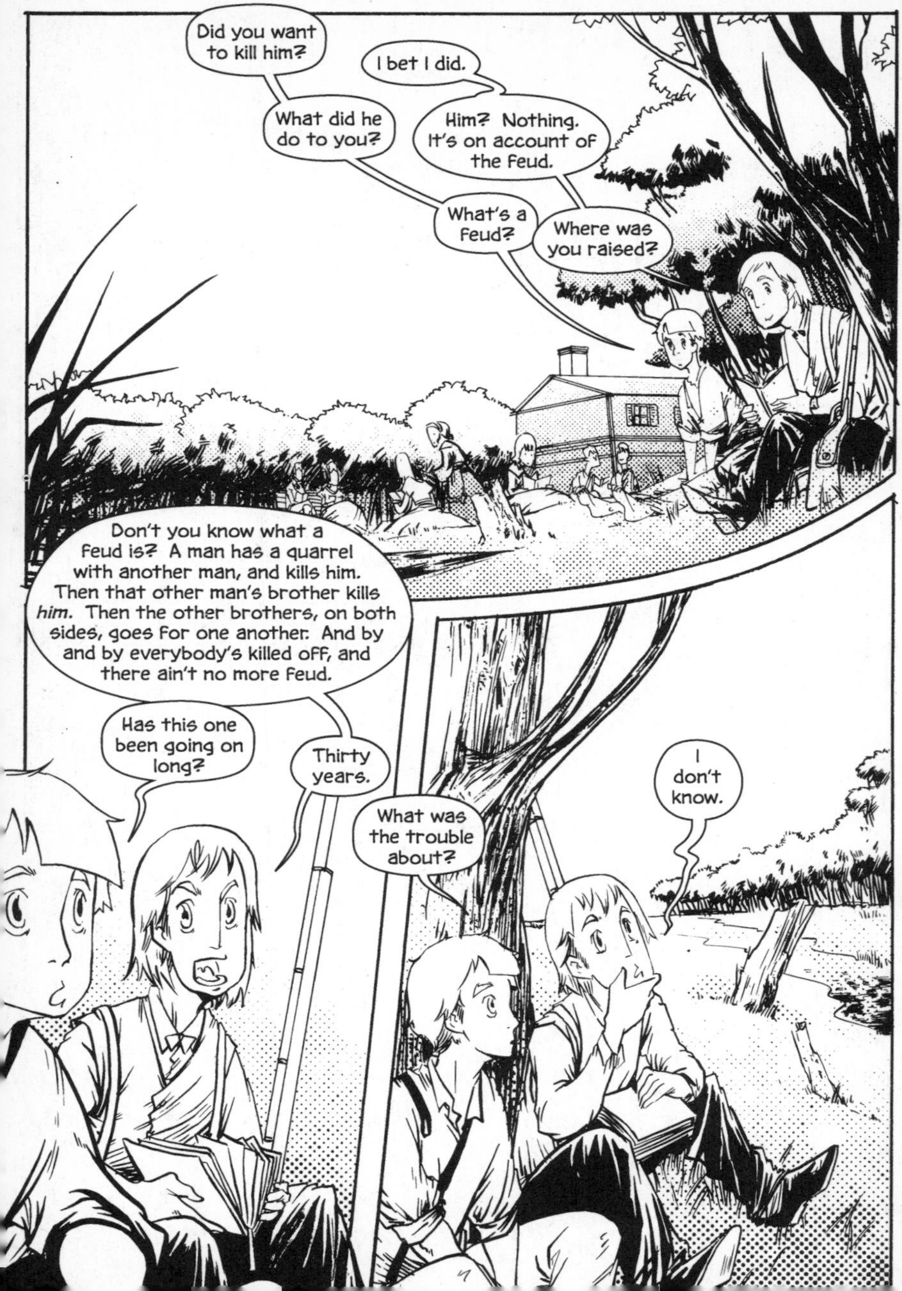

Did you want to kill him?
I bet I did.
What did he do to you?
Him? Nothing. It's on account of the feud.
What's a feud?
Where was you raised?
Don't you know what a feud is? A man has a quarrel with another man, and kills him. Then that other man's brother kills *him*. Then the other brothers, on both sides, goes for one another. And by and by everybody's killed off, and there ain't no more feud.
Has this one been going on long?
Thirty years.
What was the trouble about?
I don't know.

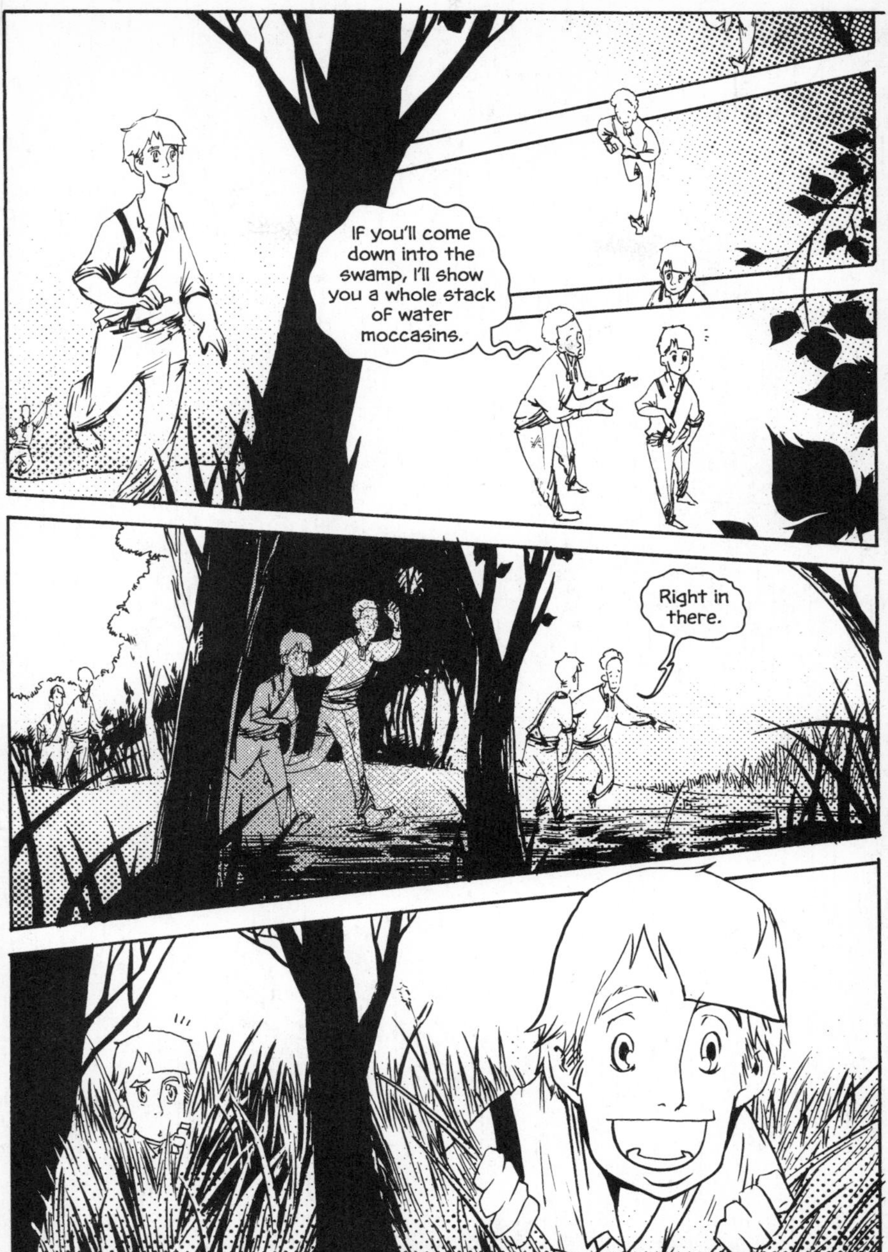
If you'll come down into the swamp, I'll show you a whole stack of water moccasins.
Right in there.

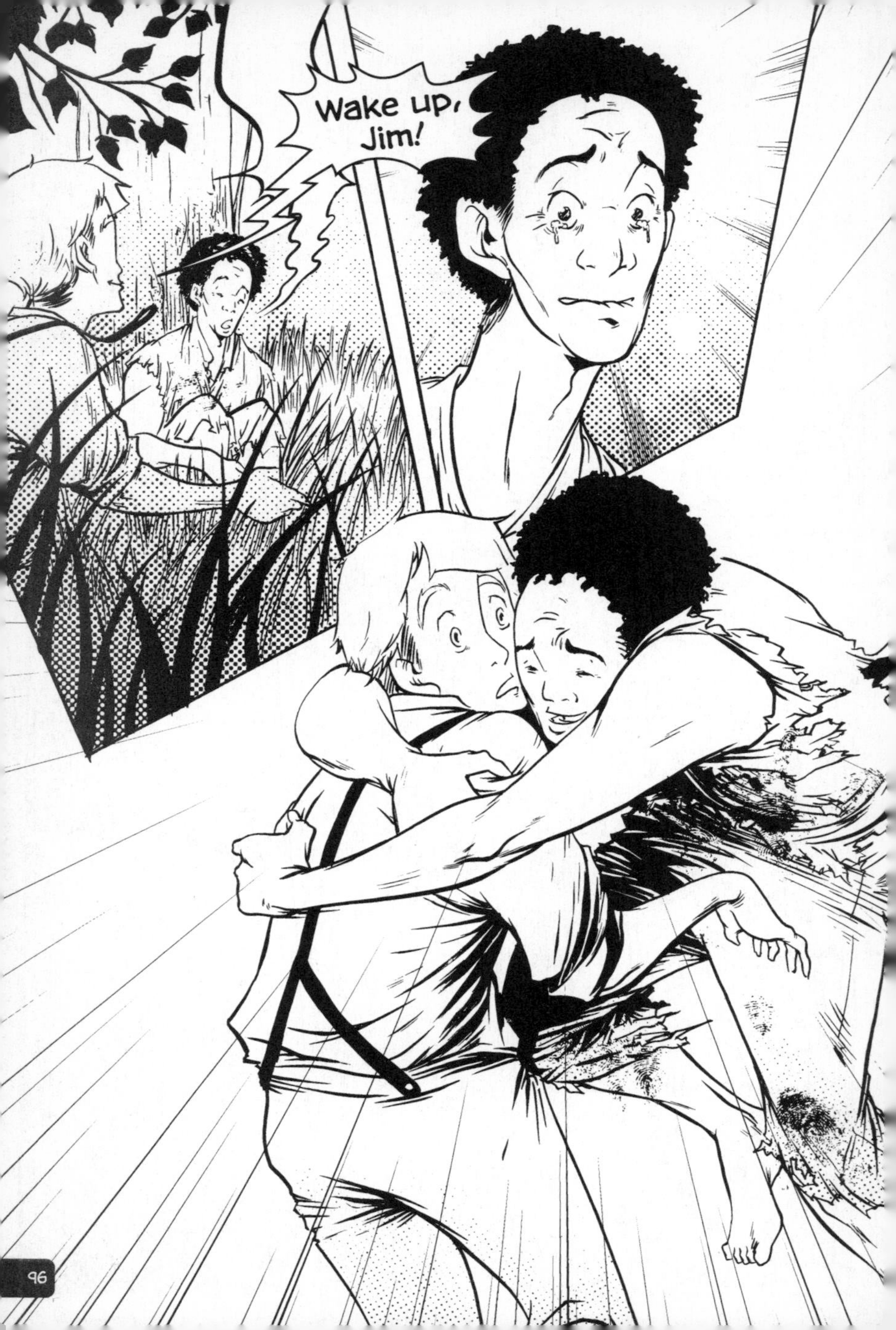
Wake up, Jim!

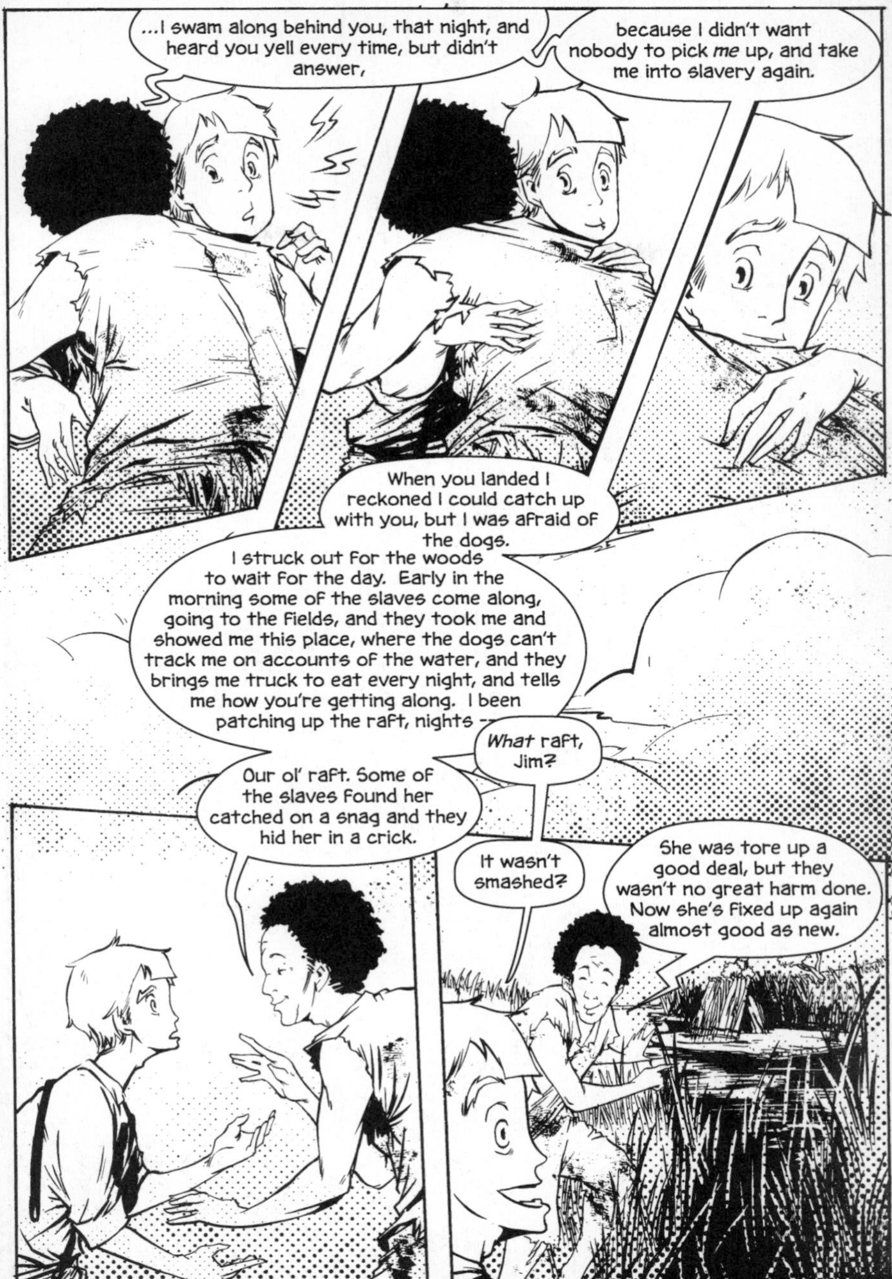

...I swam along behind you, that night, and heard you yell every time, but didn't answer,
because I didn't want nobody to pick *me* up, and take me into slavery again.
When you landed I reckoned I could catch up with you, but I was afraid of the dogs.
I struck out for the woods to wait for the day. Early in the morning some of the slaves come along, going to the fields, and they took me and showed me this place, where the dogs can't track me on accounts of the water, and they brings me truck to eat every night, and tells me how you're getting along. I been patching up the raft, nights --
*What* raft, Jim?
Our ol' raft. Some of the slaves found her catched on a snag and they hid her in a crick.
It wasn't smashed?
She was tore up a good deal, but they wasn't no great harm done. Now she's fixed up again almost good as new.

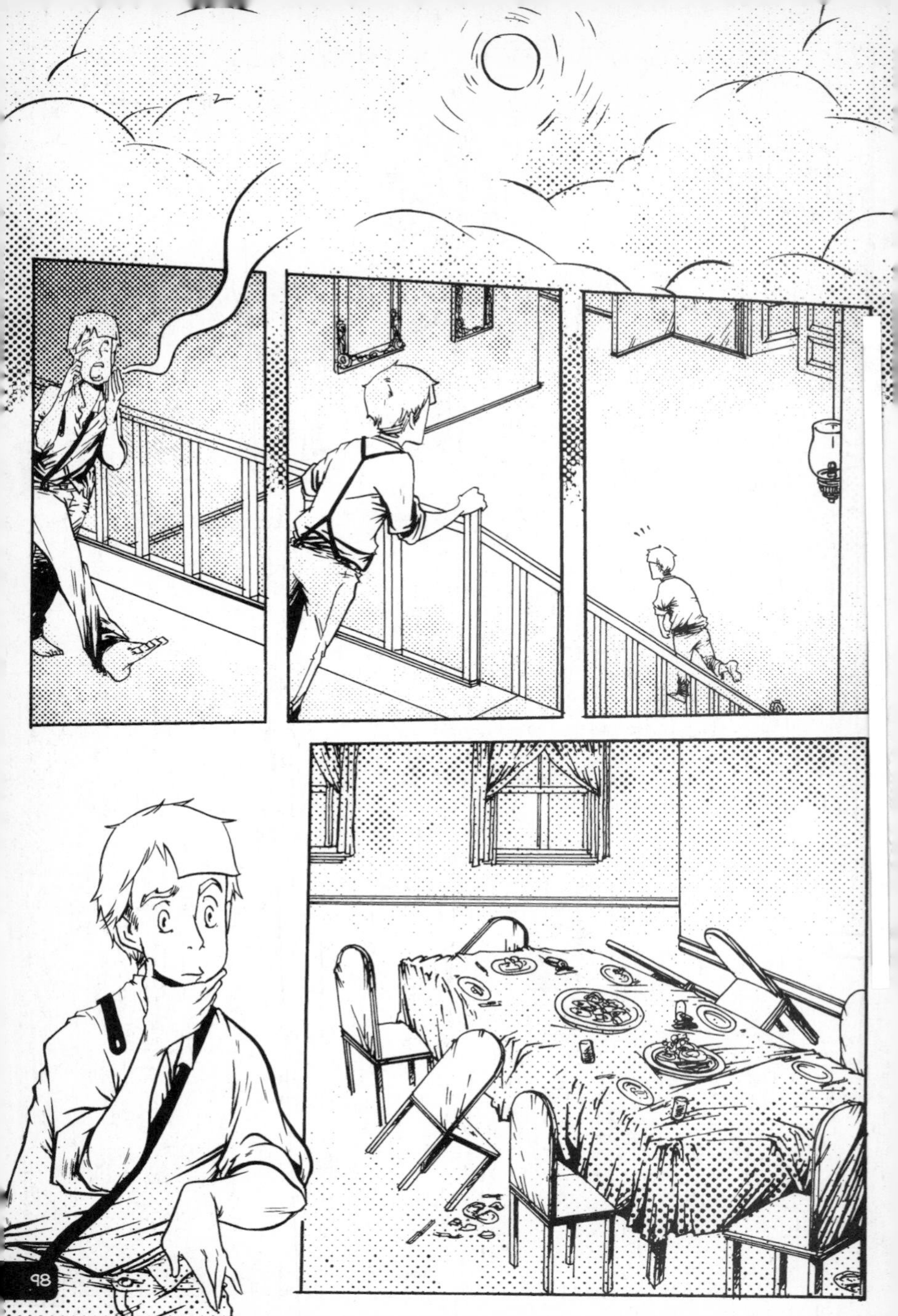

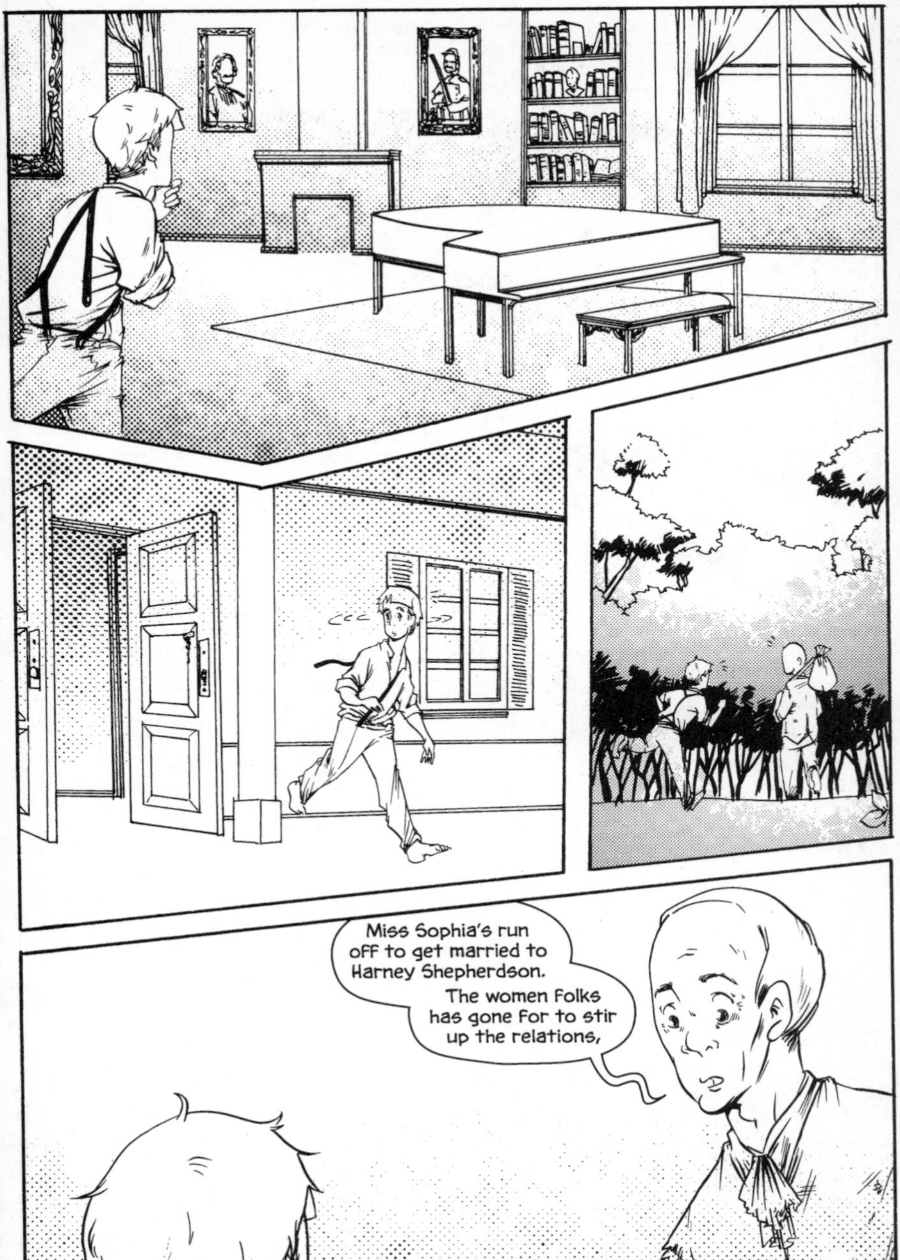
Miss Sophia's run off to get married to Harney Shepherdson.
The women folks has gone for to stir up the relations,

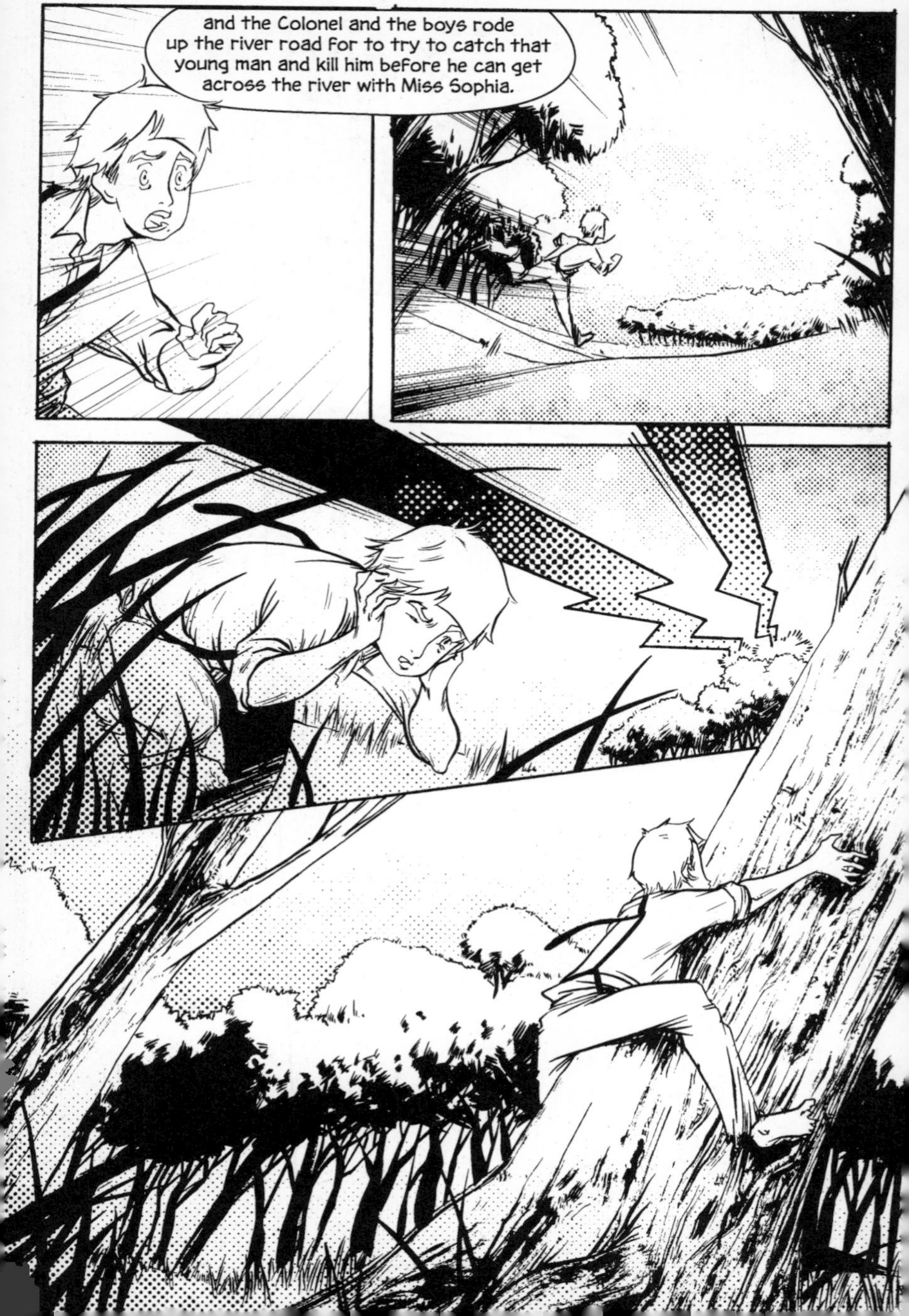
and the Colonel and the boys rode up the river road for to try to catch that young man and kill him before he can get across the river with Miss Sophia.

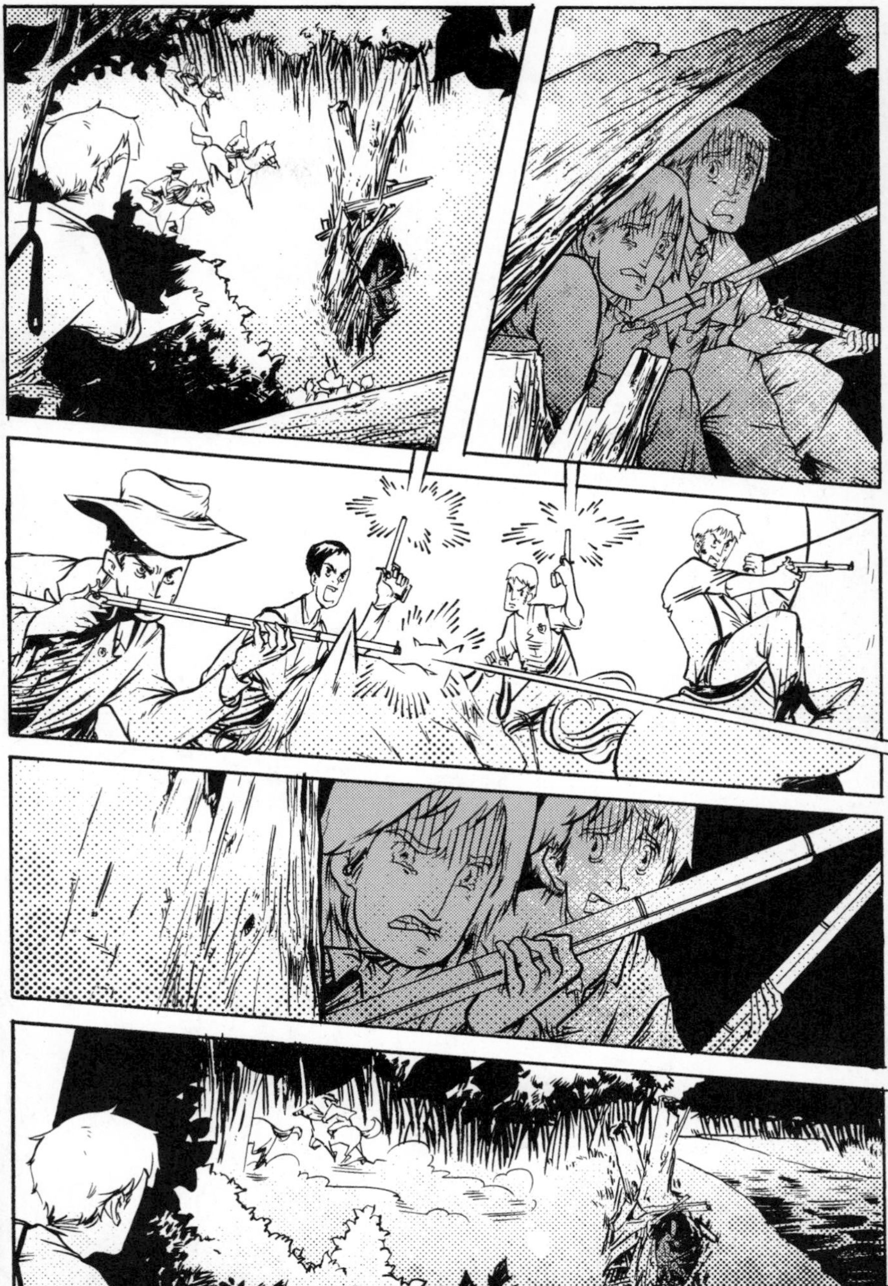

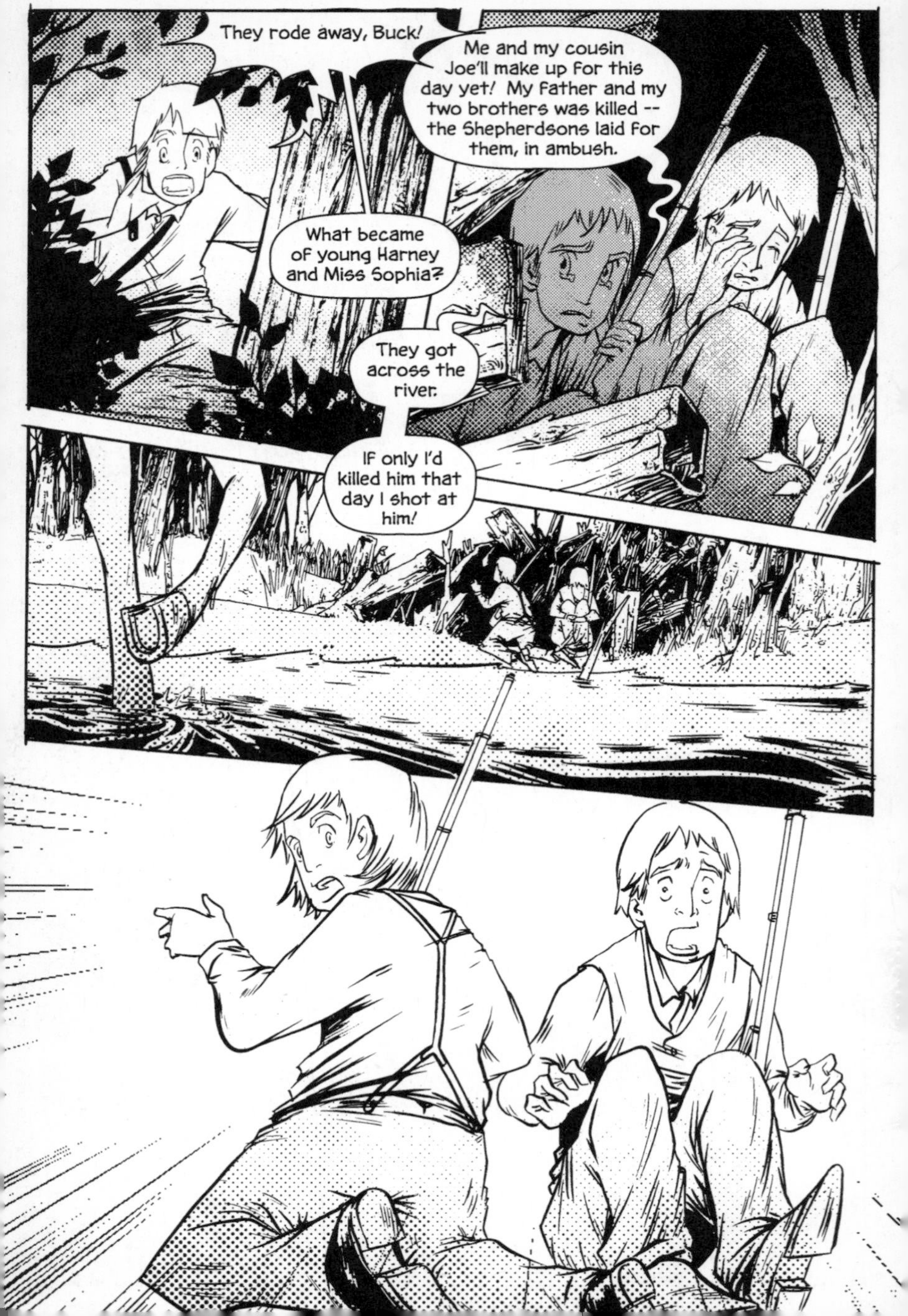
They rode away, Buck!
Me and my cousin Joe'll make up for this day yet! My father and my two brothers was killed -- the Shepherdsons laid for them, in ambush.
What became of young Harney and Miss Sophia?
They got across the river.
If only I'd killed him that day I shot at him!

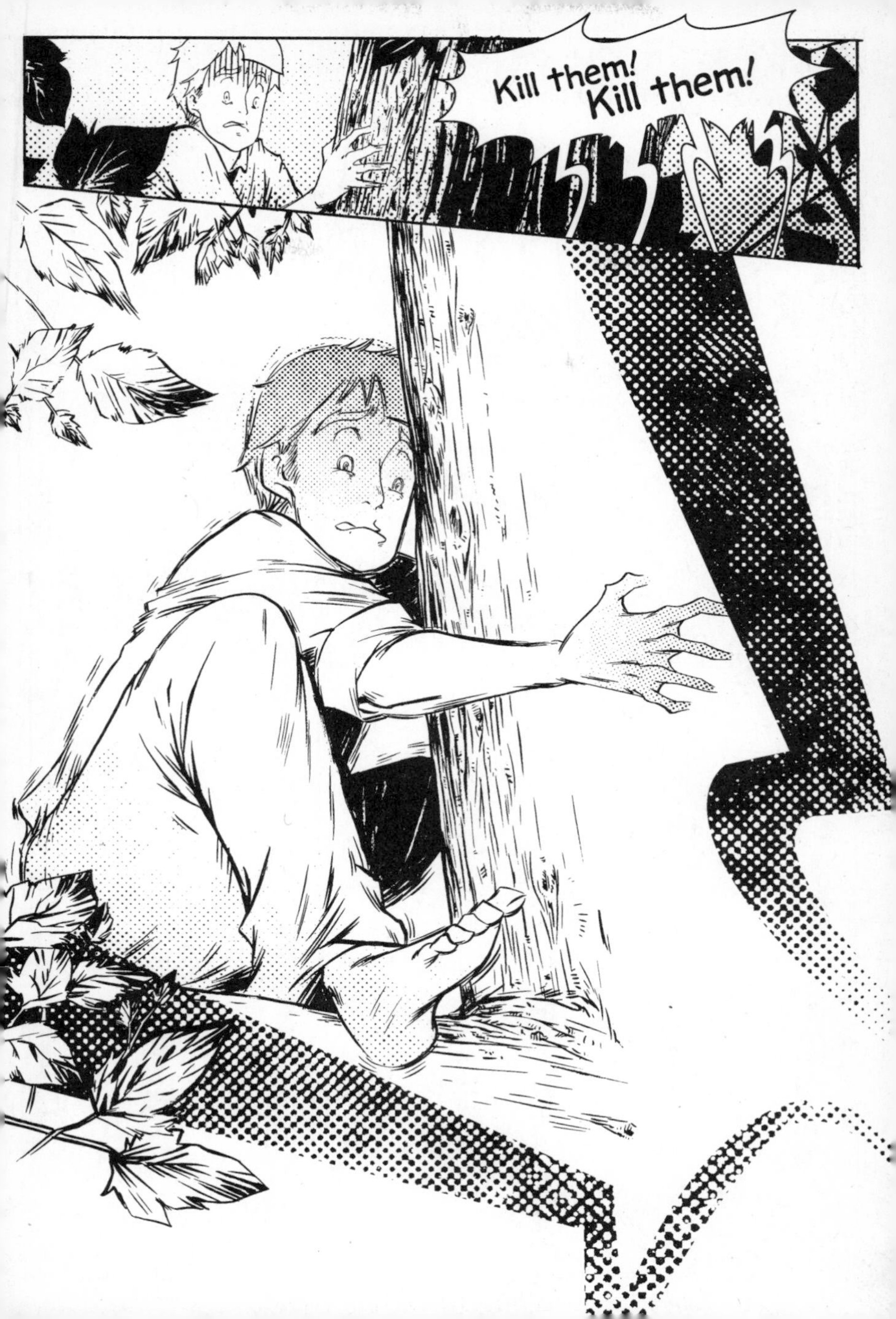
Kill them! Kill them!

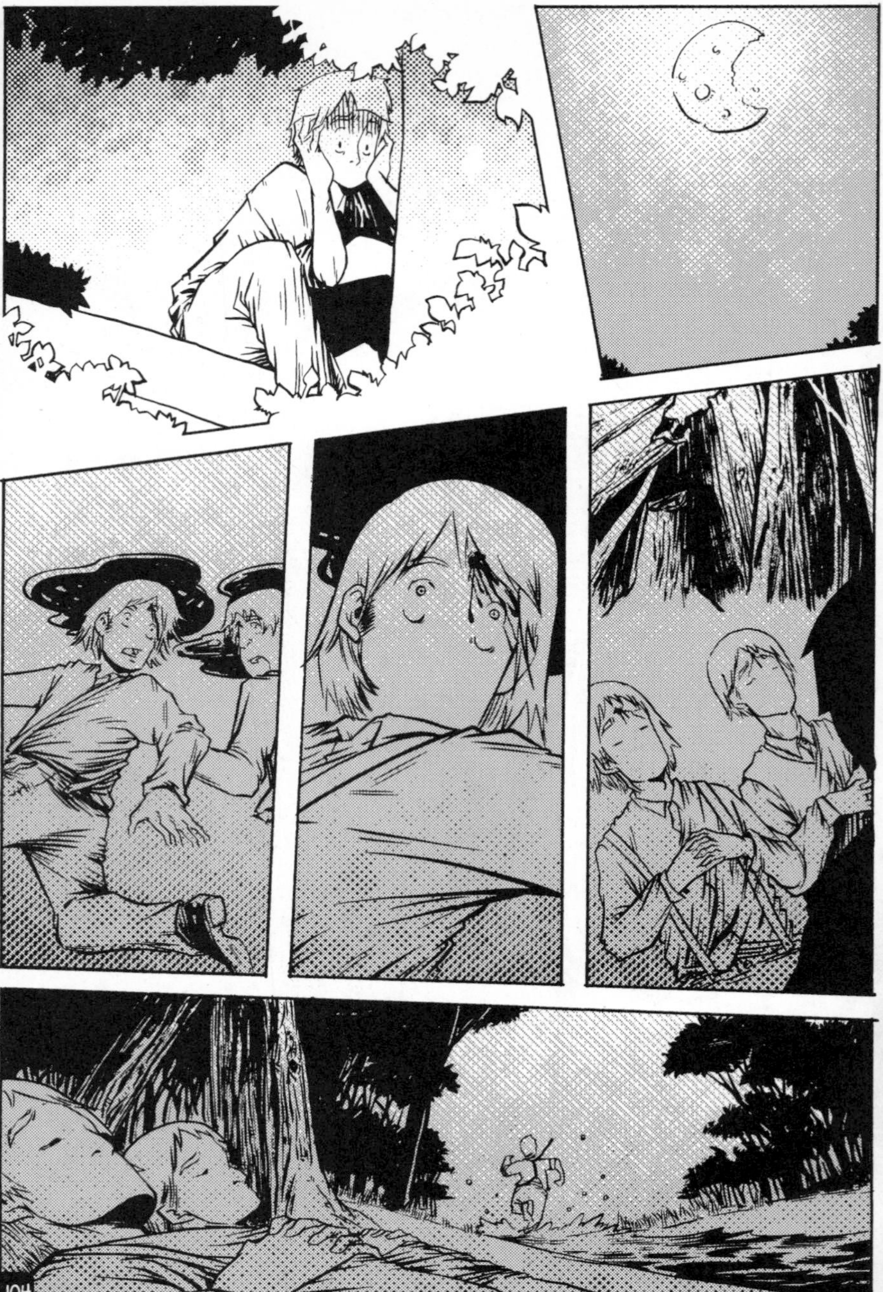

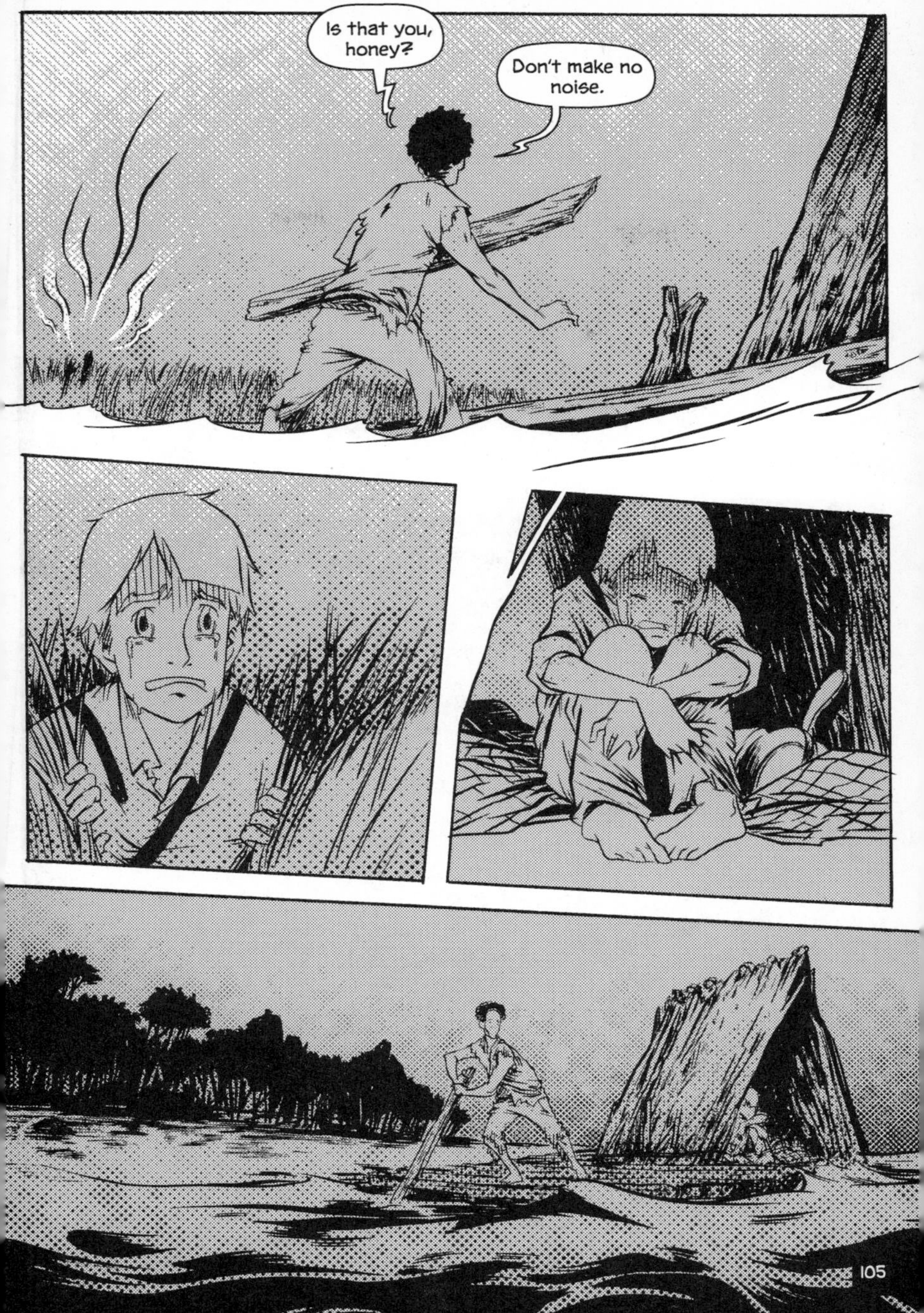
Is that you, honey?
Don't make no noise.

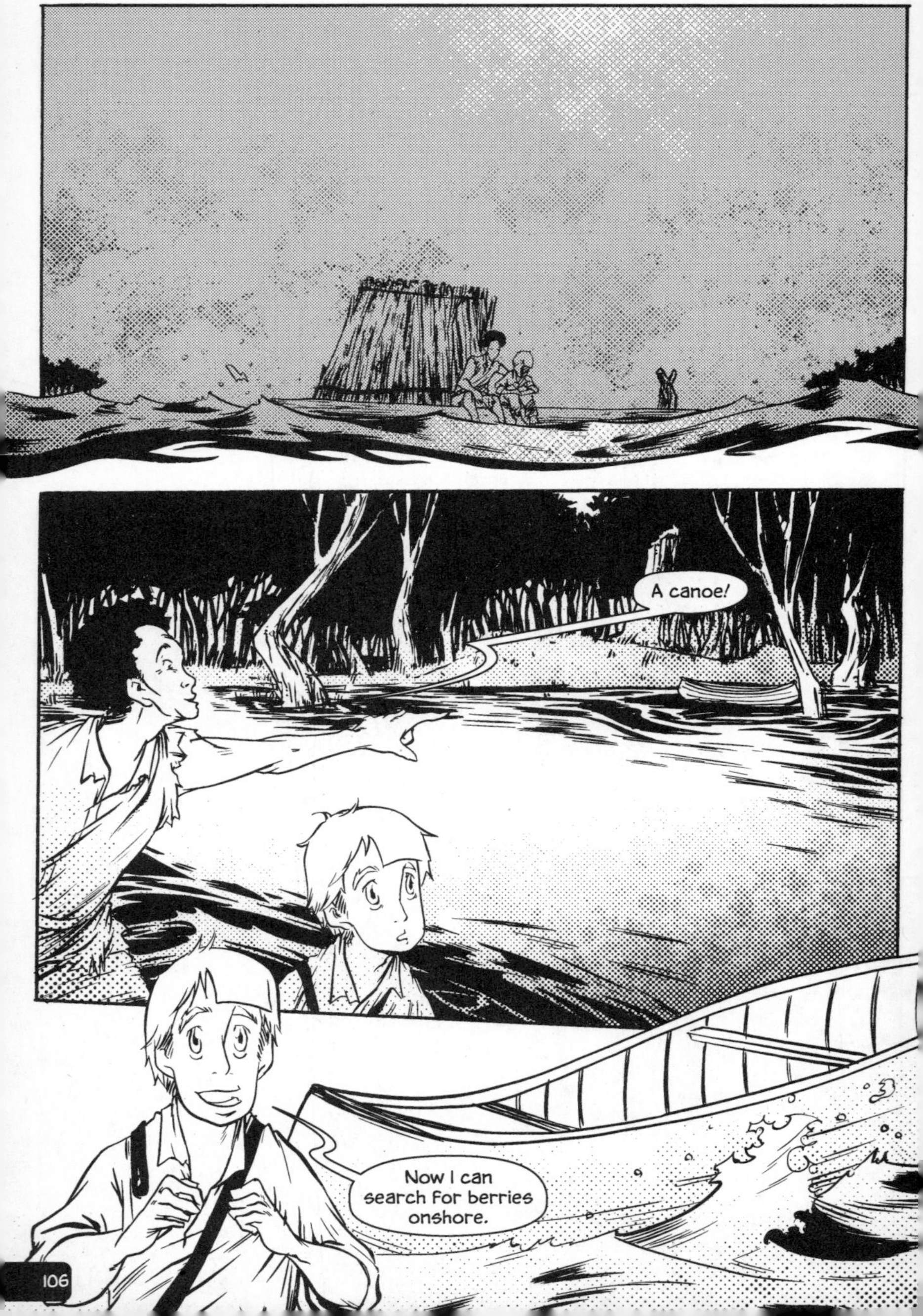
A canoe!
Now I can search for berries onshore.

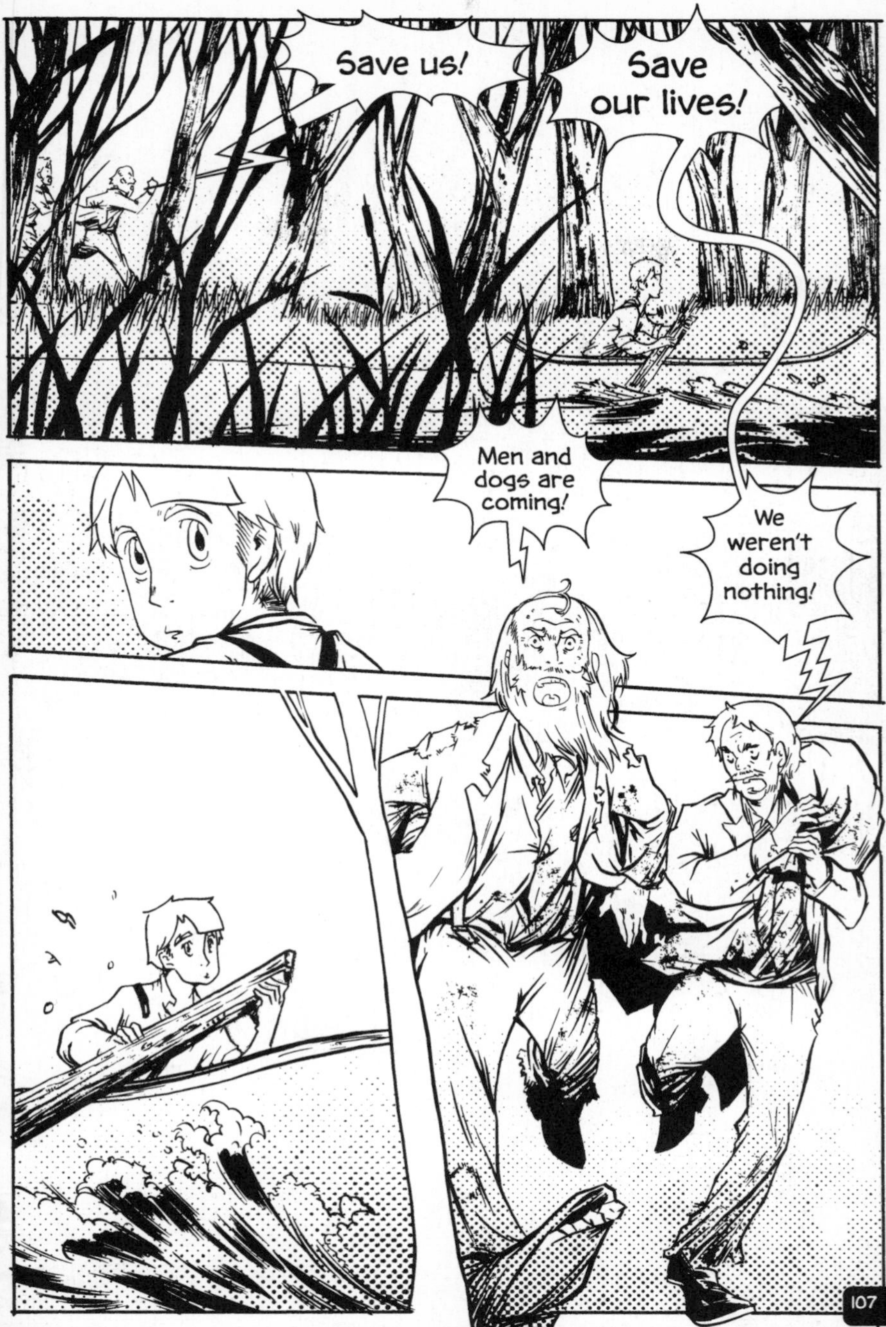

Save us!
Save our lives!
Men and dogs are coming!
We weren't doing nothing!

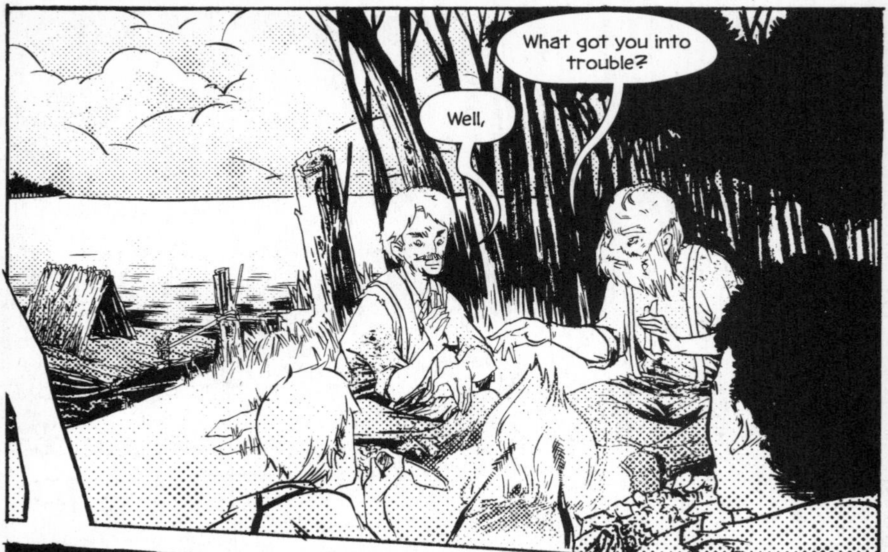
What got you into trouble?
Well,

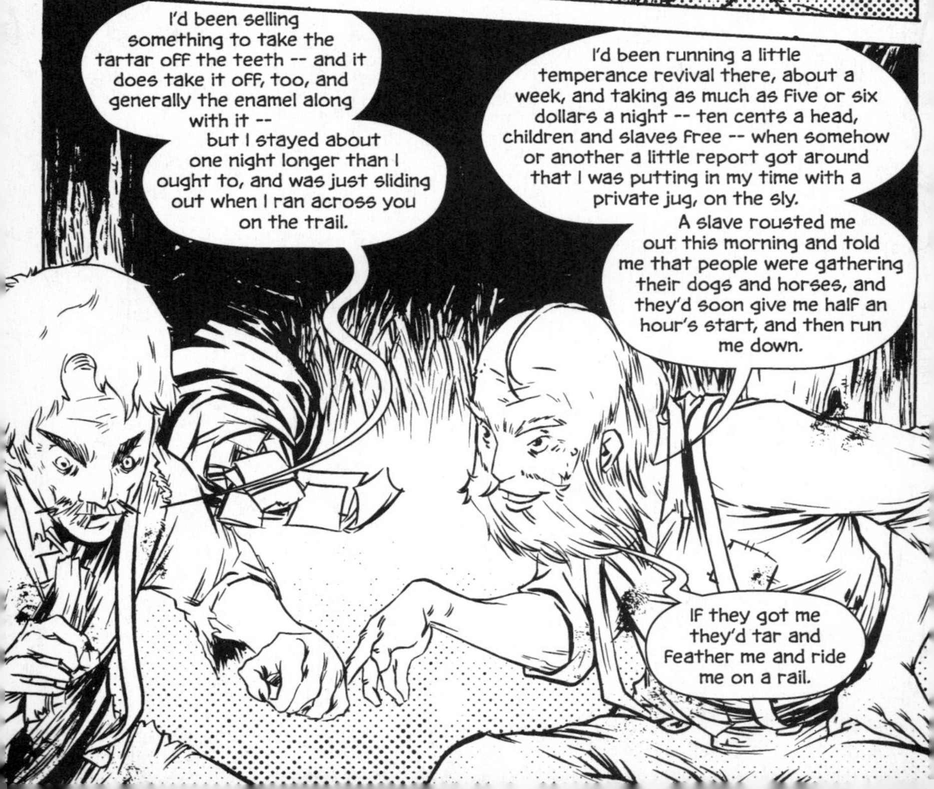
I'd been selling something to take the tartar off the teeth -- and it does take it off, too, and generally the enamel along with it -- but I stayed about one night longer than I ought to, and was just sliding out when I ran across you on the trail.
I'd been running a little temperance revival there, about a week, and taking as much as five or six dollars a night -- ten cents a head, children and slaves free -- when somehow or another a little report got around that I was putting in my time with a private jug, on the sly.
A slave rousted me out this morning and told me that people were gathering their dogs and horses, and they'd soon give me half an hour's start, and then run me down.
If they got me they'd tar and feather me and ride me on a rail.

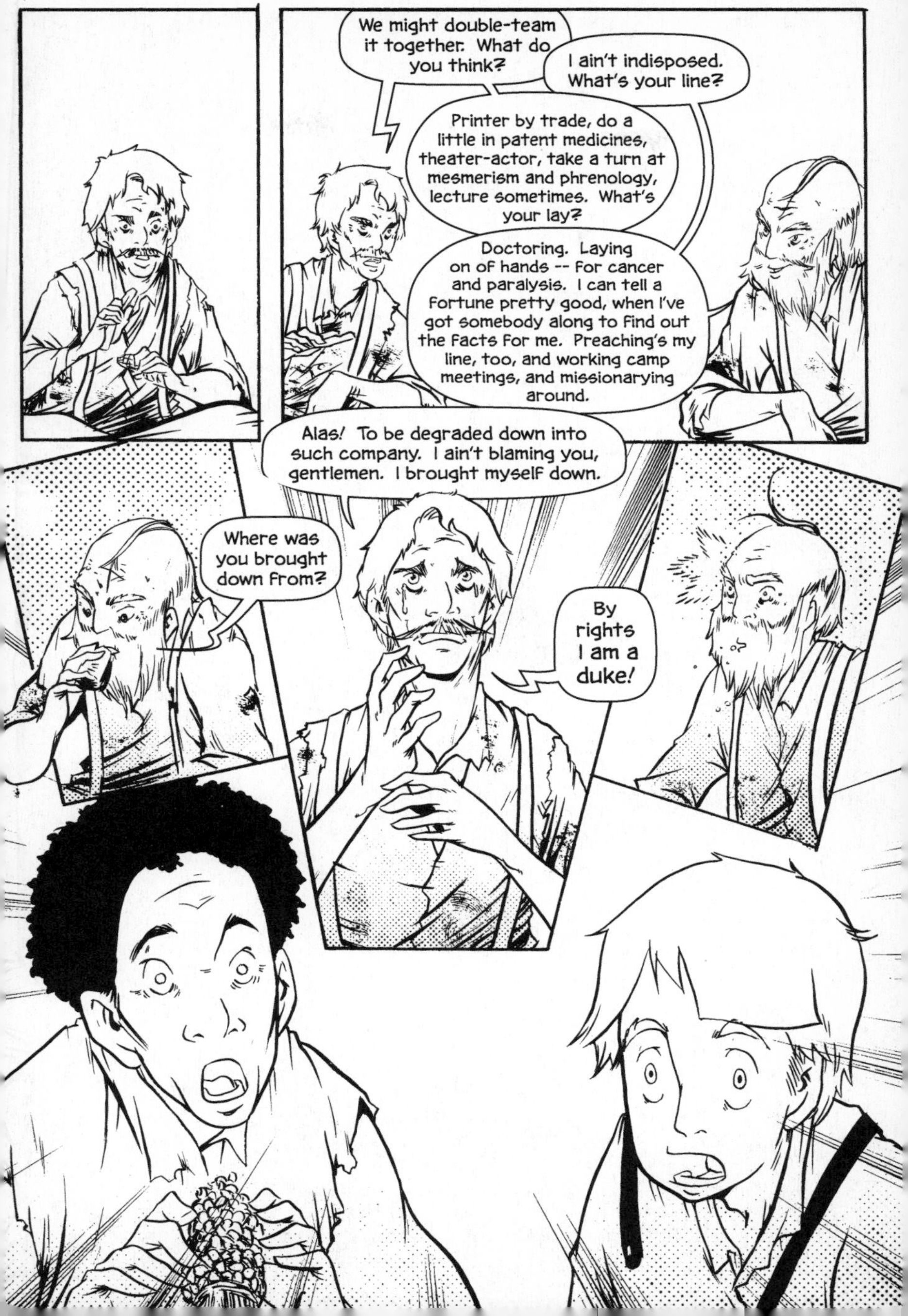
We might double-team it together. What do you think?
I ain't indisposed. What's your line?
Printer by trade, do a little in patent medicines, theater-actor, take a turn at mesmerism and phrenology, lecture sometimes. What's your lay?
Doctoring. Laying on of hands -- for cancer and paralysis. I can tell a fortune pretty good, when I've got somebody along to find out the facts for me. Preaching's my line, too, and working camp meetings, and missionarying around.
Alas! To be degraded down into such company. I ain't blaming you, gentlemen. I brought myself down.
Where was you brought down from?
By rights I am a duke!

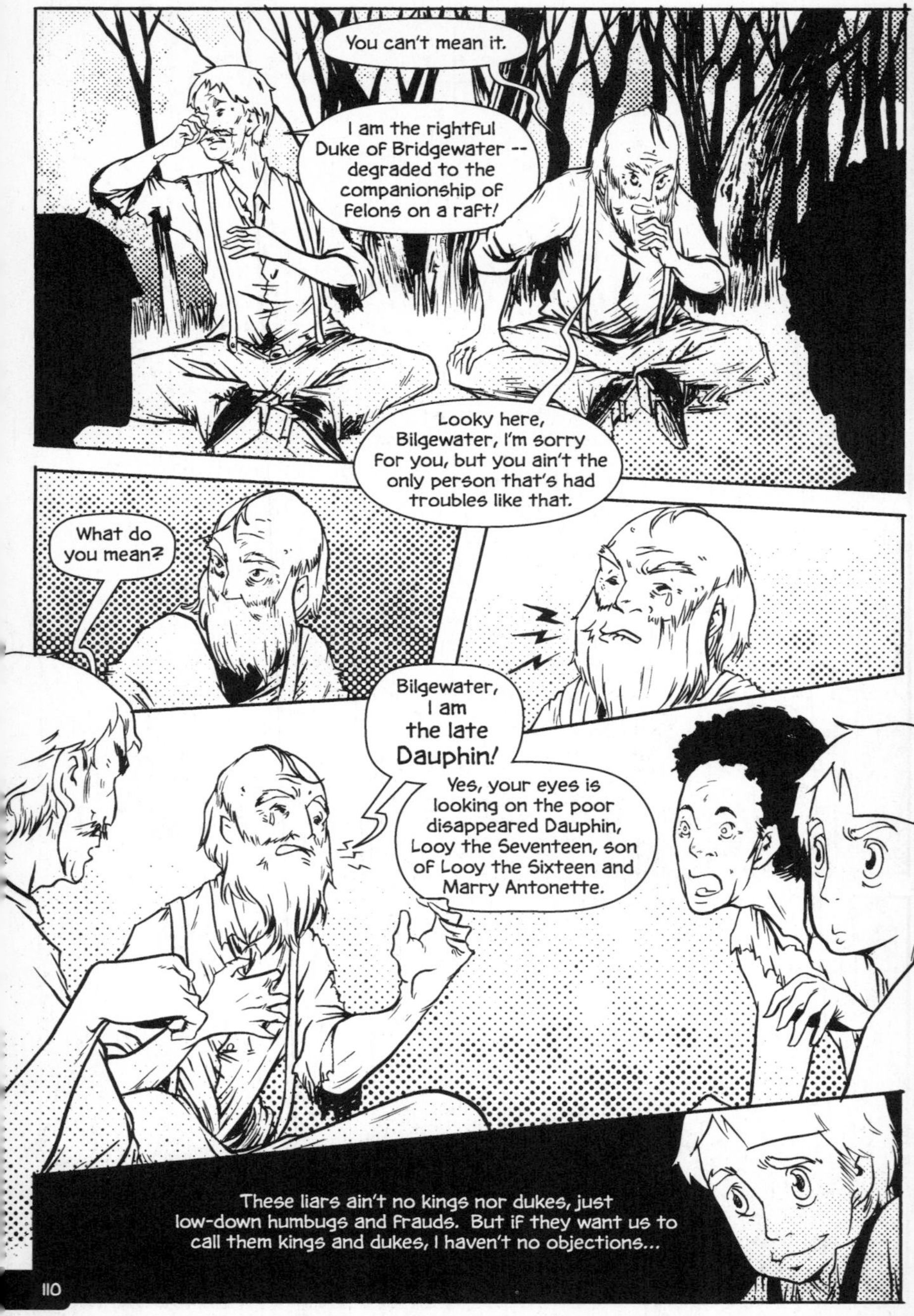
You can't mean it.
I am the rightful Duke of Bridgewater -- degraded to the companionship of felons on a raft!
Looky here, Bilgewater, I'm sorry for you, but you ain't the only person that's had troubles like that.
What do you mean?
Bilgewater, I am the late Dauphin!
Yes, your eyes is looking on the poor disappeared Dauphin, Looy the Seventeen, son of Looy the Sixteen and Marry Antonette.
These liars ain't no kings nor dukes, just low-down humbugs and frauds. But if they want us to call them kings and dukes, I haven't no objections...

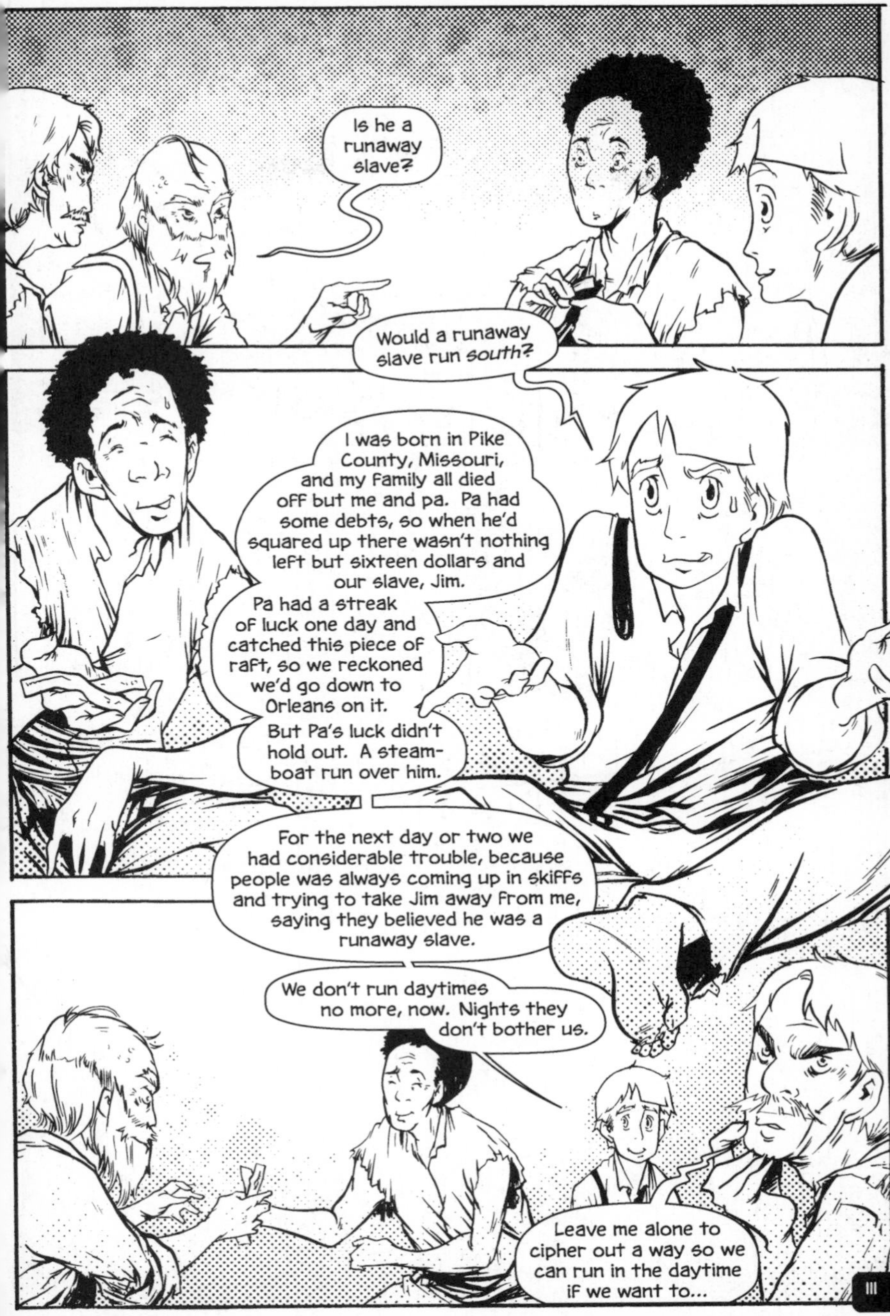
Is he a runaway slave?
Would a runaway slave run *south*?
I was born in Pike County, Missouri, and my family all died off but me and pa. Pa had some debts, so when he'd squared up there wasn't nothing left but sixteen dollars and our slave, Jim.
Pa had a streak of luck one day and catched this piece of raft, so we reckoned we'd go down to Orleans on it.
But Pa's luck didn't hold out. A steam-boat run over him.
For the next day or two we had considerable trouble, because people was always coming up in skiffs and trying to take Jim away from me, saying they believed he was a runaway slave.
We don't run daytimes no more, now. Nights they don't bother us.
Leave me alone to cipher out a way so we can run in the daytime if we want to...

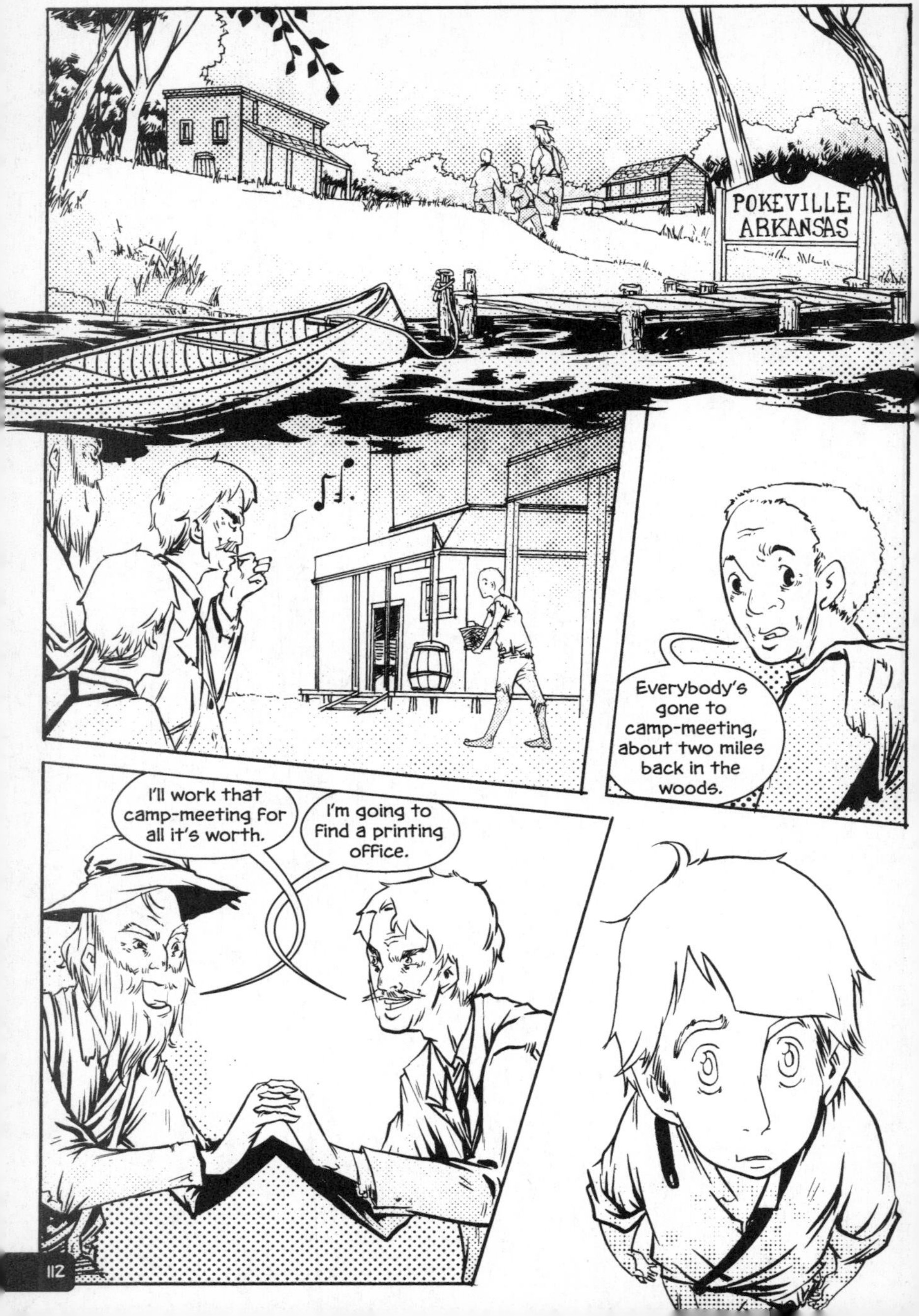
POKEVILLE ARKANSAS
Everybody's gone to camp-meeting, about two miles back in the woods.
I'll work that camp-meeting for all it's worth.
I'm going to find a printing office.

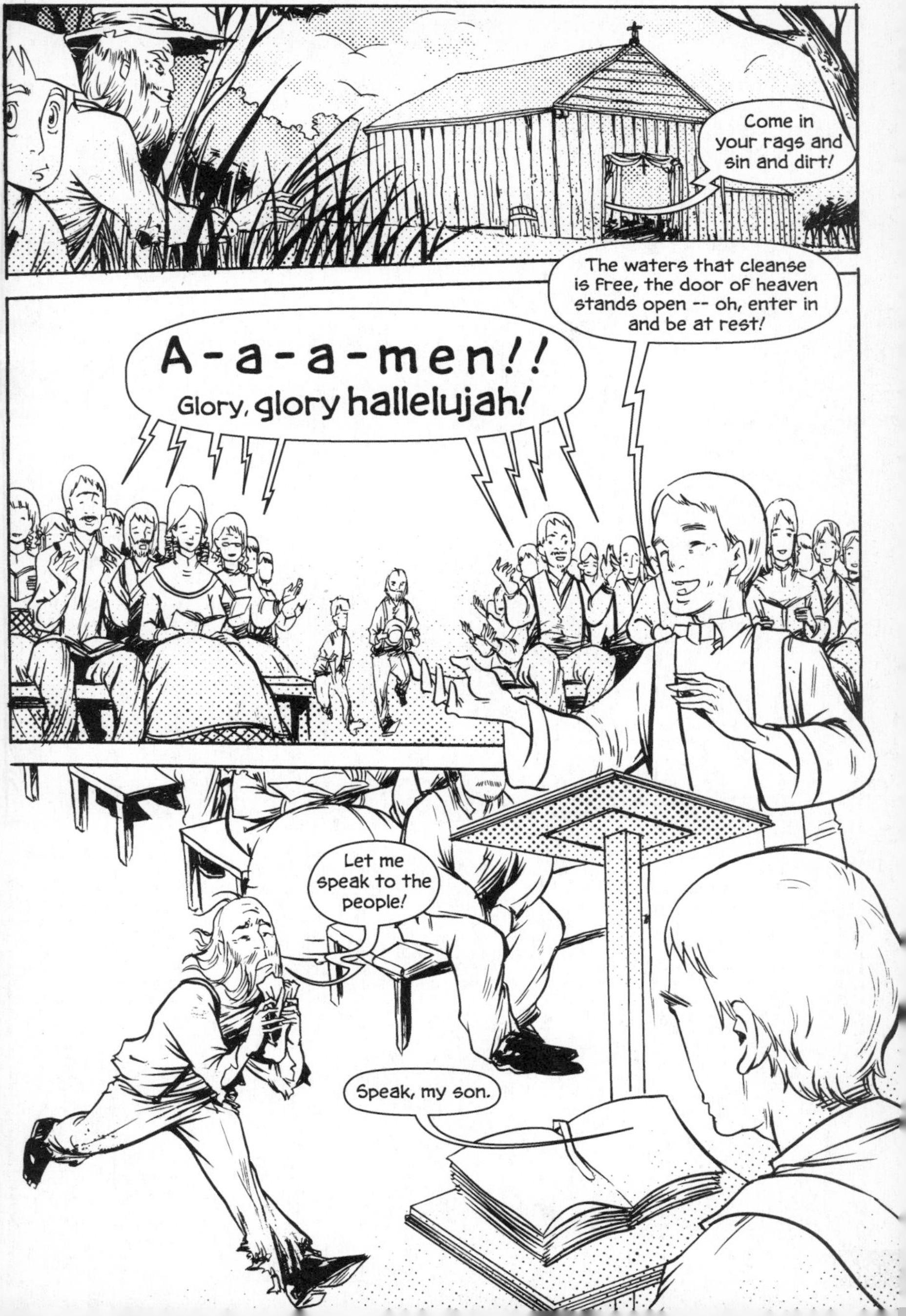
Come in your rags and sin and dirt!
The waters that cleanse is free, the door of heaven stands open -- oh, enter in and be at rest!
A-a-a-men!! Glory, glory hallelujah!
Let me speak to the people!
Speak, my son.

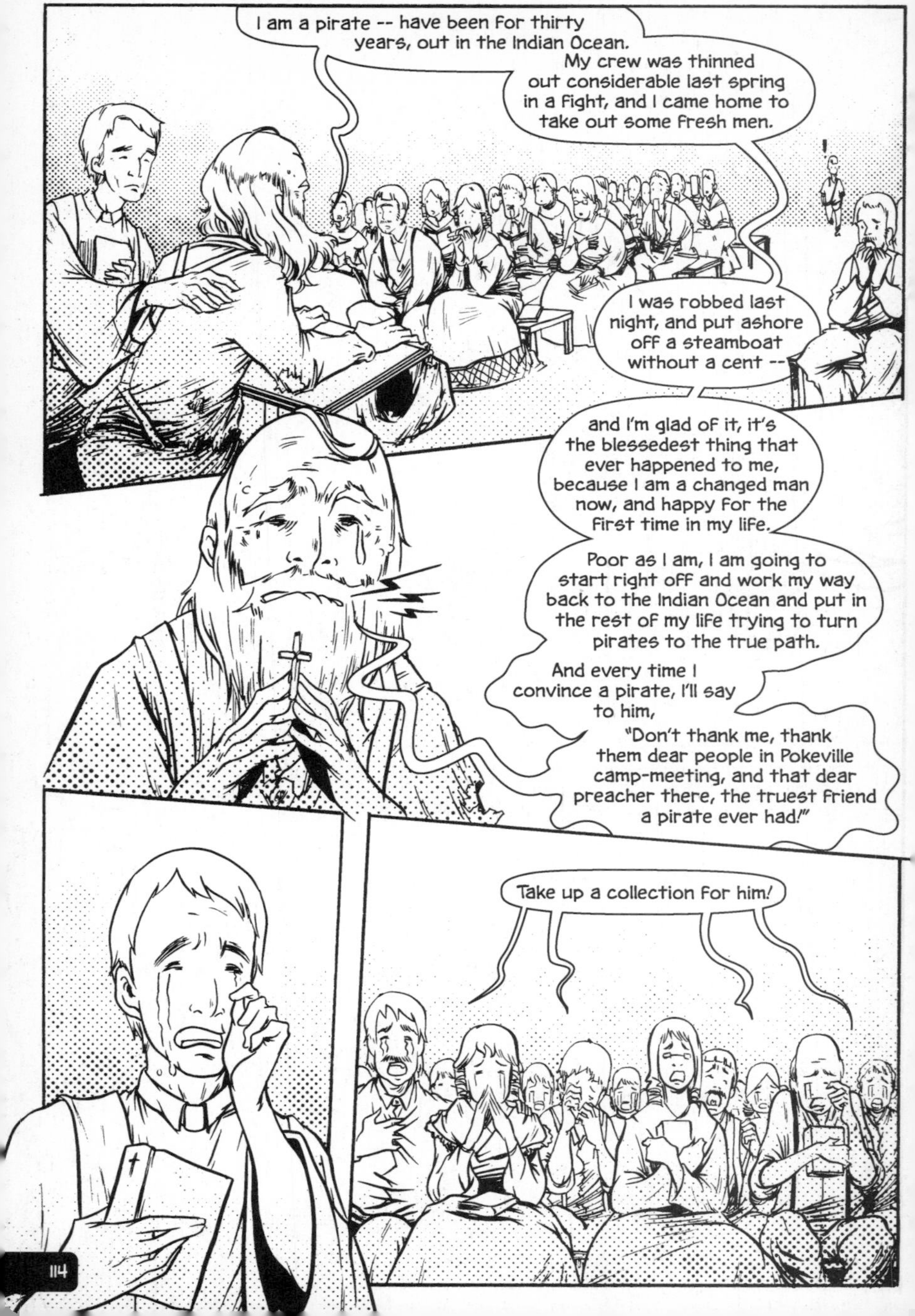
I am a pirate -- have been for thirty years, out in the Indian Ocean.
My crew was thinned out considerable last spring in a fight, and I came home to take out some fresh men.
!
I was robbed last night, and put ashore off a steamboat without a cent --
and I'm glad of it, it's the blessedest thing that ever happened to me, because I am a changed man now, and happy for the first time in my life.
Poor as I am, I am going to start right off and work my way back to the Indian Ocean and put in the rest of my life trying to turn pirates to the true path.
And every time I convince a pirate, I'll say to him,
"Don't thank me, thank them dear people in Pokeville camp-meeting, and that dear preacher there, the truest friend a pirate ever had!"
Take up a collection for him!

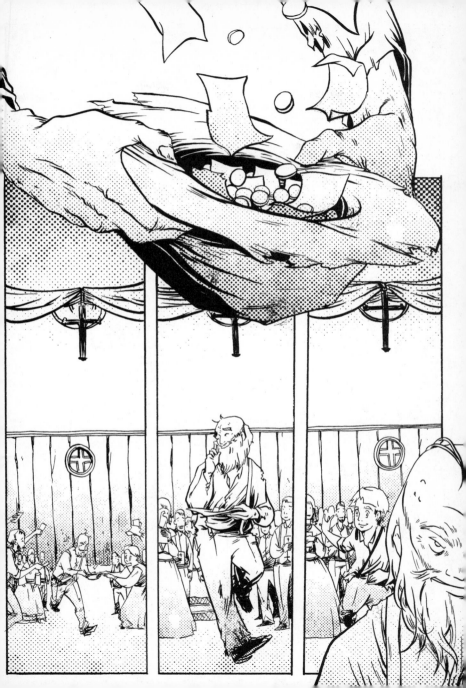

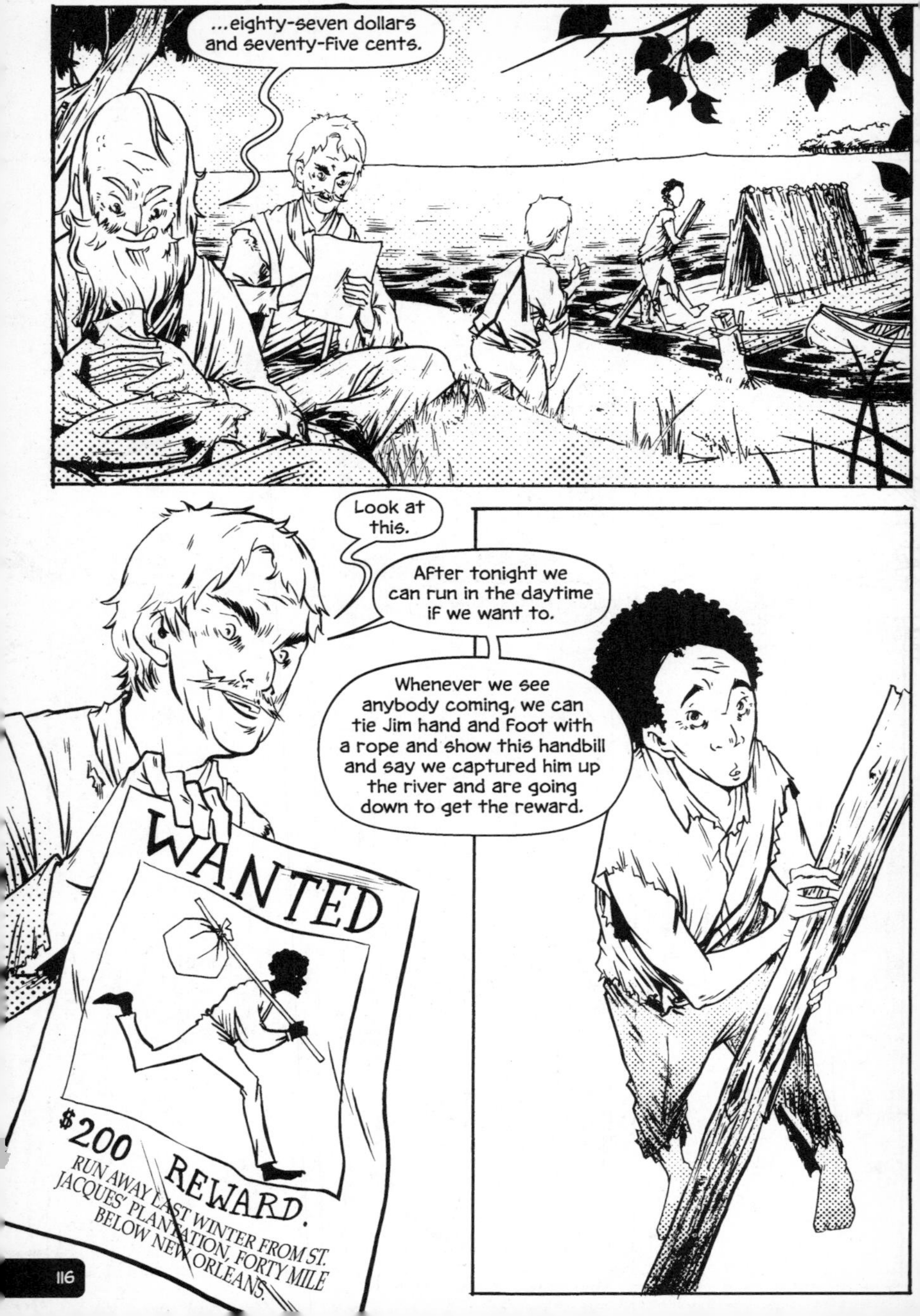
...eighty-seven dollars and seventy-five cents.
Look at this.
After tonight we can run in the daytime if we want to.
Whenever we see anybody coming, we can tie Jim hand and foot with a rope and show this handbill and say we captured him up the river and are going down to get the reward.
WANTED
$200 REWARD.
RUN AWAY LAST WINTER FROM ST. JACQUES' PLANTATION, FORTY MILE BELOW NEW ORLEANS.

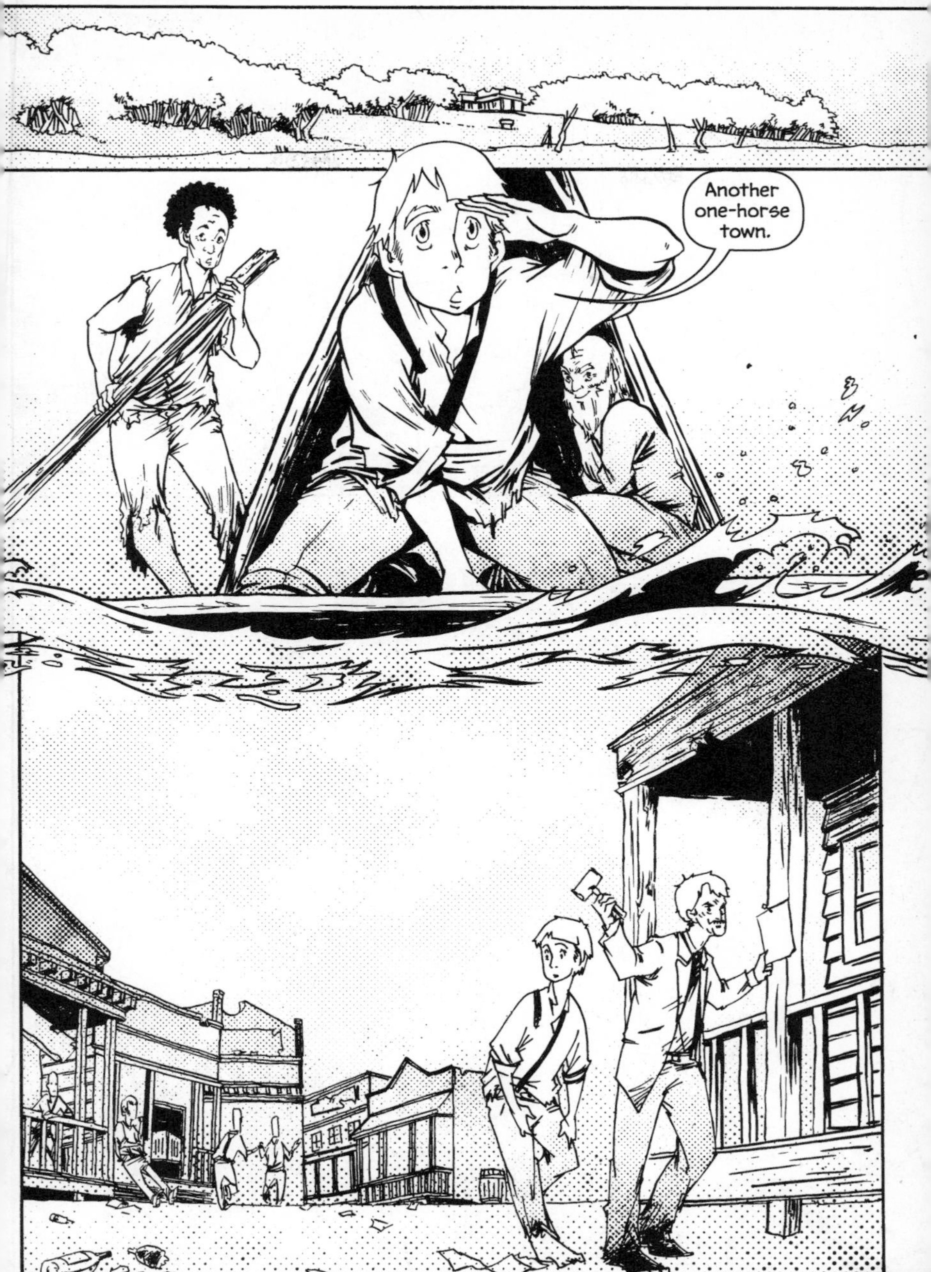
Another one-horse town.

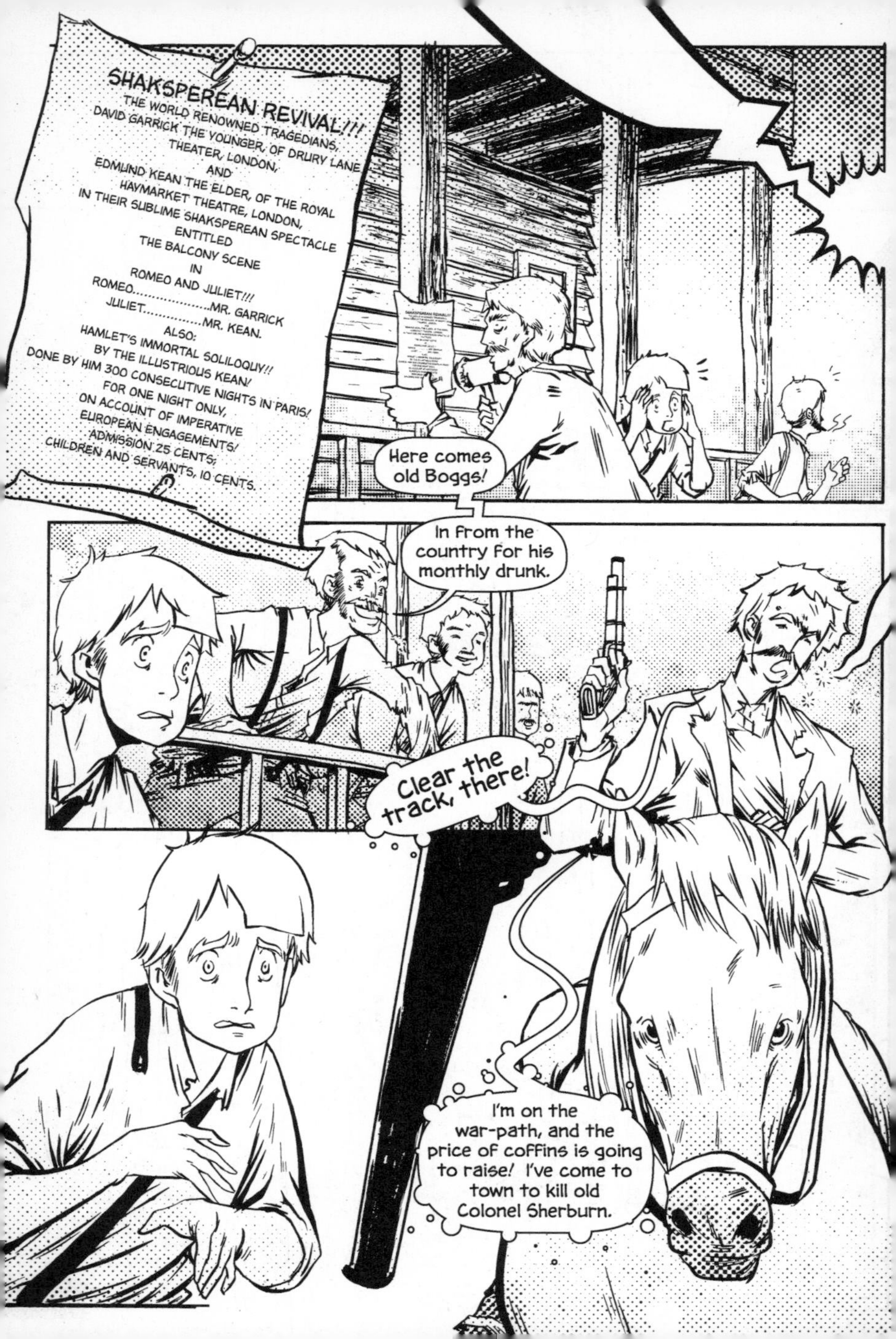
SHAKSPEREAN REVIVAL!!!
THE WORLD RENOWNED TRAGEDIANS,
DAVID GARRICK THE YOUNGER, OF DRURY LANE THEATER, LONDON,
AND
EDMUND KEAN THE ELDER, OF THE ROYAL HAYMARKET THEATRE, LONDON,
IN THEIR SUBLIME SHAKSPEREAN SPECTACLE ENTITLED
THE BALCONY SCENE
IN
ROMEO AND JULIET!!!
ROMEO...................MR. GARRICK
JULIET..............MR. KEAN.
ALSO:
HAMLET'S IMMORTAL SOLILOQUY!!
BY THE ILLUSTRIOUS KEAN!
DONE BY HIM 300 CONSECUTIVE NIGHTS IN PARIS!
FOR ONE NIGHT ONLY,
ON ACCOUNT OF IMPERATIVE EUROPEAN ENGAGEMENTS!
ADMISSION 25 CENTS;
CHILDREN AND SERVANTS, 10 CENTS.
Here comes old Boggs!
In from the country for his monthly drunk.
Clear the track, there!
I'm on the war-path, and the price of coffins is going to raise! I've come to town to kill old Colonel Sherburn.

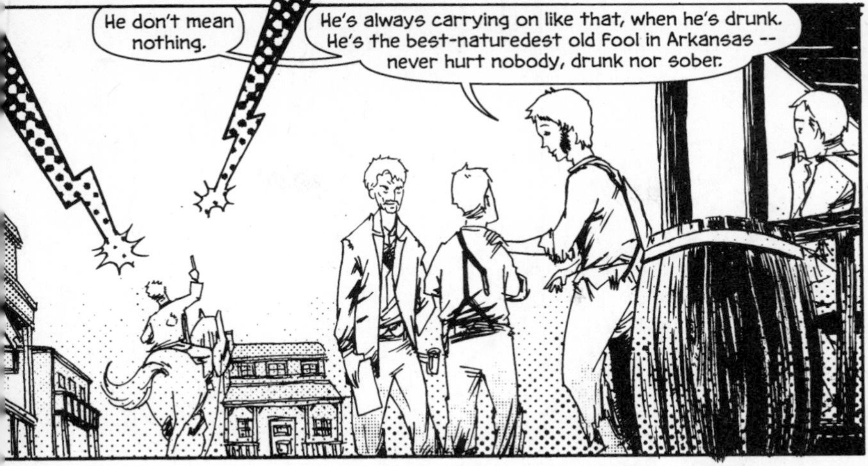
He don't mean nothing.
He's always carrying on like that, when he's drunk. He's the best-naturedest old fool in Arkansas -- never hurt nobody, drunk nor sober.

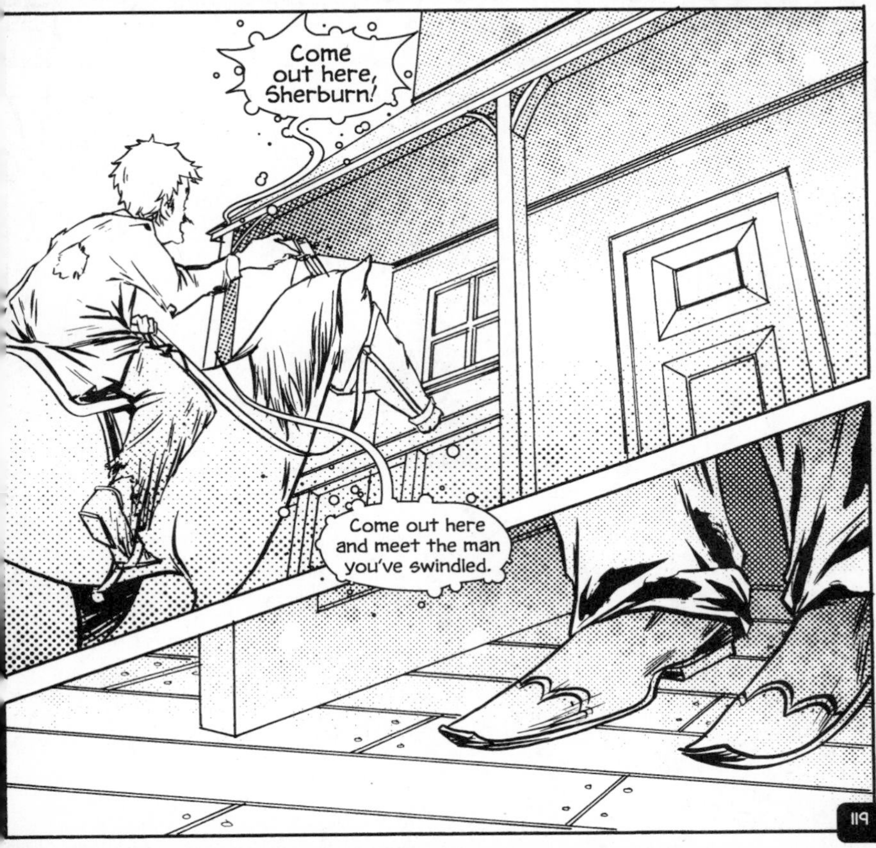
Come out here, Sherburn!
Come out here and meet the man you've swindled.

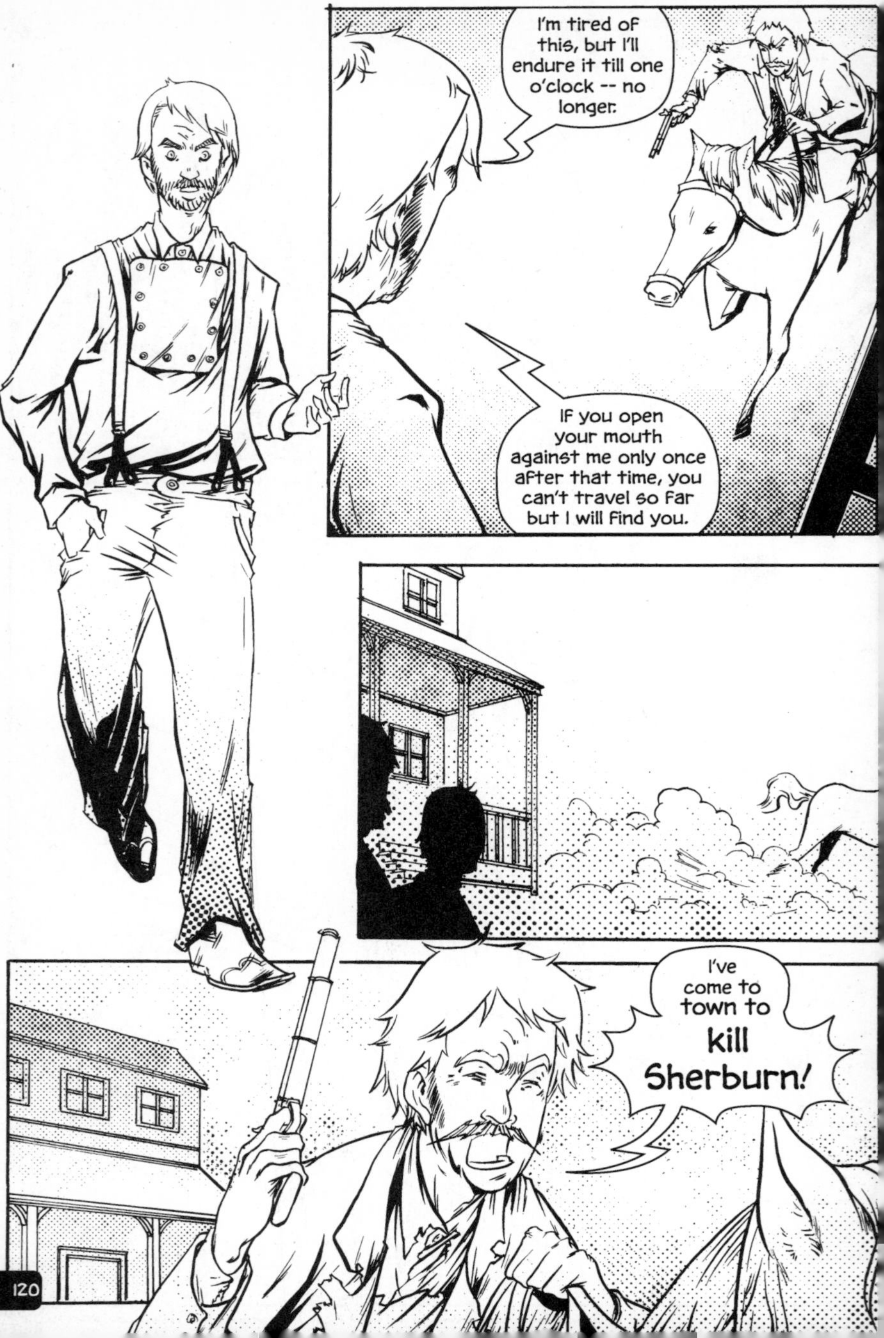
I'm tired of this, but I'll endure it till one o'clock -- no longer.
If you open your mouth against me only once after that time, you can't travel so far but I will find you.
I've come to town to Kill Sherburn!

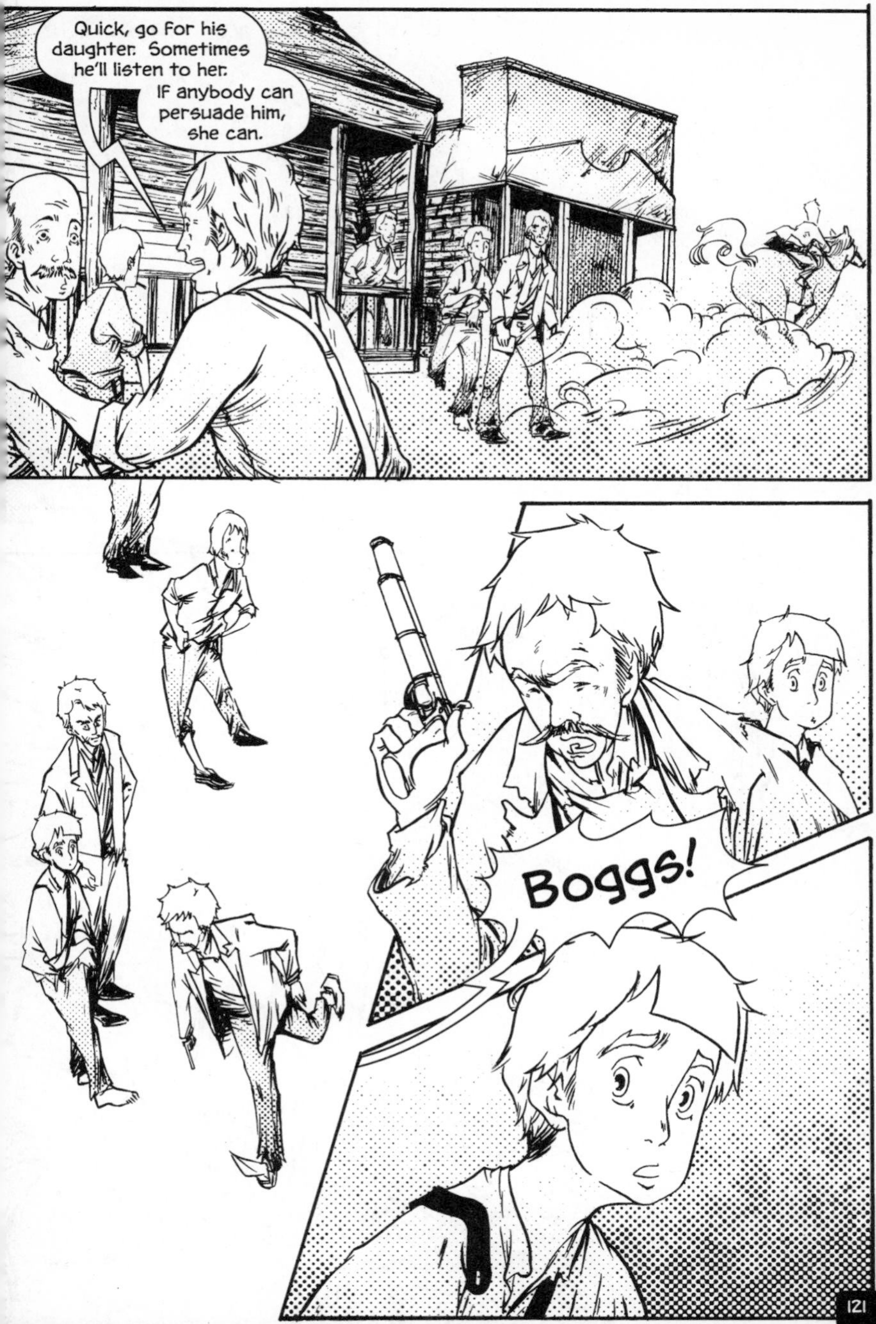
Quick, go for his daughter. Sometimes he'll listen to her.
If anybody can persuade him, she can.
Boggs!

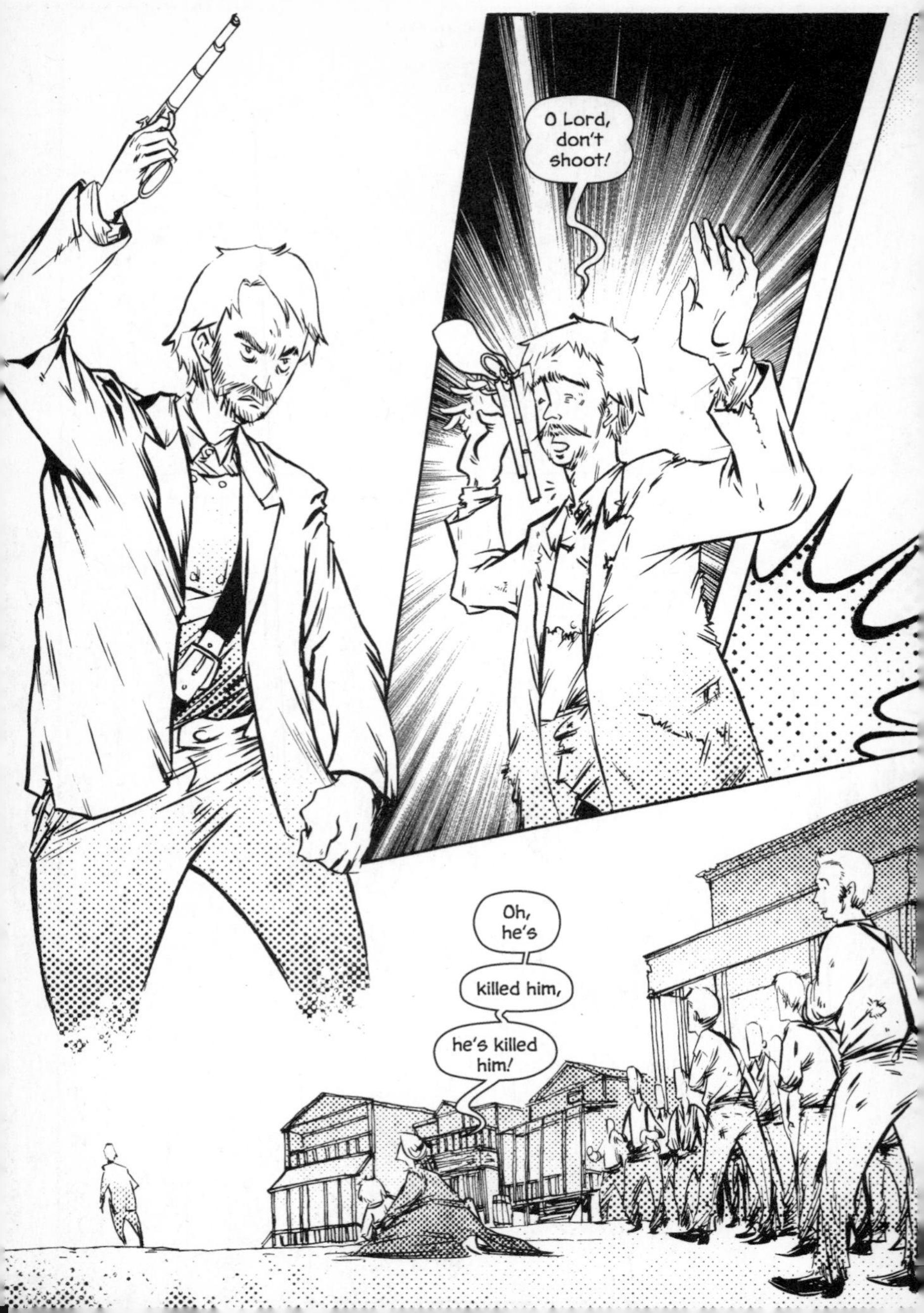
O Lord, don't shoot!
Oh, he's
killed him,
he's killed him!

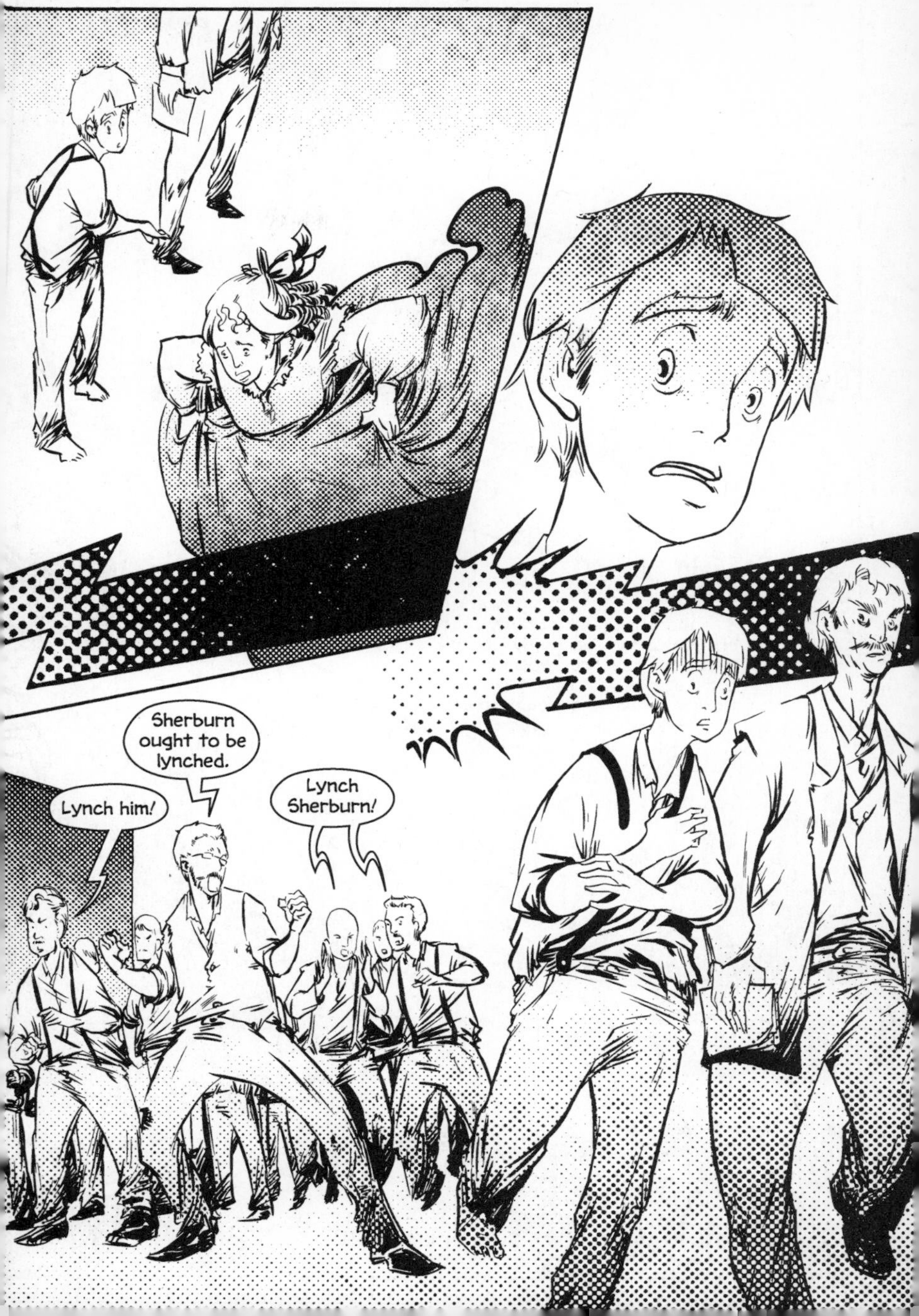
Sherburn ought to be lynched.
Lynch him!
Lynch Sherburn!

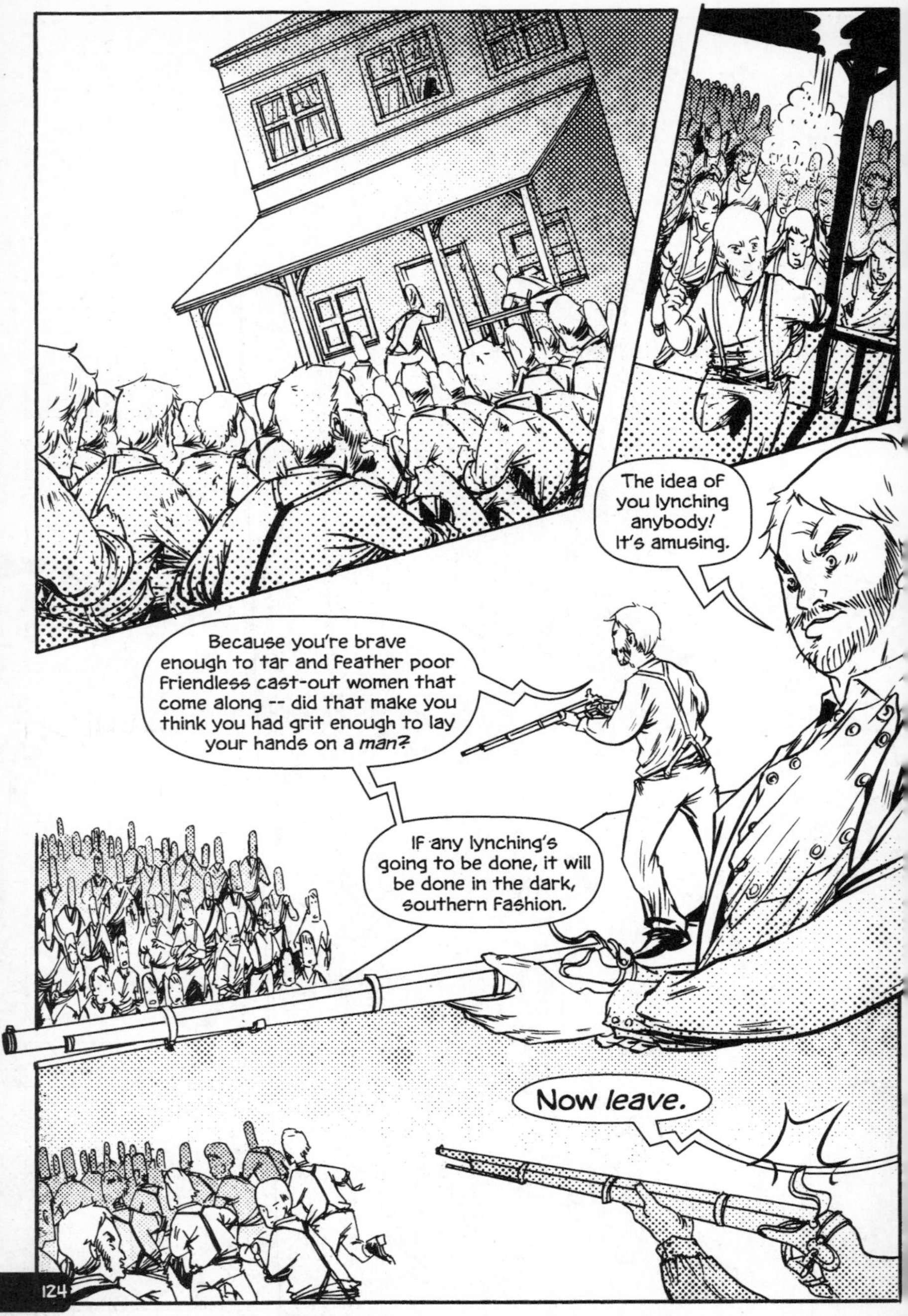
The idea of you lynching anybody! It's amusing.
Because you're brave enough to tar and feather poor friendless cast-out women that come along -- did that make you think you had grit enough to lay your hands on a *man*?
If any lynching's going to be done, it will be done in the dark, southern fashion.
Now *leave.*

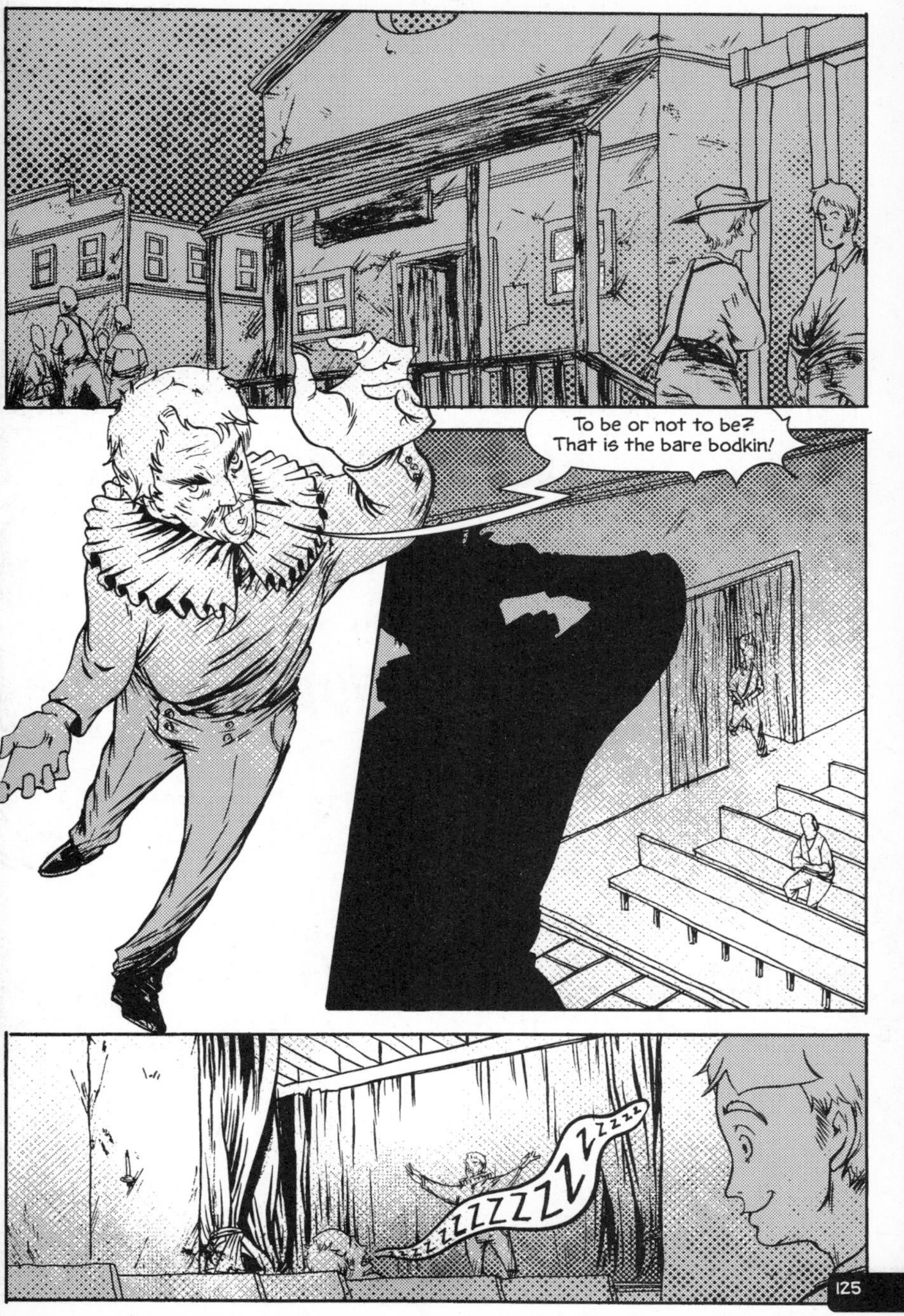
To be or not to be?
That is the bare bodkin!
Zzzzzzzzzzzzzz

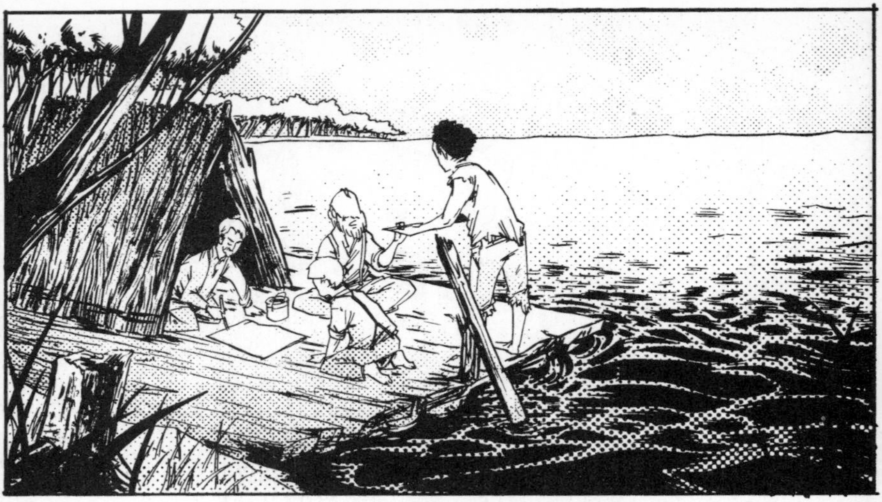

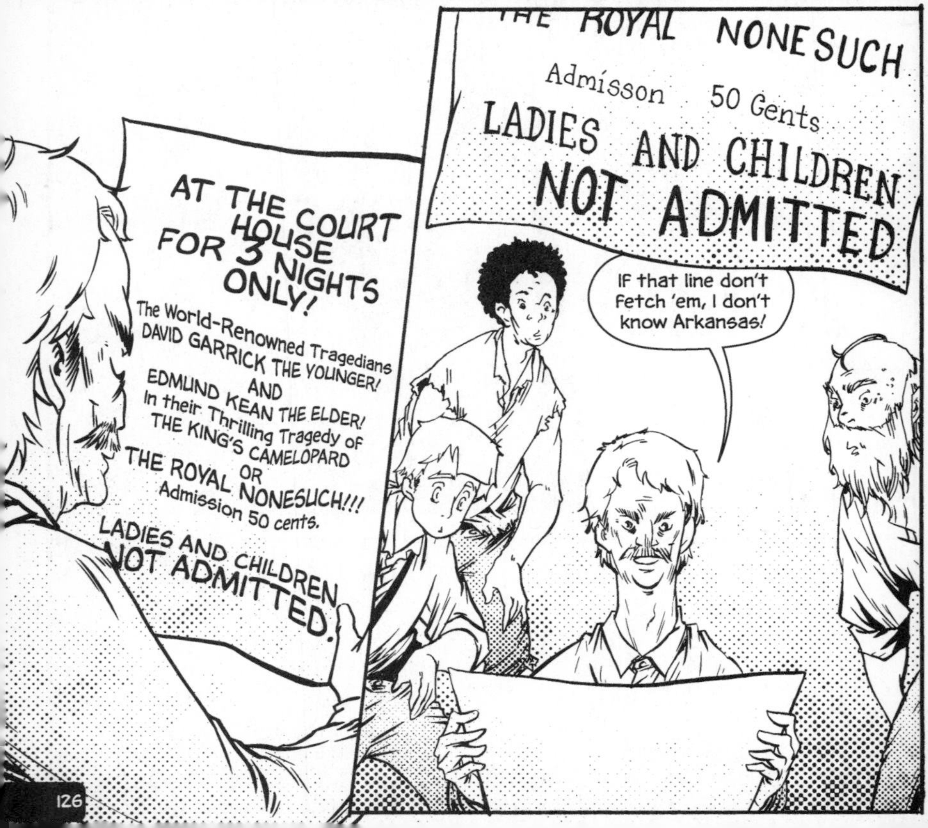
AT THE COURT HOUSE FOR 3 NIGHTS ONLY!
The World-Renowned Tragedians DAVID GARRICK THE YOUNGER! AND EDMUND KEAN THE ELDER! In their Thrilling Tragedy of THE KING'S CAMELOPARD OR THE ROYAL NONESUCH!!! Admission 50 cents.
LADIES AND CHILDREN NOT ADMITTED.
ROYAL NONESUCH
Admísson 50 Cents
LADIES AND CHILDREN NOT ADMITTED
IF that line don't fetch 'em, I don't know Arkansas!

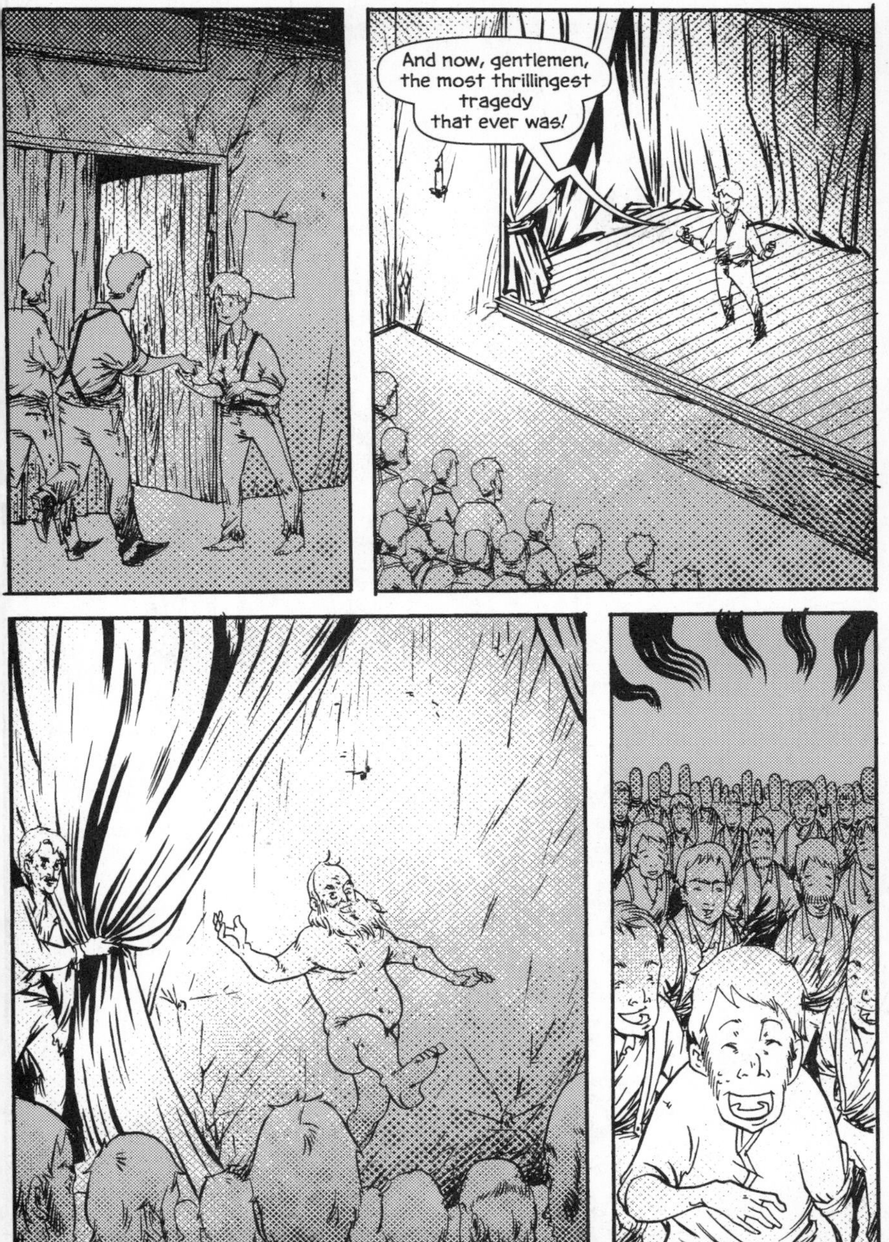
And now, gentlemen, the most thrillingest tragedy that ever was!

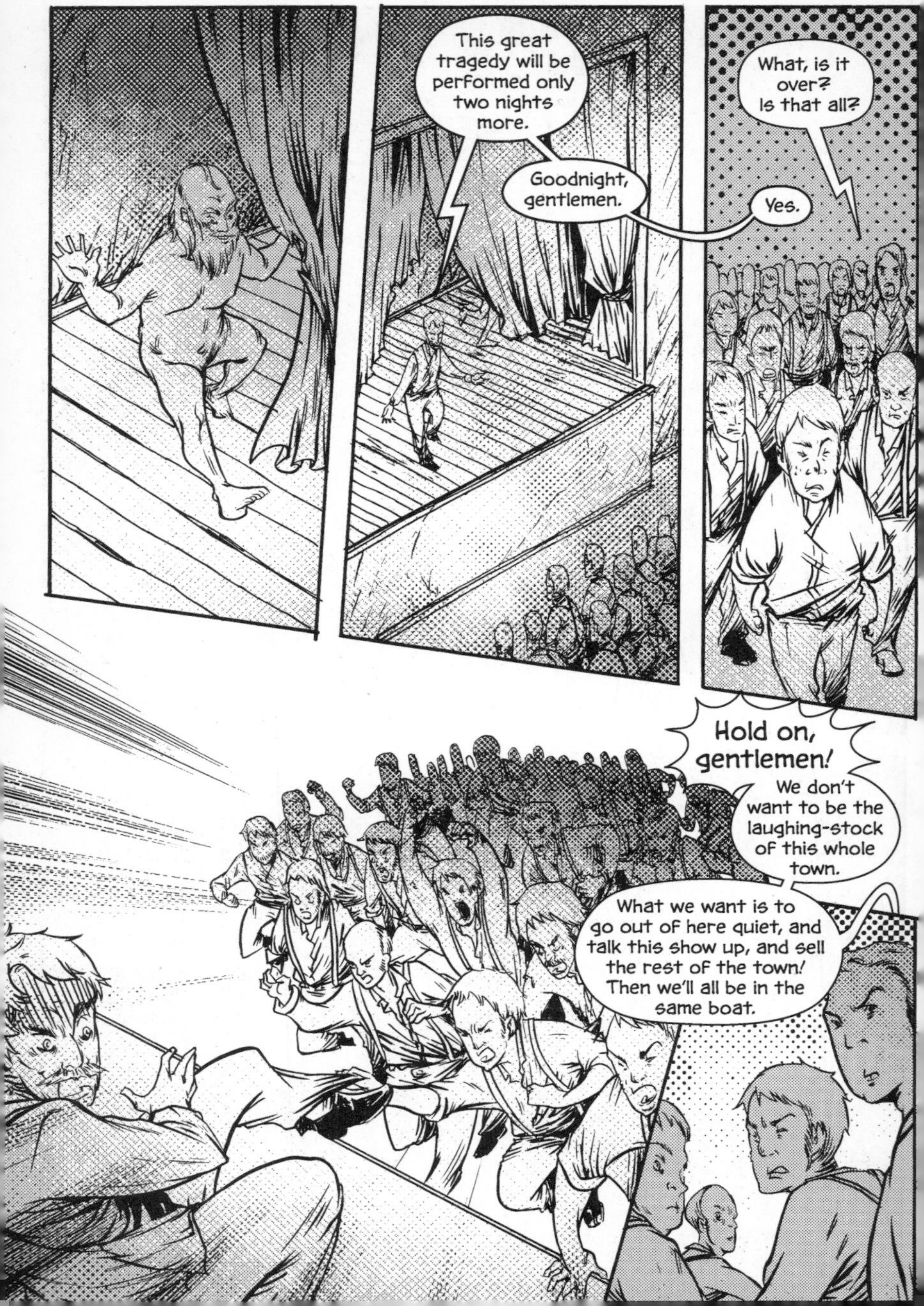
This great tragedy will be performed only two nights more.
Goodnight, gentlemen.
What, is it over? Is that all?
Yes.
Hold on, gentlemen!
We don't want to be the laughing-stock of this whole town.
What we want is to go out of here quiet, and talk this show up, and sell the rest of the town! Then we'll all be in the same boat.

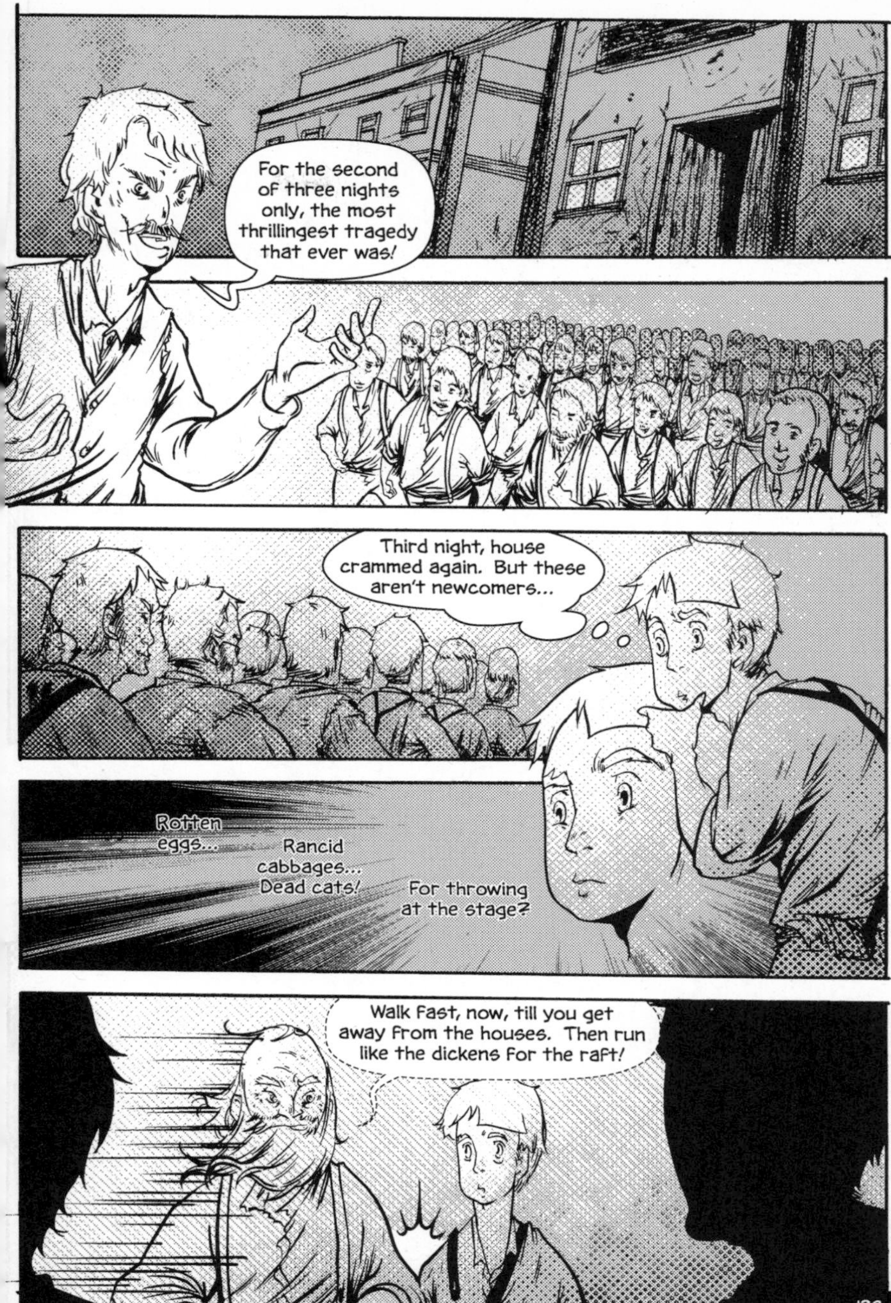
For the second of three nights only, the most thrillingest tragedy that ever was!
Third night, house crammed again. But these aren't newcomers...
Rotten eggs...
Rancid cabbages...
Dead cats!
For throwing at the stage?
Walk fast, now, till you get away from the houses. Then run like the dickens for the raft!

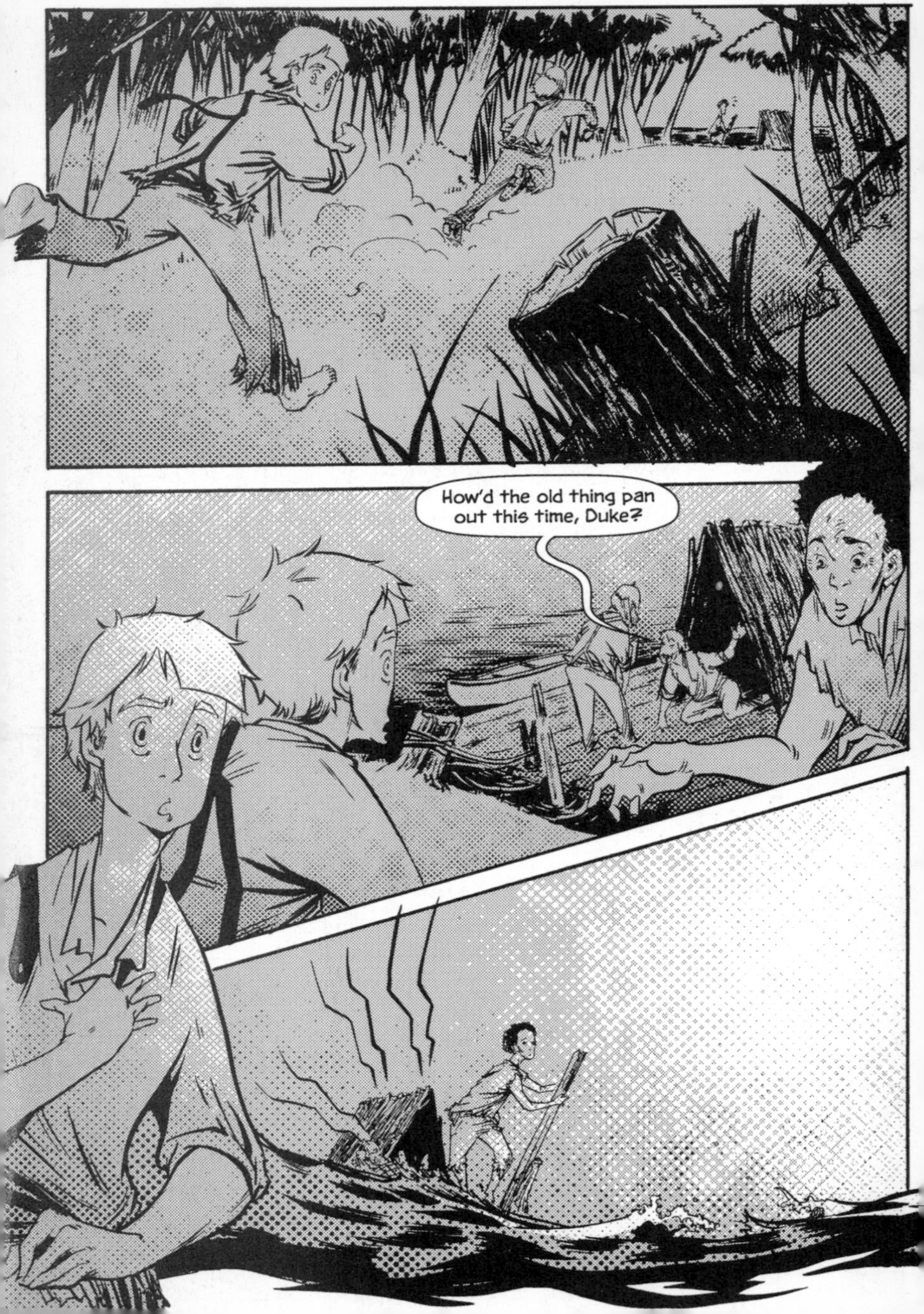
How'd the old thing pan out this time, Duke?

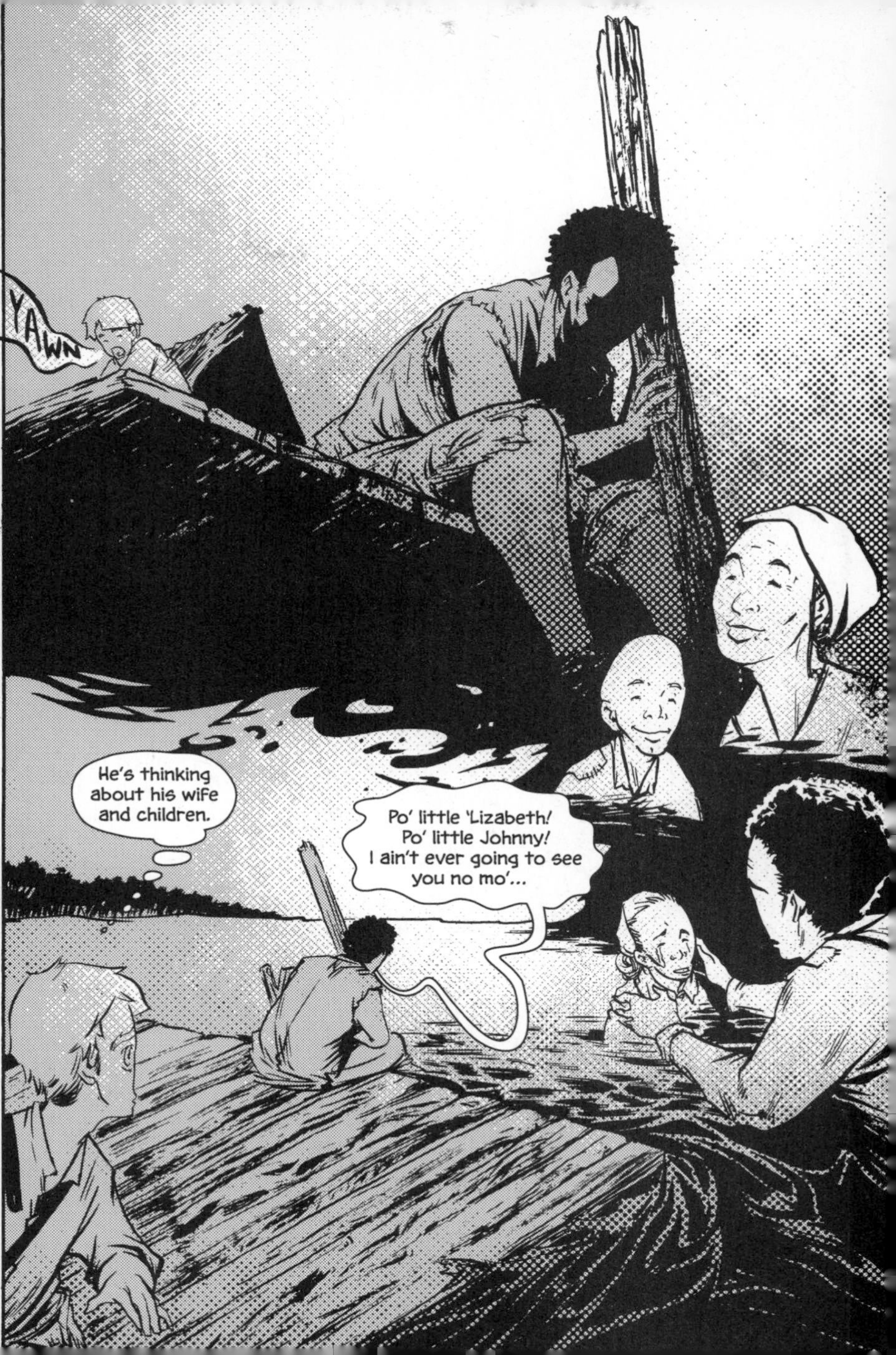
YAWN
He's thinking about his wife and children.
Po' little 'Lizabeth! Po' little Johnny! I ain't ever going to see you no mo'...

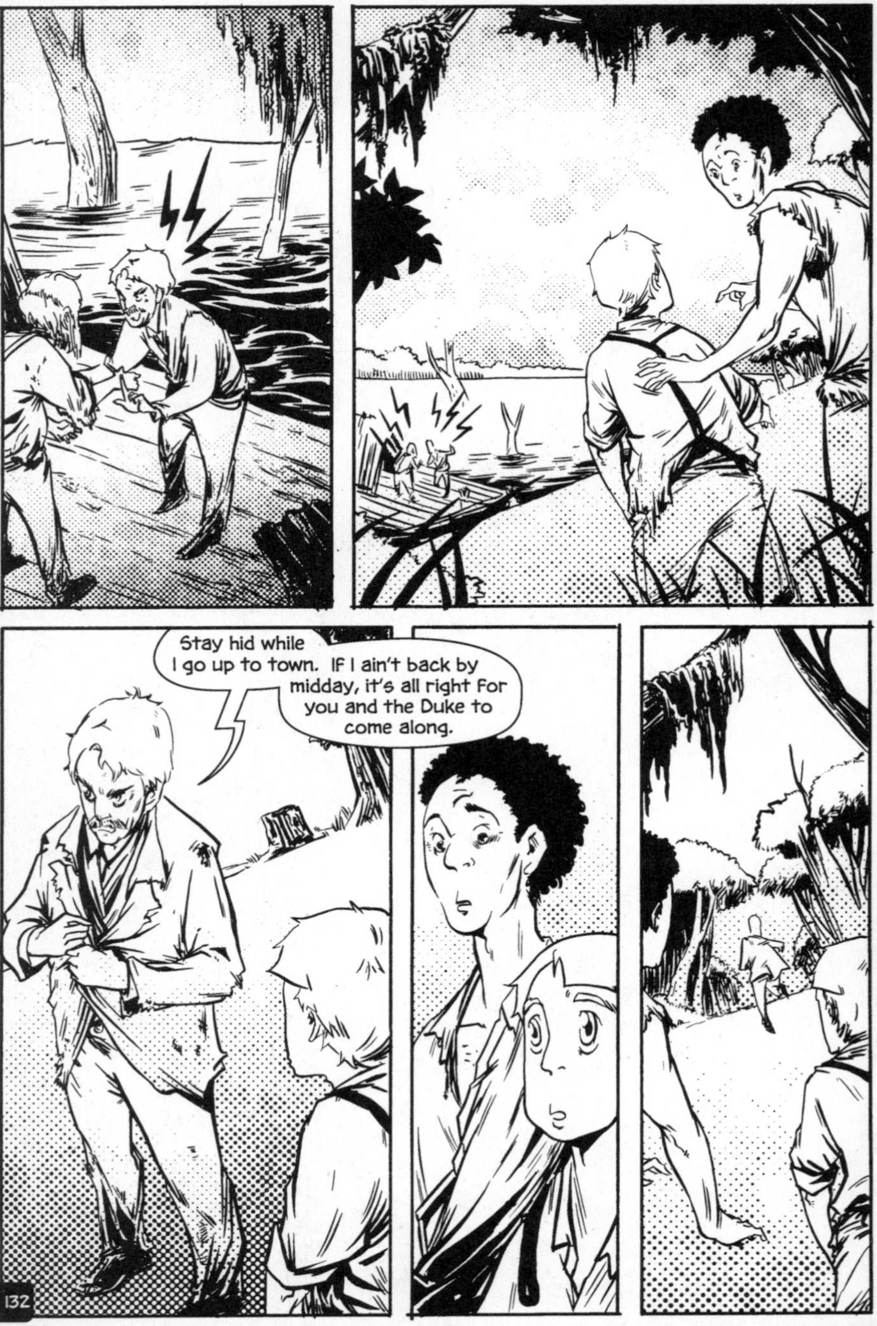
Stay hid while I go up to town. If I ain't back by midday, it's all right for you and the Duke to come along.

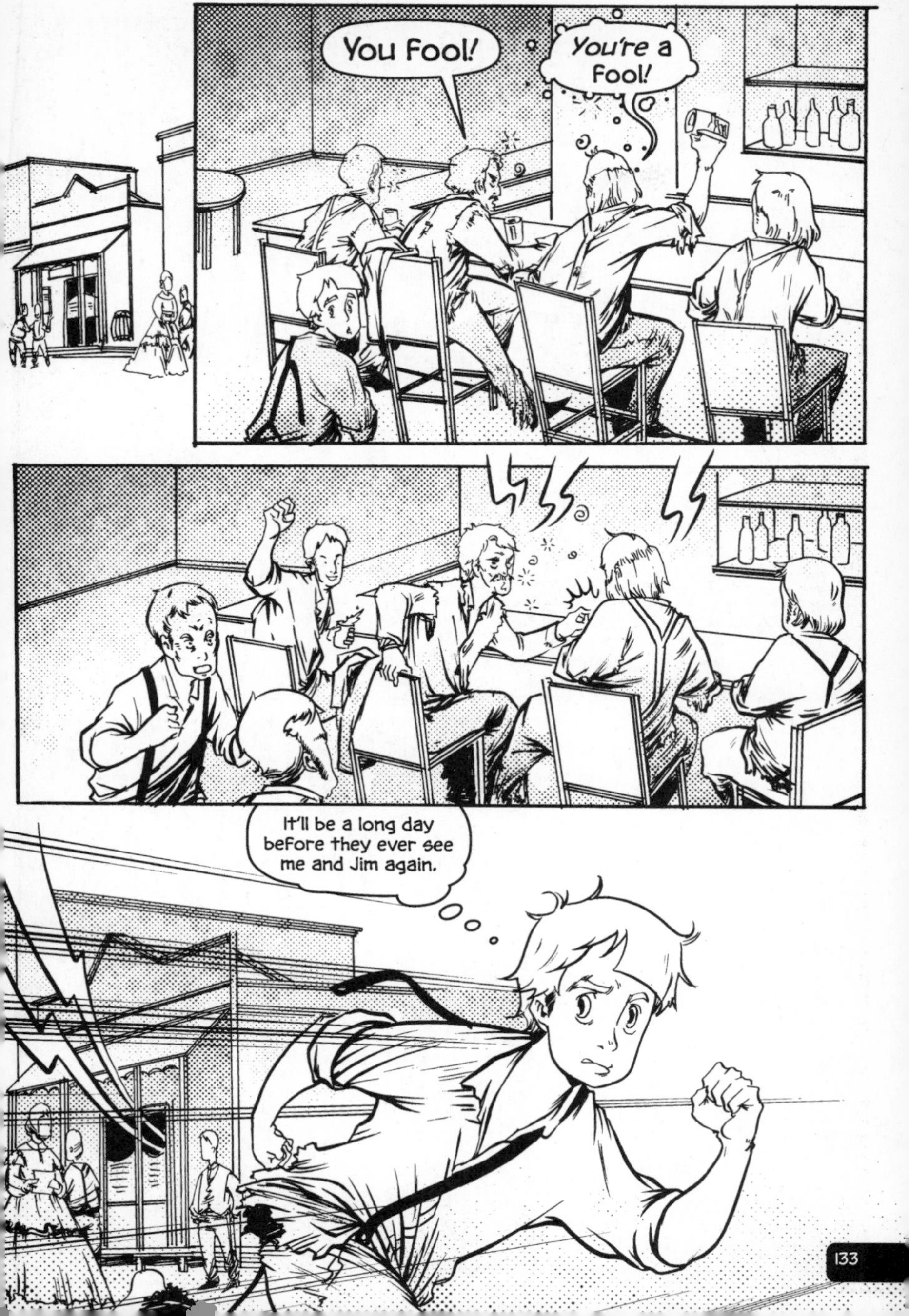
You Fool!
You're a fool!
It'll be a long day before they ever see me and Jim again.

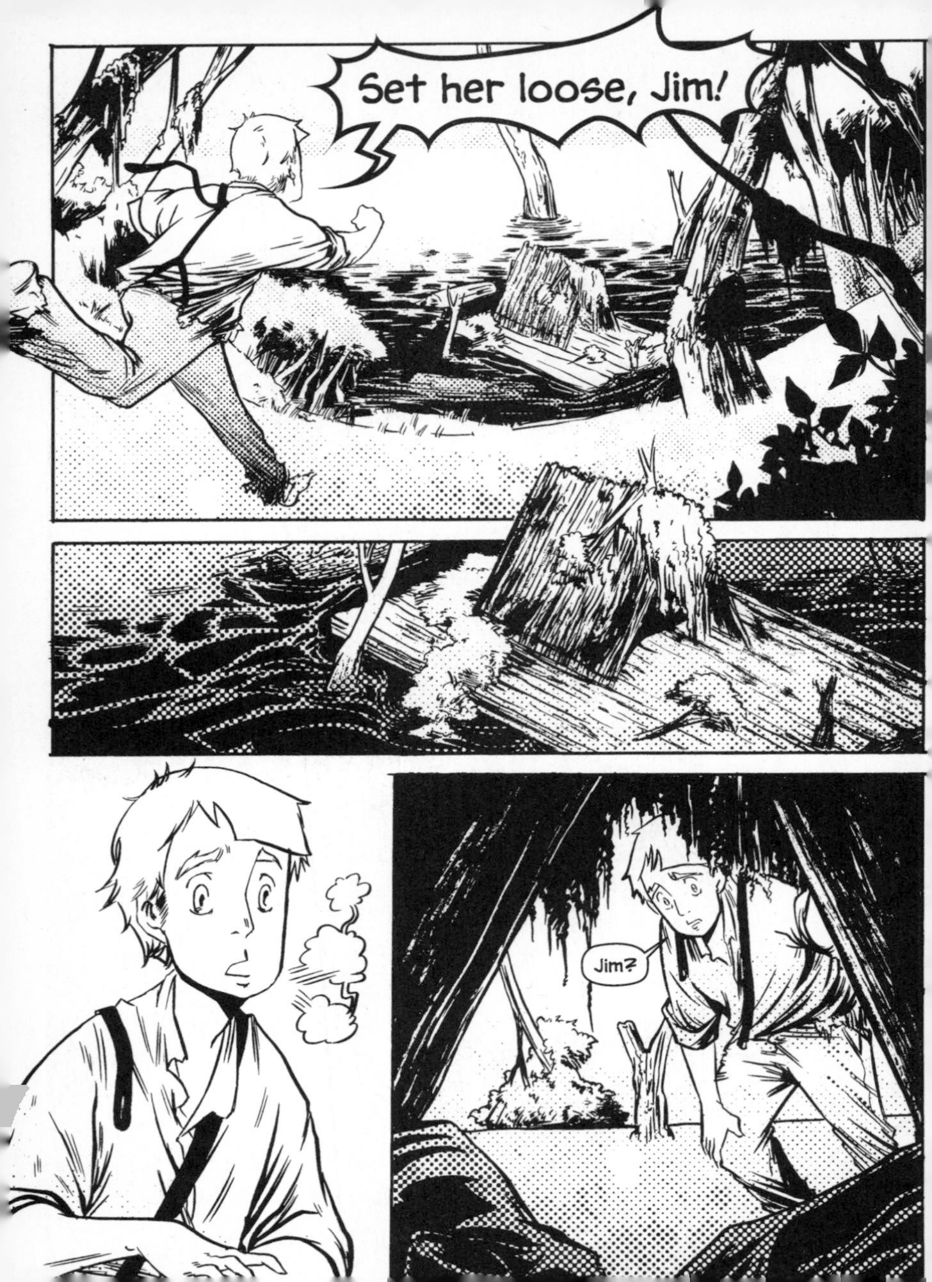

Set her loose, Jim!
Jim?

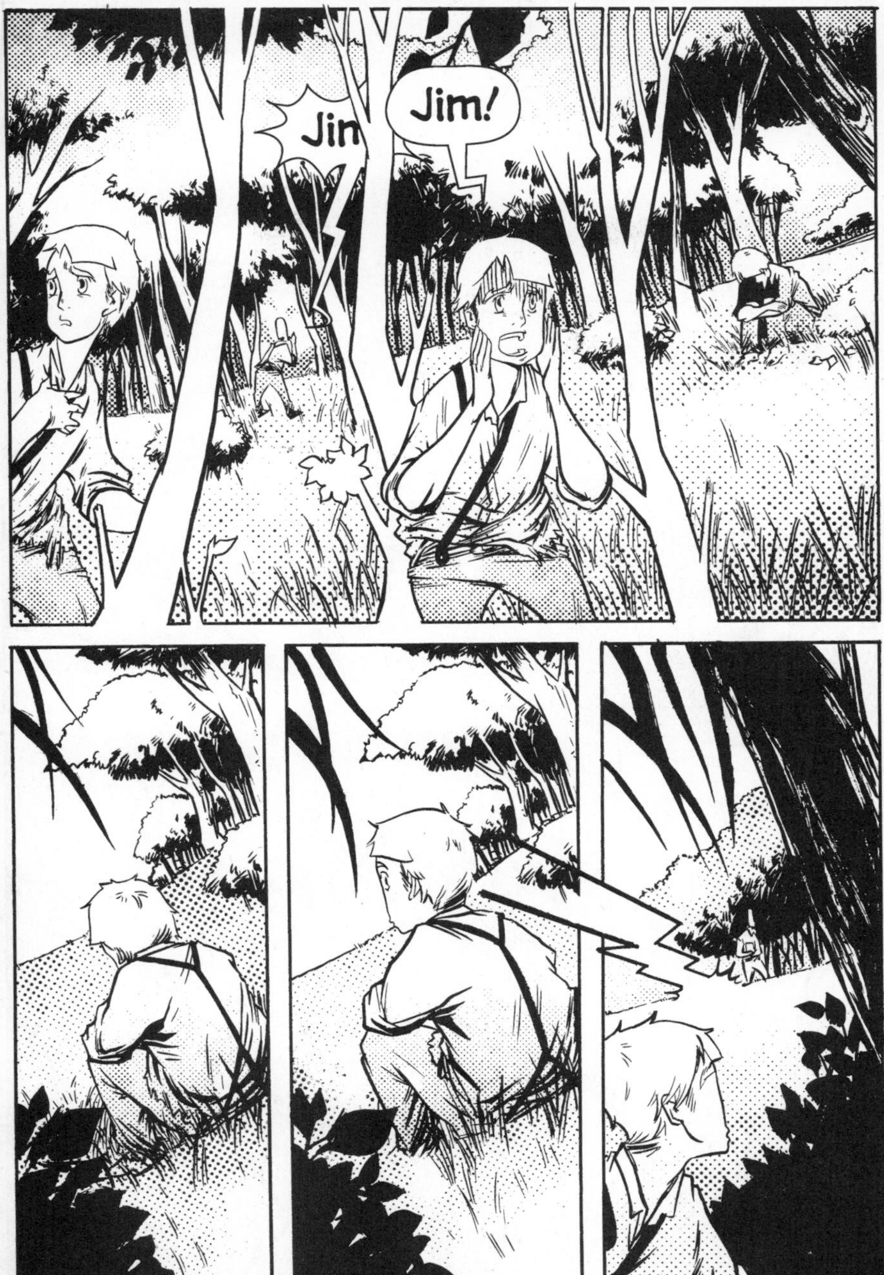
Jim
Jim!

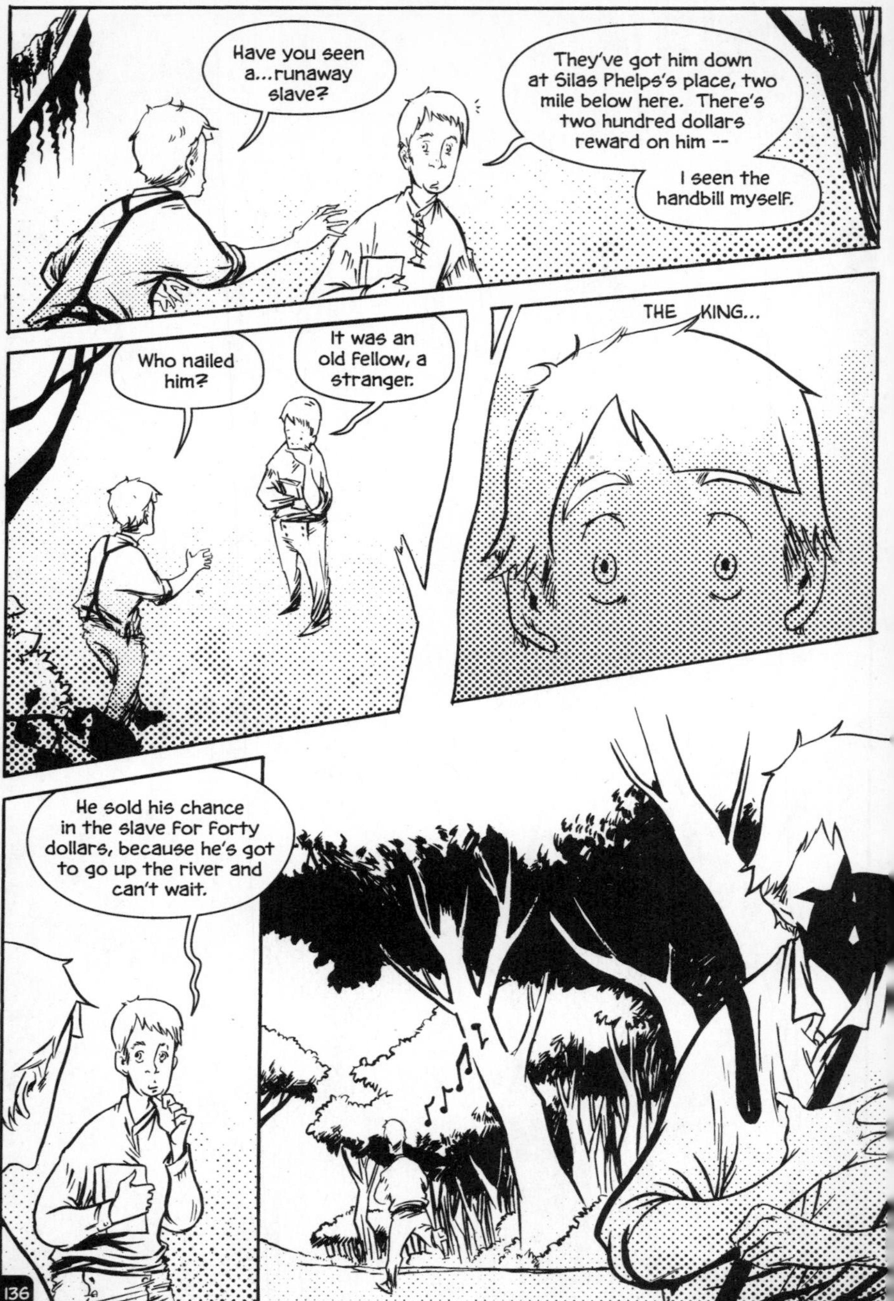
Have you seen a...runaway slave?
They've got him down at Silas Phelps's place, two mile below here. There's two hundred dollars reward on him --
I seen the handbill myself.
Who nailed him?
It was an old fellow, a stranger.
THE KING...
He sold his chance in the slave for forty dollars, because he's got to go up the river and can't wait.

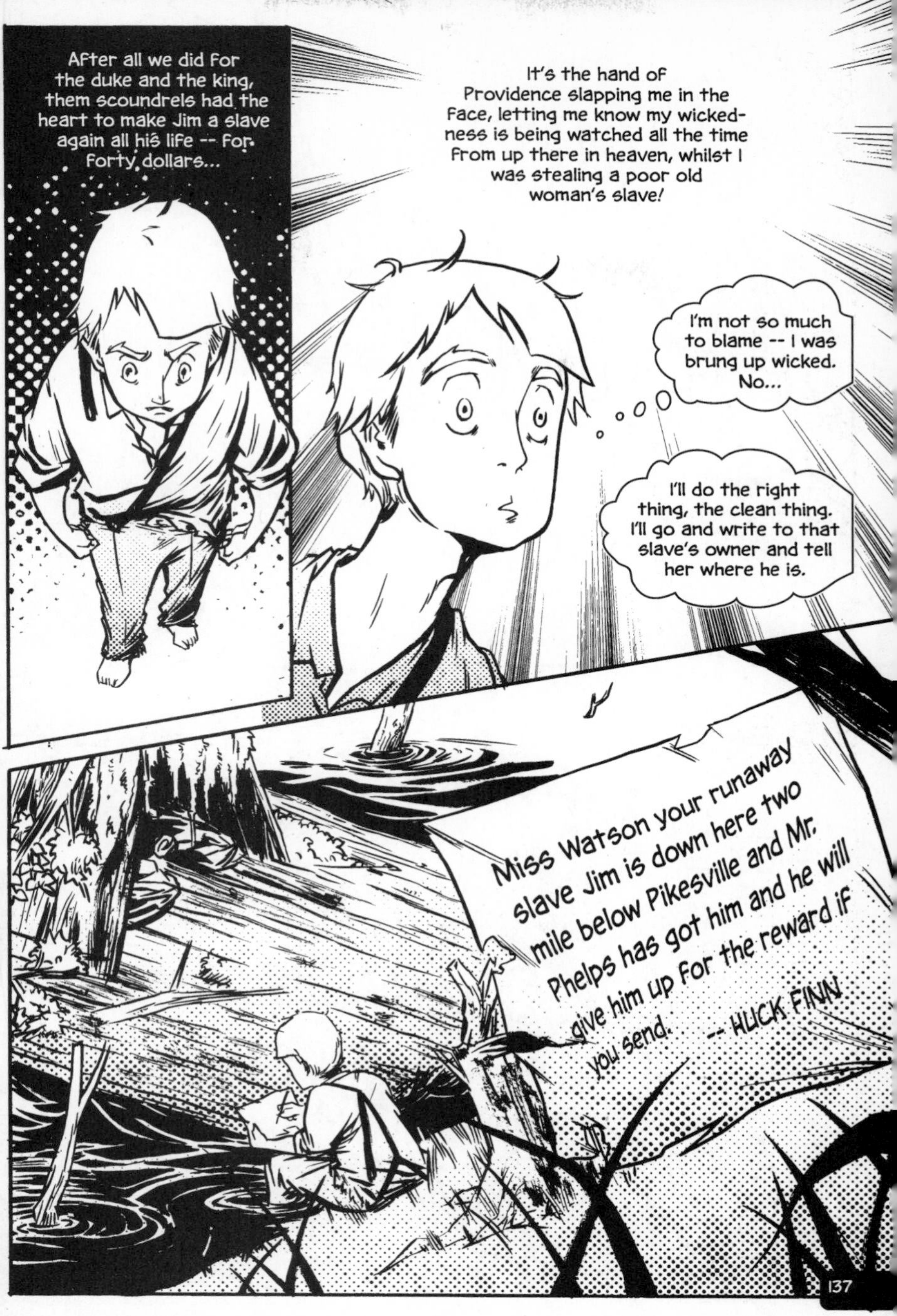
After all we did for the duke and the king, them scoundrels had the heart to make Jim a slave again all his life -- for forty dollars...
It's the hand of Providence slapping me in the face, letting me know my wickedness is being watched all the time from up there in heaven, whilst I was stealing a poor old woman's slave!
I'm not so much to blame -- I was brung up wicked. No...
I'll do the right thing, the clean thing. I'll go and write to that slave's owner and tell her where he is.
Miss Watson your runaway slave Jim is down here two mile below Pikesville and Mr. Phelps has got him and he will give him up for the reward if you send. -- HUCK FINN

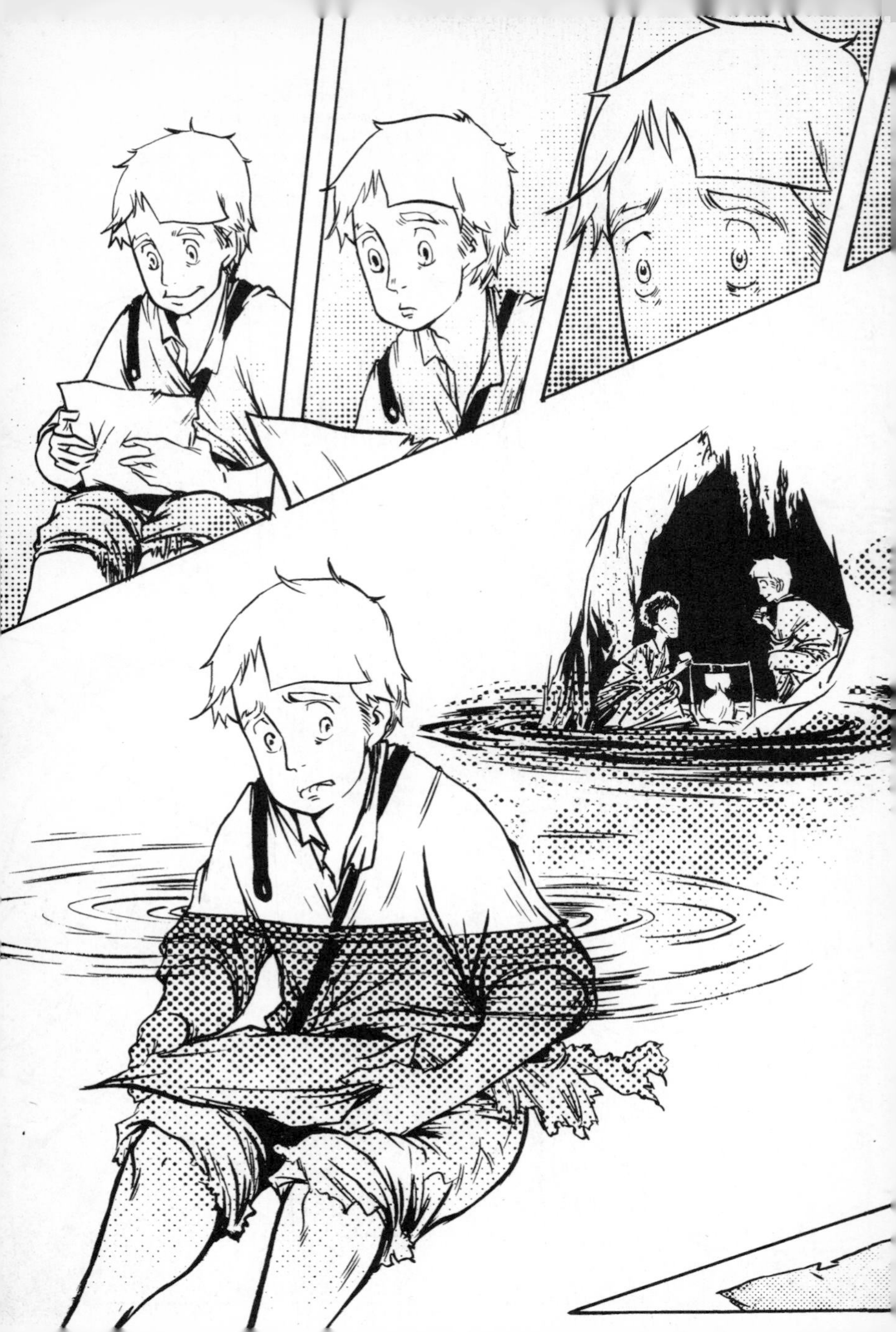

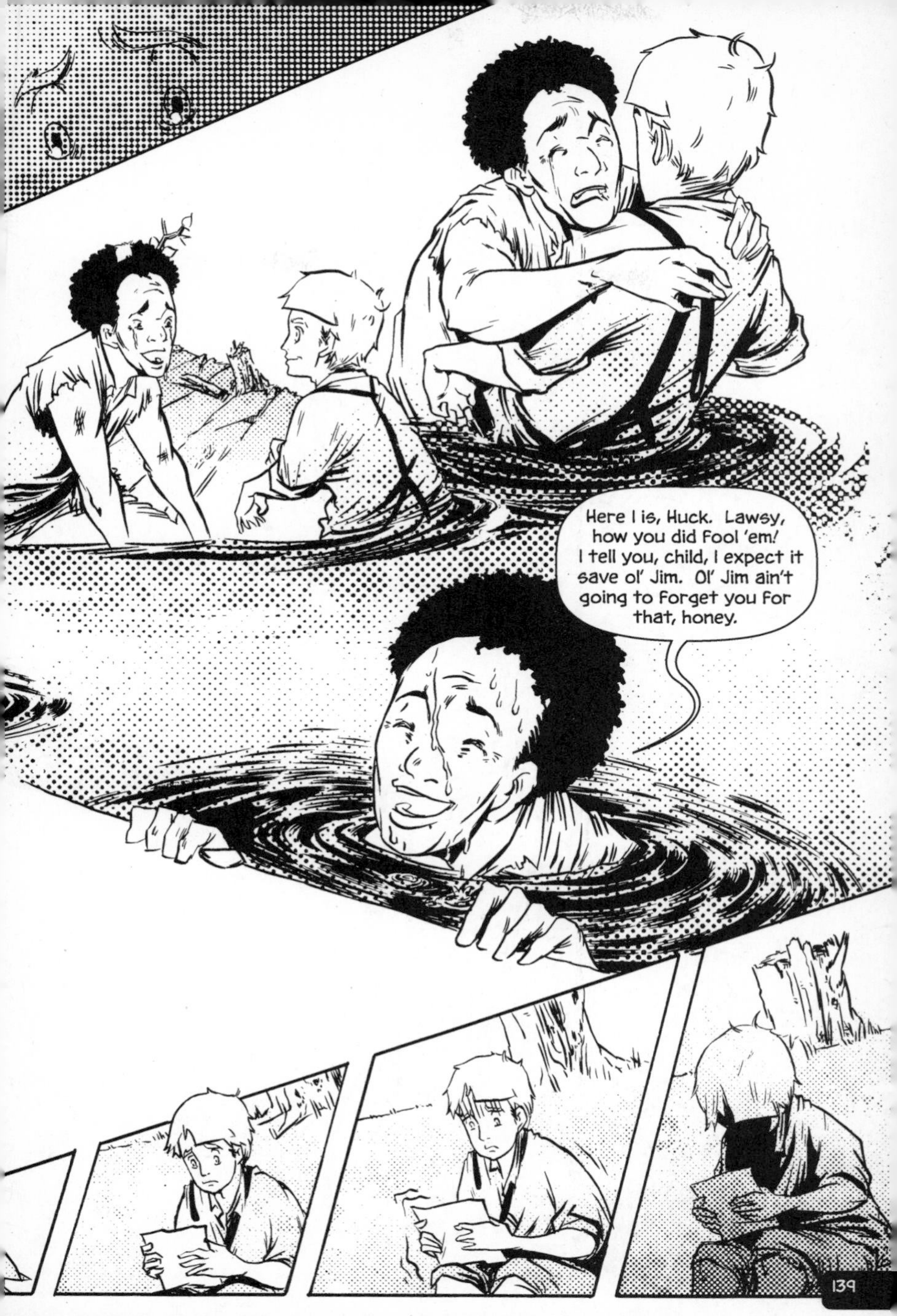
Here I is, Huck. Lawsy, how you did fool 'em! I tell you, child, I expect it save ol' Jim. Ol' Jim ain't going to forget you for that, honey.

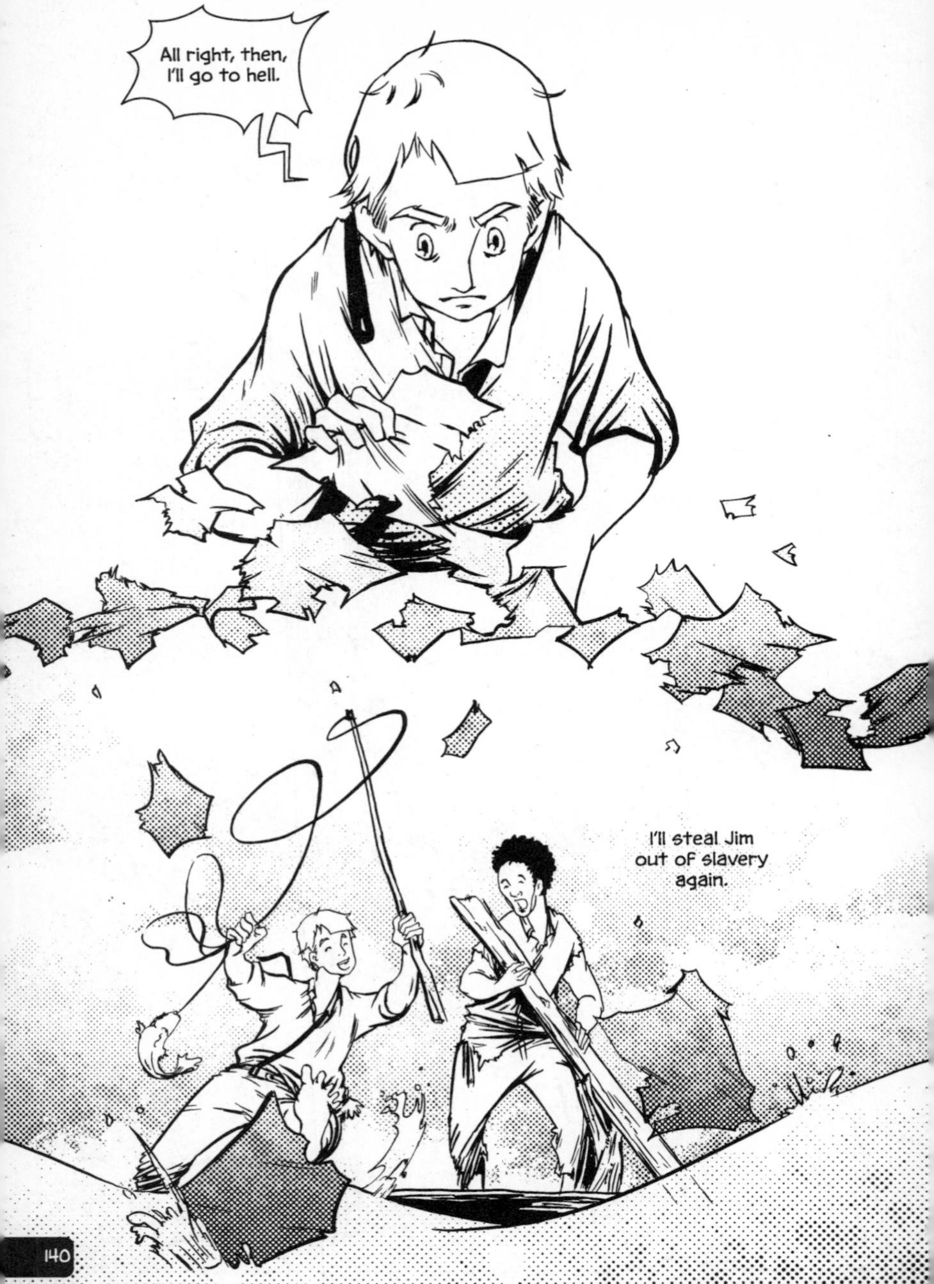
All right, then, I'll go to hell.
I'll steal Jim out of slavery again.

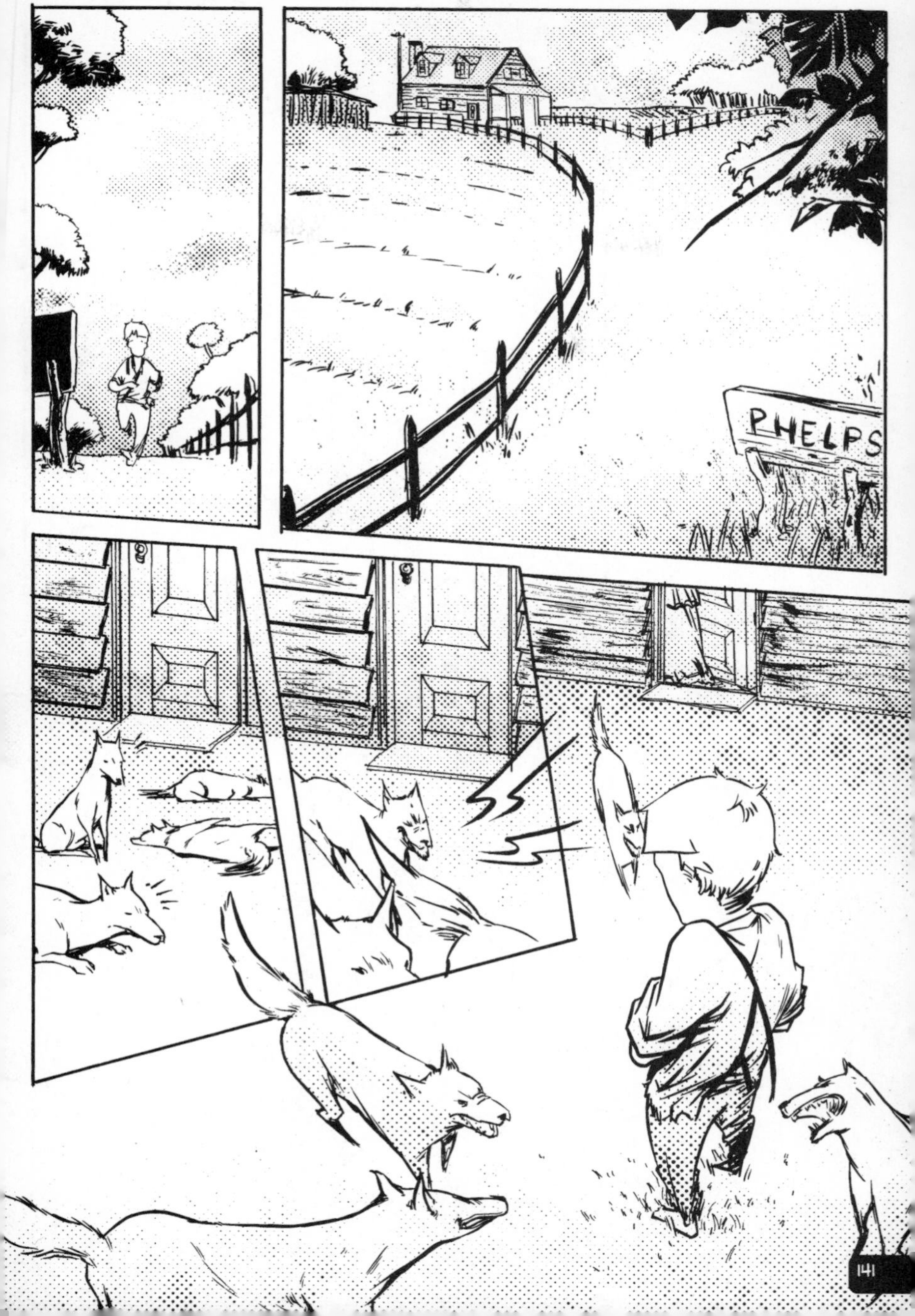
PHELPS

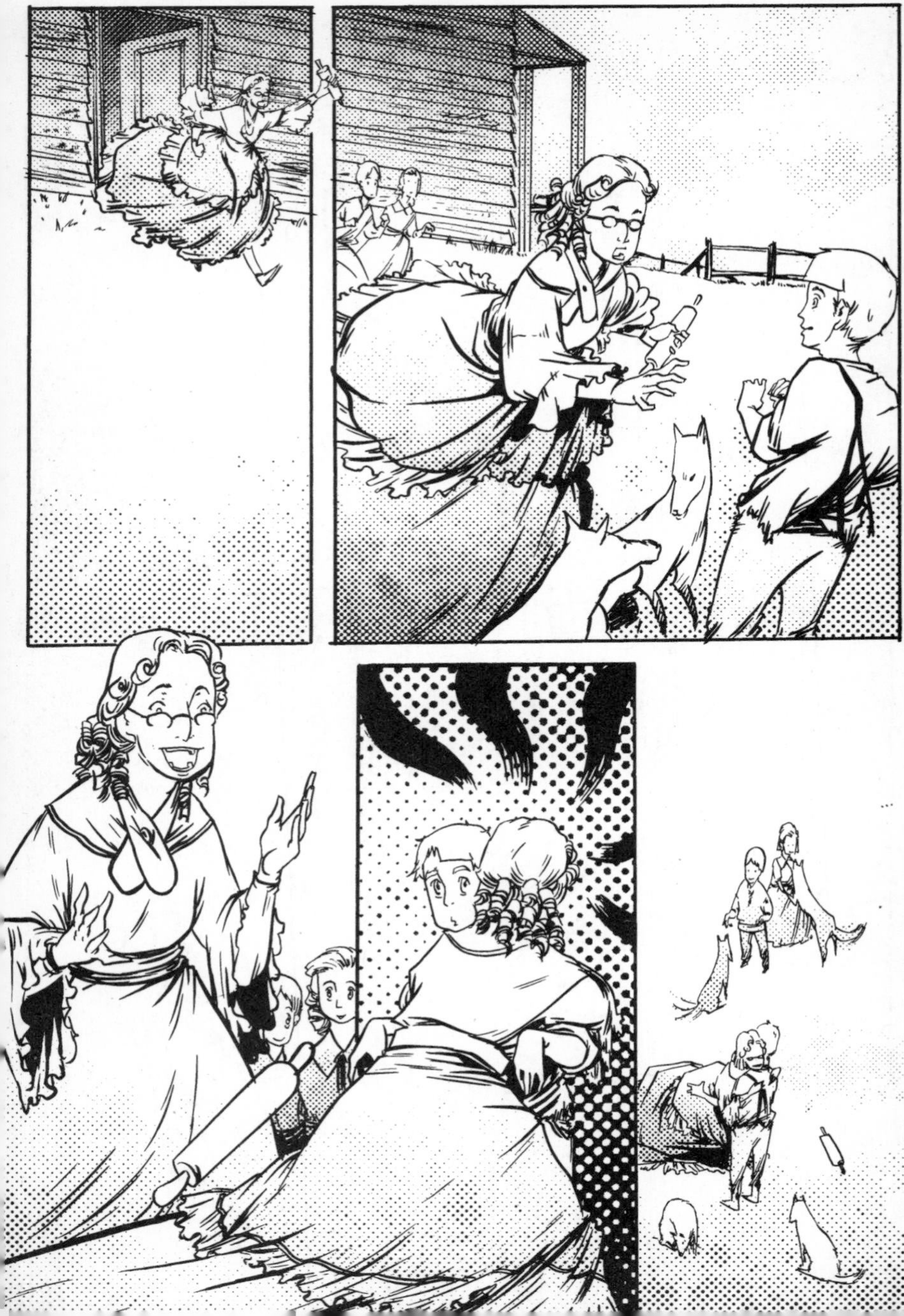

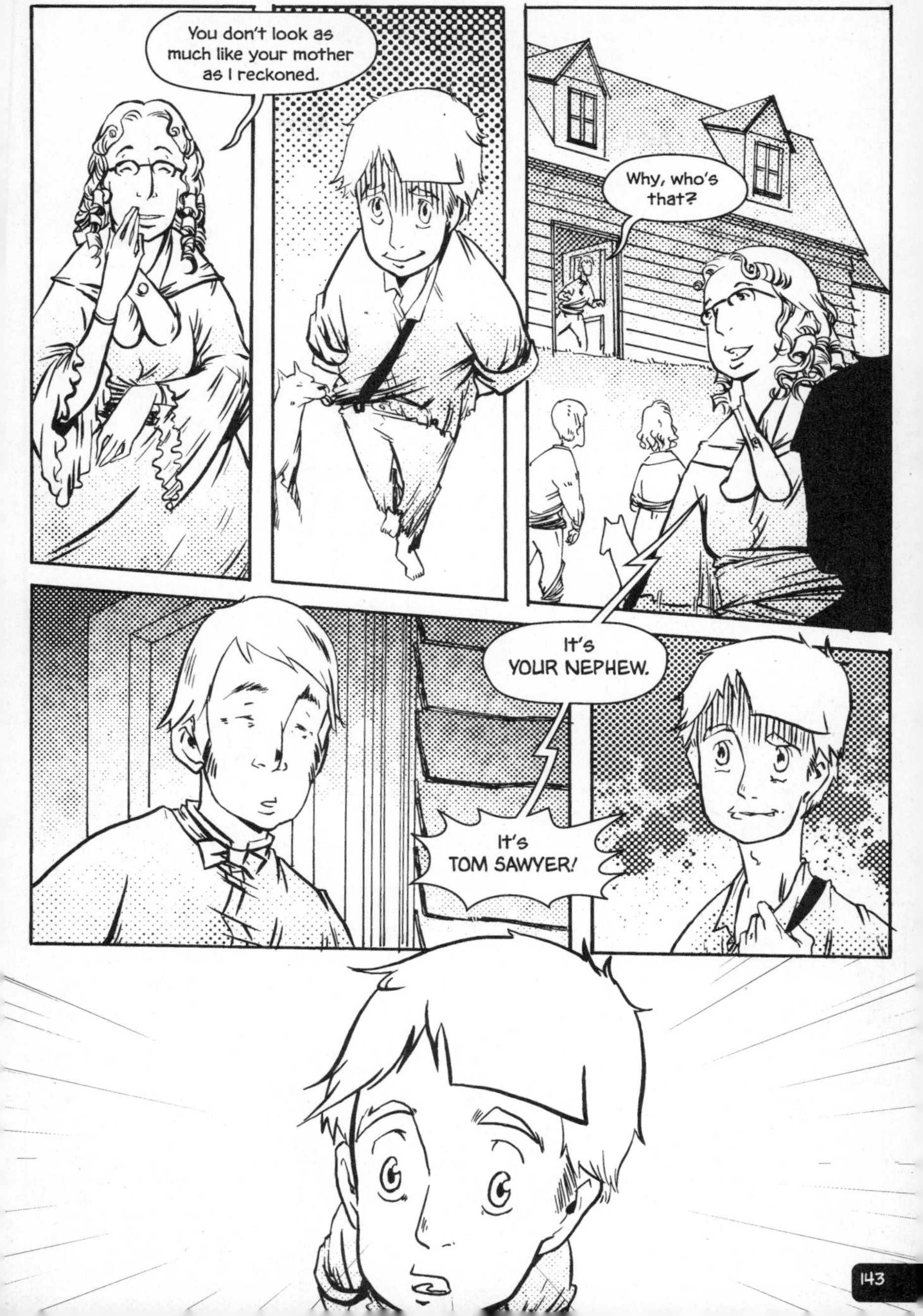

You don't look as much like your mother as I reckoned.
Why, who's that?
It's YOUR NEPHEW.
It's TOM SAWYER!

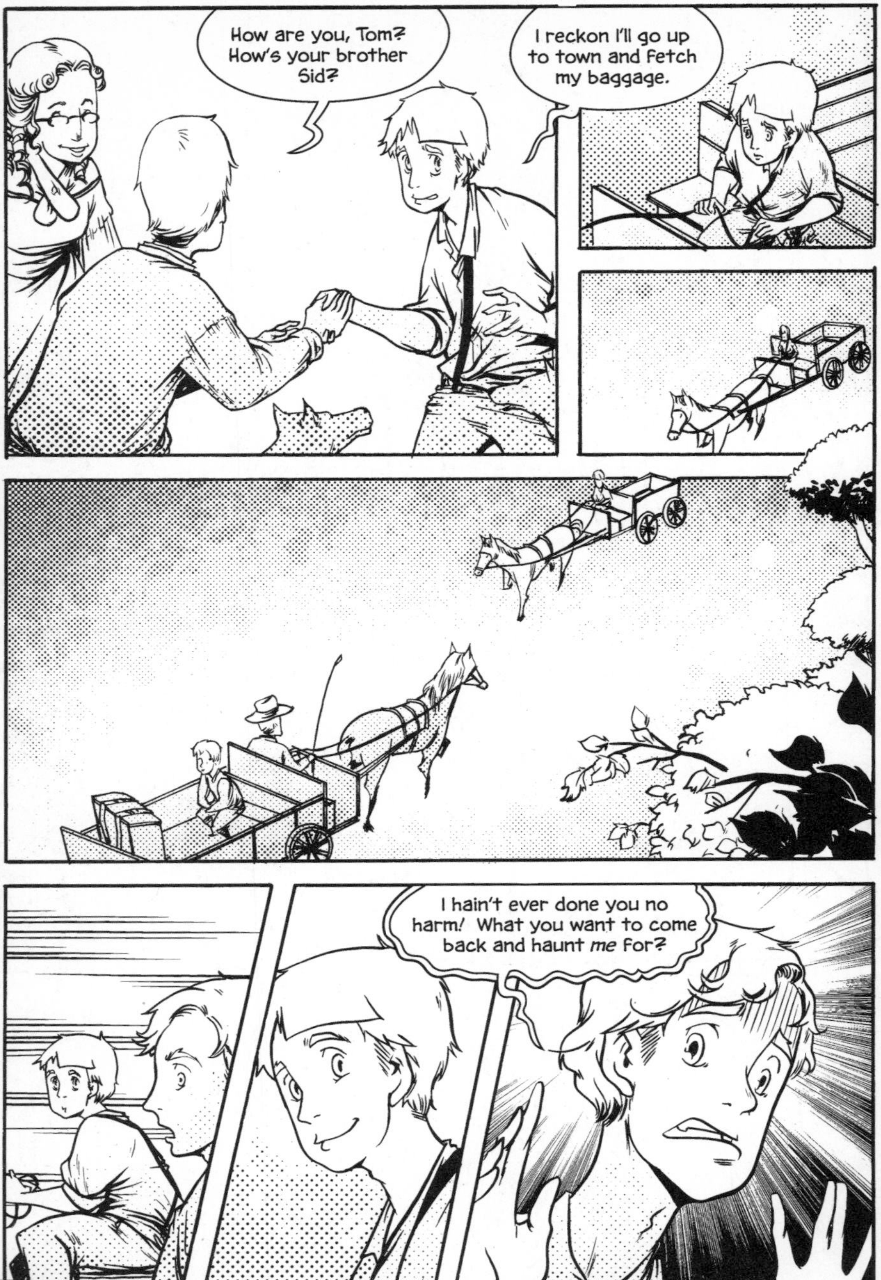
How are you, Tom? How's your brother Sid?
I reckon I'll go up to town and fetch my baggage.
I hain't ever done you no harm! What you want to come back and haunt *me* for?

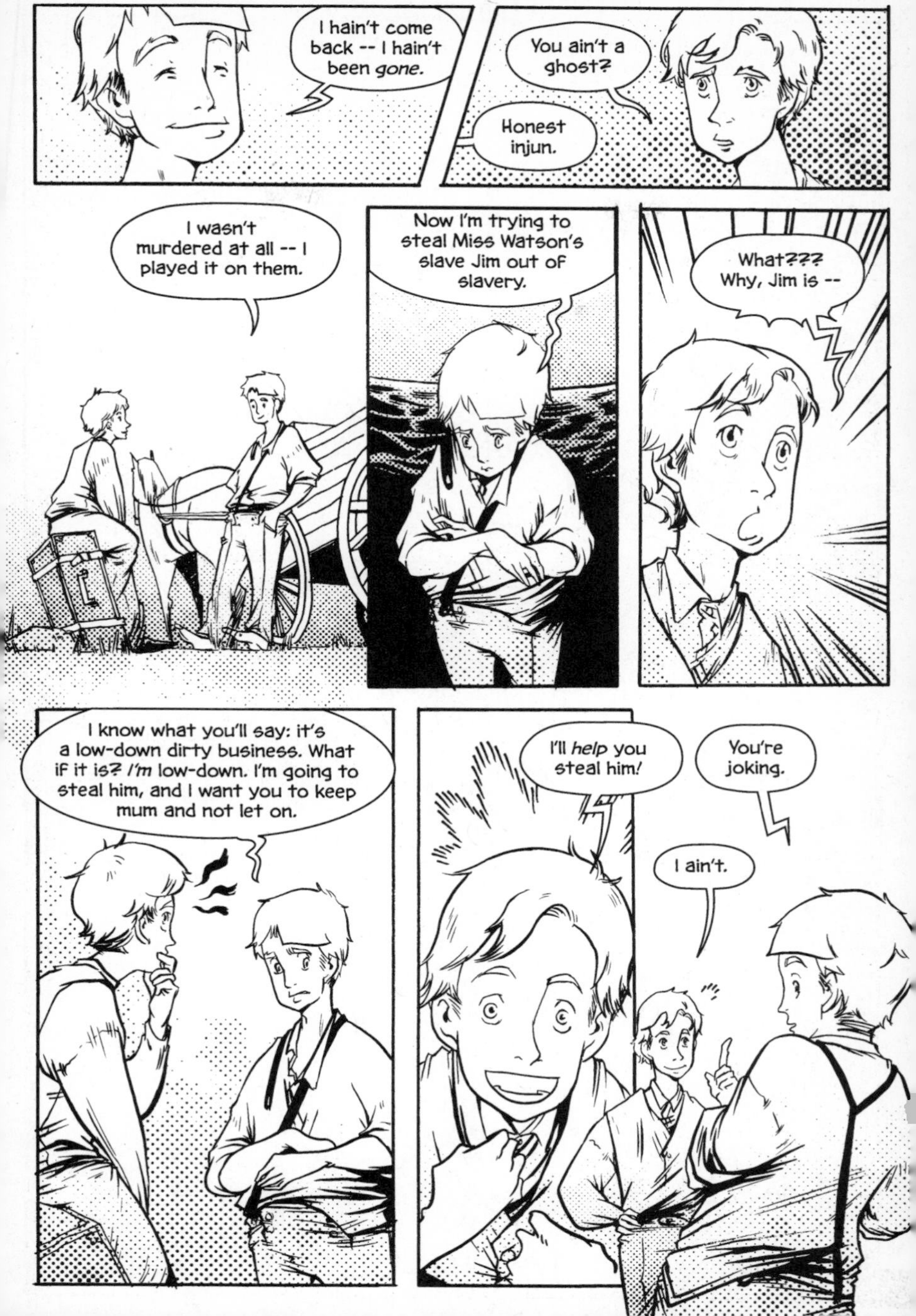
I hain't come back -- I hain't been *gone.*
You ain't a ghost?
Honest injun.
I wasn't murdered at all -- I played it on them.
Now I'm trying to steal Miss Watson's slave Jim out of slavery.
What??? Why, Jim is --
I know what you'll say: it's a low-down dirty business. What if it is? *I'm* low-down. I'm going to steal him, and I want you to keep mum and not let on.
I'll *help* you steal him!
You're joking.
I ain't.

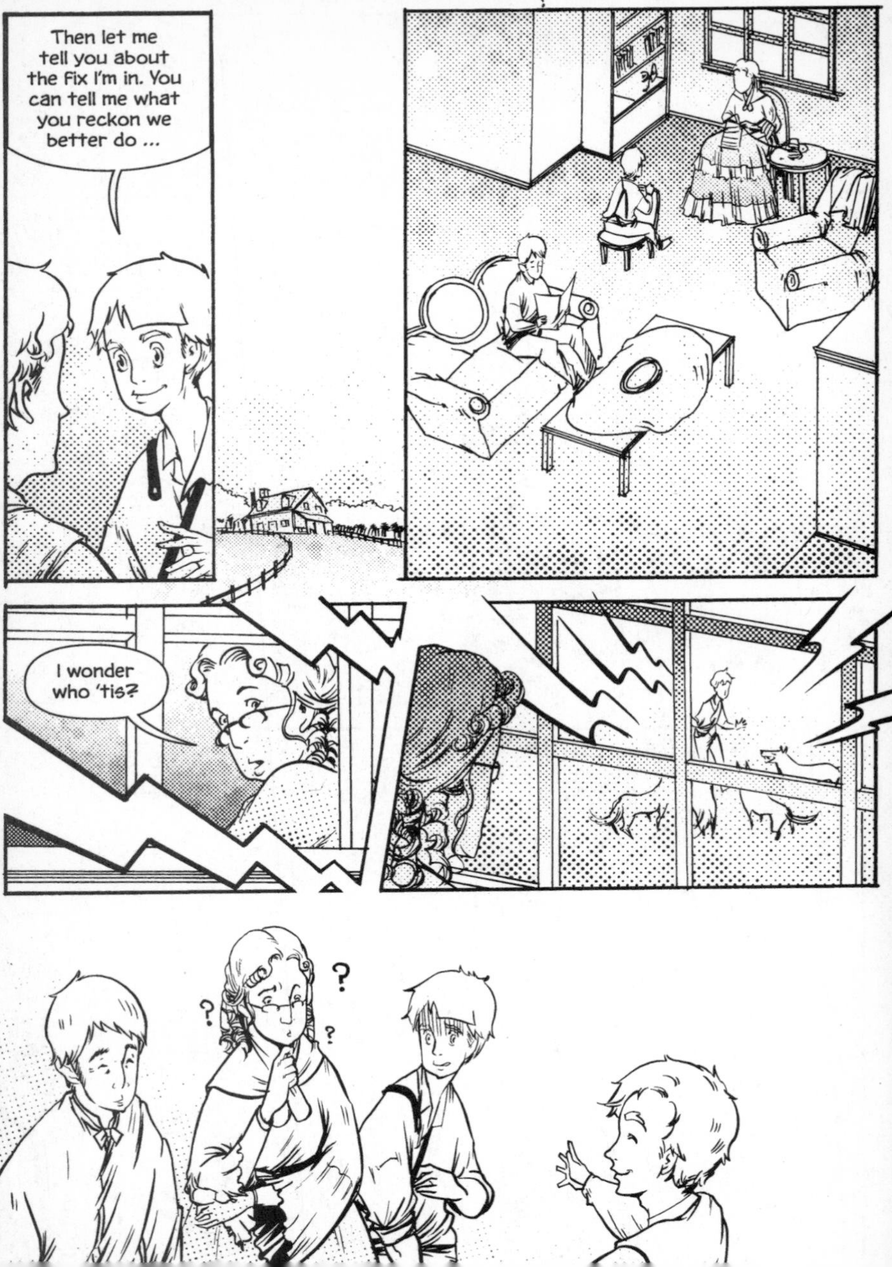
Then let me tell you about the fix I'm in. You can tell me what you reckon we better do ...
I wonder who 'tis?
?
?
?

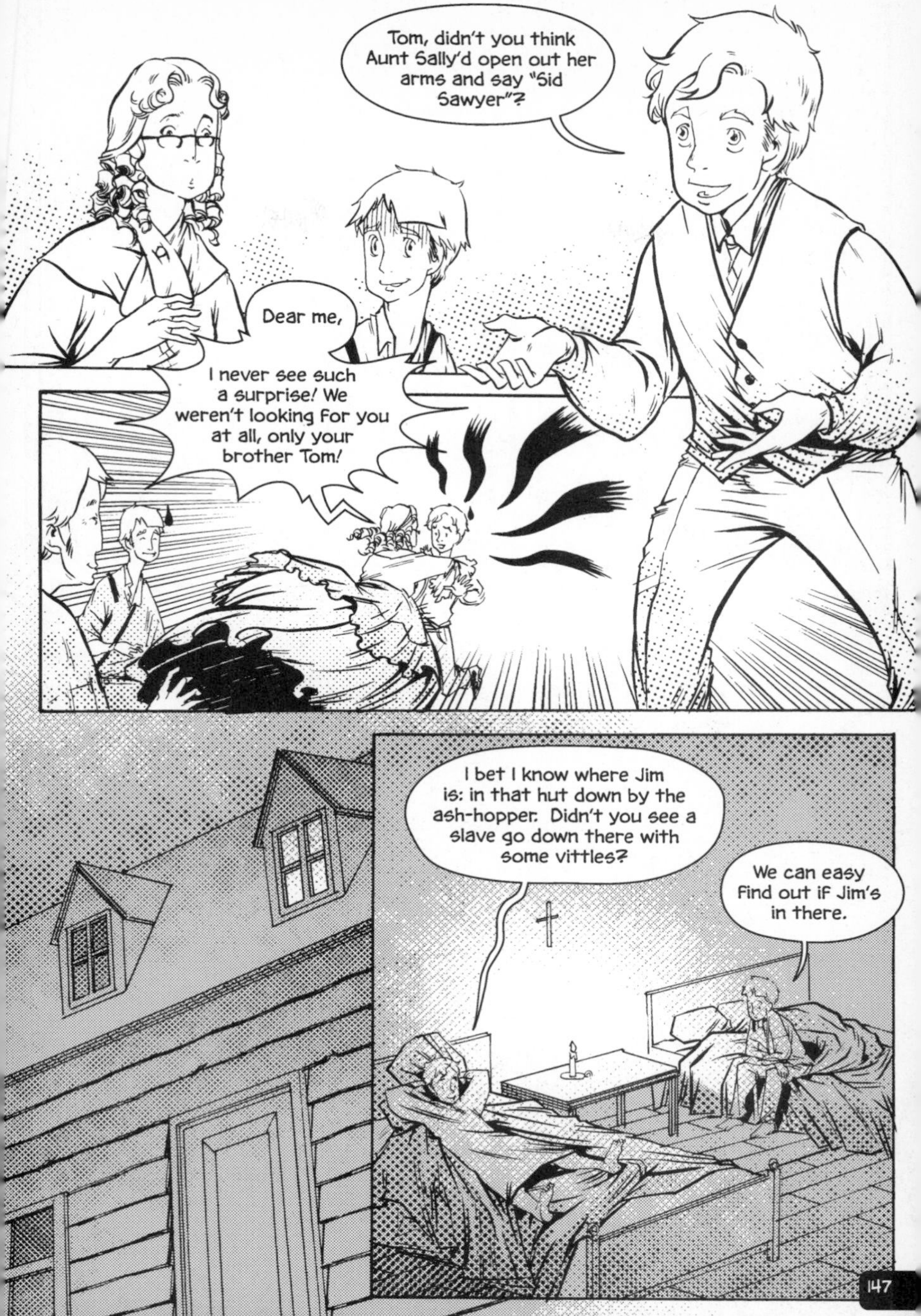
Tom, didn't you think Aunt Sally'd open out her arms and say "Sid Sawyer"?
Dear me,
I never see such a surprise! We weren't looking for you at all, only your brother Tom!
I bet I know where Jim is: in that hut down by the ash-hopper. Didn't you see a slave go down there with some vittles?
We can easy find out if Jim's in there.

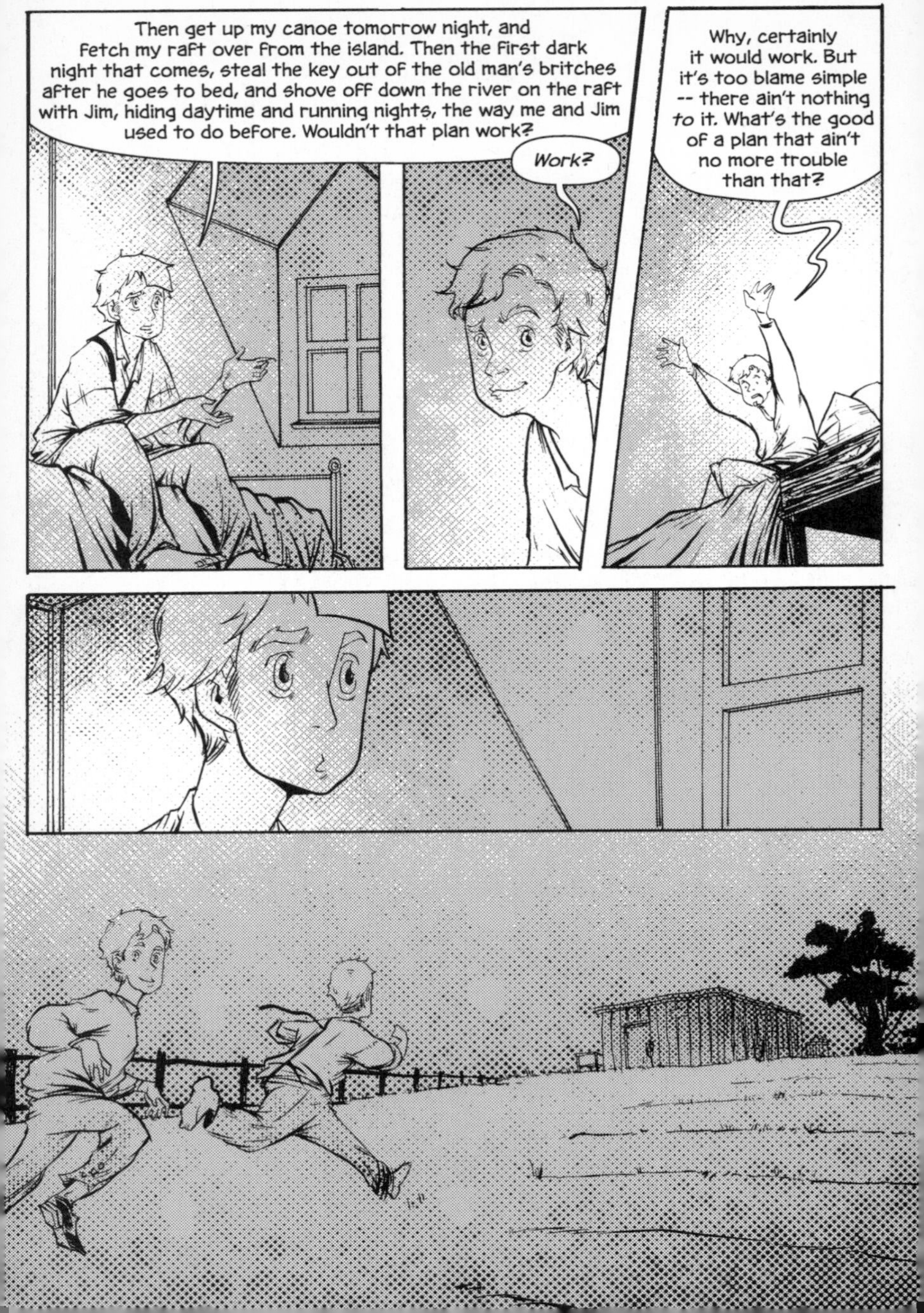
Then get up my canoe tomorrow night, and fetch my raft over from the island. Then the first dark night that comes, steal the key out of the old man's britches after he goes to bed, and shove off down the river on the raft with Jim, hiding daytime and running nights, the way me and Jim used to do before. Wouldn't that plan work?
*Work?*
Why, certainly it would work. But it's too blame simple -- there ain't nothing *to* it. What's the good of a plan that ain't no more trouble than that?

That hole's big enough for Jim to get through if we wrench off the board.

I should *hope* we can find a way that's a little more complicated than *that*, Huck Finn.

We'll *dig* him out. It'll take about a week!

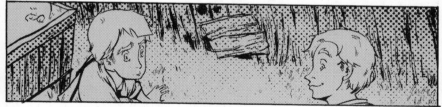

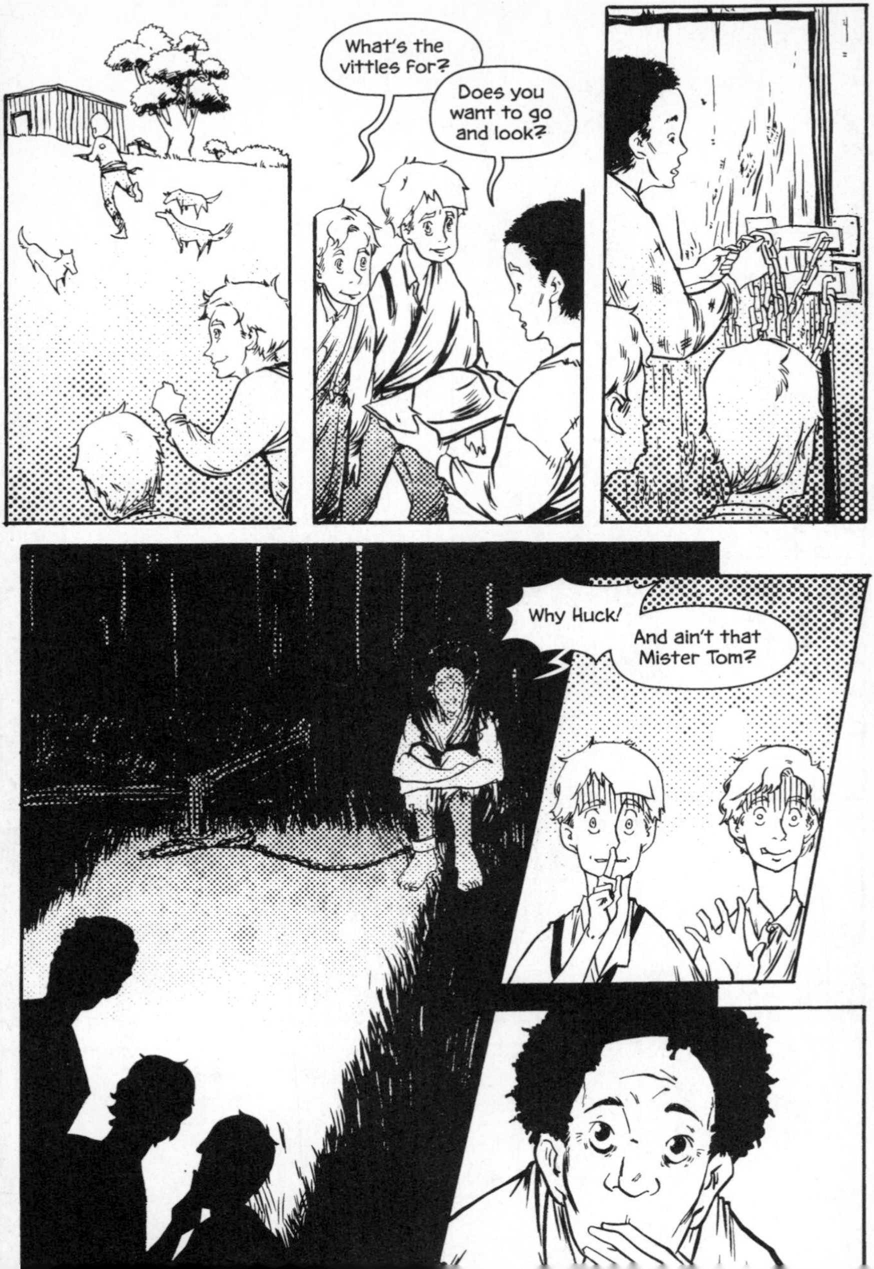
What's the vittles for?
Does you want to go and look?
Why Huck!
And ain't that Mister Tom?

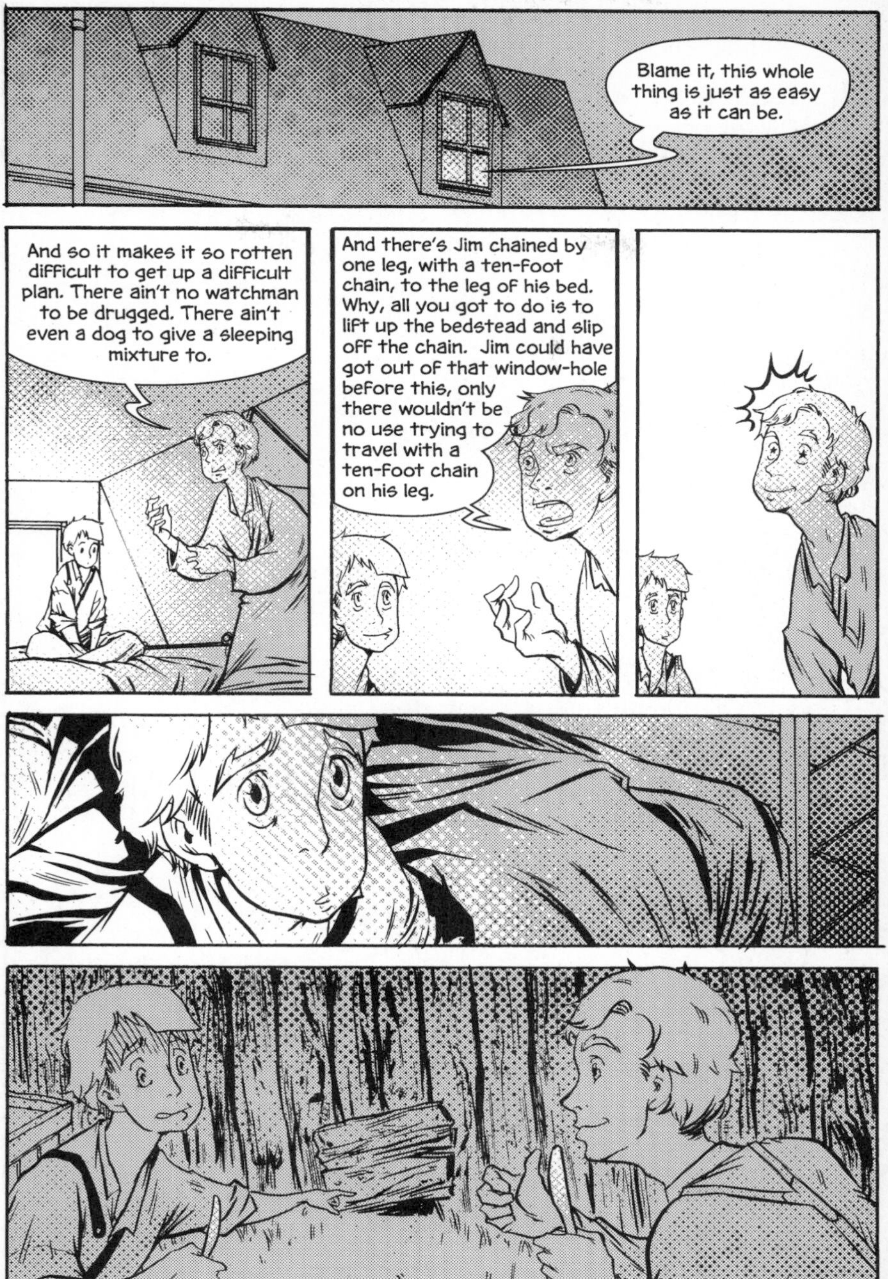
Blame it, this whole thing is just as easy as it can be.
And so it makes it so rotten difficult to get up a difficult plan. There ain't no watchman to be drugged. There ain't even a dog to give a sleeping mixture to.
And there's Jim chained by one leg, with a ten-foot chain, to the leg of his bed. Why, all you got to do is to lift up the bedstead and slip off the chain. Jim could have got out of that window-hole before this, only there wouldn't be no use trying to travel with a ten-foot chain on his leg.

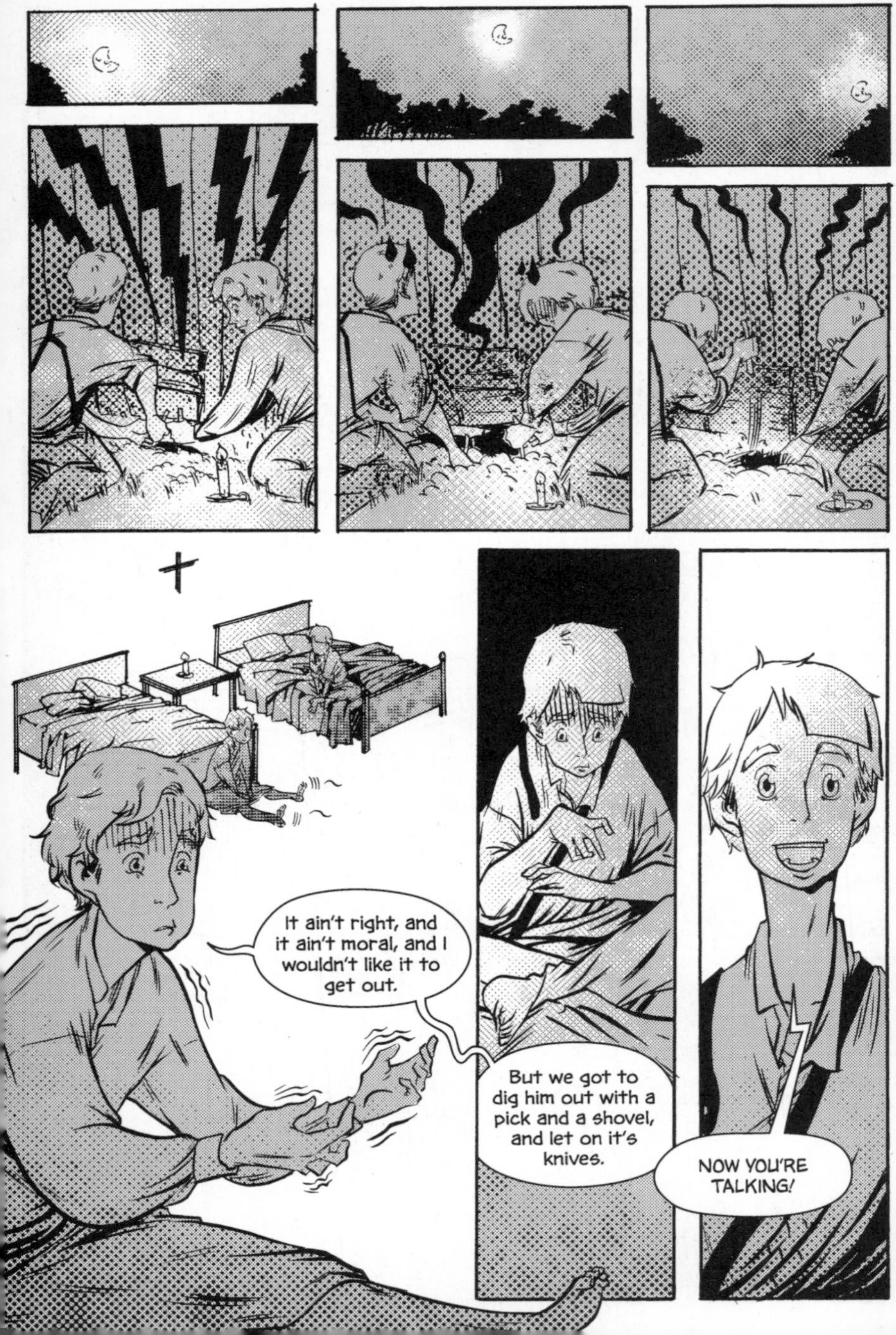
It ain't right, and it ain't moral, and I wouldn't like it to get out.
But we got to dig him out with a pick and a shovel, and let on it's knives.
NOW YOU'RE TALKING!

ZZZZZZ
ZZZZZZZZ

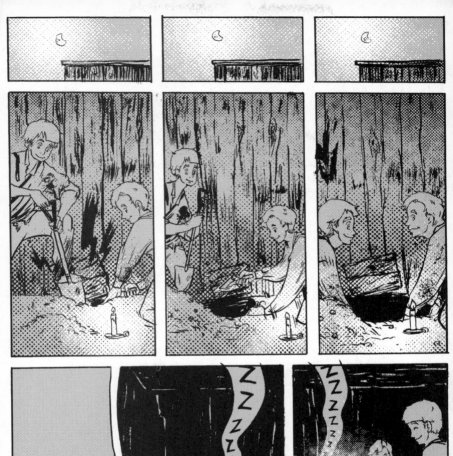

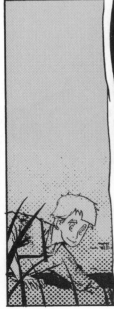

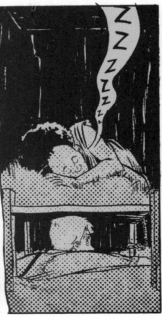

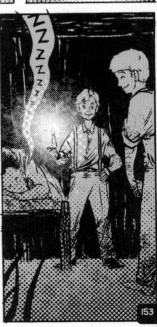

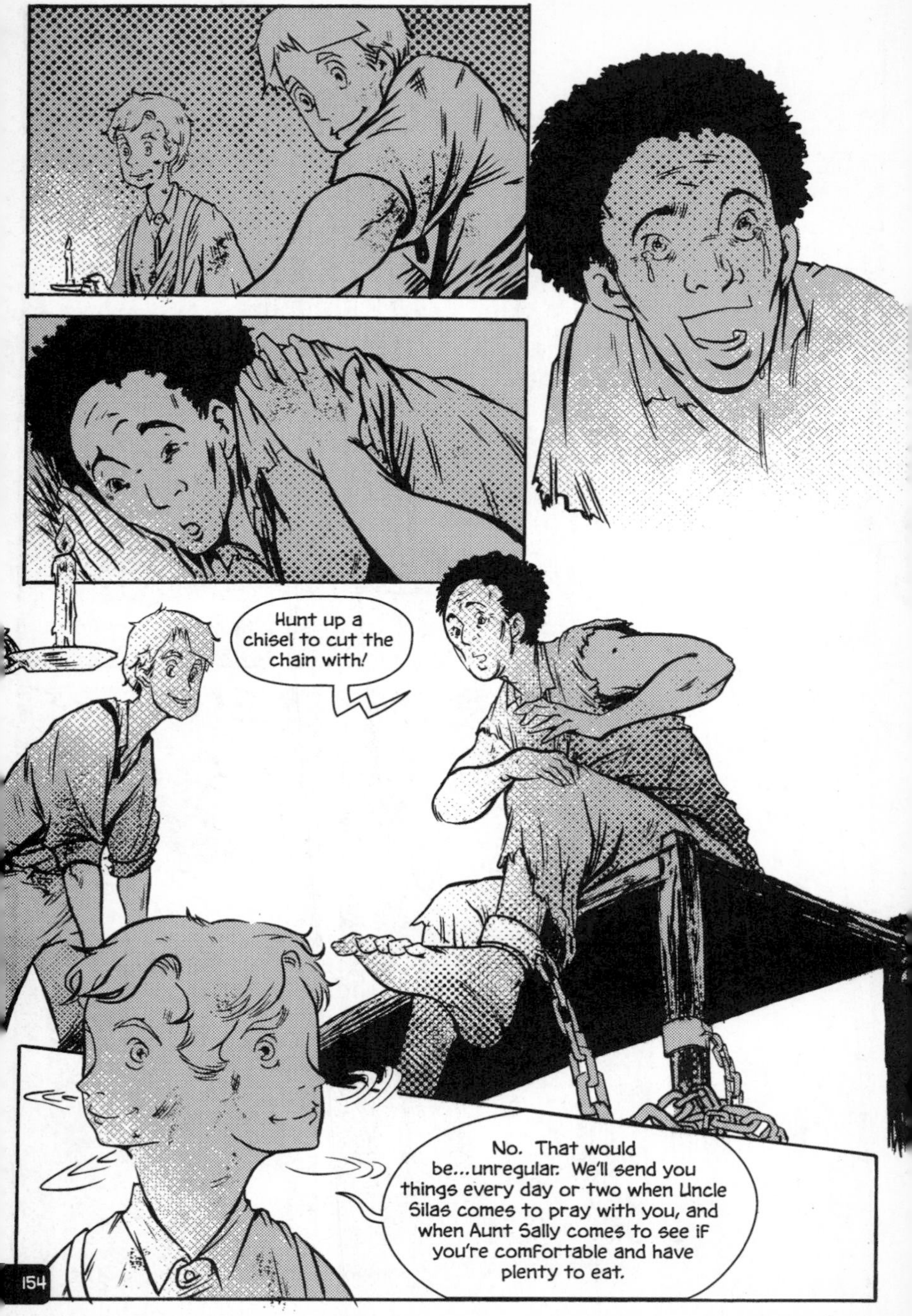
Hunt up a chisel to cut the chain with!
No. That would be...unregular. We'll send you things every day or two when Uncle Silas comes to pray with you, and when Aunt Sally comes to see if you're comfortable and have plenty to eat.

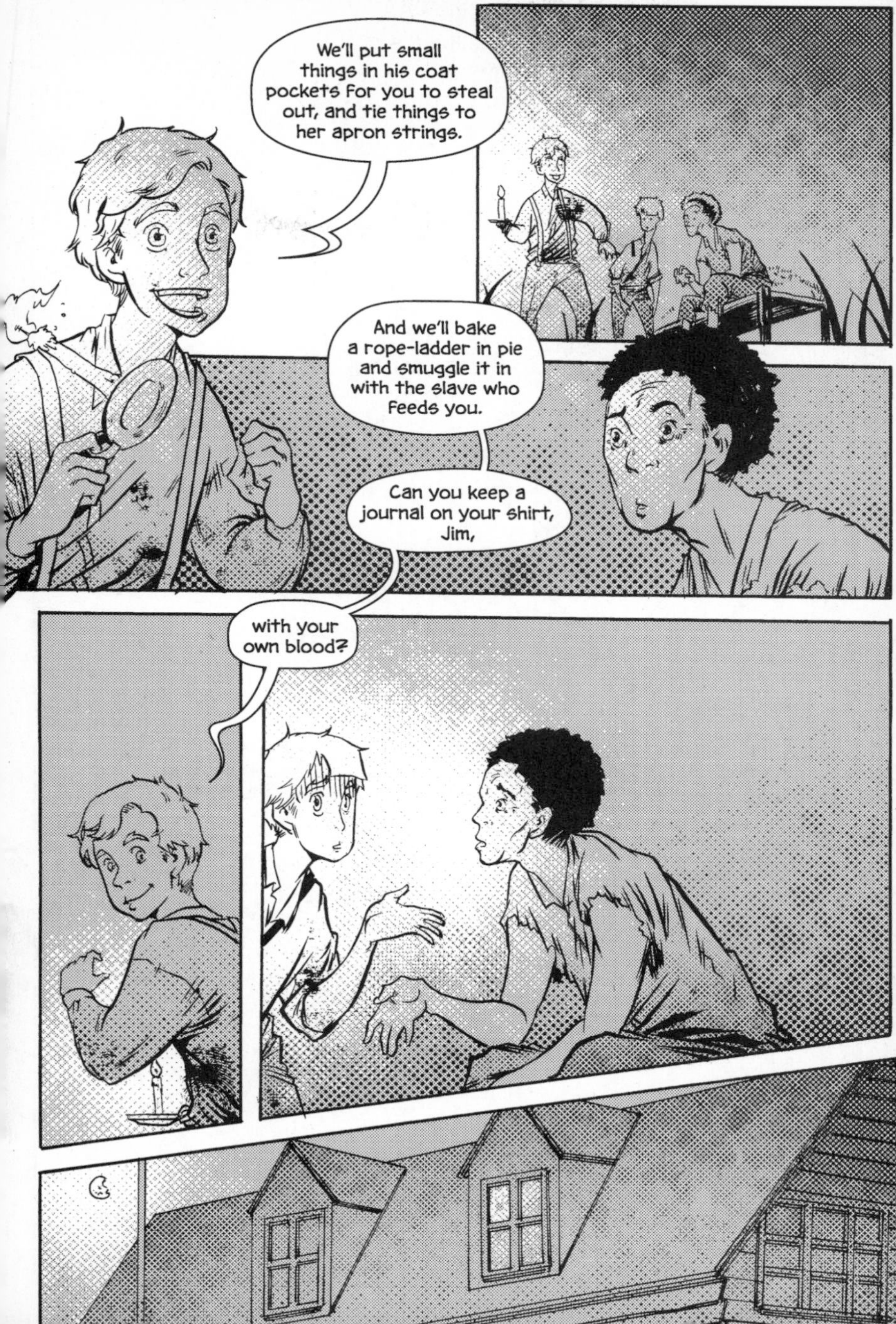
We'll put small things in his coat pockets for you to steal out, and tie things to her apron strings.
And we'll bake a rope-ladder in pie and smuggle it in with the slave who feeds you.
Can you keep a journal on your shirt, Jim,
with your own blood?

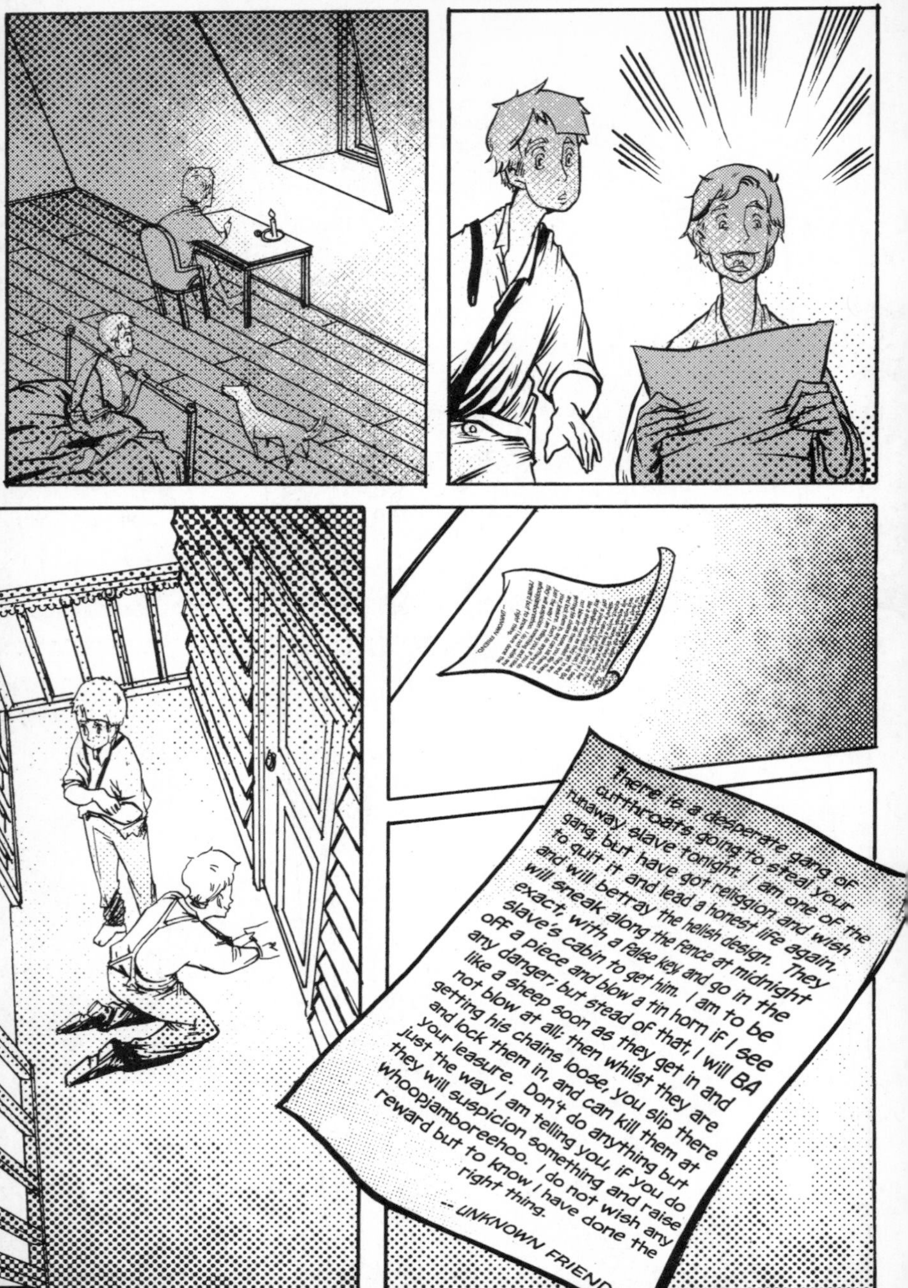
There is a desperate gang of
cutthroats going to steal your
runaway slave tonight. I am one of the
gang, but have got religgion and wish
to quit it and lead a honest life again,
and will betray the helish design. They
will sneak along the fence at midnight
exact, with a false key, and go in the
slave's cabin to get him. I am to be
off a piece and blow a tin horn if I see
any danger; but stead of that, I will BA
like a sheep soon as they get in and
not blow at all; then whilst they are
getting his chains loose, you slip there
and lock them in, and can kill them at
your leasure. Don't do anything but
just the way I am telling you, if you do
they will suspicion something and raise
whoopjamboreehoo. I do not wish any
reward but to know I have done the
right thing.
-- UNKNOWN FRIEND.

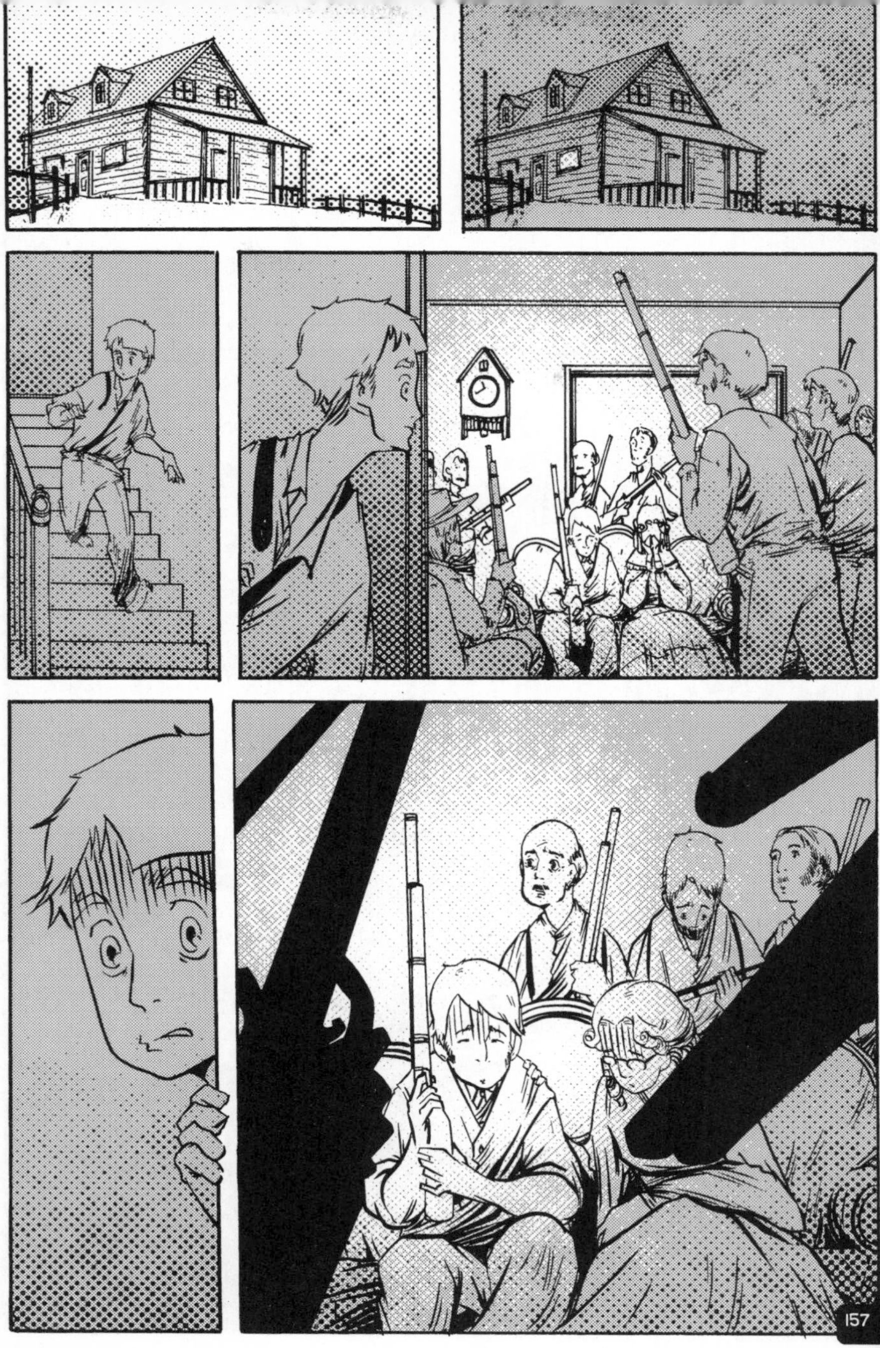

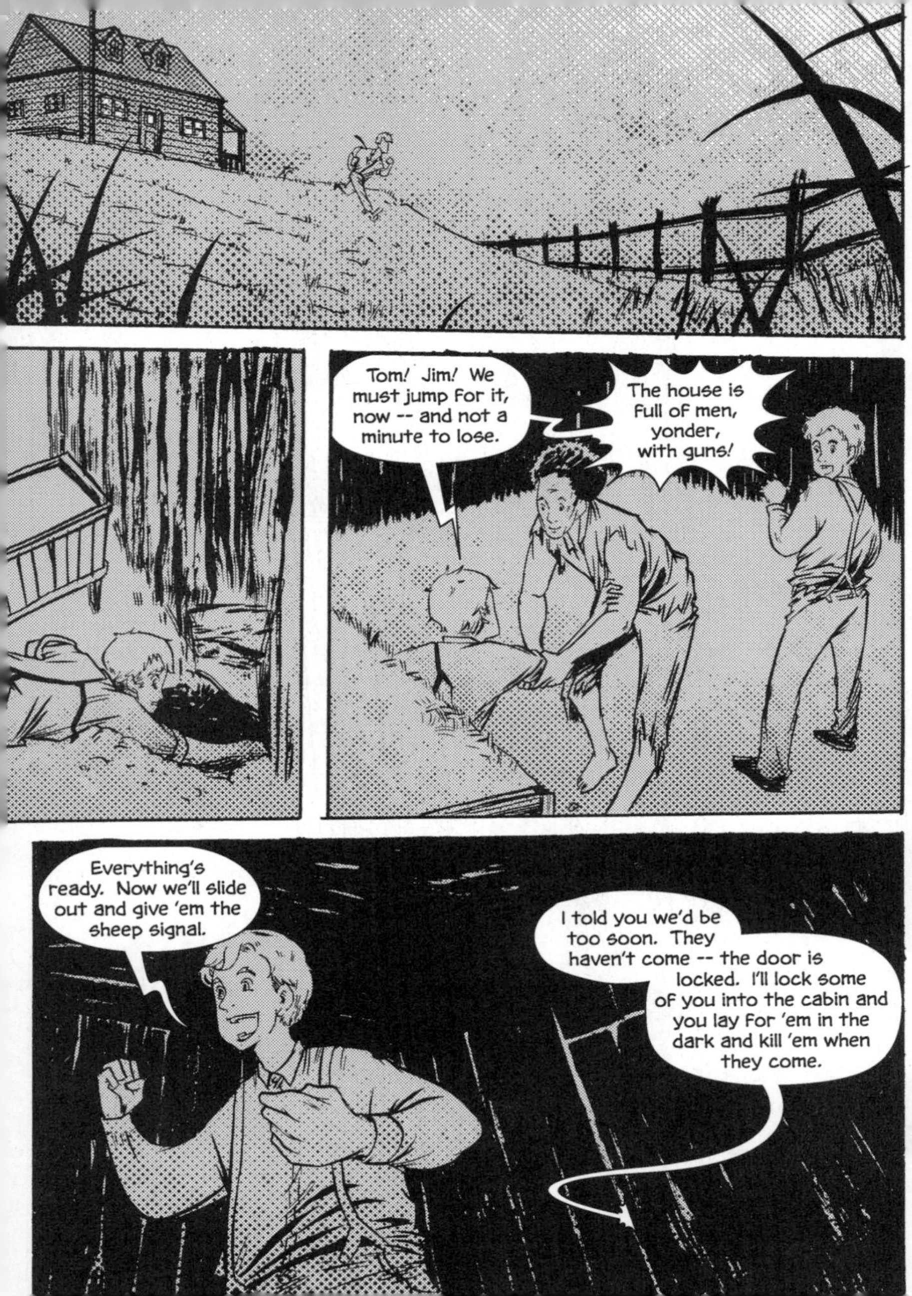
Tom! Jim! We must jump for it, now -- and not a minute to lose.
The house is full of men, yonder, with guns!
Everything's ready. Now we'll slide out and give 'em the sheep signal.
I told you we'd be too soon. They haven't come -- the door is locked. I'll lock some of you into the cabin and you lay for 'em in the dark and kill 'em when they come.

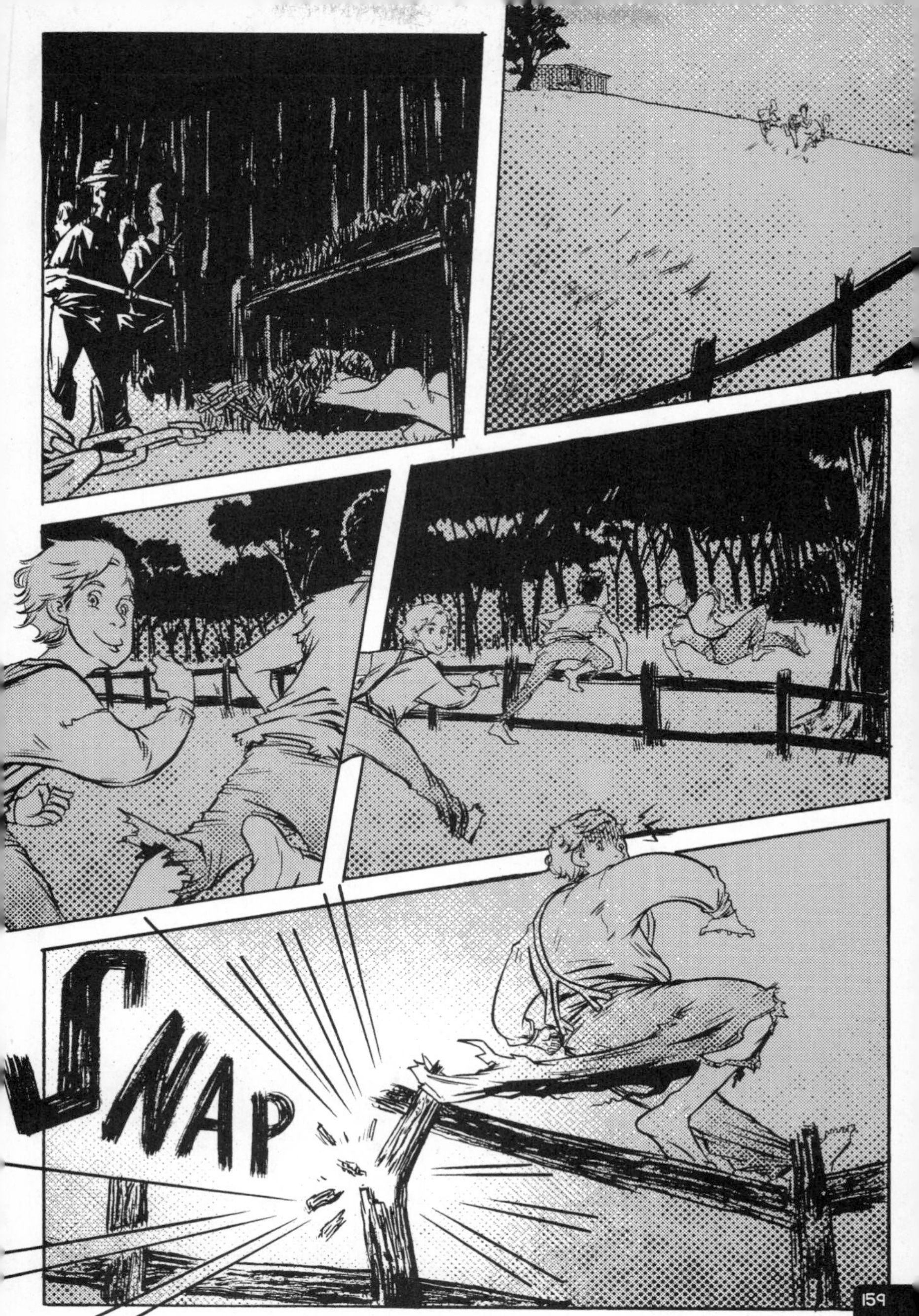
SNAP

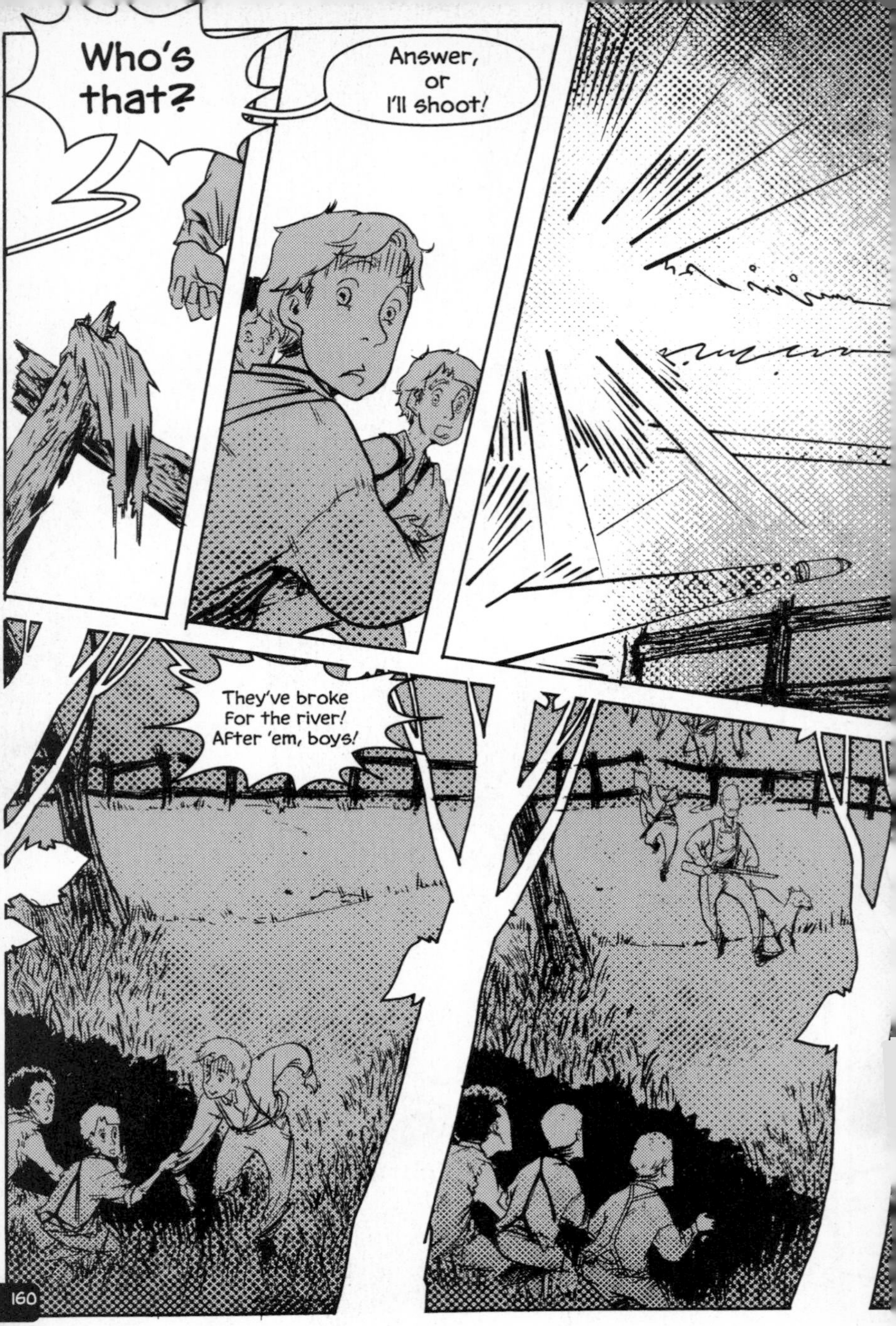
Who's that?
Answer, or I'll shoot!
They've broke for the river! After 'em, boys!

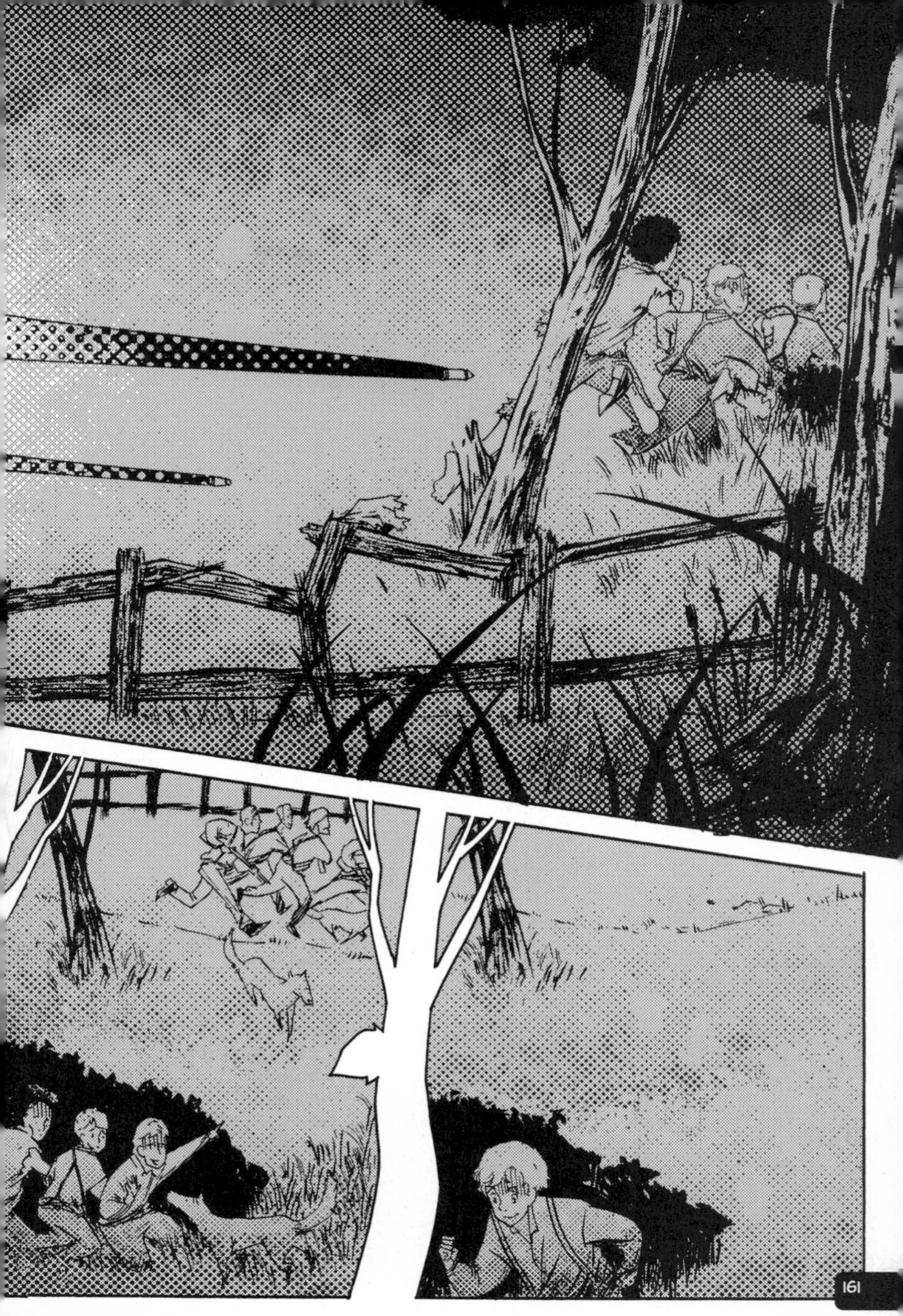

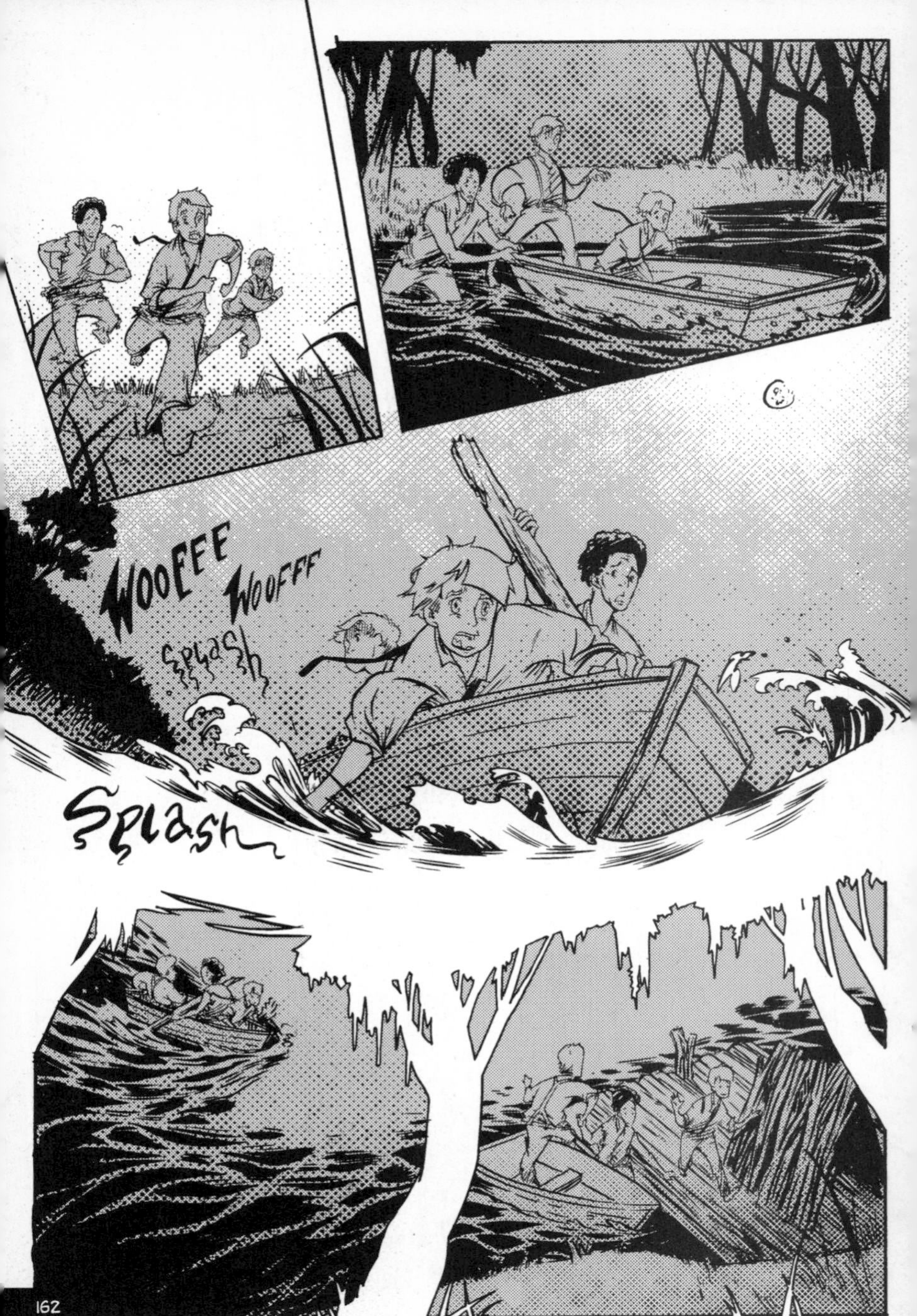
WOOFFF
WOOFFF
Splash
Splash

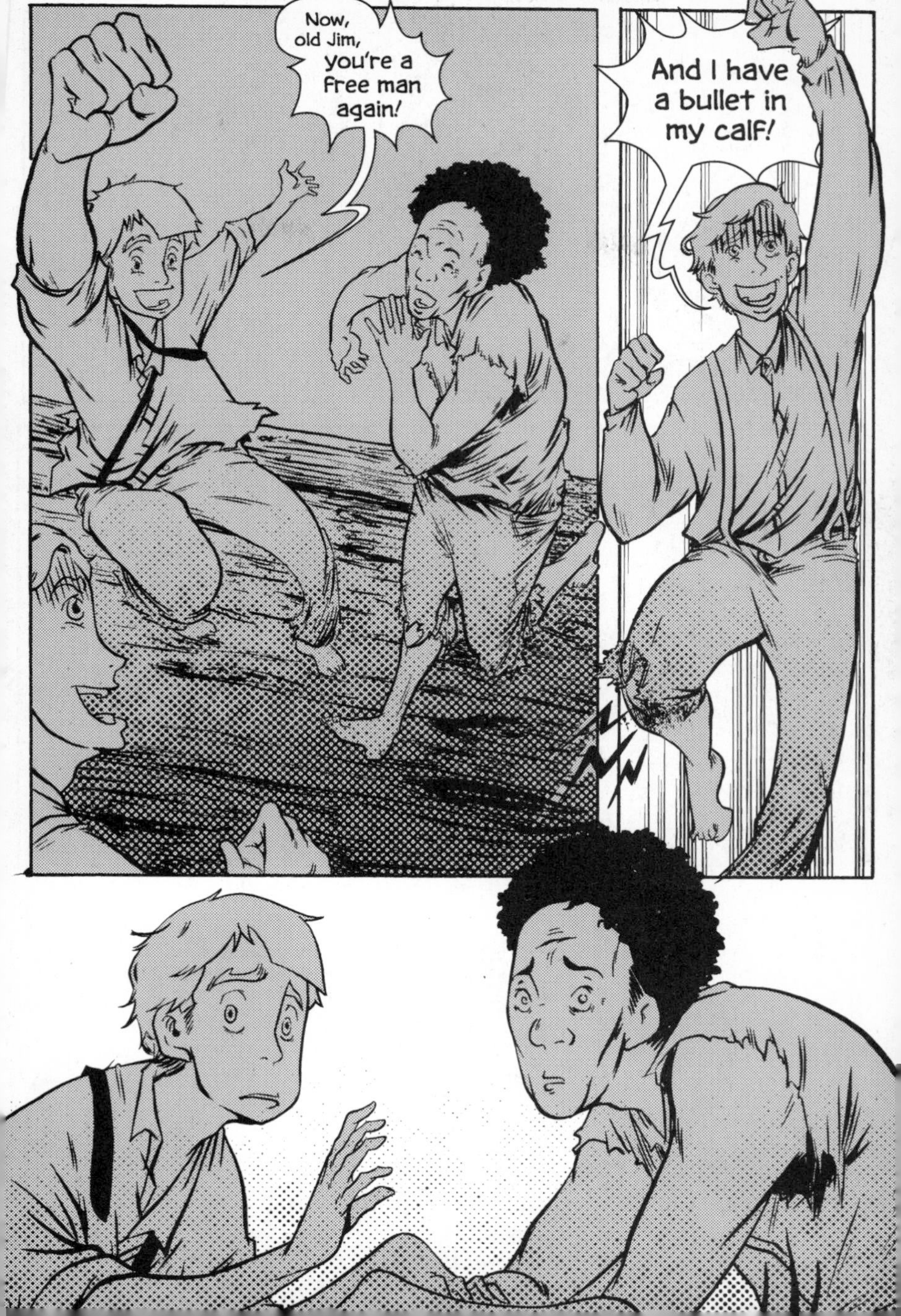
Now, old Jim, you're a free man again!
And I have a bullet in my calf!

It's bleeding.

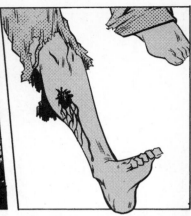

Gimme the rags, I can do it myself.

Boys, we done it elegant. Man the sweeps. Man the sweeps!

I don't budge a step out of this place without a doctor.

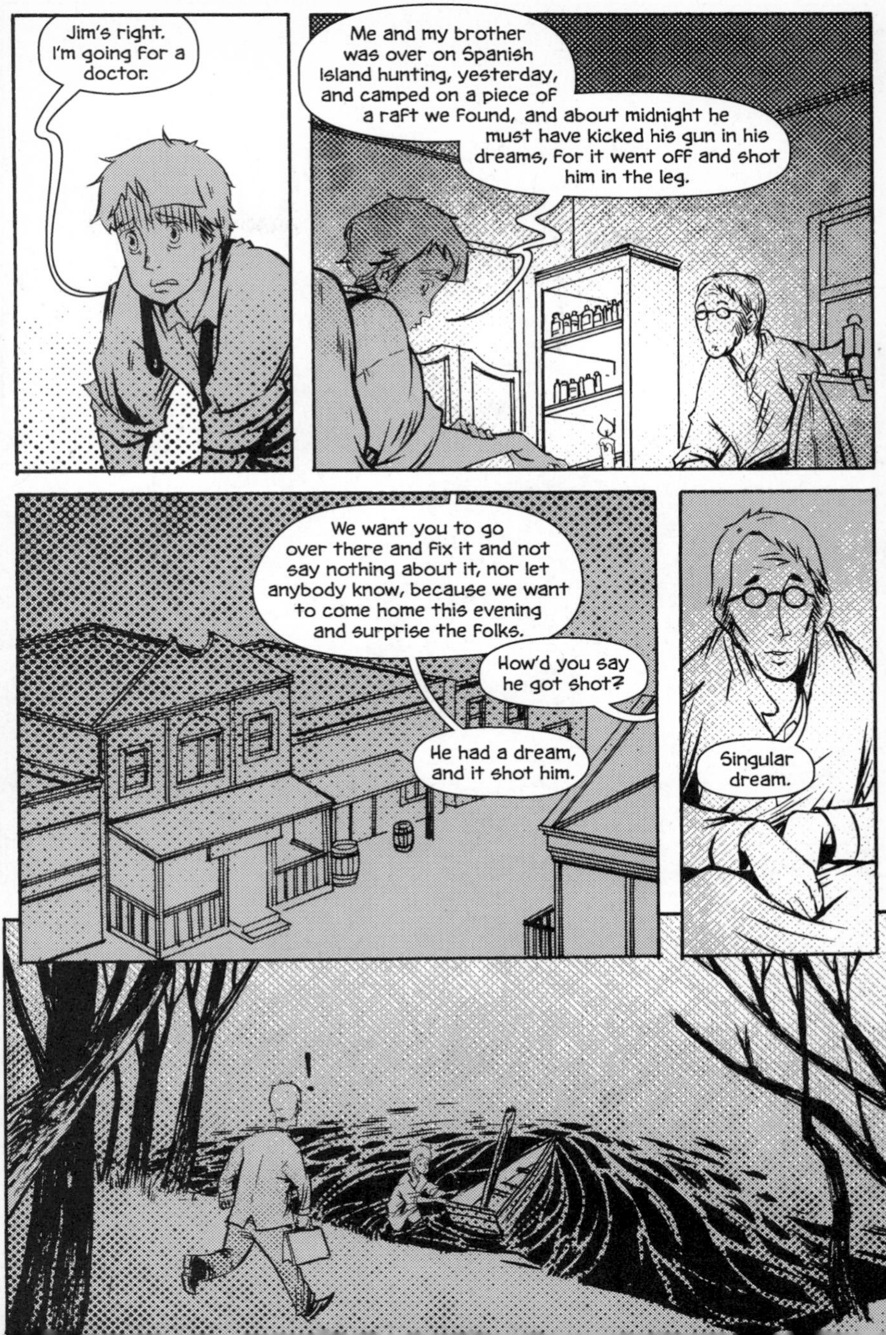

Jim's right. I'm going for a doctor.
Me and my brother was over on Spanish Island hunting, yesterday, and camped on a piece of a raft we found, and about midnight he must have kicked his gun in his dreams, for it went off and shot him in the leg.
We want you to go over there and fix it and not say nothing about it, nor let anybody know, because we want to come home this evening and surprise the folks.
How'd you say he got shot?
He had a dream, and it shot him.
Singular dream.
!

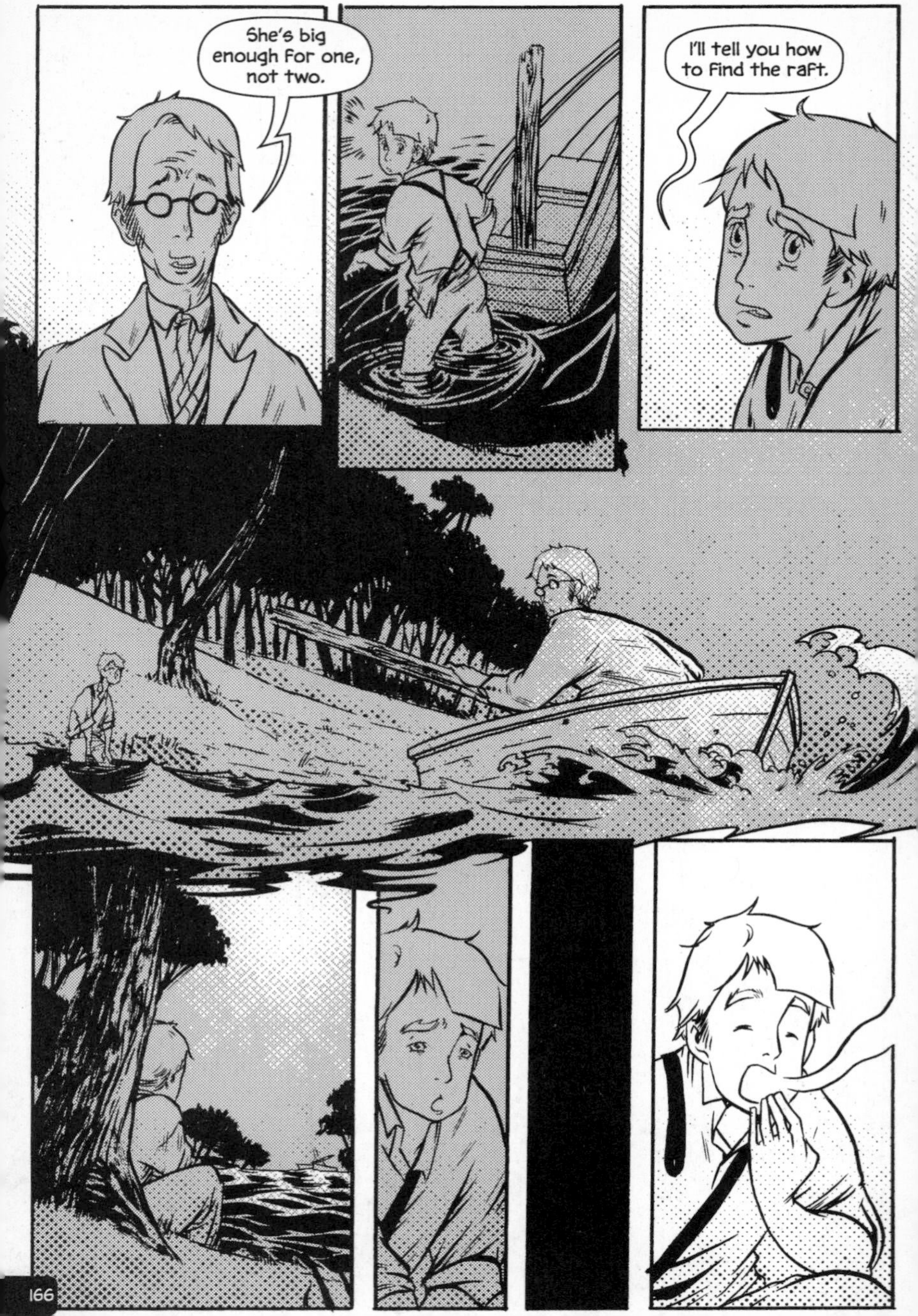
She's big enough for one, not two.
I'll tell you how to find the raft.

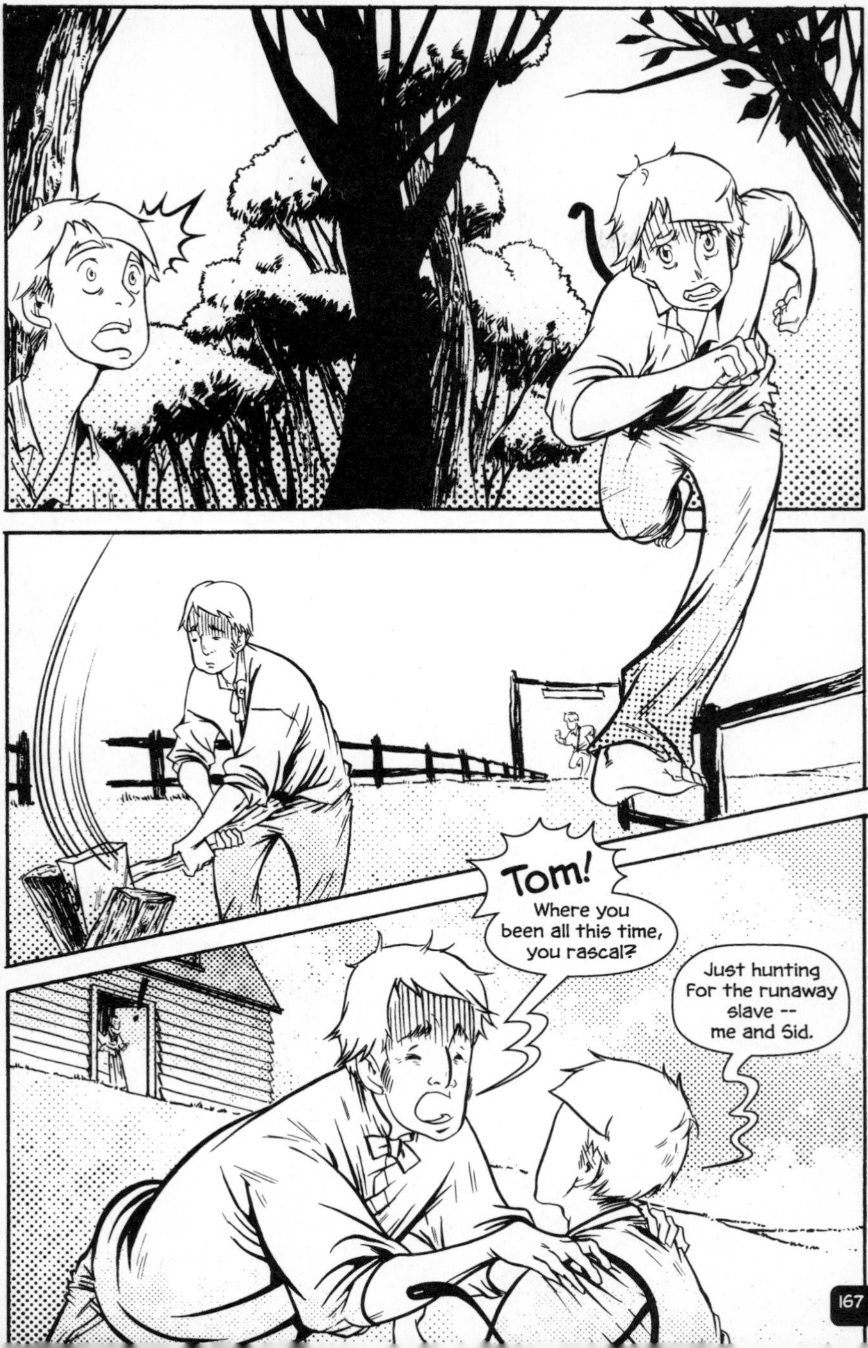
Tom! Where you been all this time, you rascal?
Just hunting for the runaway slave -- me and Sid.

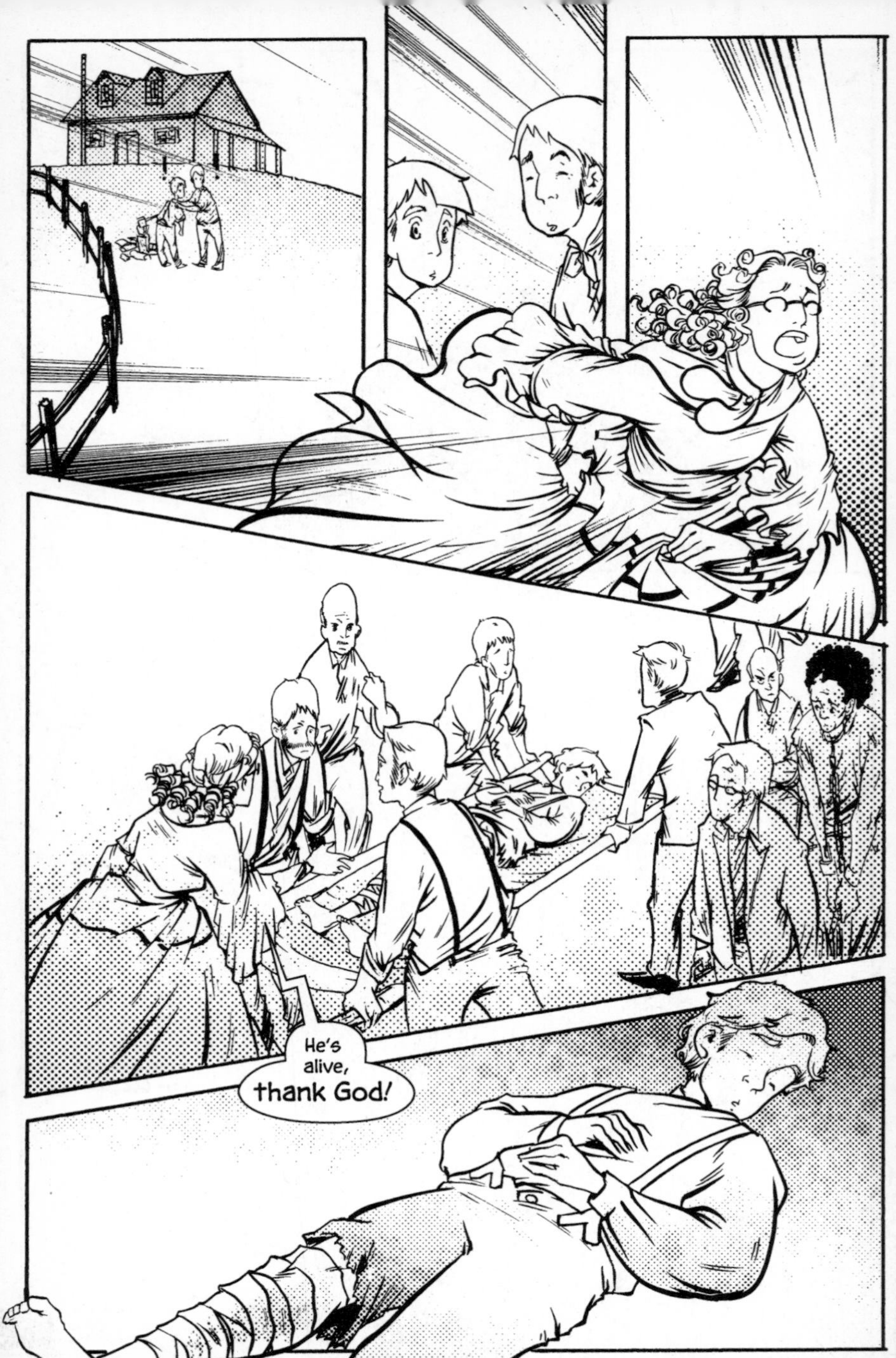
He's
alive,
thank God!

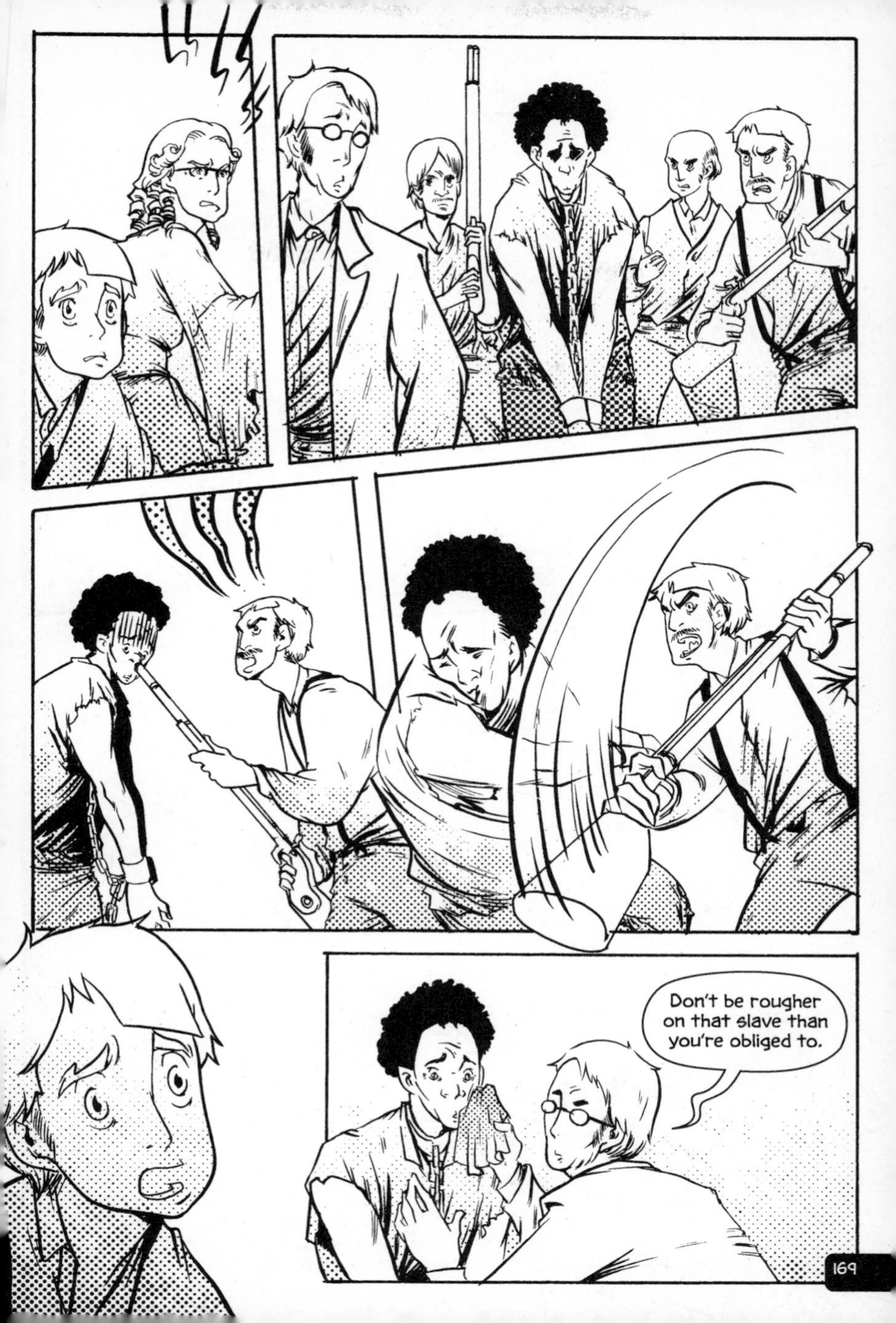
Don't be rougher
on that slave than
you're obliged to.

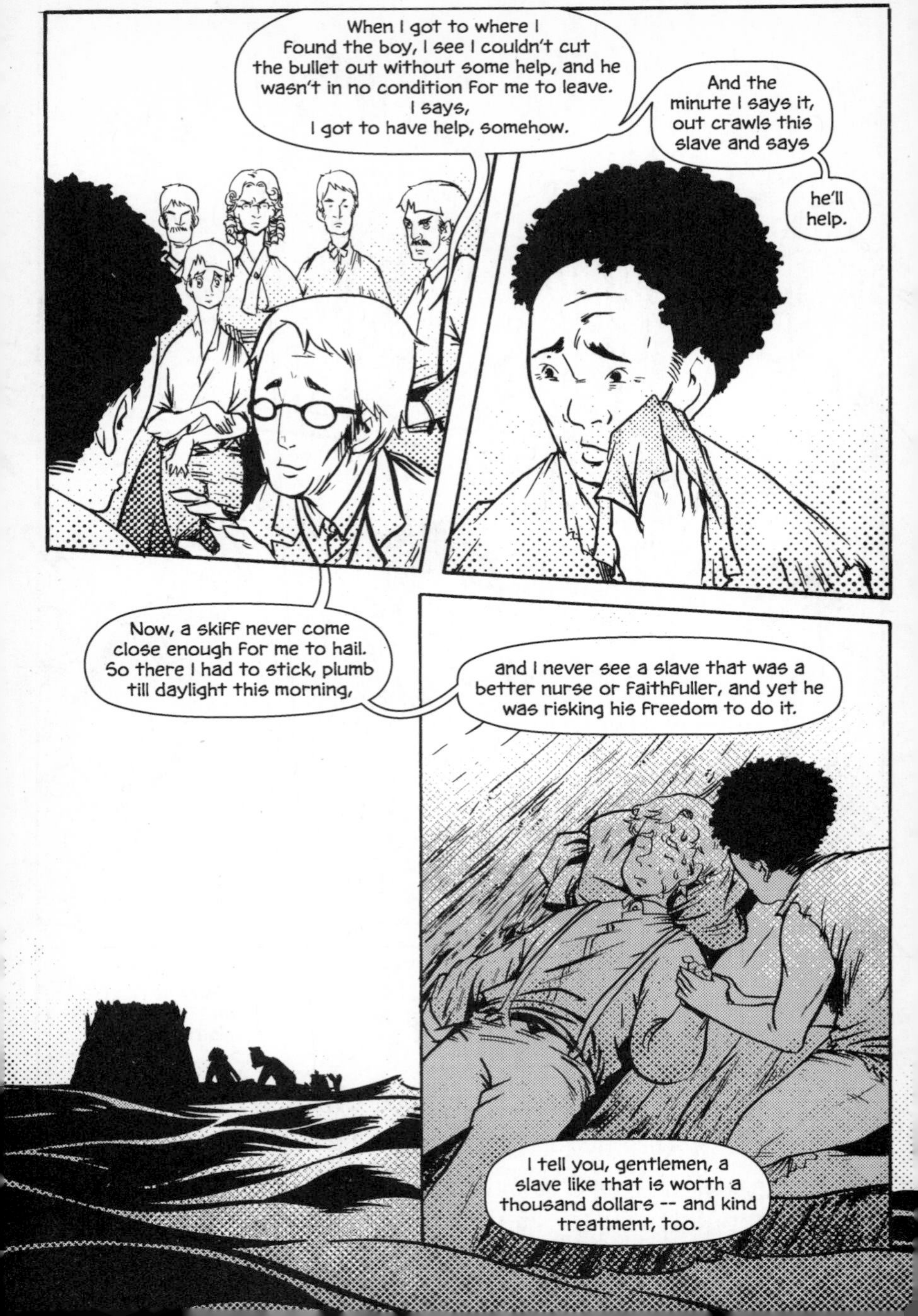
When I got to where I found the boy, I see I couldn't cut the bullet out without some help, and he wasn't in no condition for me to leave. I says, I got to have help, somehow.
And the minute I says it, out crawls this slave and says
he'll help.
Now, a skiff never come close enough for me to hail. So there I had to stick, plumb till daylight this morning,
and I never see a slave that was a better nurse or faithfuller, and yet he was risking his freedom to do it.
I tell you, gentlemen, a slave like that is worth a thousand dollars -- and kind treatment, too.

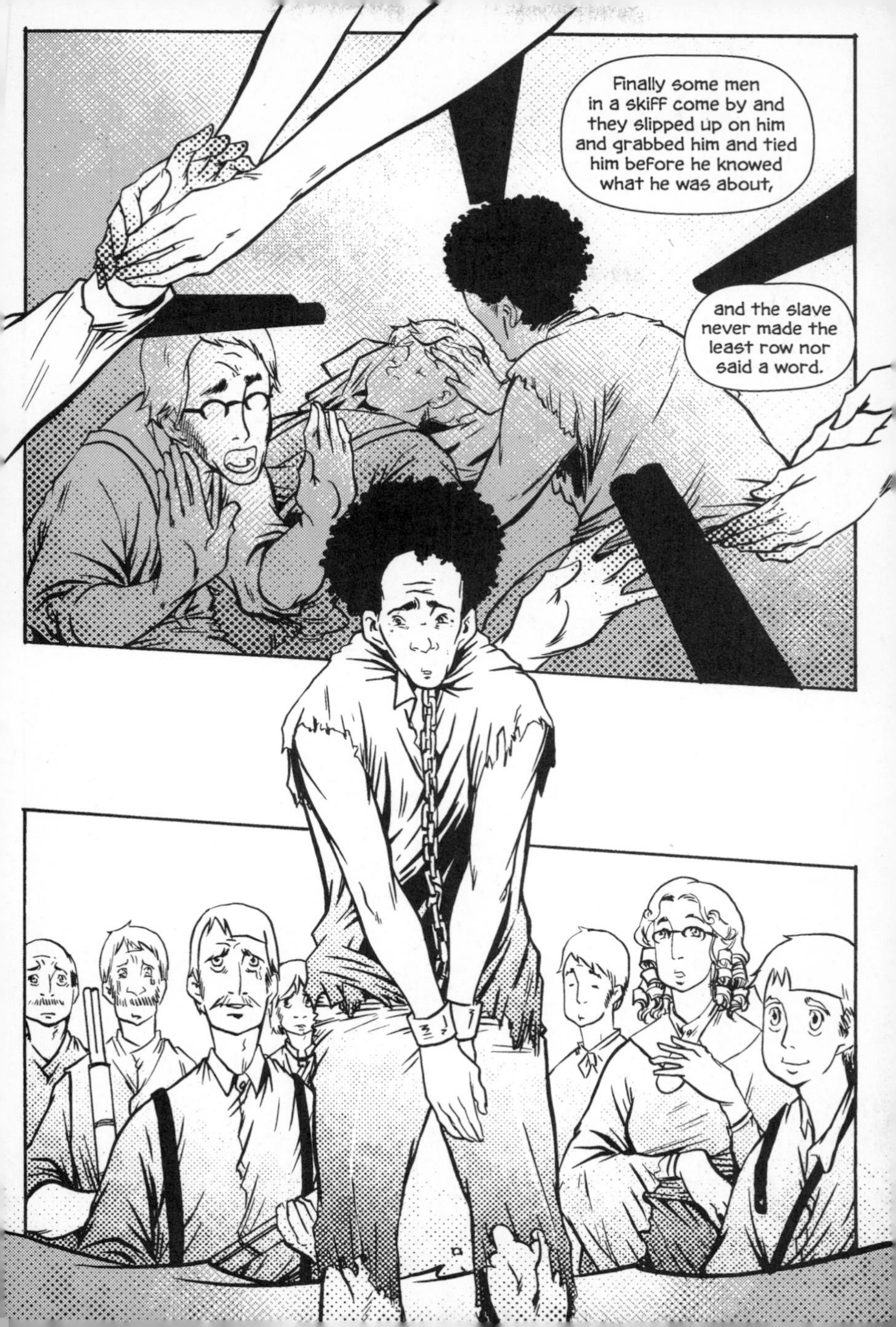
Finally some men in a skiff come by and they slipped up on him and grabbed him and tied him before he knowed what he was about,
and the slave never made the least row nor said a word.

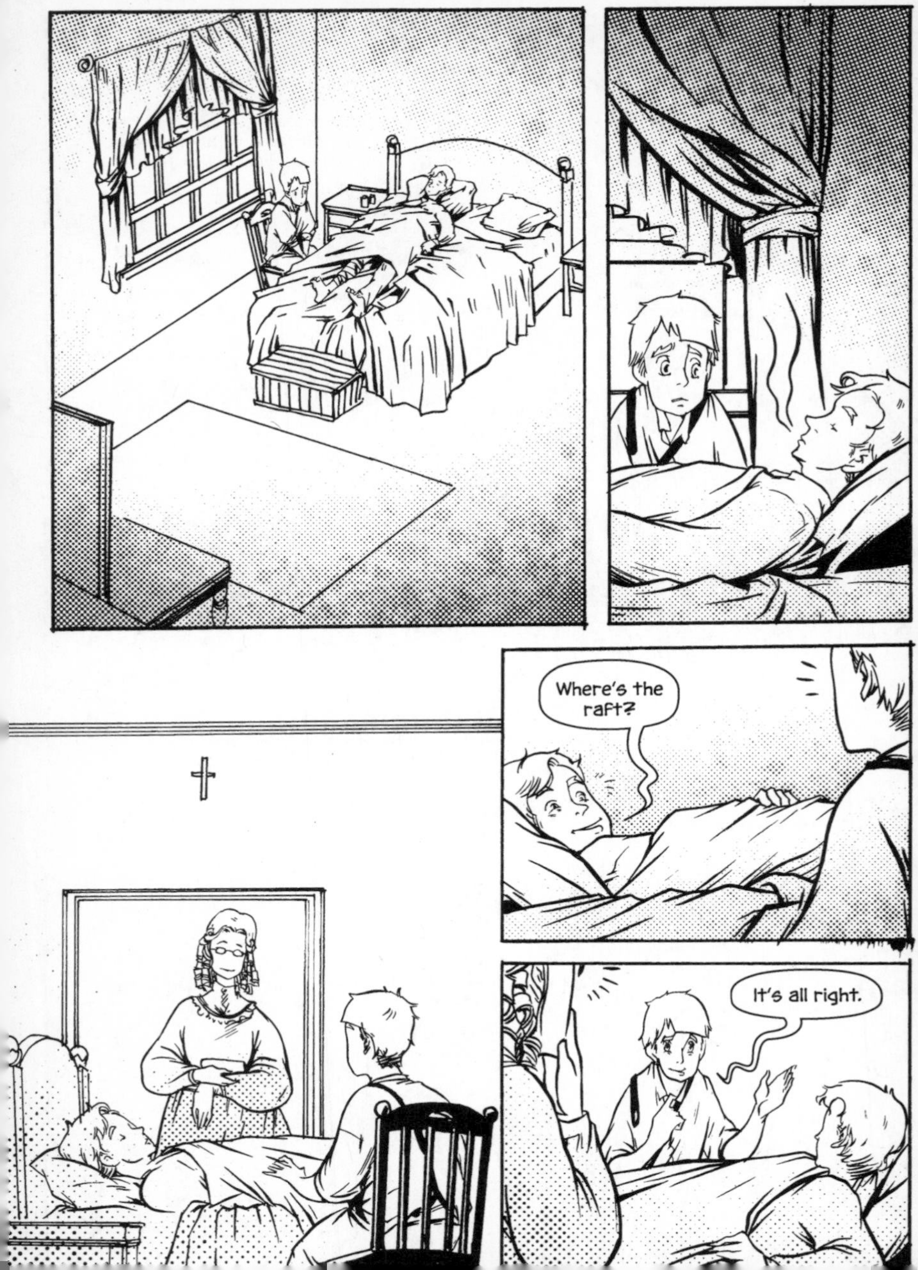

Where's the raft?
It's all right.

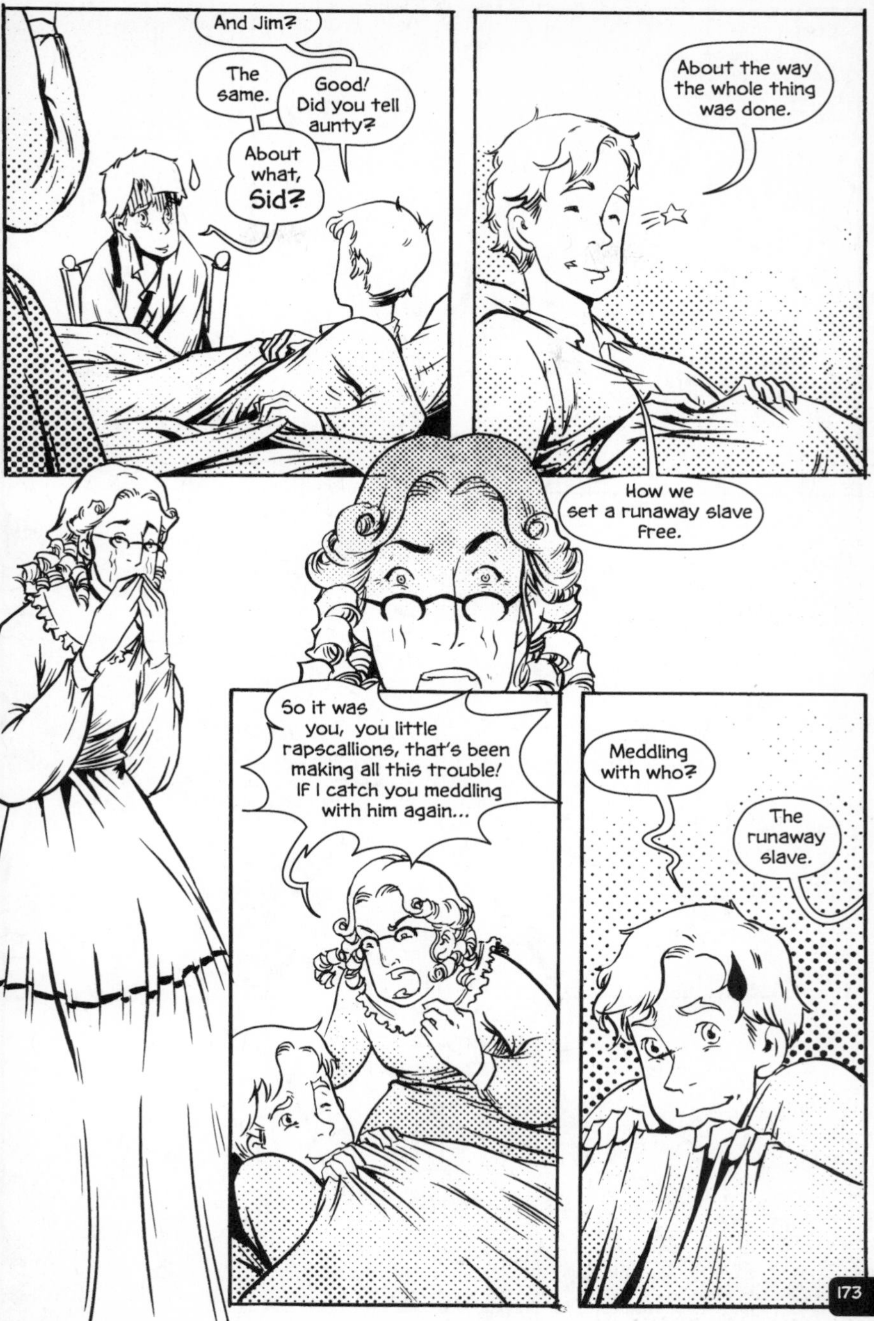

And Jim?
The same.
Good! Did you tell aunty?
About what, Sid?
About the way the whole thing was done.
How we set a runaway slave free.
So it was you, you little rapscallions, that's been making all this trouble! If I catch you meddling with him again...
Meddling with who?
The runaway slave.

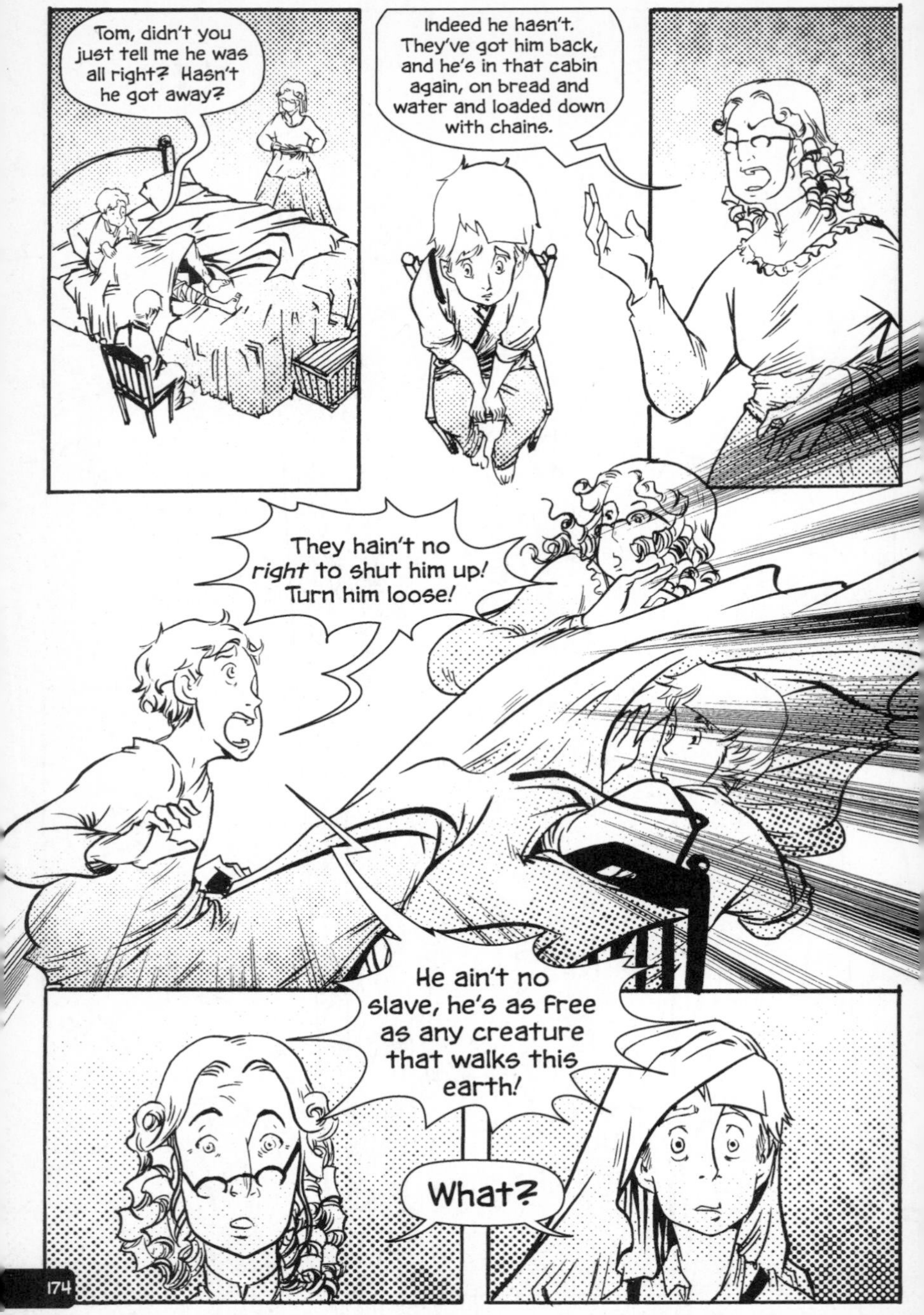
Tom, didn't you just tell me he was all right? Hasn't he got away?
Indeed he hasn't. They've got him back, and he's in that cabin again, on bread and water and loaded down with chains.
They hain't no *right* to shut him up! Turn him loose!
He ain't no slave, he's as free as any creature that walks this earth!
What?

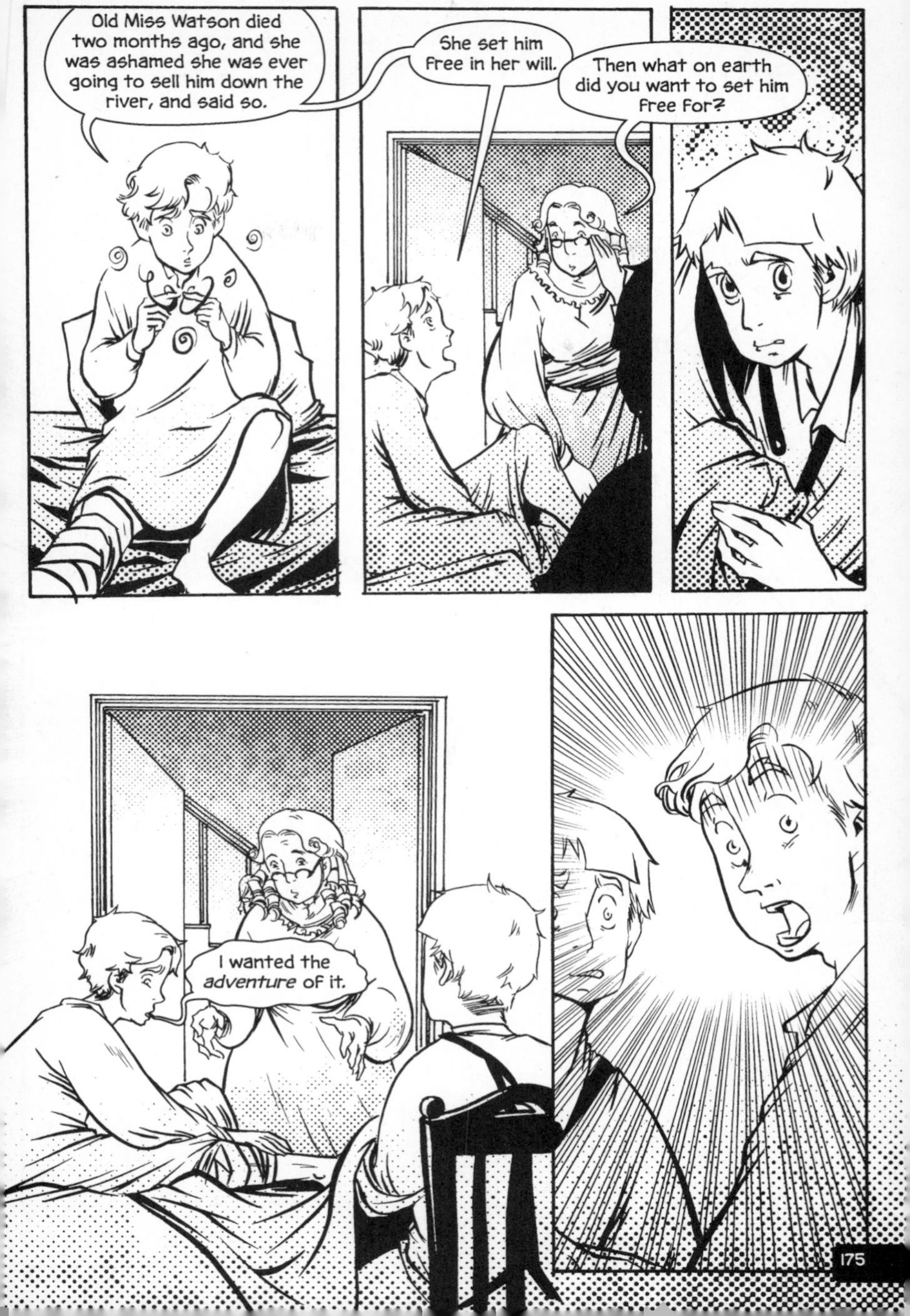
Old Miss Watson died two months ago, and she was ashamed she was ever going to sell him down the river, and said so.
She set him free in her will.
Then what on earth did you want to set him free for?
I wanted the *adventure* of it.

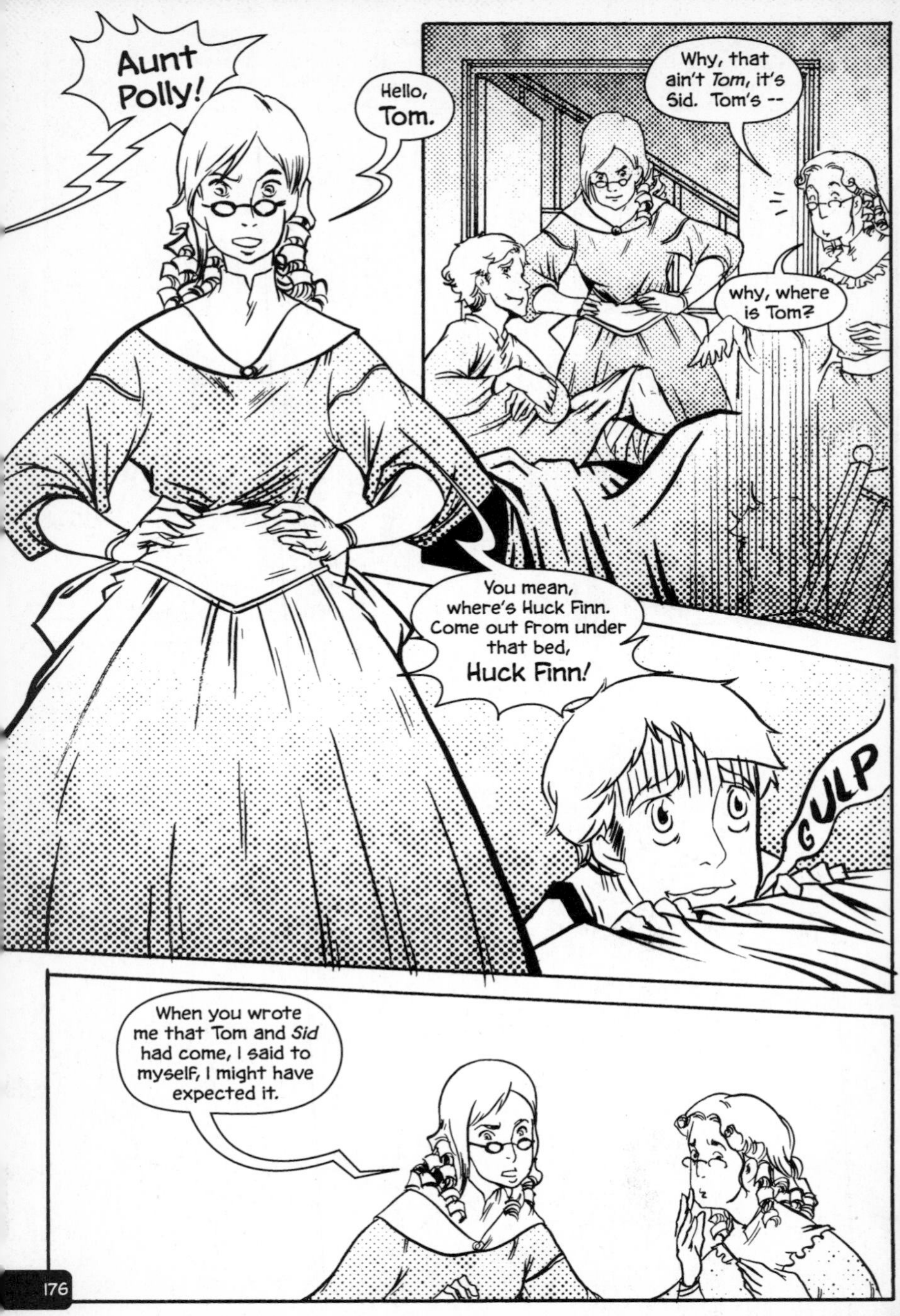
Aunt Polly!
Hello, Tom.
Why, that ain't *Tom*, it's Sid. Tom's --
why, where is Tom?
You mean, where's Huck Finn. Come out from under that bed, Huck Finn!
GULP
When you wrote me that Tom and *Sid* had come, I said to myself, I might have expected it.

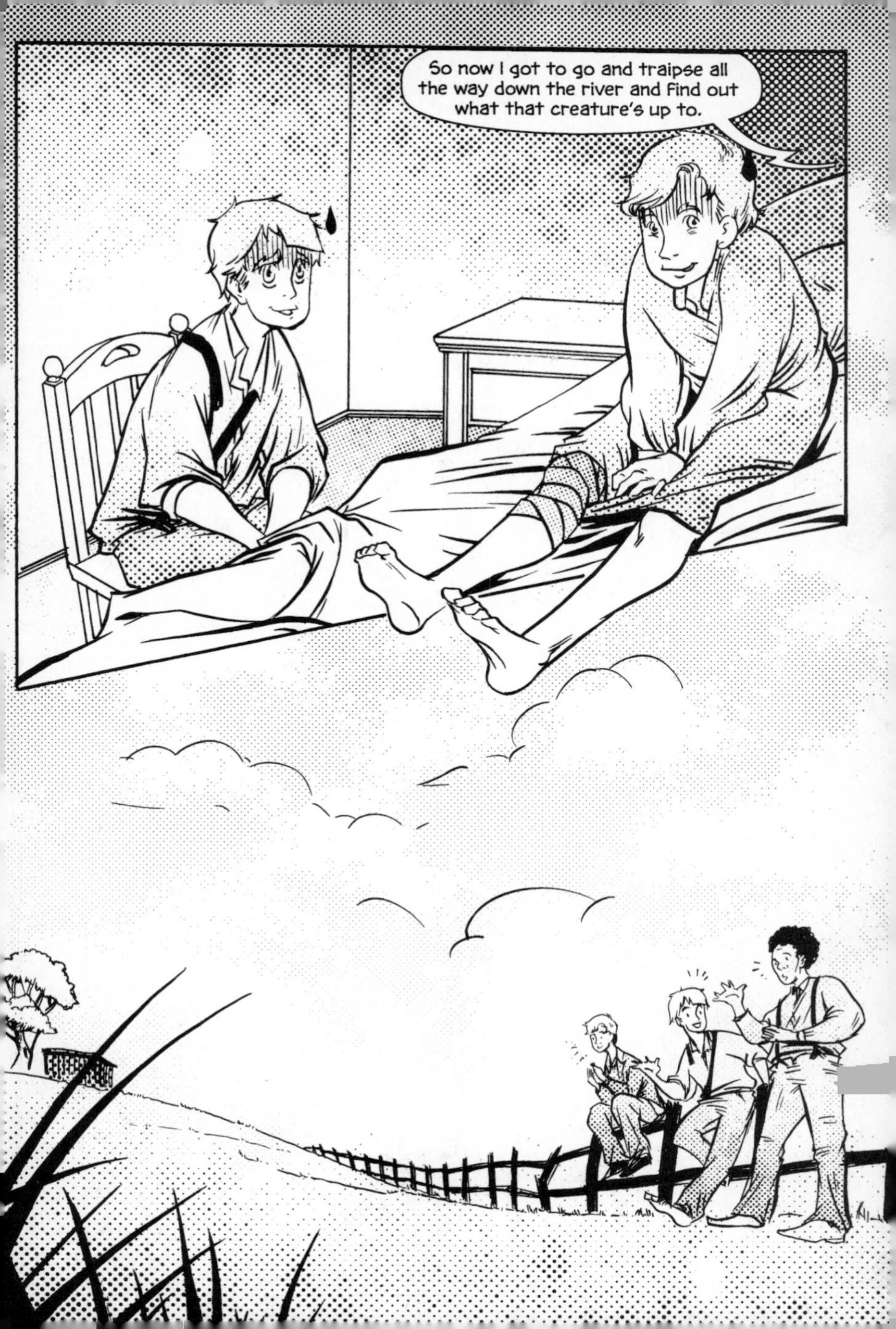
So now I got to go and traipse all the way down the river and find out what that creature's up to.

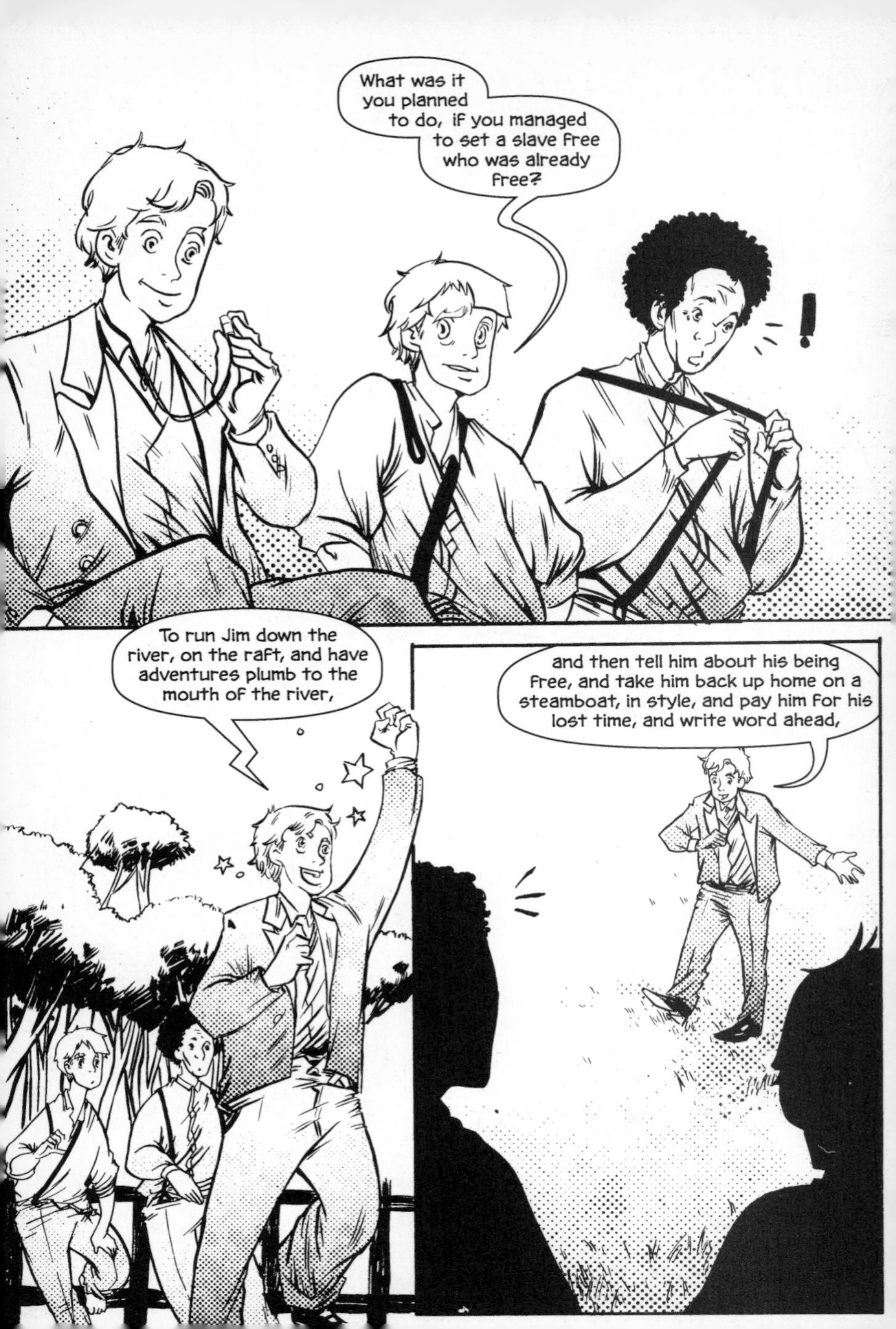
What was it you planned to do, if you managed to set a slave free who was already free?
!
To run Jim down the river, on the raft, and have adventures plumb to the mouth of the river,
and then tell him about his being free, and take him back up home on a steamboat, in style, and pay him for his lost time, and write word ahead,

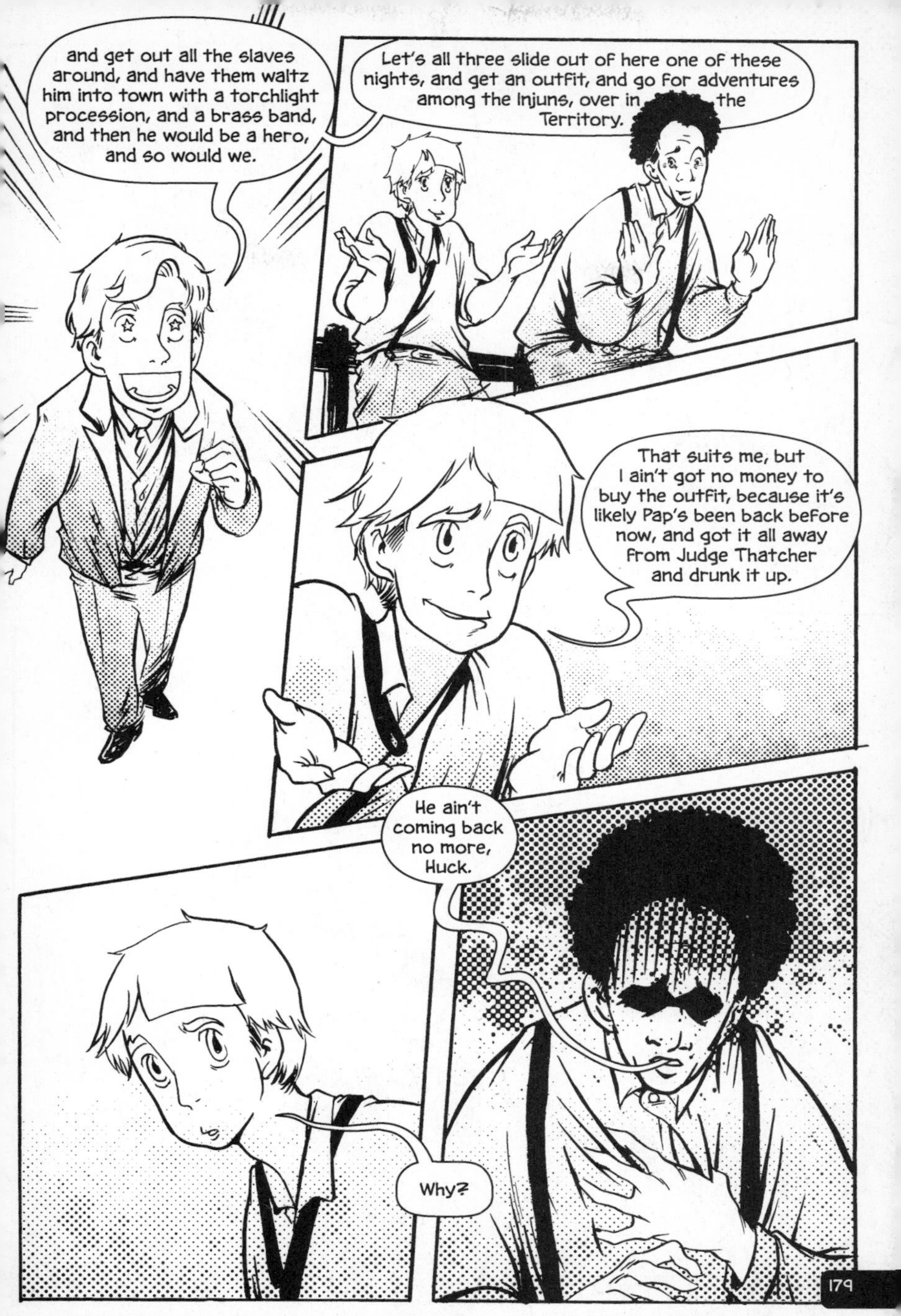
and get out all the slaves around, and have them waltz him into town with a torchlight procession, and a brass band, and then he would be a hero, and so would we.
Let's all three slide out of here one of these nights, and get an outfit, and go for adventures among the Injuns, over in the Territory.
That suits me, but I ain't got no money to buy the outfit, because it's likely Pap's been back before now, and got it all away from Judge Thatcher and drunk it up.
He ain't coming back no more, Huck.
Why?

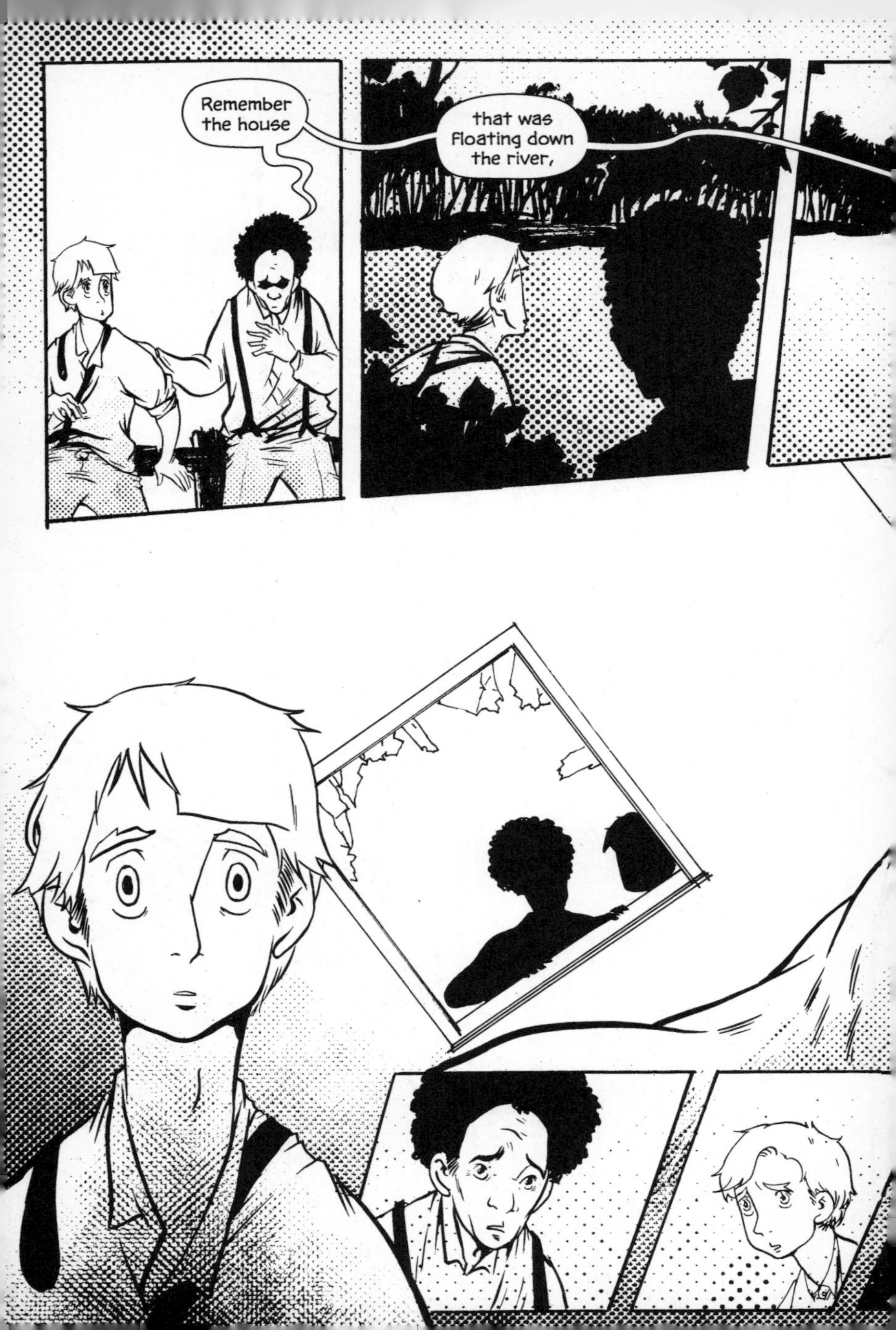
Remember the house
that was floating down the river,

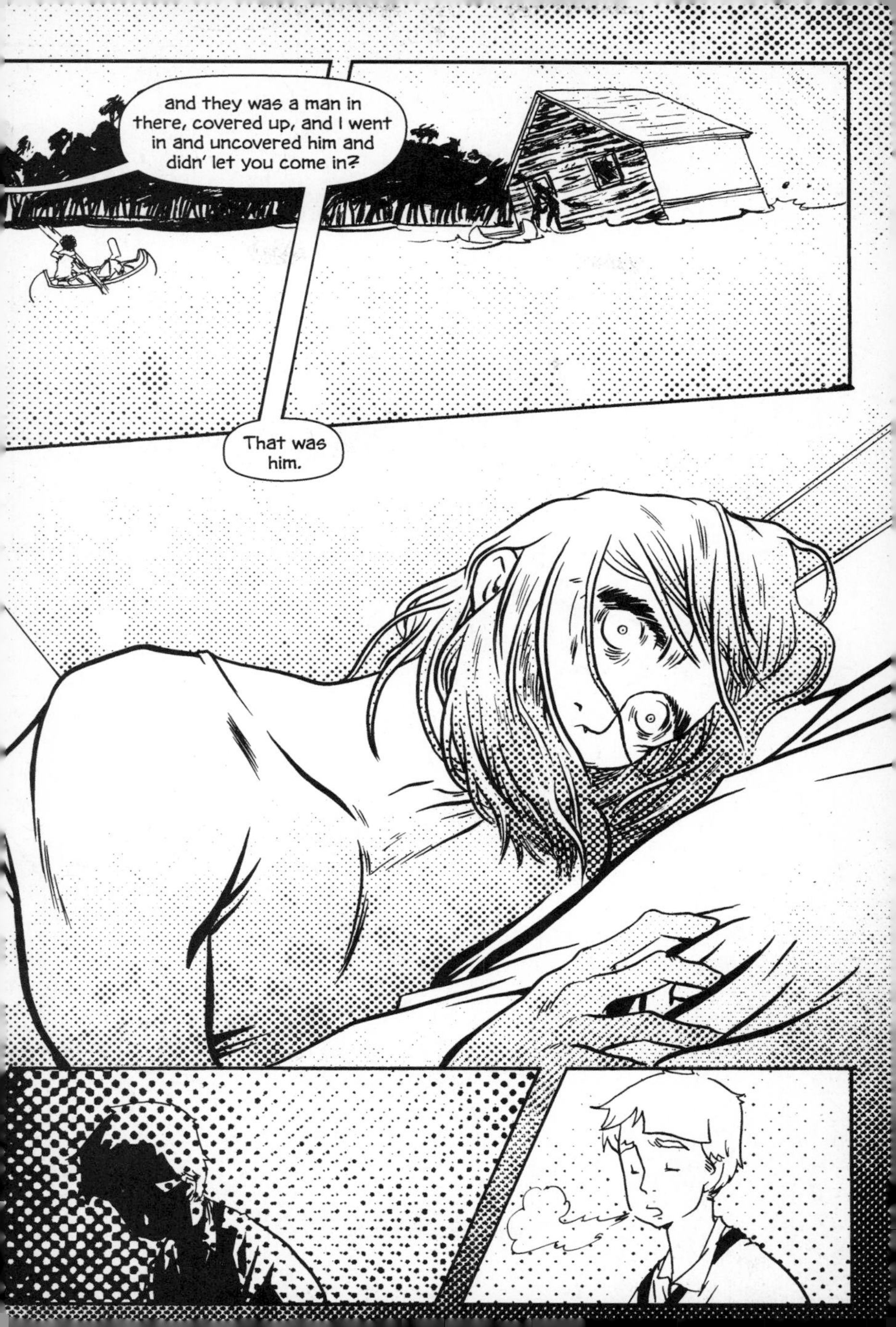
and they was a man in there, covered up, and I went in and uncovered him and didn' let you come in?
That was him.

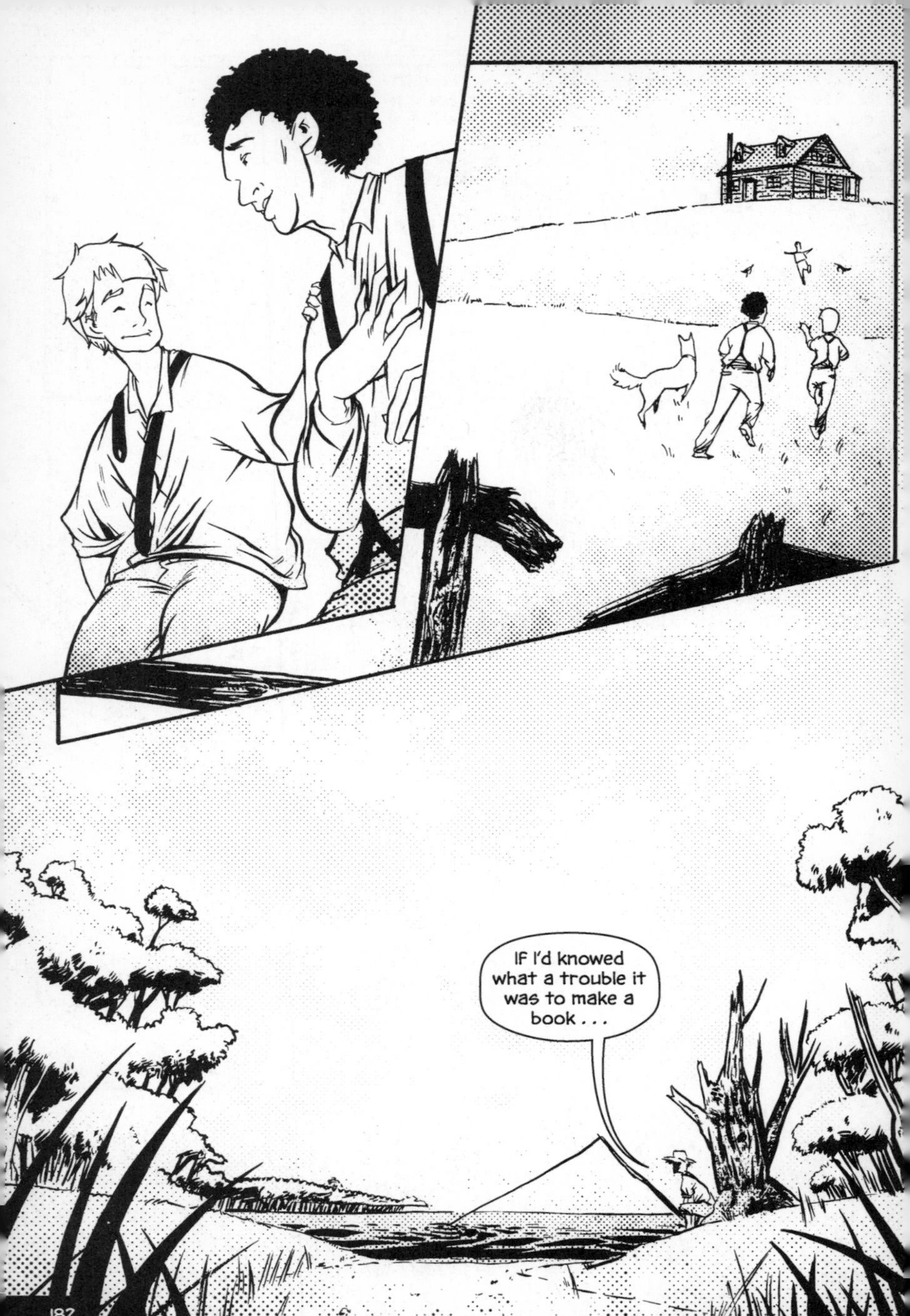
IF I'd knowed what a trouble it was to make a book . . .

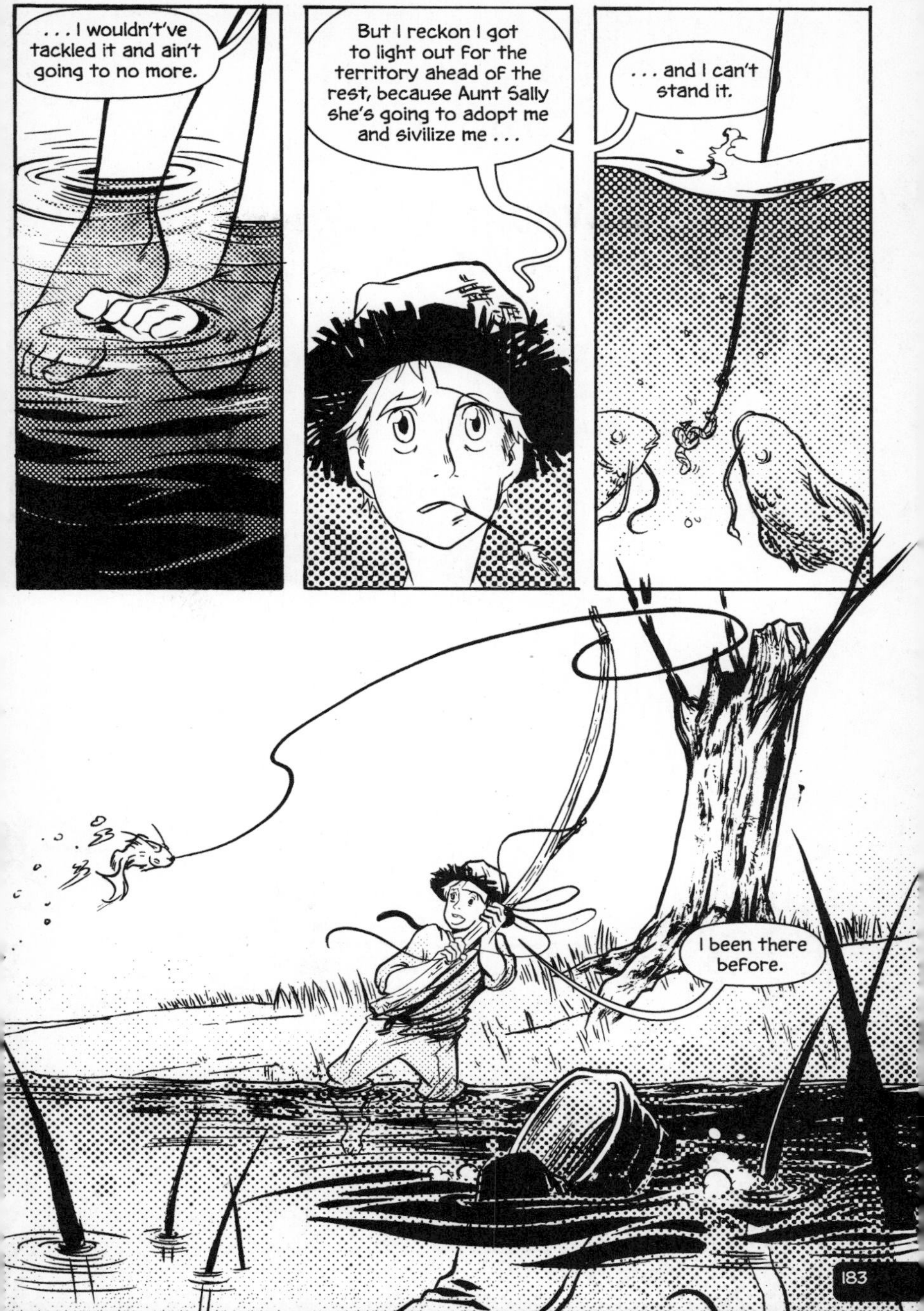

. . . I wouldn't've tackled it and ain't going to no more.
But I reckon I got to light out for the territory ahead of the rest, because Aunt Sally she's going to adopt me and sivilize me . . .
. . . and I can't stand it.
I been there before.

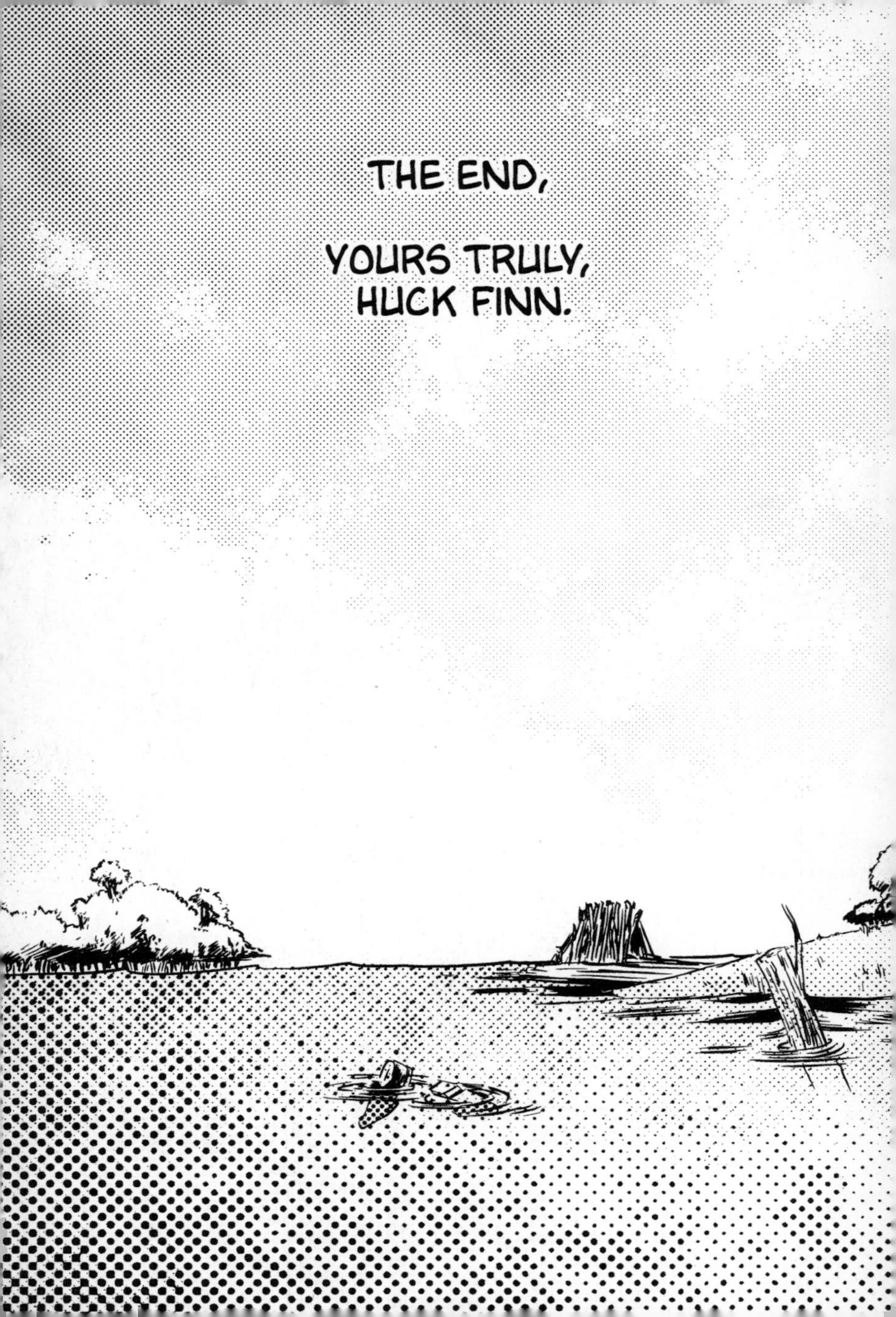
THE END,
YOURS TRULY,
HUCK FINN.

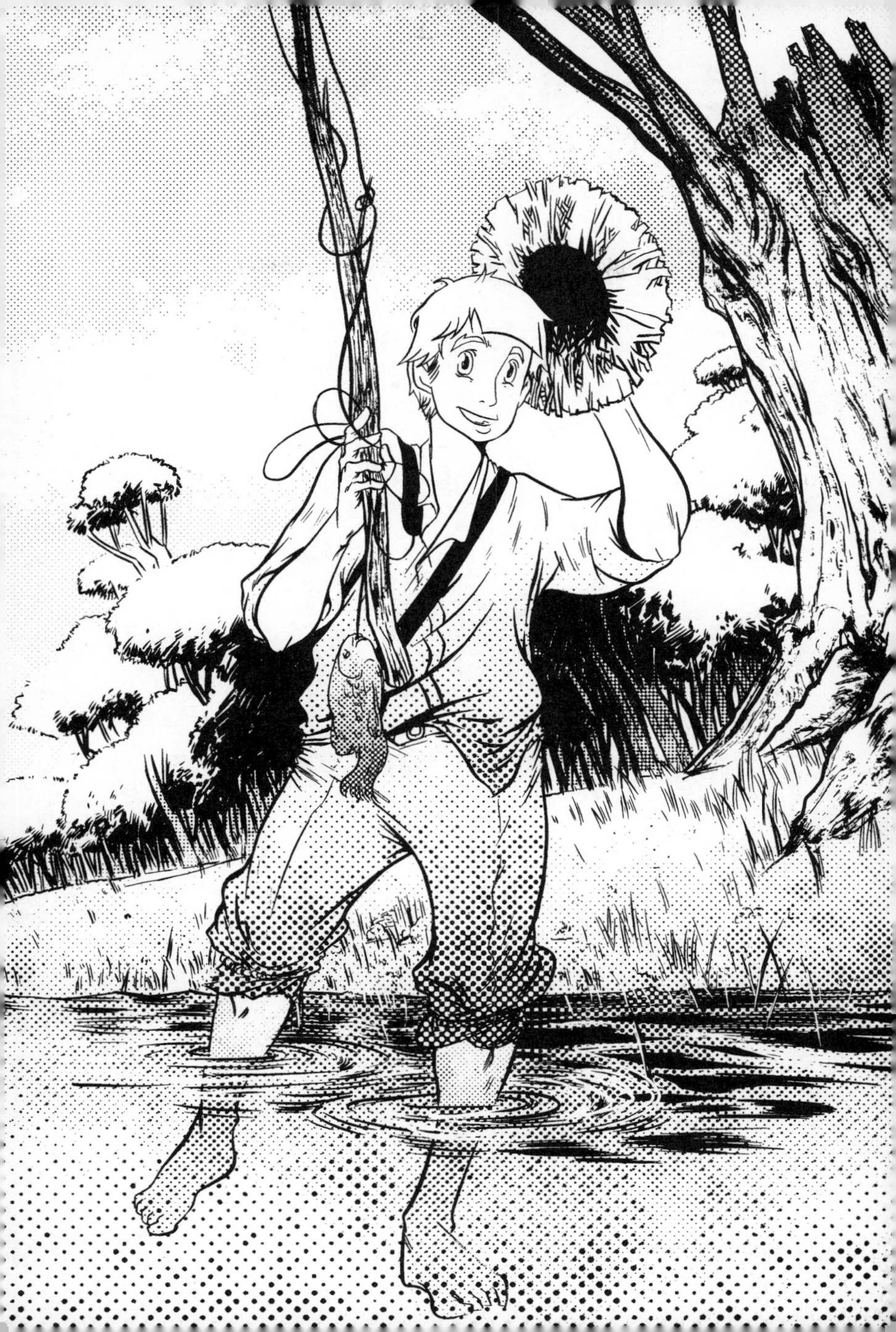